I0764476

Splintered Lives

by
Grace Anselmo D'Amato

iUniverse, Inc.
New York Bloomington

SPLINTERED LIVES

iUniverse books may be ordered through booksellers or by contacting:

iUniverse
1663 Liberty Drive
Bloomington, IN 47403
www.iuniverse.com
1-800-Authors (1-800-288-4677)

ISBN: 978-0-595-48150-7 (pbk)
ISBN: 978-0-595-71813-9(cloth)
ISBN: 978-0-595-60243-8 (ebk)

Printed in the United States of America

iUniverse Rev. Date 12/2/2008

In Memory of My Grandmother: a Noble Lady

Special Thanks to Lisa, My Daughter

1

Messina, Sicily—1900

Hot, southeast winds blew through the city; the fragrance of citrus fruits permeated the region as dawn shed its cloak. Blue skies welcomed the morning, etched in variegated shades of pale orange and pink. Franca Raimondi awakened, glanced out the window, relishing the view of the flotilla of ships crossing the Strait of Messina that was twenty-four miles long and two miles wide. She poured water into a bowl, washed with castile soap, and dusted with lavender scent. Her eyes were glued to ships halting at the port as crews unloaded merchandise from all over the Mediterranean Seaport. Ferries crossed the strait from Reggio di Calabria to Messina, with passengers arriving en masse on foot, horses and wagons.

Franca dressed, walked into the dining room where her family breakfasted on cappuccino, blood red oranges and toasted bread. She noticed her mother's eyes glued to her attire and wondered if something was wrong. But Elena Raimondi studied Franca's flawless complexion, oval blue eyes, light brown, waist-length hair, straight nose and perfect teeth.

"Franca, you look lovely."
"Grazie, Mamma."

"If only she would concentrate on marriage, rather than her studies," Elena pondered.

Elena and Giacomo Raimondi belonged to the last vestige of nobility in the city of Messina, and they encouraged their daughters, Franca and Maddalena, to be teachers. Franca wanted to be a doctor, much to her parents' chagrin. Although, Maddalena did not have Franca's intellectual prowess, men surrounded Maddalena with her blond hair, brown eyes, and petite figure. Roberto, her brother, an academic like Franca, had olive skin, black hair and green eyes.

Their father constantly spoke about the land that had sustained the Raimondis for many generations. Roberto was attentive but his mind wandered. He did not have the emotions and passion about the land that his father loved with such reverence.

"I have to go now," said Franca, grabbing her books.
"Don't be late," her father called out.

Tonio, Franca's driver, waited near the carriage to take her to the university.

"Buon giorno, Tonio," Franca said as she covered her face with her veil and climbed into the carriage.

Tonio, a bulk of a man and a friend of Giacomo, whipped the horses, battled torrid winds and dust that pricked his face like a thousand needles, finally reaching the University of Messina, a mile away. Students lolled around the university inside high wrought iron gates, wiping their faces and eyes from smarting particles of sand while majestic cypress trees provided some relief from the heat.

Franca removed her veil and shook it out as Dottore Rossi, her mentor and pathologist at the university's medical school, called out to her. Dottore Rossi was a diminutive man with a receding hairline, wispy black hairs at the nap of his neck, and black gentle eyes that peered above wire-rimmed eyeglasses.

"I have a cadaver … three o'clock?"
"Si, Dottore, grazie."

Despite her parents' objections, Franca continued her furtive participation in postmortems, and studied about malaria and typhoid fever, prevalent diseases in the region. After her mid-day dinner with her family, she returned to the university, descended the concrete steps into a dark, dank cavernous basement, with walls a foot thick.

"Signorina Raimondi, we've been waiting for you. Gentlemen, please show the young lady due respect."

The doctor summoned the students around the cadaver on a cracked marble slab, where he dissected the male cadaver, handed the organs to Franca who, in turn, explained their functions while a student turned pale, keeled over, gagging as other students assisted him.

"Get him outside!" Dottore Rossi ordered.

After the completion of the postmortem, Dottore Rossi made the Sign of the Cross on the forehead of the cadaver, called out to the waiting drivers, who placed the man into a wooden coffin for proper burial. Franca and the other students removed their masks, aprons and gloves, dumping them into buckets of carbolic acid and scrubbed their hands. Then she sprinkled gardenia scent on her clothes.

"Franca, let me try again to persuade your parents."
"No, please, they don't want to hear it."
"Peccato."[1]

At the sight of her father pacing the verandah, Franca moaned.
"Oh, Tonio, I'm in trouble."

Giacomo Raimondi had a mane of dark brown hair, peppered with gray at the temples; a formidable man, he challenged anyone who dared to defy him. His black eyes penetrated into a man's eyes, sizing up his demeanor, honesty and motives during business dealings. Those eyes were now focused on Franca, who held her head down, pretending not the see his reddened face. He shielded his eyes against the setting sun that resembled half-an-orange, glanced around at the formal gardens, designed in geometric patterns, with fountains that usually spouted upward and downward. The water had dried up from the oppressive heat, spinning the color of maize over the city with the arrival of the Levante, bitter-east winds, the Maestrale, northeast winds, and the Sirocco, southeast winds that belched across the island from Northern Africa."

"Papa′, I lose all sense of time at the university, there's so much to learn."

"When you graduate, start thinking of marriage. Your mother and I will find someone suitable."

"Papa′, no disrespect, but I will choose my own husband."

Silence prevailed.

They entered the winged-symmetrical house that spread out like the wings of an eagle. The family lived on the first floor while the second and third floors accommodated visiting relatives and guests. Tapestries hung on the living room wall on each side of large mirrors but the rest of the wall had family portraits. Velvet chairs, brocade couches, and marble tables graced the room. Crystal chandeliers, with lit candles, hung from the ceiling and a rosewood concert grand piano stood regally, overlooking the garden. Franca's mother, Elena, stood in the foyer, arms akimbo, and waited for an explanation. A petite woman with light brown hair, she had delicate features with bony cheekbones and a cast in her right eye did not diminish her patrician beauty.

"Sorry, Mamma," said Franca, kissing her mother on both cheeks. Elena threw up her hands in futility.

"Why do you always insist on getting your own way? I know … you were studying."

Franca sighed.

"Get ready; we're going to the interior."
"Yea, Mamma."

With the earth scorched from the oppressive heat, the Raimondis and their servants loaded the carriages, closed the house, departing from the city in their annual journey to the mountains. They rode along the ocean drive, overlooking the Ionian Sea, four hundred feet below. The horses neighed in rebellion, fearful of the fragile earth that bordered the hazardous edge of the road. Ships crossed the sea, upon a depression of fifteen thousand feet, resembling toy boats that sailed to and from Greece.

Two hours later, they entered a gravelly landscaped road arrayed with leguminous Judas trees, blooming with pink and purplish flowers. Suddenly four fawn-colored mastiffs halted the carriages; their powerful bodies climbing and clawing at the carriages, their bark echoed through the mountains.

"Papa′, I hate those dogs!"

"Franca, once they recognize us, they'll calm down. Men, put their leashes on!" Giacomo ordered.

"Si, Signore Raimondi, *subito*."[2]

Contadini[2] rushed toward the carriages, controlled the mastiffs that weighed one hundred and fifty pounds each, held them into submission, patting them and led them away. The cool moderate winds danced through the stately columns of palm trees, prodded their fronds while massive growths of pink, white and red geraniums bloomed side by side with prickly thistles. A mixture of white, pink and yellow daisies tilted to the music of the winds. Delicate angel trumpets gently swayed and overgrown agave grew wild behind the house, thwarting prowlers with sword-like leaves.

Elena, Franca and Maddalena entered the terra-cotta villa, an upside-down house with bedrooms on the first floor. The kitchen, dining and living rooms were on the second floor, which provided an expansive view of the mountains. While the women checked the house to make sure all was in order, Giacomo and Roberto rode out to the field, where fruits and vegetables burst with life. Giacomo beamed; Persephone, the goddess of agriculture, had blessed the crops.

"Roberto, this will be yours someday."
"Thank you, Papa′," Roberto replied, turning his head away.
"It is your heritage, my son."

Roberto nodded, climbed back onto his horse and waited for his father who glanced at him with puzzlement. They rode back in silence. Giacomo sped ahead of him and reached the stables, with Roberto trotting along.

Quietude pervaded throughout supper, and Roberto avoided his father's eyes that castigated him. Elena, aware of the tension, chatted incessantly but Giacomo remained mute. Outside the larks' song lifted the gloom while dusk illuminated the azure skies with lavender and orange hues. Finally Giacomo stood up, excused himself, went outside and grabbed one of the mastiffs from the contadino, and strolled the fields with a torch, relishing the abundance of Nature's bounty, finding solace in the bucolic setting.

"Roberto, what's going on? Did you have an argument with your father?"

"No, Mamma, I wouldn't argue with him. I respect him too much."

"Well, something is wrong?"

"He constantly lectures me about the land. I am not really interested in farming."

"You should be interested. Your forefathers have fought and worked hard for this land. Why your uncle was killed during the Reunification of Italy in 1860. Your father does not talk about it. The pain is too great."

When Giacomo returned from his stroll, the millennial stars topped the mountains, and his family sat outside waiting for him. Roberto leaped to his feet and embraced Giacomo; words were unnecessary. Elena ordered the servant to serve fruits, pastries and espresso.

Giacomo strummed his mandolin, singing ballads about the land with its turbulent history; conquerors ravaged Sicily, causing the assimilation of many cultures.

"Papa′, we have the blood of many nations running through our veins."

"Yes, Franca. In our particular genus, we have Greek, Carthaginian, Roman, Spanish, French, Jewish and German."

"Jewish? How can that be?" Roberto asked.

"The Jews lived here for fourteen hundred years, and in 1492 under Spanish rule, they were forced to convert to Christianity or leave. Some went to parts of Southern Italy, Rome and Northern Italy as well as Northern Africa."

Now the full moon hid behind towering mountains. Tonio put out the torches and went to his cottage, where he lived with his wife Maria and daughter Costanza. Then the Raimondis retired to a benign sleep. The next morning, Giacomo toured the village with his contadini and was visibly upset at the illnesses of the children and elderly.

"Why don't you go to the clinic in the city?"
"Too far for us," an elderly woman replied.

Giacomo nodded, rode back to the villa and called out to Franca.

"The villagers need a doctor. We have to notify Dottore Rossi."
"Papa′, he is busy at the clinic. I can examine the patients and the ones that are seriously ill, we can send to the clinic."
"You? You've been studying with Dottore Rossi!" He shook his head.
"Please don't be angry. I know a great deal."
"I'm sure you do. I'll have the men set up a tent. Only women and children … understood?"
"Yes, Papa′."

Was there a glint of pride on his face?

"I'll pick up the supplies tomorrow."
"Tonio will go with you."

During the first two days, the farmers' wives shunned Franca; only two women straggled in with their ill children. She examined them and gave them medication, reassuring the mothers that their conditions were not serious. The women kissed Franca's hand, much to her embarrassment.

"Please, do not do that. Just persuade your neighbors to come here. If I can't help them, I'll send them to the clinic in the city."

"Si, Dottore, grazie."
"Prego." Franca did not correct the woman.

The following morning, a parade of women with infants and children queued up in front of the tent. Franca could not hide her astonishment, welcoming them with open arms; perhaps embracing them would lessen their fears. At sunset she finally sat down, tired but pleased, when a young woman ran in, begging her pardon.

"Can I help you?"

"Si, Signorina, my four-year old daughter has a rash. I had the mal'occhio[3] removed but she still has it."

"Signora, that is primitive. Those ways must stop. I'll give you some salve and in a few days, she'll be fine."

Soon word spread about Franca's gentleness and competence. She lectured the women about personal hygiene, urging them to relinquish the old superstitions. Young women nodded their heads in approval, while an older women stood up, shaking her finger.

"No, Signorina, you have your ways and we have ours."

"Signora, with all due respect ... do you want to remain ignorant peasants?" Franca exclaimed, unable to hold back her frustrations. But instantly, she regretted her outburst as the women streamed out of the tent. She sat down and wept. That was the end of her medical work in the village.

The evil eye was ingrained in the nature of the people and women visited certain women who had the gift to remove the curse. Those women poured water into a dish, added a whiskey glass of olive oil, and if the oil and water did not blend, someone had cast the evil eye upon them.

Men did not visit the women, but sent their wives with their ties cut off, wanting an explanation for their headaches. *Who had wished evil upon them?* Shrewd women understood their husband's tension headaches, and their warm, receptive lips and bodies alleviated their anxiety when their bodies exploded in a torrent of passion. Elderly women warned young mothers to place something red inside of their babies' cribs and never allow anyone to compliment their children's beauty. That was considered envy, a curse, and could mar the children's beauty.

Now with the end of summer came the arduous task of carting fruits, vegetables and wheat along the roads. At dawn, women, children and elderly parents emerged from their homes in the roseate mountains, applauding the procession of donkeys, horses and men. Wagons were painted with tiny designs encircling the rims, and large panels depicted splendid knights and paladins—heroic champions—from the twelve peers of Charlemagne the Great's court during his conquest of the West. The dreaded Moor and his vanquish were scorned in the paintings.

Finally, the parade reached the port of Messina for shipment to the rest of Italy and Western Europe, aboard ships that navigated along the Tyrrhenian Sea. Giacomo, relieved at the completion of the first harvest, supervised the contadini as they set the land on fire, returning nutrients to the soil. Three days later they prepared the ground for the second harvest.

Now Giacomo, Elena and Maddalena returned to the city. Giacomo and Elena strolled along the sickle-shaped harbor, and watched the giant steamers crossing the Strait of Messina. When sailors came ashore, Giacomo conversed with Greeks, Spaniards, Frenchmen, Ottoman Turks and Arabs. With Sicily facing three continents, Africa, Asia and Europe, it was a natural progression to learn different languages. Franca and Roberto returned to classes at the university. She was in her last year and continued her studies with Dottore Rossi, while Roberto entered his second year.

In mid-October, guests arrived from Palermo, Catania, Siracusa, the Italian mainland, France and Germany. Most came by ferry, while others came by carriage. Women alighted from carriages, dusting off and primping themselves while their husbands pounded the dust from their knickers and loosened their ascots. They arrived in Messina for the annual ball.

Elena and Giacomo welcomed their guests on the verandah; the men kissed Elena's gloved hand and shook hands with Giacomo. Refreshments were served on the verandah and they led their guests through an octagon-shaped chapel for prayers of thanksgiving for a safe journey. Some guests were accommodated at the Raimondi home, while others were driven to the Grand Hotel on Viale San Martino.

Maddalena, now seventeen years old, vied for the first bath with Franca, stripping and splashing into the water, laughing, amid Franca's giggling.

"Just don't pee in there," Franca said.
"I won't or maybe I will," Maddalena teased, giggling.

After Maddalena bathed, the servant added additional hot water and Franca submerged into the trough. Then the servant brought out their gowns and set them upon the bed.

"Signorina, your mother gave me strict orders … you must look beautiful. Sometimes you dress too plainly."
"I know. She wants to find a suitable husband for me."

Then she called out to Maddalena.

"Come over here … want to tell you something."

She whispered into Maddalena's ear and her eyes opened wide at the news.

"You like Edoardo!"
"Yes, always have, since the first time I saw him."
"Now, wait a minute." Maddalena cautioned.
"Shh, I don't want the servant to hear."

Edoardo Privitera was the illegitimate son of Count Privitera, a friend of Giacomo's. The count had had an illicit affair with his mother, who was a governess in his household. She became pregnant and died giving birth to Edoardo. Count Privitera had two daughters from his marriage and wanted Edoardo raised in his home. His wife was furious at her husband, and forbade Edoardo from entering their home. The count placed Edoardo into an orphanage, where he visited him frequently and supervised his education.

When Edoardo was eighteen years old, his father died, and Giacomo offered his friendship to Edoardo. Edoardo thanked him, but decided to leave Sicily for America. The journey was traumatic with the mass of humanity herded together, but Edoardo was determined to succeed and return to Messina a successful man.

In 1885, he arrived in America, rented a room, found employment as a waiter, studied English, diligent in his study and only associated with Americans. Two years later, he strolled through the large department stores, fascinated with the array of merchandise, but he noticed that the linens and fabrics did not have the quality of Italian goods. That was the answer! He had found his niche. He learned about merchandising, and sailed back to Italy, not in steerage, but in business class, where he met other business people and made connections.

When he returned to Messina, no one knew him. He resembled a prosperous, young American, not the thin, emaciated young man who had left Messina's shores with a cloth bag. After he settled at the Grand Hotel, he hired a carriage and sought out Giacomo, who embraced him and invited him for dinner.

While they dined, Edoardo explained the opportunities, and Giacomo, impressed with his business acumen, offered to help him, putting up money and hiring women to embroider the linens.

"Giacomo, thank you. Once you offered me your friendship and I thought you felt sorry for me."

"No, not at all. Your father and I were friends. His wife was cruel toward you."

"Giacomo, that is the past. Are we partners?" Giacomo embraced him and they shook hands.

Later they went into the salon, and Franca sat beside Edoardo, smiling at him. His brown eyes avoided her smile, fearful of disrespecting Giacomo and Elena who motioned Franca to move near them.

Giacomo and Elena were angered by Franca's flirtatious ways toward Edoardo and asked her to leave the room. Franca's face reddened, she held her head down and ran out of the room.

"Edoardo, I apologize for Franca's behavior."

"That's quite all right. She is only a child. Well, Giacomo, let's talk about our business."

"A pleasure. Let's go to the library."

Franca and Maddalena dressed for the ball. Franca wore a burgundy velvet gown with apron-folds pulled backward in a waterfall of velvet. The servant braided her hair with a pearl rope encircling her head, and added a pearl necklace and pearl-drop earrings. Maddalena wore a simple, emerald green velvet gown.

"Franca, you look beautiful. I look like a child in this gown," Maddalena sighed.

"You look precious," Franca said and embraced her.

Dust cloaked the city in a mantle of mauve and orange. The sound of music filtered through the house as the two sisters entered the salon. Giacomo leaped to his feet, sandwiched himself between Franca and Maddalena, escorting them to the family's table. His eyes drifted around the room for eligible young men.

"Someone will find Franca appealing. I just hope she acts a little stupid. Maddalena, I'll have to chase the men away," he thought.

"Franca saw Edoardo and smiled at him. He stood up and held the chair out for her while Giacomo assisted Maddalena to her seat.

"May I have the honor of this dance?"
"Yes, Edoardo … Papa′, may I?

Giacomo nodded, grinning, and sat next to Elena.

"Franca, you are a beautiful young lady."

Franca shyly put her head down, decided to act demure, and delighted to hear him say those words. She melted into his arms, her heart pounded while they danced the waltz.

"Your father told me about your activities and your studies. I'm honored to know you. He's proud of you."
"Thank you."

Suddenly her brother, sister and cousins formed a circle, dancing the mazurka and laughing until they were exhausted. Later they joined the adults in a waltz. During intermission, Giacomo announced that Franca would perform a Scarlatti Sonata, and escorted her to the rosewood piano. She sat down, anxious, not about her ability but aware of Edoardo's presence. She felt his gaze upon her and a warm feeling stirred within her. After her performance, applause resounded throughout the room. And then she saw Edoardo coming toward her to escort her back to the table.

"You were wonderful."
"Thank you."

Giacomo and Elena glanced at each other, surprised at Edoardo's attentive manner toward Franca.

"Giacomo, he likes her," whispered Elena.

Giacomo agreed.

The orchestra stopped playing at Giacomo's signal. He asked his family and guests to sit down for dinner. He remained standing, lifted his glass of wine, and silence was pervasive.

"To my family and friends, buona salute e cent'anni a tutte."[4]

Applause resounded through the dining room and the family and guests returned the toast.

"Don Giacomo, Donna Elena, cent'anni a lei."[5]

Servants served a sumptuous dinner of salad, cheeses, proscuitto and salami, vegetables, veal, poultry, and wine produced on Giacomo's lands. Espresso and a plethora of desserts completed the meal.

Meanwhile, Edoardo, not used to such opulent dining, excused himself and went out on the verandah. As he glanced at the darkened skies with millennial stars, he signed; it brought back fond memories, when in his youth, he slept outside during the summer months.

"It is a beautiful sight."
"Franca! Come near me."

He grabbed her hand and she snuggled close to him.

"Your parents … I don't want them to get angry with me."
"They won't."
"I hope you're right. I think I'll ask them if I may court you."
"Oh, Edoardo, I liked you the first time I saw you."
"And I, you, but you were too young. How old are you now?"
"I'll be twenty. I'm graduating this year. And you?"
"Thirty"
"That's perfect," she replied, giggling.

And the courtship started with her parents' blessing. Edoardo had an inner peace when he was with Franca; yet, he felt alive with her. He had known many women, but she was exciting, interesting and livened up his life.

Until now, he had been a serious, ambitious young man, devoid of emotion for any woman, only seeking biological needs.

It was time for Edoardo's departure, and Franca appeared despondent, but he reassured her the months would go quickly.

"Oh, Edoardo, I wish I could leave with you."

The next morning, Giacomo called Edoardo to his study, and he noticed concern clouded Giacomo's face. What could be wrong? They had agreed on the modus operandi for their business affairs.

"Edoardo, do not be offended but we must do something about your illegitimacy."

Edoardo turned crimson and slumped into the chair. The stigma of his illegitimacy had lain dormant, but now surfaced like a sword into his heart. Giacomo placed his arm around his shoulder.

"I have the greatest respect for you, but we must think of your unborn children. You will be listed in the Nobilario di Sicilia."

"Giacomo, isn't the social register becoming obsolete?"
"No, not at all. Besides, you will have influential connections."
"I use my father's name in America."
"But here you are known only as Edoardo, the illegitimate son of Count Privitera. I can help you," he assured him.

Tonio drove Franca and Edoardo to the docks, waiting for the ferry to arrive for his trip to Reggio di Calabria, then to Naples and America. Tonio left them alone while they embraced and their lips met with such fervor and yearning for each other.

"Tesoro, I love you … only six months," moaned Edoardo.
"Please take care of yourself … I love you."

During Edoardo's absence, Franca, besides her courses, worked at the clinic and studied ancient manuscripts at the library. The Pearl of the Mediterranean suffered at the hands of many invaders, who ravaged her women and children, tortured and killed her men who defended their families and lands. Sicily's art and sculpture, from her Greek heritage, had been pilfered. Her past forged her future, and hostility became part of her personality, directed against those rapacious nations who devastated her earth. But with the diversity of invading cultures, Sicily became the America of Antiquity. Franca sighed, and returned the manuscripts that would be preserved for future generations.

2

Edoardo arrived in May, amid Franca's jubilation, as she prepared for her graduation. After the festivities, Giacomo told Edoardo to follow him into the library. Giacomo unlocked his drawer and handed Edoardo a document. Edoardo's hands shook as he read it, tears rolling down his face.

> It has been decreed that Edoardo of Messina will now and forevermore be know as Edoardo Privitera, the son of COUNT RUGGERO PRIVITERA of MESSINA.
>
> Signed and sealed this tenth day of May 1903
> UMBERTO I
> *Umberto I*
> Re' D'Italia

Edoardo wept without restraint. Giacomo leaped to his feet and put his arm around him.

"Giacomo, I am grateful."
"One favor I ask of you … call me Papa′ from now on."
"With honor, replied Edoardo."
"Papa′, can the countess prevent me from using my father's name?"
"No, not at all. There is power in the king's signature."

Edoardo sought Franca while Giacomo needed seclusion in the library and recalled the past. His eyes glazed over, remembering when his father represented the Province of Messina at a meeting with Giuseppe Garibaldi, the Italian patriot, in Palermo. In the beginning, Sicilians regarded Garibaldi as their messiah but later considered him a man like other rulers. Garibaldi, despite his battle for reunification, became disillusioned, and promises made to the Sicilians were not kept. Garibaldi had received his orders from Count Camillo Benso Cavour of Turin, who spoke French, not Italian, and assumed Sicilians only spoke Arabic and considered Sicily an Islamic society. After the meeting, funds were set aside for the redevelopment of the Mezzogiorno (Southern Italy and Sicily) but rumors abound that the House of Savoy had squandered funds and lands reverted back to the aristocracy and the Honored Society, the Mafia.

"Giacomo, Giacomo, are you all right?"
"Yes, Elena, I was just thinking."
"Dinner is ready."

The family rejoiced at the news, elated for Edoardo and Franca. Giacomo questioned him about America.

"Naturally, your home will be here. But what is it like for immigrants in America, especially New York City? I wasn't particularly interested until now."

Edoardo explained large families were crowded together in a single room, hot in the summer and freezing in the winter. He hesitated for a moment, lowering his head.

"A friend of mine, who was kind to me and helped me out, fell from a scaffold as high as the mountains, crushed to death, his brains splattered over the sidewalk. It was horrible."

"Madonna! Sicilians are foolish to leave this beautiful island, where they can grow their own food, sleep under the stars, surrounded by flowers and plants and the magnificent blue sea … one never tires of the view."

"Papa´, that is true and live in perpetual poverty and ignorance, exploited by absentee landlords who hire hoodlums to keep the peasants in line. Papa´, three-quarters of our people are illiterate."

Giacomo leaped to his feet, his hands trembled, his face reddened, his voice roared, and he banged on the table, knocking over the wine.

"This land has been handed down to me from hundreds of years of sweat, blood and toil."

"Papa', please forgive me, but I don't mean you. You are good to the peasants. Perhaps we should have democracy here."

"We want autonomy, we want to rule ourselves. We are tired of the many masters and rulers who have stolen from our island and abused our people."

Cold silence enveloped the room, gelid faces but one stared at Edoardo, who stood up and begged forgiveness.

"Papa', it was not my intention to offend you. Please believe me."

"I know that. My great-grandfather could have purchased the title of count, duke or baron when the Bourbons ruled, but he chose to remain one of the people, close to the land."

Franca interrupted the quietude, stood up, and told Edoardo she had learned a new Scarlatti sonata.

"Please excuse me," Edoardo said, extending his hand to Giacomo who nodded in deference.

As they walked toward the piano, Edoardo whispered to Franca.

"Your family will call me il grande boca."[6]

"No, they'll say you have cugnuni."[7]

They covered their mouths to muffle their laughter.

After the performance, Edoardo grabbed her hands, kissed her palms, and thrilled her with his fervor. At that moment, Giacomo strolled into the salon; Edoardo released Franca's hands.

"Papa', I would never do anything to offend you."

"Edoardo, I know."

"Papa', how do you know the king?

"My father knew his father and he always backed his policies, and now I support Umberto."

After an uncomfortable silence, Edoardo asked,

"Papa´, may I have Franca's hand in marriage?"

"Why, yes, of course. You will have to ask her mother, too. Elena! Elena!"

"I'm here. What is wrong?"

"Mamma, may I have Franca's hand in marriage."

"Oh Edoardo, I would be happy to have you as a son."

Then Edoardo placed a square-cut diamond ring on Franca's finger, linking his arm through hers, their hearts bursting with love, webbed together for life.

"Edoardo, you planned this evening."

He grinned. Then Giacomo called out to the servant to chill a bottle of champagne in their well while Franca waved her hand, showing off her ring to the rest of the family.

In the middle of June, guests and family assembled in the Madonna of the Letters Cathedral, where freshly picked pink and white roses adorned the three alters. Masses of the island's prolific, tubular freesias created an indoor garden with dew drops glistening on the leaves, and sunbeams pouring through the Gothic windows.

The doors opened wide, and the choir sang Ave Maria by Bach-Gounod. While Roberto, Edoardo's best man, waited for him at the altar. Edoardo looked debonair in a gray frock coat with silk lapels, a white dress shirt, and a gray, knotted cravat. Maddalena walked in alone and Elena waited in the pew. Franca and Edoardo had decided the bridal party would be minimal since he had no family.

Giacomo escorted Franca down the aisle as guests and relatives craned their necks for a view of Franca. She wore a slight bustle, ivory silk gown with seed pearls on the bodice. Her headpiece was a crown of seed pearls and an ivory veil masked her face. She held ivory rosary beads her mother had given her and her blue eyes shone with excitement as she held onto her father's arm.

"Franca, you look beautiful. I am so proud of you."

"Thank you, Papa'."

They reached the altar and Giacomo pulled her veil back, kissed her and handed her over to Edoardo. Franca winked at Edoardo who broadly smiled at her, but the eminent Cardinal D'Amico of Messina frowned at her lack of decorum. His dour face revealed his annoyance as he adjusted his vestments of red, trimmed with gold.

The cardinal sang the High Mass in Latin while the choir of nuns responded. After the Mass, Franca went over to a statue of the Madonna on the side altar, placed a single, white rose into an empty vase. Franca and Edoardo went outside on the pavilion, lingering amid showers of confetti and congratulations.

Dusk shrouded the city when Franca and Edoardo returned home from the photographer's. A sumptuous meal consisting of wedding soup, salads, pastas, roasted pigs and roasted lambs were served with a plethora of vegetables, ending with an array of desserts and the wedding cake.

When the skies glistened with millennial stars, Giacomo summoned his family and guests out to the verandah, where an assemblage of young men on horses, mounted with longhorns and scarlet and green feathers, encircled the gardens, raised their torches to Franca and Edoardo in tribute to their marriage. The young women's costumes matched the men's, and they danced the tarantella. Guests removed their shoes, joining the dancers. Their inhibitions thrown to the wind, they danced until their feet were encrusted with a mixture of grass and soil.

Two days later, Franca and Edoardo departed for Naples, reaching the docks at sunset. She held Edoardo's arm, mesmerized with the mass of emigrants boarding third class, transatlantic liners for their voyage to America.

"It's heart-breaking," murmured Franca.

"Franca, they'll have a chance in America. It is a terrible journey. On my first trip, people peed, vomited, lost control of their bowels … the stench was unbearable. I would sneak up to the upper decks, then I'd get caught and the stewards sent me back down."

"I'm sorry … so many people are leaving Italy. It's sad leaving your homeland."

"Our class system must change," Edoardo sighed.

Franca remained silent.

Prostitutes tarried around the docks, raised their dresses, exposed their thighs, swung their hips and heaved their breasts to the rhythm of mandolins in the background. Their sultry smiles enticed men to come closer to them with a promise of love and passion.

"They are brazen … flirting with you in front of me."

"Franca, I would never get near those kinds of women. Besides, I have you … young and beautiful."

"And I have you. Oh, goodness, look at that man. He's got syphilis," she whispered, hanging onto Edoardo.

The man peered out of the darkness, moving toward them, hesitating for a moment under a gas lantern. His face was lined with ridges and half of his nose was gone.

"Just ignore him … keep walking."

Children, in tattered clothes, barefoot and frail, ran up to them, rubbed their thumbs on their index and middle fingers, begging for money. Edoardo succumbed to their cherubic faces, nothing could detract from their innocence as he handed them each twenty liras.

"Grazie, Signore!" They yelled, running to their fathers who lurked in the darkness.

Edoardo did not relax his guard for a moment. The sinister-looking men, now and then, revealed themselves in the murky background.

"Let's hurry up the gangplank."

When they reached their stateroom, Franca sighed with relief, removed her hat, gloves and shoes. The steward knocked on the door, brought in a chamber pot, a metal bathtub, a screen for privacy, towels, and a pitcher and basin.

"Steward, please fill the tub."

"Yes, Sir."

Franca glanced at the full moon through the porthole, extended her hand to Edoardo, and he put his arms around her waist.

"Edoardo, the moon never looked so beautiful."
"Nor you," he said.

He kissed her earlobes, his hands caressed her body, and he led her to the tub. They removed each other's clothes and dropped them to the floor as he climbed in first, studying her nakedness.

"You are like a Greek goddess."
"And you, a Greek god," she giggled.

Edoardo stepped out, put a towel around him, and assisted her out, wrapping the towel around her, pulling her close to him.

"I adore you. How was I so fortunate to have found you?"
"Edoardo, I discovered you first … remember?"

He grinned, lifted her up, carried her to the bed, loosened her hair, and their lips met in a frenzy of emotion. He kissed her breasts, ran his fingers up and down her body, entered her, and their bodies molded together with a hunger and yearning for one another as their bodies undulated to symphonic rhythms of passion until they succumbed to their ecstasy.

"Edoardo! I love you!"
"I adore you. My life was empty before you came along."

They held onto each other, delighted in each other's arms.

"You amaze me … you are not shy."
"Edoardo, how could I be shy? I participated in postmortems?
"What?" He exclaimed, sitting up.
"Yes. I'm used to naked bodies. I wanted to be a doctor."
"I'm sure your parents did not allow it. Please, no more."
"They never knew, don't let it slip out."

He shook his head, embraced her and they fell asleep in each other's arms.

Two weeks later, bullhorns resounded at six a.m., waking them up as the steward brought in juice, coffee and rolls, and welcomed them to New York City. They packed their trunks and went to the upper deck. The morning mist shrouded the harbor but burned off at sunrise, exposing the skyscrapers that loomed over the city. Boats gathered around the gigantic liner, as captains tooted their horns, welcoming newcomers to America. Franca stared at the immensity of the lofty buildings, exclaiming,

"They're like mountains made of granite."
"Here it is … New York City … quite a sight."
"Amazing!"

Police patrolled the docks, banging their clubs, chasing away tramps that slept with toothless mouths, opened in the direction of the sun. They leaped to their feet, urinating without shame. The police, furious at their behavior, clubbed their legs, and backed off from their fetid bodies.

Crippled sailors in wheelchairs, carved miniature ships out of wood, dreaming about their former days at sea, held out their hands for contributions. One elderly sailor combed his shoulder-length white hair and beard, adjusted his wooden leg, and hobbled around with pride. His tattered, faded uniform was adorned with full medals and shredded ribbons from his younger days of valor at sea.

Young hoodlums lurked behind trunks and barrels of merchandise, hammering the sides. Policemen grabbed them, but they wrestled out of the policemen's grip, taunting and cursing them as they ran away. Edoardo pushed aside the peddlers hawking figs and dates from pushcarts. The persistent ice cream man offered them a small ice cream cone for one cent and a soda for two cents. Finally Edoardo used his walking stick to ward off irksome peddlers. One man was resolute, exaggerated his smile, exposing perfect white teeth.

"Sir, may I brush your and the lady's teeth?"
"No, Toothpowder Man, we brush our own teeth."

After their trunk was put into a carriage, Edoardo ordered the driver to take them to the Plaza Hotel.

"Edoardo, how did you manage when you first came here?"

"I learned fast. On the first day, I had to go to the bathroom and I couldn't find the men's room. So, I positioned myself on an imaginary pot. A policeman saw me, laughed and led me to the bathroom. What a relief!"

"You have had a difficult life."

"In comparison to whom? There are millions like me. Tomorrow, we will go on tour of the department stores where they sell our fabrics and linens."

"Sounds wonderful."

The array of merchandise impressed Franca, but when she saw the label, she frowned.

"Edoardo, why not *Made in Sicily*?"

"We are Italians now."

"Do you think we well ever be accepted as Italians."

"Perhaps we prefer it that way," replied Edoardo.

They left the department store. Edoardo hired a carriage and ordered the man to drive them to a courtyard in Little Italy, where his old friend from the orphanage, Paolo Monte, had a restaurant. Paolo sat underneath a black and white awning, a white handkerchief around his neck, and one in his hand wiping his face.

"Edoardo! Paisanu![8]" He said, leaping to his feet.

"Paolo, I want you to meet my wife, Franca."

Paolo's eyes bulged.

"She's beautiful … classy. Son-of-a-gun, he's got all the luck."

"Franca, Paolo, my old friend from Messina."

"Signora, a pleasure. I wondered who had captured Edoardo's heart. Come in."

"I'm honored to meet you."

Paolo led them to a table covered with a white oilcloth, ordered a bowl of fruit, a chunk of provolone and hot Italian bread. He excused himself, returned with the handkerchief removed from his neck and changed into a lightweight navy blue jacket.

"Here is some of my best wine. Edoardo, how long are you staying this time?"

"About three weeks. We're going to Atlantic City for our honeymoon."

"I wish I could go to get away from this heat."

"Paolo, do you ever get homesick for Sicily?" Franca queried.

"Signora, I never want to set foot there again," he replied, curling his lips in disgust.

"Oh, forgive me for asking."

Edoardo glanced at Paolo with disdain, annoyed at the acrimony oozing out of him. Edoardo had spoken with affection about him, but now disquietude pervaded their meeting. Edoardo stood up, signaled Franca who excused herself and went to the ladies' room.

"Paolo, what the hell's the matter with you? Not everyone hates Sicily. I will always love Sicily like one loves a poor mother, but I like America better."

"Edoardo, are you ready? Paolo, it was nice meeting you."

He nodded. They could not get out of there fast enough. They climbed into their carriage and France sighed.

"What a nasty man."

"He is bitter about his childhood. He was left at the orphanage, never knew his mother or father; he had no one. I guess I was lucky that my father looked after me."

Edoardo ordered the driver to tour the tenements where he had lived upon his arrival to America. Various nationalities lived there, each in their own enclave. Franca frowned at the general malaise of the people, living in abject poverty with crowded streets and stagnant air. Hucksters peddled pots and pans, clothing, vegetables and fruit. Their carts piled up high like a pyramid, filled with bananas, apples and oranges. The hucksters cursed the boys who stole apples and oranges, sometimes turning over their carts, and running away laughing. Clotheslines were strung across porches and balconies. Hot winds puffed up pajamas, nightgowns and towels while shirts and dresses that had been starched, hung limp like lifeless bodies. Malodorous smells permeated the hot, humid air and Franca held her stomach, feeling nauseous.

"At least we have mountains, trees, flowers … and when we cook, it smells delicious."

"That's true. America has the same. I just wanted you to see where I lived when I first came here. You'll like Atlantic City; it reminds me of Messina without the mountains."

On Saturday morning, they boarded a train at Grand Central Station. They arrived in Atlantic City at noon, where Edoardo hailed a carriage and ordered the driver to take them to a small hotel on South Mississippi Avenue near the Boardwalk. They entered a turn-of-the-century hotel with latticed-wood awnings that dripped like lace over guests seated in white rattan chairs.

"It's lovely here," exclaimed Franca, inhaling the sea air.

"I knew you would like it. At least we will cool off."

After unpacking, they had a leisurely lunch and walked up to the Boardwalk. Edoardo hired a rolling chair for a tour along the length of the Boardwalk.

"Imagine, a wooden walk framing the ocean," Franca remarked.

"I've been here a few times. It would be a nice place to live."

She ignored his last statement.

Bathers hastened to the beach en masse. Children ran to the water's edge, dove into the water, tumbling and churning over and under the water, emerging and screeching with delight. While adults tested the water, wading up to their knees until they became accustomed to the cold and took the plunge. Expert swimmers dove in, swimming out toward the dolphins that went upward and downward, balletic in their movements.

Edoardo and Franca reached one end of the island at Maine Avenue. They got out of the rolling chair at the concrete bulkhead, where waves overlapped along the inlet. The spittle from the ocean sprinkled on their faces. Sailboats, yachts and fishing trawlers filled the harbor. Fishermen sold their catch of the day as owners of restaurants and fish markets queued up. Men with pushcarts yelled:

"Hot puppies for sale! Delicious hot puppies for sale!"

"Edoardo, what is he selling?"

"Hot dogs … they are not real dogs." He laughed, glancing at the expression on her face.

"I don't want any. Look over there, they have clams."

After they enjoyed their little neck clams, Edoardo hired a carriage for a tour of the island that included Ventnor City, Margate City and the other end of the island, Longport. In Margate, they stopped at the Elephant Hotel, where Lucy, the huge pachyderm was constructed of wood and plaster and "guarded" the entrance to the ocean. She was surrounded with mounds of sand, dunes, tall grasses and reeds dancing to the cool breeze along the shore.

They removed their shoes and hose, walked along the water's edge and later returned to their hotel for an interlude of love. As dusk descended over the city, Franca and Edoardo were spent from their excessive ardor for each other; their bodies limp from their passion.

"Franca, you are ravishing, free and uninhibited. I adore you."

"Tesoro, thank you."

After two languorous weeks, they departed with a promise to return.

On Sunday night, tourists departed from Atlantic City en masse, tanned, rested and reluctant to leave the barrier reef. Edoardo and Franca arrived at Grand Central Station, where men hawked newspapers, proclaiming the news:

KING UMBERTO I OF ITALY ASSASSINATED

Edoardo purchased a newspaper, shaking his head as he read the story. An anarchist, who detested King Umberto's policies, killed him. The king had instituted policies that led Italy into disastrous conditions with his nationalistic and imperialistic ambitions. Dissension grew among anarchists for the elimination of the monarchy because it was alleged that the king had spurred Italy into an armament race, a costly action for Italians who had limited resources.

"Edoardo, we must go home. My father must be so upset."

"He's lost an important ally."

"I just hope there isn't any turmoil in Italy. See if we can leave as soon as possible."

"I'll try. It's difficult during the summer months."

Edoardo managed to get them a cabin, paid off an acquaintance, and Franca and he departed. Despite their sadness about the death of the king, they enjoyed dining with many dignitaries who were artists, musicians and opera stars. Without Franca's knowledge, Edoardo spoke to the orchestra leader about her talent as a pianist. The orchestra leader approached Franca.

"Signora, please honor us with a piano rendition of your choice."
"Oh, Edoardo, you told them."
"Yes, please play a Scarlatti sonata."

The orchestra leader extended his arm, escorted Franca to the piano, and silence prevailed as she performed. As she finished, Edoardo was at her side amid the passengers' applause.

"Tesoro, you were wonderful."
"Grazie, I can't wait to tell Mamma and Papa′."

Upon their arrival in Messina, temperatures soared to one hundred degrees. The sun burned the earth, lawns appeared jaundiced, flowers wilted, fountains dried up, and a mantle of opaque orange hung over the city.

"The streets are deserted. Let's get something to eat and drink and leave for the interior before it gets too dark." Edoardo said, wiping his face with his handkerchief.

A path of dust preceded them and followed their carriage to the interior. They finally reached the villa, where cool mountain breezes caressed their faces. Dusk descended upon the massive verdant mountains, now tinged with brown, and stars glittered with majesty while a full moon lit their path. Edoardo brought the horses to a halt and immediately, the mastiffs surrounded the carriage, barking and snarling at them.

"Get away from here!" Giacomo yelled, his voice reverberating throughout the mountains.
"Papa′, it's wonderful to be home."
"Welcome home … Elena, they're home!"

They spent the evening speaking about Franca's first trip to America and the assassination of King Umberto I.

"Papa′, what will you do without his influence?"

"Franca, you've heard the expression *il mondo camino.*" (the world goes on)

Two days later, Maddalena and Roberto asked them to accompany them to Taormina for a candlelight play at the ancient Greek Theatre on Mount Tauro, where the gods reigned. They had an expansive view of Mount Etna, the great volcano, rising almost eleven thousand feet above sea level, spouting sulfurous fumes from its entrails.

"It's frightening, I want to leave," said Maddalena, shuddering.

"There is nothing to be afraid of … it's quiet. Tomorrow morning we'll go to Catania to get a closer view," Roberto stated.

In the morning, they reached Zafferana in Catania, settled in their hotel rooms and directed their gaze at Mount Etna. Despite the barrenness at the top of the crater, with its venom subdued, flowers and plants grew profusely on the sides. The earth at the bottom of the volcano was rich and dark, a haven of fertility, where fruits, vegetables and nuts flourished. Residents lived along its slopes, mindful of its power, but also appreciative of its benefits.

"Mongibello!" Edoardo exclaimed.

He bowed to the volcano, the largest in Europe, and recalled when the Arabs ruled Sicily from the eighth to the eleventh century and named Mount Etna: Beautiful Mountain.

"Let's go to Casale before the afternoon sun," suggested Roberto.

An old Roman dome had been erected in Casale in 400 A.D. and archeologists had uncovered mosaic walls that had been plastered over paintings of six Greek girl athletes in bikinis.

"Franca, at least they kept cool. I'm going to have the dressmaker make me a suit like that," Maddalena said, laughing.

"Me, too, a red one" Franca replied, grinning.

Later in the day, they toured the yellow countryside of Etna, where peasants worked in dangerous, sulfur mines for export to Western Europe. Anxious women milled around with little children and wiped their faces with their aprons. At the sight of their fathers, husbands, brothers, and sons, they rejoiced as their men emerged with faces and eyes coated with sulfur. The mines were dangerous, with narrow, hot tunnels. Men discarded their clothes, working naked in the mines; sometimes children were used as slave labor.

"I can't stand the way our people are exploited. The owners of these mines are greedy, strangers to this land," Edoardo remarked.

"Our system must change."

"Roberto, why don't you try? Everyone speaks about change but nothing happens," Edoardo commented.

They spent the night in Etna, rising at dawn and returned to the villa, where they spent the rest of the summer. Then Edoardo prepared for his departure. Despite the fact that she knew he had to leave, Franca paled at his announcement, holding onto him.

"I want to go with you."

"With the business, I will have to leave you alone. What will you do until you learn English?"

"I suppose you're right."

Despite Edoardo's absence, Franca kept busy, studied English, enjoyed her teaching position at the university, where she taught Graeco-Roman literature, and volunteered at the clinic with Dottore Rossi. But her nights were empty without Edoardo at her side and his arms caressing her.

After supper with her family, Franca went to her apartment on the second floor, undressed, put on her nightgown and robe, played the piano, and read Edoardo's letters that were filled with love for her. She touched her face and yearned for his arms around her, her lips upon hers, his hands caressing her body.

Then she anxiously waited at the port with Tonio, anticipating Edoardo's arrival for Christmas. The ferry was crowded with residents returning from other parts of Italy and Western Europe. Franca ran to the gangplank into his arms and kissed him.

"Edoardo, Tesoro … oh, I missed you so much."

"Franca, Franca, I love you."

"I can't stand to be away from you. I'm going next time. Did you stay away from Greenwich Village?"

"Of course, I didn't want to see my so-called friend, Paolo … bastard."

On Christmas Eve, the family gathered for the traditional meal of seven fishes that included tuna, whiting, eel, mackerel, swordfish, baccala (salt-dried cod imported from Norway) salad, pesce stocco (cod air-dried on boat sails in Norway), cooked in a tomato sauce with celery, onions, sweet basil, capers, green olives and potatoes; truly a delicacy. The pasta dish consisted of linguini with an anchovy sauce with roasted breadcrumbs sprinkled on top.

Tonio, his wife Maria and their daughter, Costanza spent Christmas Eve with the Raimondi family. Costanza was a beautiful child with wavy black hair, brown eyes, and exuberant with an infectious smile.

"Costanza, what grade are you in now?"

"Uncle Edoardo, seventh grade. When I grow up, I want to go to America."

"Perhaps, you will."

She grinned.

A few days later, Costanza went shopping with her mother for fabrics on Viale San Martino and wandered outside. Suddenly a man covered her mouth, carried her behind a warehouse, holding a knife at her neck. She wept with fright and he warned her in Sicilian, if she screamed, she would die. He stuffed her mouth with a handkerchief, lifted up her dress, pulled down her stockings and raped her. She stiffened up; it appeared as if she went into shock. Then he ran. Costanza wept. What should she do? She screamed! Men and women came to her aid, consoling her, wiping her face, and the women put her clothes back on.

Her mother ran to her.

"Costanza, what happened?"

The child shook her head, unable to speak and hung onto her mother, who took her to Dr. Rossi.

And they found Franca there.

"Who did this to her," whispered Franca.

"She said he spoke Sicilian to her but later he sounded differently. He was dark-skinned."

"She's ruined for life," sobbed her mother.

"A lot of people who come here speak Sicilian. We'll find him. Tonio should be here any moment."

"Maria, take her home. I'll give her some medicine to make her sleep"

"Si, Dottore, Grazie."

Tonio ran in as Maria held Costanza. He was enraged, sobbed incoherently and Franca put her arm around him.

"Who did it? I'll kill him! I'll kill him!"

"Tonio, we will find him. Come to our house. Papa´ will get men together."

"No, Franca, I'll take them home. I'll be back."

In the morning, when the roosters crowed, Giacomo and ten of his men climbed onto their horses. They began the search around the docks, where men from many nations unloaded and loaded merchandise. Giacomo asked permission from the captains to search their ships, and they protested only once. They directed their double barrel shotguns at their heads, and the captains relinquished their authority. Giacomo and his men searched a plethora of ships in the harbor, frustrated and exhausted. Suddenly a man climbed up a ladder, nervous and anxious to get away. If he dove into the sea, they could get him, so he decided to climb to the top of the mast. But a fellow sailor grabbed his leg and pulled him down as he rattled on the Ottoman Turkish, pleading for his life. His beady eyes darted from Giacomo to his men. The he implored them in a form of Sicilian.

"I fear you people!"

"Merda![9] You only have to fear us if you are guilty. We revere our children and to hurt one," Giacomo bit his lip.

A cold sweat came over the man, wetting himself, looking around for some escape. There was none, only eyes staring at him with virulence and wanting vengeance. The ship's captain confronted Giacomo and declared the man should be returned to his country. Giacomo turned crimson, pointing his gun at the captain's chest.

"No, then he will get away with it. He remains here for our punishment."

The men shackled the rapist, whose eyes protruded with terror as he averted obdurate gazes that foretold his future. They shoved him into the carriage, drove up to a desolate area of the mountains, where they threw him into a shack.

Tonio, Maria and Costanza arrived and when she saw the rapist, she screamed, cowering at the sight of her abuser. Maria held her close and brought her outside while Tonio confronted him.

"Maladetto!"[10]

Tonio emptied his gun into the rapist and watched him squirm as he died.

"Mori con un cane! Mori con un cane![11] You have ruined my daughter."

Giacomo came in, embraced Tonio, and led him outside into the fresh air.

"Tonio, it's over … he's dead."

The next day, tarantulas, ants, and mice nibbled at the wasted flesh; then the men set the shack on fire.

Edoardo had not participated in the killing and admonished Franca when she returned home.

"The police should handle these matters. This eye for an eye must end," Edoardo exclaimed.

"Police? If you had seen her, you would have shot the man."

"No, I wouldn't."

A wall of silence separated them. Tears welled up in Franca's eyes for a few minutes and then he lifted her chin, kissed her upturned lips, whispering:

"You are my weakness. I adore you."

After Christmas, Franca and Edoardo departed for Paris where he planned on purchasing fabrics. While they dined at Cafe′ de la Paix restaurant, across from the opera house, Franca excused herself.

"Have to go to the bathroom. I'm nauseous."

"I'll wait for you outside the bathroom," replied Edoardo.

After regurgitating, Franca splashed cold water on her sallow face, but managed a smile when she came out.

"Edoardo, I'm pregnant."
"What? Are you sure? We'd better leave right away."
"We don't have to rush."
"We'll go to the train station right now for a reservation and leave tomorrow."

Franca leaned her hand on Edoardo's forearm.

"Are you happy?"
"Delighted, I love you."

During the next several months, Franca and Edoardo became enraptured with her body that blossomed with their child. They basked in the sunlight, strolled along the sickle-shaped harbor; at night they attended concerts and plays at the university. Life was idyllic.

One night at the beginning of June, after they had retired, Franca sat up as severe back pains contorted her face. She nudged Edoardo to wake him.

"I'll call Mamma?"
"Not yet. Get Dottore Rossi … please hurry."

When Tonio returned with the doctor, Edoardo explained to Elena about Franca's plans.

"She's always different, doesn't like to conform. I ordered the servants not to speak about this to anyone."
"But Mamma, that's what I love about Franca. She's courageous," Maddalena said.

Six hours later, amid tears streaming down her face, the primordial forces of Nature disgorged her baby from its security.

"It's a girl," Dottore Rossi exclaimed.
"A girl … how wonderful," said Franca, exhausted but exhilarated.
"Yes. Would you like to cut the umbilical cord?"
"Oh, yes, Dottore."

The nurse handed her a pair of sterile scissors and Franca released her baby's life from her own. For a moment, melancholy came over her. Why? Was it some kind of omen? Nonsense, it was just the strain and emotion over the baby's birth.

"Grazie, Dottore … it was a beautiful experience."

"I'm glad. Nurse, clean up Signora Privitera and the baby while I talk to her family."

Her parents, Roberto, Maddalena and Edoardo came into the room and Edoardo rushed to Franca, held her hand, bent down and their tears mingled.

"Look at our daughter … what a gift."

"Yes, she is," murmured Edoardo, adding, "What shall we name her?"

"Giulia, after your mother."

Edoardo's throat knotted, gazing at Franca with such love, holding her hand, and searching for words that were elusive. He kissed the baby's head and whispered:

"I hope you have a better life than your grandmother."

"She will. We'll see to it," Franca assured him.

And so Giulia became a source of joy to her family who showered her with love and attention. When she was two months old, the servant swaddled her like an Indian papoose, ensuring her straight limbs and well-formed body. On her first birthday, she was placed in a wicker-walking frame with an insert of crinoline, which enabled her to walk within two feet of furniture and walls without injury.

During that year, Edoardo had become accustomed to life in Messina once again. He added a store near his and Giacomo's factory on Viale San Martino and hired additional women for madeira work on linens, exporting them to America.

Giulia, under her grandparents' tutelage, was taught French, but Edoardo spoke English to her, and conversations between family members vacillated between French, Sicilian and Italian. Now five years old, Giulia had dark brown hair, large amber eyes, and a disposition that matched her beauty.

Edoardo realized that his income had somewhat dwindled and he must return to America, where his business needed his personal touch. The last week before his departure, he took Giulia to the docks, where she saw her grandfather's merchandise loaded onto boats that sailed to America. Suddenly she screeched with delight at the Baraculli walking by, carrying their feluccas; handsome, strong young men attired in black pants, white-striped cotton shirts with colorful scarves, and jauntily cocked, black berets. Their sailboats, with lateen sails, resembled Chinese junkets with large eyes painted on each side of the bow, with mermaids heralding their launch out to sea for tuna and swordfish.

"Signore Privitera, how are you? Would your daughter and you like a short ride close to shore?"

"Yes. Grazie. Giulia, don't tell your grandparents, they worry about you."

They climbed aboard, and the Baracullo sailed along the shore while the towering mountains manifested the beauty of the island against the azure sea. Suddenly, cool winds swerved the sailboat, black clouds cast a shadow over the sea and rain pelted them. Edoardo removed his jacket, covered Giulia and held her close to him.

"Signore, I'll take you back to shore."

As he dropped them off, the rain ceased and the sun emblazoned the skies once again. Edoardo and Giulia went home.

"Papa´, when I'm older, may I go to America with you?"

"Yes. That is why we must always speak English."

Three days after Christmas dinner with the family, Franca and Giulia retired to their apartment. Franca put Giulia to bed, sat down at her piano, a nightly ritual, with Edoardo glancing at the lists of clients he must see in America. An hour later, she kissed him.

"Edoardo, I'm going to bed."

"I have lots of work to do."

Four hours later, Edoardo snuffed out the candles, climbed into bed, twisting and turning, and sleep eluded him. He crept out of bed, held onto the wall until he lit a candle, and glanced at his watch: 5:00 a.m. He tiptoed into Giulia's room, kissed her on the forehead, and groped his way back into the living room. He hesitated for a moment, felt dizzy and held onto the furniture. Snuffing out the candle, he leaned against the wall and tried to regain his equilibrium.

"I'm sick … need some fresh air."

He opened the French doors, deeply inhaled the cool morning air and glanced up, where stars still glistened in the dark blue sky. Now and then a ship glided by on the calm waters that resembled a sheet of blue grass. An unnatural quietude pervaded the city, and Edoardo had a visceral, sensory perception of horror. A flock of birds flew in all directions, gaggling, ignored their leader as they flew in circular directions, confused about their destination. Donkeys brayed with fear, while tethered horses stricken with terror, neighed unnaturally, jumping in their stalls with every muscle in their sinewy bodies distended. Suddenly church bells pealed impending doom throughout the Provinces of Messina, Catania and Siracusa, but alas, the warning came too late.

"Giulia! Giulia! Edoardo bellowed as Franca ran toward Giulia's room, but the floor rolled beneath them. Edoardo and Franca held onto each other, tottered, and grabbed the piano leg. The crystal chandelier oscillated like a giant pendulum above them.

"Move!" He yelled, grabbing her leg, pulling her away.

The chandelier crashed to the floor; concrete walls collapsed around them and the floor opened up like a giant chasm, swallowing them up. Large chunks of plaster crowned them as they howled for Giulia. Another eruption plummeted them down into an abyss. Piano keys clinked, furniture toppled, and massive cornices entombed them. The stillness was dreadful.

In December of 1908, Mount Etna, located in the town of Zefferana, Etnea, had regurgitated, causing widespread earthquakes in the provinces of Catania, Siracusa and Messina. The mighty volcano had disgorged its venom, illuminating the skies with fountains of fiery lava, resembling an orange-red reptile, hissing, slithering and cremating animals and humanity. Seven minutes after the earthquake, a tidal wave roared over the shores of Messina, scooped up survivors, hurled them across the mountainside, crushing and absorbing them. Cement boulders and blocks of concrete weighing up to twenty tons, were flung sixty to eighty feet away. Waves that were forty feet high continued the slaughter against humanity and the magnificent buildings.

Finally the waves subsided, survivors crawled over rocks, their blood mixing with mud, sobbing and cursing the gods who had deserted them. Those who reached higher ground, before the onslaught of the tidal wave, were tossed like broken toys; their bodies crashed against rocks, bellowing their anger before they succumbed to Nature's fury.

"Terra bruciata![12] Terra bruciata!"

When the water ebbed, the after-shocks ceased, survivors crawled out of their crevasse, avoiding fires that lit the region, searching with raw bare hands for family amid lamentations and curses. Ships had overturned and struck the rocks. Howling was pervasive as people sought assistance, groping around, trying to pull themselves out the abyss, but it was a futile attempt without assistance.

As the morning sun shone upon the sea, Captain Ugo Martinelli, in charge of rescue operations, arrived. He wept with Russians who launched boats from ships, anchored offshore, looking for their fellow sailors who had decided to spend the night in Messina. Their friends had been buried under the debris of third and fifth-story buildings. Then English and Russian sailors from other ships joined in the rescue, assisting the Sicilians. Survivors were shocked that that their rescuers were not Italians but English and Russians who had felt the seaquake. When it was safe, they launched boats to haul survivors for other islands, parts of Sicily, Italy and Naples, which became the demarcation area for survivors who had family in America. In the meantime, men were handed picks and shovels. A survivor screamed and hurled the pick and shovel.

"Please be patient," Captain Martinelli said, trying to console the desperate people.

"Patient! When my wife and children could be dead!"

"As soon as we can, we will help you dig."

The man sat down and sobbed.

Soon pandemonium ruled among the survivors who furiously dug on their hands and knees, blood oozing out of their wounds, immersed in bitterness and rage, furious at Nature and the gods who had brought such destruction. Four days later, soldiers heard voices wailing from the rubble. Rescuers removed boulders, cornices and a keyboard wedged in between massive chunks of plaster. Three hours later, a bloodied hand flailed at them. Edoardo! Sailors pulled him up out of the pit, his pajamas stuck to him with a mixture of blood, encrusted with plaster, and blood gushed out of his right eye. Suddenly, the earth rumbled and no one moved or breathed. Then the earth rested. An English sailor gently cleansed Edoardo's eye and told the captain:

"Captain Martinelli, I know Signore Privitera and his family."

"Young man, we will do our best. It is a disaster, a tragedy but who can control the force of Nature."

"My wife was next to me but my daughter," he sobbed, and then glanced around at the destruction. Men, women, girls, boys, babies and animals lay strewn about like discarded rag dolls on top of demolished houses, stores and boulders.

"Oh my God!"

"Signore Privitera, the Russians are bringing up your wife."

Edoardo walked over where the sailors had dug. They pulled up Franca; her nightgown was shredded, exposing her breasts and thighs. Edoardo grabbed a blanket out of a sailor's hands, covering her and embracing her. Words eluded them for a moment, their emotions buried deep within them.

"Giulia, my parents, Maddalena and Roberto," Franca cried out.

"We were the first to be rescued. Sit here; let me see your wounds."

"Your eye! Oh, Edoardo, we've got to get help."

He glanced around at the devastation.

"Where?"

"I don't know. I don't know."

Franca had a large gash in her thigh, blood spurted out like a fountain, and her body ached from the descent into the nether world. Edoardo caressed her face, kissed her scratches and bruised, weeping.

"Franca, my love, we will find her and your family," Edoardo assured her.

"We've got to find Giulia before it gets dark."

She climbed over the rocks, and Captain Martinelli held her arm.

"Signora, we've set up tents for survivors ... maybe she's there."

A ray of hope cloaked their faces.

The sailors entered the tent first, cleared a path for them. The children's wail was heart wrenching, disheartening and pitiful as they stretched their arms while their frail bodies shivered with fear of abandonment. Franca and Edoardo searched through the sea of desperation; elderly men and women sat stoically on the ground, staring into oblivion.

"Let's get out of here. Capitano, do you have any idea how many people have died."

"Signore Privitera, we figure about 200,000 here in Messina, Catania and Siracusa ... why even Calabria ... how can one count the dead that are buried underneath the rubble?"

"Madonna! That's horrible. Please help us dig for out family."

The captain's reply struck a chord of dissonance, despair, and fury within them.

"We can't. We'll set up a tent, give you blankets, water, two picks two shovels and a few oranges."

"You can't leave us," Franca cried, grabbing his arm, thrashing her head from side to side.

"I'm sorry, so many people need help. If you hear voices, then we will help you out."

Franca and Edoardo leaned against a boulder; desolation and fear crawled up their spine.

"Lovely Messina, the earth's fury has destroyed you, gushed out its bitterness and fury. Your fury has been unrelenting." Her voice cracked.

"Franca, please, we must keep strong. We have a lot of digging to do. Stay here while I look around for pots or anything we can use."

Eventually emergency relief arrived such as doctors, nurses, soldiers, firemen, engineers, and the Red Cross. Additional sailors from England, Germany, France, Russia and the United States arrived. The news spread throughout the world as Europe's worse earthquake, a worldwide catastrophe.

Two hours later he returned with utensils, muddied linens, clothing, and towels. Franca helped him wash everything in the blue sea that was now tranquil and unusually beautiful. Then they threw everything over boulders to dry. But Edoardo's biggest find was a sword and candles.

They went to their tent and she froze, unable to utter a word, just pointing her finger toward the tent.

"Franca, what's wrong?"
"Uh! Uh!"

He saw it. A python! He put his finger on his lips, picked up the sword and started cutting it as the python unfurled, aiming for Edoardo. He chopped the head off and then picked it up with the sword and threw it outside. He sat down and wept.

"How awful. Suppose snakes or rats are near her?"
"Franca, don't think like that. It will drive us crazy."

Edoardo padded their knees with torn sheets. They dug and kept watching the sky, hoping darkness would be delayed. Soon the midnight blue sky twinkled with stars and Edoardo's yelled.

"Why are you so beautiful when we are suffering here below?"

They huddled together, the cold air chilled their bruised flesh, and they fell asleep in each other's arms. During the night, Franca screamed, something furry gnawed at her wound. Edoardo lit a candle and two rats as large as cats peered defiantly at them; their teeth large and ugly, still aiming for Franca's leg. Edoardo handed Franca the candle, grabbed both rats by their tails, went outside and pounded them to death on a boulder. Blood splattered all over him. Suddenly, dawn appeared. He walked to the sea, despite the cold, immersed himself, diving under; soaring up he felt cleansed. He ran back to the tent, removed his wet clothing, and dried himself with a blanket.

"After I dress, I've got to find some cats … emaciated ones."
"I'll continue to dig."

While he was gone, Franca removed debris and rocks with an unknown strength consuming her. She placed her ear close to the earth.

"Giulia, it's Mamma … Giulia … Giulia."

She continued digging, her tears mixing with debris and mud. Then Edoardo returned with two cats, one in each pocket, and placed them in the tent. He bent down, grabbed the pick and shovel away from Franca, and he held her for a moment.

"My darling, rest a while."

He dug relentlessly, rolled boulders over, called out, and then a hand thrust up at him; a sapphire ring glistened … Giacomo!

"Papa´?"
"Edoardo? Help us."
"Franca, hurry! It's Papa´, talk to him while I get the English sailors."

Within minutes, sailors dug, pulled out Giacomo and Elena, whose faces were covered with dirt and blood. Giacomo cried out in pain.

"I think my leg is broken. Take care of Mamma."

Russian sailors came over and wrapped blankets around them. Franca embraced them and cried with them.

"We've got to get Dottore Rossi … I hope he's alive."
"Giulia? Maddalena? Roberto?" Giacomo queried.

Edoardo shook his head.

"Not yet."

Franca tore up a sheet, made a sling for her mother's broken arm and cleaned her up while Edoardo searched for a tree limb. He stumbled over a basket of oranges and lemons, washed them in the sea, returned to the family, and helped Franca make a cast for her father.

"Mamma, Papa´, Franca will stay with you while I dig for the rest of the family."

Now the sunset provided lighting of ethereal beauty, with its shades of pink, lavender and pale orange. While the majestic mountains stood smug in their strength and power, the earth had been uprooted, despoiled and disintegrated into a filthy ocean of mud, dead bodies and animals. Soldiers and survivors piled up dead bodies, resembling a pyramid of carrion. Ravenous, bearded vultures hovered overhead, waiting to feast on the decay and resembled falcons with long, angled wings and diamond-shaped, dark tails with vivid breasts. Men querulously fought the vultures, throwing rocks at them; a futile attempt as they shot them dead with their luparas.

Later that night, perennial stars blazed through puffs of clouds, reflected upon the blue sea, which intensified the brilliant stars. The cumulous clouds moved slowly, the full moon peeked through, creating a mirrored trail on the blue sea. Edoardo diagrammed the area, figuring out where Giulia's room had collapsed: to the right or the left, forward or backward. At what angle did it fall? His patience dwindled. Then his fury reached its zenith, unexplained strength came over him. He rolled over a boulder and saw a large cornice of Spanish tiles and raised it. He gasped! A child's hand, it must be her!

"Franca! Hurry! It's Giulia!"

Franca chipped away at the plaster covering the child, with Edoardo urging her to hurry, his arms aching. Then, Franca wept at the mass of dark brown hair with plaster stuck to it. She pulled her out of the way. Edoardo dropped the cornice and the earth rumbled. When they brought her to the tent, Franca removed her pajamas, washed her and checked her injuries. She was unconscious but soon was alert.

"Mamma, I had bad dreams … I was so afraid."
"My darling, you're fine now, in our arms."

Franca turned away, hiding her tears while Edoardo spoke to Giulia.

"Giulia, my sweet, beautiful daughter."

Edoardo kissed her and then whispered to Franca.

"What's wrong with her?"
"Concussion and broken arm. She'll be all right. We've got to get a doctor for all of us."

Despite the massive destruction, some churches, cathedrals, and the Museo Nazionnale D'Arte had not been completely destroyed. A huge tent had been erected nearby the museum. Edoardo ran ahead, snaked his way through the mass of survivors who sat on the earth dazed, bewildered, with general despondency. Men and women had masks of hatred, disillusionment and fury. Only children wept. He searched for a doctor but to no avail. Hundreds were waiting for medical attention. Then he ran to his family and shook his head.

"Let's try the cathedral of the Madonna of the Letters; maybe we can find someone."

Edoardo opened the tall, wide wooden doors and saw Dottore Rossi. He went to them and expressed his sorrow and embraced them.

"Why has this terrible thing happened to our beautiful island," he questioned.

No response.

"Sit down and let me look at you. Franca, we could use your help."
"Dottore, not yet. Let her heal a bit, she has a great deal of pain," Edoardo explained.
"Of course, she can sit down."
"Dottore, when the pain eases up, I'll gladly help."

Giacomo, Edoardo and Elena glanced at each other with dismay, shaking their heads. Dottore Rossi motioned to the family to follow him to pews that were not destroyed, and had been reserved for the elderly and nursing mothers. Suddenly a young woman came in screaming, holding her baby at her breast; a soldier gravitated toward her and asked if he could help.

"The nurse said that my baby is dead. She is not!"

She leaned against a marble column, squeezed her breast replete with milk, and put it into her infant's mouth, murmuring:

"Figghia bedda da mamma … take my milk."[13]
"Signora, I'm Dottore Rossi, sit down and let me look at the baby."

Dottore glanced at Franca who sat next to the woman.

"Rigor mortis is setting in."

Franca grabbed the woman's hand, wanting to console her, but she pulled away.

"Signora, I'm sorry but your baby is in heaven," Dottore Rossi said.

"No!"

Her voice echoed as she ran out of the cathedral, onto the pavilion, threw herself down the mountainside, holding her baby, screaming the child's name. And then silence. Those who had watched the unfolding scene, cried for her, her baby, and for themselves.

Dottore Rossi took care of the family. Edoardo's loss of his eye appeared to be the worse injury. He gave him a black patch to wear so the deformity would not show. Franca promised to be back and assist the doctor as soon as the intense pain subsided.

"Maddalena and Roberto?" Dottore Rossi asked.

"They have not been found yet," replied Giacomo.

3

Upon returning to their tent, Giacomo, accustomed to getting things done, spewed out his impatience at the sailors who did not understand him; he ordered them to dig for his children. Then to their amazement, he got on his knees; imploring them that time was essential for their survival. They, in turn, were shocked, yet, sympathetic to that man; they complied and a team of five sailors dug feverishly.

"Papa', I'll speak to them."
Giacomo wept.

Five hours later, Maddalena's body was recovered; her waist-length hair a mass of entanglement, her face masked in plaster, and decay had set in. Her nightgown outlined the crevices of her body and a soldier removed plaster from her face; two large brown eyes stared at them, frozen in time.

"That's not Maddalena," Giacomo cried out.
"It is Maddalena. I had that nightgown made for her," Elena sobbed.
"It's strange. Remember when we saw Mount Etna and she trembled. I thought she was too emotional," Edoardo whispered to Franca.
"She had a premonition," she replied, weeping.

Her little sister dead, a sweet, unsophisticated girl, who resembled a Norman beauty with her blonde hair and brown eyes, now forever young and beautiful in death.

The family huddled together while Maddalena's body was placed into a wooden coffin on their former home site, until she could be transported to the family's ancestral cemetery in the interior. Her name was listed in a common Mass for the Dead at the cathedral.

Edoardo told the family to rest while he searched for food. On the way, he met people he had known growing up, offered their condolences, and one man offered him two aged horses.

"Grazie, I'll pay you when the banks open."
"Please, no money."

Riding a horse proved easier. He found a one-story house with a sale sign that contained two bedrooms, a kitchen and a living room. The owners told him they were leaving for America, where they had family. They were spent from that cauldron of destruction: Mount Etna, who ruled over them and dominated their lives. Almost the entire city of Messina had been destroyed.

Slowly, there was some semblance of order to their lives, while never giving up hope that Roberto was still alive. Fishermen once again sold their daily cache, but there was a lack of vegetables, wheat and fruit. As yet the highways had not been cleared of massive destruction.

Elena and Giacomo remained home with Giulia, desperate for some news of Roberto. Their tragedy had stolen their zest and verve for life. Somehow Giulia's playfulness, affection and laughter drew them out of their despair. Meanwhile, Franca began feeling better and worked with Dottore Rossi at the cathedral, where doctors healed battered faces, set broken limbs, but their patients' spirits had been shattered and splintered into a million pieces.

Two weeks later, an outbreak of cholera, malaria and typhoid fever spread throughout the city. Pandemonium erupted. Men refused to bury the dead; soldiers had arrived and were ordered to shoot protestors who did not assist in cremating bodies. Residents were horrified; cremation was practiced in ancient times. Pyramids of dead bodies were burned with soldiers supervising, and men covering their noses and mouths with rags. The pyre of bodies burned day and night for weeks until the fear of diseases had vanished.

Franca, overwhelmed with the mass of humanity, entered the cathedral and asked Dottore Rossi if she could treat the children rather than the adults. He agreed. Unexpectedly, people banged on the door, disrupted the routine of patients lining up. A crowd pushed their way inside, and their leader, a young man, confronted Dottore Rossi and Franca.

"We want the truth! Our families have been cremated … how bad are the diseases? Should we leave this godforsaken place?"

Immediately, soldiers flanked Franca and Dottore Rossi, and Franca shuddered at the ugly faces, etched in fury. Perhaps, they were justified with their vexation, and for a moment, she recalled history.

The Black Death—the bubonic plague—decimated one-third of the population of Europe that began in October of 1347 in China and Turkestan, and then transmitted to sailors aboard ships headed for Russia through the Crimea, a peninsula between the Black Sea and the Azov Sea, and reached Genoa. From there they sailed to Messina, docked, and many on board were dying from the plague. Within days the disease was like a malignant rain, spreading throughout the city and the countryside. Sicilians tried to leave the city but they were too late. Fathers abandoned their families, especially sick children, and chaos ensued. Boccaccio, the Italian writer, wrote:

"Victims ate lunch with friends and dinner with their ancestors in Paradise."

And what started the calamity? Fleas infected mice and then infected mankind.

Dottore Rossi raised his hand for order, attempting to allay their fears, stating the situation was under control, assuring them that Nature creates disasters but then rewards you with beauty. Messina would soon return to her former self.

"Fancy words! The nobility have the money to rebuild their homes, but what do we have?" The leader exclaimed, clenching his fists.

Franca wept. Soldiers pushed the protestors out of the cathedral.

Heavy equipment arrived from Palermo as well as food and clothing. Slowly residents' anguish and fears were tempered, especially when obstruction was removed from the highways. Giacomo and Edoardo rose at dawn, prepared for their trip to the interior where they hoped to find vegetables and fruit. They fed the horses, hitched them to a borrowed carriage, and they were on the way. They reached the outskirts of the city, when a man ran up to them, selling rabbits and calves' brains. Giacomo glanced at him ad nauseum, enraged, his face turned crimson, and he swung his cane at him.

"Who do you think you are fooling? Merda! Dead cats! Animals' offal! For pigs, not for us. Get away from me before I kill you."

"Papa', please calm down," Edoardo pleaded.

"If you are hungry, you'll eat anything," the man yelled.

"Bastardu! fa n'culu,"[15] bellowed Giacomo.

Edoardo hit the horses and they were on their way again.

They passed scores of injured men, women and children who dragged along the highway, downtrodden, hopeless, and begging them for assistance. Giacomo shook his head, opened his hands, and they realized the futility. Suddenly, a man with a bandaged head ran up to the carriage, got on his knees and sobbed.

"Giacomo, it's me … Tonio."

"Oh, my God, Tonio."

Edoardo jumped off the carriage, embraced Tonio, whose tears poured out like a fountain.

"Maria? Costanza?" he asked.

"Morte! Terra maladetto."[16]

Edoardo assisted Tonio unto the carriage and Giacomo sobbed as he related the loss of his children and the destruction. Tonio explained his home was gone and he did not know where to live.

"Tonio, you're living with us now," Giacomo said.

On the road leading out of the city, the road Giacomo had traveled his entire life, was strewn with dead animals and humans. Egyptian vultures hovered overhead, diving down, ripping putrefied bodies open, while survivors leaped out of the way. Men piled those bodies that vultures had not touched and burned them in the pyre. The stench was unbearable.

"Let's go, it's horrible here," Edoardo said.

A young woman got in their way, holding two young children. Coagulated blood covered their wounds as her children wailed, squatted on the earth, and relieved themselves.

"Why are you leaving the countryside?" Edoardo asked.
"Death hangs over us," she replied without further utterance.

Edoardo beat the horses out of frustration. He lacked enthusiasm for the trip that he feared would be futile. Finally, they reached the villa. The palm trees that once greeted them were swallowed up into the earth and a skeleton of a house remained with twisted, hammered-iron railing resembling a giant spider. The larks' song had ceased and insects no longer hummed.

Edoardo stepped down from the carriage, disillusioned and depressed, not for himself but for Giacomo. Within seconds, wild dogs surrounded Edoardo. He resembled an inert piece of sculpture, afraid of moving or breathing, frozen to the ground. Giacomo blasted the dogs with his lupara, one after another, until the dogs collapsed around Edoardo.

"Edoardo, you can breathe now! They're dead."

He climbed back into the carriage, threw his head back and sighed with relief.

"I've never been so terrified in my life. Papa´, thank you."
"I've got to teach you to use a gun."
"Papa´, I'm a city person. I don't need a gun."

Edoardo grabbed the reins, drove through the fields, and the ruination of the earth traumatized them. The earth had regurgitated; olive, nut and fruit trees, as well as vegetables, had been swallowed up into the earth's bowels. Where were the sheep, lambs, cows, horses, and most importantly, the villagers? Everything and everybody was gone. Desolation prevailed.

"This is the end." Giacomo screamed, thrashing about until Edoardo put his hand on his shoulder.

"Papa′, please."

They descended from the carriage and Giacomo leaned against a boulder with his gun, while Tonio and Edoardo clambered over precipices looking for something or someone.

"Tonio, stay with Papa′. I'll be all right."
"Here, take this small gun."

Edoardo glanced at it and Tonio explained how to shoot it.

Edoardo climbed over debris. He noticed a horse's head buried, its rump stuck up, and its tail gracefully spread over the ground. He continued on, hoping to find food and stopped at the sight of an infant sucking his mother's breast; mother and child were coated with ash, molded together for eternity. Her hand gripped a basket of oranges and lemons. He disengaged her hand from the basket and touched her and the baby's face and cried for them. There was nothing to bury them with, but searching around, he found tree branches and covered them. Then, to his amazement, he discovered a bottle of wine covered with ash.

Meanwhile, Giacomo became restless and asked Tonio for his arm, wanting to glance around. He spotted a sprig of mint, which he pulled out and ate. Hope glimmered within him because the earth was renewing itself. They sighed with relief. Edoardo returned and showed them the baskets. As they rode back to the highway, Giacomo startled him.

"Roberto is not dead."
"Papa′, how do you know that? Why hasn't he been found yet? Maybe he drowned or was buried in one of the mass graves."
"No, I feel he is alive … in trouble, but alive."
"If he is alive, where would he be? Why didn't he come home or get in touch with us."
"I don't know. I must do something or I'll go mad. I can't sleep."

Riding along the highway, men, women and children sought refuge in the caves, but an onslaught of bats swarmed around them and they scurried outside en masse back onto the highway. A young woman cuddled her baby, stretched her neck and glanced into the carriage. Her pitiful gaze moved Edoardo and he handed her two lemons and four oranges. She bowed her head in gratitude.

They returned home and Elena saw Giacomo's distraught face and eyes. No words or questions were necessary; his face revealed the trauma of the day. Elena urged him to sit down, having baked mackerel and squeezed lemon juice on top. Then Edoardo washed the outside of the bottle of red wine and poured it in cups."

"Wine, where did you get it? Elena asked.

"In the field, just wanted to surprise everyone."

Giacomo paused for a moment and then proposed a toast.

"Well, here's to the ancient Cyclops who still rule Mount Etna. Those giant shepherds in Greek mythology still protect their domain and we are at their mercy. We will never forget December 28, 1908, the year of our demise, with the terrible loss of land and life."

All wept in agreement.

Giacomo's nightmares about Roberto never ceased. He spoke about him as if he were alive. Finally, Edoardo decided something had to be done to alleviate his persistent torment. They had to find Roberto, alive or dead. When he explained his idea to Giacomo, his face lit up with resounding hope. They consulted Naval authorities, inquiring if naval or merchant ships had pulled survivors out of the water after the tidal wave. An officer stated he heard several survivors were saved and he was certain many other vessels had done the same.

"Captain, suppose my son was picked up, injured and brought somewhere else along the Mediterranean area?"

"Could be, it's a remote possibility."

"Then why didn't he come home?"

"I can't answer that."

"I know. I want to speak to all the captains whose ships passed through here after the earthquake. Don't your ledgers show the names of the ships and their captains?"

"Yes, it's going to be quite a task."

"I can't rest, I must do this."

For a month, Giacomo and Edoardo remained at the port, renting a hotel room, where they watched the harbor. They had the list of the ships that were important to their search. Edoardo was impressed with Giacomo's knowledge of many languages.

"Papa´, it's amazing, where did you learn?"

"Since I was a youngster, I liked spending time at the docks, talking to people from all over the world."

At dusk one evening, Giacomo sat by himself, glancing at the setting sun sinking slowly until a mantle of orange with lavender hues covered the sky. He sighed. Word had spread throughout merchant ships about Giacomo's vigil and a naval officer approached him.

"Signore, your son could have gone to Sardinia, Corsica or Malta. That ship sailing by is Maltese and it's stopping."

"You're right. Malta is only fifty-eight miles away. Grazie."

Giacomo boarded the ship. He spoke to the captain who was curious but evasive until Giacomo spoke the Maltese language, a combination of Arabic and Sicilian.

"Captain, I am a father looking for a lost son. Did you pick up any survivors after the earthquake?"

Giacomo faltered for a moment, tottering, and the captain led him to a seat.

"Yes, mostly young people. There was one young man from here, seriously injured and didn't want to go home. He asked me where I lived and he pleaded with me to take him to Valletta."

"I'll pay you whatever you want. Take my son-in-law and me to Malta."

"I can't now. I have to deliver merchandise to Corfu. I should be back in a week."

"A week!"

"I'm sorry."

"What is the young man's name?"

The captain shrugged his shoulders.

Giacomo and Edoardo returned home, haggard, their clothes rumpled and they apologized for their unkempt appearance. Giacomo explained all that had occurred at the dock and for the first time since the earthquake, hope and alacrity prevailed in the home. He told them he was on an implacable quest to find Roberto. Elena was worried about his fixation that Roberto was alive; nonetheless, he must find some respite.

It was time for Edoardo and Giacomo to board the ship to Malta, but turbulent seas and dense fog delayed their voyage for another day. The following morning, when the fog burned off and the sun glistened on the sails, the ship sailed. They leaned on the railing; their thoughts vacillated between despair and joy, refraining from any utterance. If Roberto was alive, how bad were his injuries? Why hadn't he come home? Suppose he wasn't there?

Malta resembled a dot in the Mediterranean Sea until the ship sailed close to the island with few islets around. The captain ordered his men to moor the ship and escorted Giacomo and Edoardo to his waiting carriage. Valletta was a fortified city of concrete, with villages high on the hilltops, and gardens cascading along the hills. The captain stopped the horses in front of a stone house.

"I'll go in first and explain to the landlady."

After an explanation, she led the captain to the garden.

"There he is, a very sick man."
"Thank you, I'll get his father. What is his name?"
"He wouldn't tell me. I think he comes from an important family. He's educated."

The captain motioned Giacomo and Edoardo to follow him into the garden.

"There is the man I told you about."
"He's an old man. My son is twenty-five years old."
"Signore, that's him. When you get closer, you can see that he's young."

They walked toward him. A gaunt man with a handkerchief masking his face stared at them in disbelief. He coughed incessantly, blood spewing out of his mouth onto his handkerchief and he pulled it off.

"Roberto! It's you, my son, I knew you were alive."

Roberto sobbed and Giacomo went to him, holding him, kissing him.

"Why didn't you come home?"
"Look at me, Papa′."

His face was mapped with scars as if he had been beaten. His left eye was shut and he covered his right eye from the glaring sun.

"I'm not the son you knew. I'm paralyzed on one side."
"My son, I love you dearly."

Edoardo approached them, assisted Roberto to his feet and hugged him.

"Your mother waits to see you," Edoardo said.
"And I yearn to see her," Roberto replied.

The captain drove them to his ship as Roberto explained what happened to him.

"I was dazed, found myself outside, when a gigantic wave swept me out to sea. I was thrown around, battered against the rocks. It felt as if my body was coming apart and then I lost consciousness."
"We found him floating and picked him up," the captain interjected.
"Papa′, is the rest of the family alive?"
"No, Maddalena is gone."
"Oh, no, Maddalena, so sweet and lovely. I'll never forget how she was trembling when we saw Mount Etna, almost as if she knew. Papa′, let's go home."

Giacomo nodded.

On the ride back to Messina, Roberto remained in the cabin, coughing constantly; blood spurted out of him like a spigot. Giacomo cleaned him up, covered him and fed him broth, a spoonful at a time. Then Roberto gasped for air. Edoardo picked him up and carried him to the upper deck, where he breathed in fresh cool air.

"Edoardo, thank you for finding me. I would have died like a dog."
"Your father found you. He kept having nightmares. He said you were alive and he was right."

They reached Messina as dusk scrolled above the mountains. The evening star appeared and Roberto wanted to stand, anxious to see the beauty of the sea and the stars glimmering in the darkened blue sky. He was frail and his legs gave way on him. Edoardo called for a stretcher and sailors placed Roberto on it, carrying him out to a carriage, where Tonio waited for them.

"Tonio, how did you know we would be coming in?"
"Giacomo, I asked the authorities. Welcome home, Roberto."
"Grazie, Tonio. I am sorry about your family."

Tonio acknowledged his condolences.

"Papa′, when we get home, I want to walk into Mamma's arms."

Giacomo's throat knotted but he held back his tears.

Meanwhile, Tonio sent a courier to Elena and Franca informing them that they had found Roberto, sick but alive.

"Franca, he's alive! Your father was right. I can't wait until I can hold him."

Edoardo assisted Roberto out of the carriage. Giacomo flanked him and he sauntered into his mother's arms. Elena felt his skeletal body, trembling, but held back her tears.

"Roberto, I am so happy you're home. I've missed you, my darling son."
"Mamma, Mamma."

Edoardo saw Roberto's legs giving way on him, slowly slipping through his mother's arms, and he leaped to hold him up. He carried him into the bedroom, started to put on a blanket, when Roberto pushed the blanket off the bed, coughing continuously.

"Franca, can't you help him?"
"We've got to get Dottore Rossi; it's tuberculosis. I'll warm up some milk; put a shot of whiskey in with sugar and a lump of butter."

As Franca spoon-fed the concoction, Roberto eased up on his coughing and wanted to speak.

"I should have come home, but I didn't have the strength. Then I didn't want Papa′ and Mamma to see me this way. Call Papa′ and Mamma in here, I have something to say."

"Roberto, we're here," Giacomo said, leaning against the door.

"Forgive me for not appreciating the land that was so important to you, but when I was in Malta, I realized what we had. And now everything is gone. I promised myself if I got well, I would run for office and try to change our system."

"My son, it doesn't matter now. Here is Dottore Rossi."

Dottore Rossi concurred with Franca's diagnosis. He gave Roberto some medication, stating he was close to death. Tears poured down Elena and Giacomo's faces and Franca put her arms around her parents and wept with them.

Ten days later around midnight, Roberto panicked, gasping for air, yelling for Edoardo. Edoardo ran in, wrapped him in a blanket and brought him outside into the cold air. Acquiescence came over him; he became limp in Edoardo's arms and expired. Edoardo carried his body into the house, placed him on the bed, and his parents stood on each side of him. Elena sobbed, bending over him. Giacomo combed Roberto's hair, the tears falling on Roberto's face, as he lay by his side.

"Roberto, my son, your mother and I love you. Now you will be buried next to your beloved sister."

4

Messina's port once again bustled with commerce; official buildings opened throughout the city. Giacomo and his family now concentrated on life. He built a three-story apartment on the site of his former palazzo. The Central Government in Rome had sent sparse aid to the victims of the earthquake and as time went by, the aid dwindled. Sicilians in America sent money and clothing to their families left behind.

Giacomo became livid at the neglect from Rome, always viewing Sicily as Italy's stepchild, unwanted but useful for her strategic position in the Mediterranean. Houses and apartment buildings were needed; people still lived in tents. Food production had increased and the sea always brought forth its bounty, but a general malaise of apathy and desperation existed.

"I am going to Rome," Giacomo declared.

"Do you think it will do any good?" Elena asked.

"Who knows? I can try. Can you imagine the English and the Russians came to our help?"

Three weeks later, Tonio and Giacomo packed for the trip. But, during the night, Giacomo awakened with chest pains, perspiring profusely. Elena yelled for Franca who ran in and examined him.

"Papa′, you've had a heart attack. Tonio, get Dottore Rossi … hurry."

Dottore Rossi arrived, told Giacomo he must rest and should not go to Rome. He could have another heart attack that could be fatal.

"But I had to use influence to get an appointment."
"Giacomo, I'm sorry."
"Papa′, I'll go," said Franca.
"Are you sure you can handle it?
"Yes, I'll try. I don't have your skills at negotiating."

In the privacy of their bedroom, Edoardo glanced askance at Franca, shook his head in exasperation.

"Franca, I'll go to Rome."
"No, I'm sorry. I must do this for my father."

Edoardo realized that once Franca made up her mind, there was no discussion, no argument and no alternative. Since he had the utmost respect for her capabilities and intelligence, he had no doubt she would succeed.

At six o'clock the next morning, Franca dressed in a black suit with an ivory blouse, rolled her hair up and wore a black wool slouch hat.

"You look beautiful. I wish I were going with you, but I'll never leave Giulia again."
She embraced and kissed him.

"I love you. I'll be back in a few days."

From the ferry, Tonio and she went to Reggio di Calabria, where they boarded a train to Naples and then to Rome. Upon reaching the Eternal City, Tonio hired a carriage, ordered the driver to the Quirinale Palazzo, where the official greeted Franca with respect.

"Madam, your credentials, please," he said.
"I am Signora Franca Raimondi Privitera. Don Giacomo Raimondi is my father. Last night my father became ill and I have come in his place."

The official glanced over her credentials that revealed the Raimondis belonged to the Sicilian Nobility.

"Signora Privitera, we have sent help, but what can I do for you?"

She related the conditions of the people since the great earthquake and their needs.

"We did send some commodities. I suggest you go to the Minister of Agriculture, perhaps, he can help you."

"Is that all you have to tell me?"

"Well, I am very sorry."

"So am I, Signore. Do you know it took two days before medical help came to us? Two days!"

And she turned, slamming the door as Tonio leaped to his feet.

"Tonio, we have to go to the Minister of Agriculture on the second floor."

The ministered welcomed her, focused on her lovely face, her full lips, the air of assurance about her, and those blue eyes.

"Signora, with all due respect, I thought the Sicilians were dark, like the Arabs. I did not realize Sicilians educated their women."

"Signore, unfortunately, there is a great deal that the mainland of Italy does not know about us."

"My apologies. How can I help you?"

Franca explained the dire conditions and needs of the people in the Provinces of Messina, Catania and Siracusa.

"But we did send assistance."

"A pittance! Do you realized that the English and Russians came right away to our aid, not the Italians!" she said firmly. Then she took a deep breath and continued.

"Most of our people are living in tents and we need building supplies to rebuild homes for thousands of people. Do you know how many people died?"

"Fifty thousand?"

"Two hundred thousand from Messina to Reggio di Calabria."

"I'm sorry to hear that. Can I help you with supplies?"

"And workers?"

"No, you are on your own."
"Signore, people are injured, incapable of working."
"Well, let's see if we can get volunteers."
"Who works for nothing?" she asked.
"There's nothing more to discuss. Good day, Signora."

She turned, holding her head up high and met Tonio in the reception room.

"Itta sangu … itta sangu."[17]
"That bad?" Tonio asked, roaring with laughter.
"Yes, I didn't accomplish anything."
"Your father will be proud of you."
"I don't think so. Tonio, let's take a walk and have dinner. We'll go back tomorrow."

As they walked around, Franca stopped at a newsstand and something caught her eye in the newspaper.

"Tonio, please pay the man for the newspapers."
"Sure, what's in it?"
"Interesting, an article about women's emancipation."

Franca read the article.

Catholic women's groups have separated from the movement of the National Council of Italian women over civil rights for women, concerning divorce, suffrage and the Church's influence over schooling.

"Tonio, when we get home, I'm becoming a member of the National Council of Italian women."
"Do you think you should? In Sicily, we are a more contained society than the rest of Italy." He asked timidly.
"Of course. Women should have rights."

Upon their return to Messina, Giacomo was disappointed, yet, not surprised at the outcome. He had hoped, at least, for a promise of future aid. The cost of restoration to the land was prohibitive and Giacomo decided to sell parcels of the land, only to Sicilians. Elena agreed with him, wanting the pressure off him since his heart attack.

Then Franca told them about her intention to join the National Council of Italian Women for civil rights of Sicilian women. Her parents frowned at her.

"Why? You can't change our ways. I'd rather you didn't get involved. You have a great deal of freedom."

"Yes, I do because we are part of the nobility. But there are many illiterate, peasant women who are dominated by their husbands. They don't have any rights. Education will set them free."

"Franca, enough. I don't want to hear any more." Giacomo exclaimed.

That evening, Edoardo discussed his plan with Franca; he must return to America and check out his investments. He insisted that Giulia go with them.

"Mamma and Papa´ will be so upset. She brings them such joy."

"Tonio will be here with them. I will never leave her again."

Elena and Giacomo appeared chagrined at the news, imploring him to leave Giulia.

"Vossia,[18] I can't. I'm sorry."

"As you wish," Giacomo replied with resignation.

At the end of the school year, Giulia and her parents boarded a transatlantic ship for Naples. Now eight years old, Giulia's lustrous, dark brown hair fell to her waist, her round amber eyes, under think lashes, sparkled. She skipped along in a pink cotton dress with rag-a-muffin sleeves, button-down kid shoes, and a pink silk bow flopped in her hair.

Aboard ship, Giulia had an opportunity to speak English. Edoardo was delighted but Franca teased them about excluding her.

"Giulia, your English is better than mine."

"Don't worry, Mamma, I'll translate for you." She said giggling.

Two weeks later, the ship crawled into the harbor. The morning sun reflected upon the windows of the skyscrapers and Edoardo raised Giulia up as they watched giant liners entering the port. They immediately descended the ship and headed for an apartment in Greenwich Village.

Once Franca familiarized herself with the area, Edoardo went to his stockbroker and the bank. He hired a carriage for Franca and Giulia to tour the city and wrote an address where they were to meet for dinner. Later they walked outside; it was a balmy evening. Salmon and charcoal hews colored the sky with clouds brushing the top of the granite buildings.

Edoardo ordered a carriage for a ride through Central Park. They rode over balcony bridges, under arched trees, near brilliant borders of flowers that created a setting for graceful swans, resting on crystal lakes.

"It's lovely here," commented Franca.

Men lit lanterns, exposed lovers on park benches, huddled together, their arms entwined, their lips together, and ignoring the gaping strollers.

Edoardo heard the sound of an orchestra revving up for the evening concert, and ordered the driver to halt. But, Franca touched his arm; Giulia had fallen asleep on Franca's lap. He asked the driver to take them back to their apartment. While he carried Giulia inside, Franca unlocked the door, picked up an envelope on the floor and read it while Edoardo carried Giulia to her bed. Franca's hands trembled, disbelief masked her face, her lips quivered, and she handed the note to Edoardo as tears poured down her face. He read the note, scowling, and implacable rage and fear terrorized him as she saw the imprint of a black hand with a request and a warning.

We want ten thousand dollars or your daughter will die.

"Goddamn bastards! We've got to get out of here tonight." He said in a muted tone, his hands shaking.

"What are you going to do?" Franca cried out.

"Shh, keep your voice down; I don't want to frighten Giulia. I would call the police but they'll think it is just one Italian against another. Besides, *La Mana Nera*[19] gets information from the police. I'll call Paolo, I've done him favors, lent him money."

"Are you sure you can trust him."

"We need help, I have to trust him. Lock the door, pack the trunks, and do not open the door to anyone but me."

Edoardo ran down through the back stairway into the restaurant's kitchen and saw waiters putting on their jackets for work. He grabbed one and put it on.

"Say, Mister, first night?"
"Yeah, where's the telephone?"
"Outside. You'd better not be late; the boss ain't gonna like it."
"I won't. I need the job."

Paolo answered the telephone and was not surprised to hear from him, which puzzled Edoardo. Could Paolo be involved in the threat to Giulia? No. He knew Paolo was jealous of his achievements, but they had known each other since their days in the orphanage in Messina.

"You knew I was here?"
"Yeah, a girlfriend of mine is a salesgirl at one of the department stores and she recognized you. How come you didn't call me?"
"I haven't been here that long. Look, I need help. My daughter's life has been threatened."

Silence.

"Paolo, did you hear me? My daughter's life has been threatened!"
"Sure, I heard you. You've done well through the years, living like a *grand signore.*"
"What the hell are you talking about? Are you mixed up with these people?"
"Sort of."
"Paolo, you are or you're not. What do you want?"
"They want ten-grand; I can help you for five-grand."
"You bastard! Friendship means nothing to you."
"Edoardo, cut out the shit and make up your mind now."
"I have no choice. Just make sure nothing happens to my family or me or else."
"Or else? You're too much of a gentleman. Here is what you do."

Edoardo listened, returned to Franca and Giulia who pondered about Paolo's involvement. He never realized the full extent of Paolo's bitterness. But now, he heard his jealousy oozing out like a snake's venom, threatening Giulia, his beloved daughter. He removed five thousand dollars from his money belt, put it in a brown envelope, and urged Franca to hurry. An electric taxicab would arrive for their department to a hotel near the docks.

"Are you coming with us?" Franca asked, distraught that he would not leave with them.

"I'll meet you at the hotel. If anything happens that I don't make it, get on board ship in the morning. I called someone at the docks. He is waiting. Give him the envelope. He'll look after you. His name is Giorgio Antonelli."

"Edoardo, can't we stay with you."

"Please, you have to get out of here. It could be dangerous."

Once Paolo saw Franca and Giulia ride away, he emerged from the darkness, held his hand out, and Edoardo handed him the envelope.

"I'm sure I don't have to count it. One thing I gotta say about you, you're honest."

Edoardo turned away; fury crawled up into his gullet, wanting to punch Paolo in his mouth. Suddenly, two sinewy figures cast their shadow underneath gas lanterns, conspicuous in Panama hats. The men leaped across the street, as three other men pursued them, grabbed them from behind, and shoved them into an overturned garbage wagon, rubbing their heads in the slime. One bulk of a man assigned to special duty stomped on the men's necks with heavy boots until they were dead. Edoardo shuddered. Paolo offered his hand to Edoardo, assuring him he had nothing to fear any longer.

"You cold-hearted bastard, I never want to see you again."

Paolo shrugged and joined his men in a carriage. Edoardo sighed with relief, entering the electric taxicab and a carriage followed with their trunks. He wanted to be certain that Paolo did not follow him. Franca was relieved when he got to the hotel, crying as he held her close.

"It's all right. Now we can enjoy our voyage. Giulia asleep?"

"Yes."

When they arrived in Naples, fear of the Camorra, the Neopolitan Mafia, hovered over them. The men crouched near the docks, hawk-eyed, cunning and dangerous, placing bets on the worth of the tourists, especially targeting the English and the Germans.

Before arriving, Franca had sewn their money and her jewels into the linings of their clothes. She walked down the gangplank in a tattered black dress and heavy black stocking. Her hair was wrapped with a bandana and she carried a worn leather handbag, tied with rope. Edoardo rumpled his full head of salt and pepper hair; a shadowed beard added to his unkempt appearance, and his eye patch revealed a mystery about him. Giulia wore a drab brown dress, white cotton stockings, and high-top, laced brown shoes.

Handsome young men strummed their guitars and mandolins under gas lanterns, while balladeers sang famous Neopolitan love songs. After their performance, they held out their caps for tourists but bypassed Edoardo and his family.

"We must look desperate." He whispered to Franca, grinning.

The aroma of roasting chestnuts counteracted the stench of garbage, which stewards had dumped into the sea. Sea gulls swarmed about, scooping up the flotsam.

On the train going home, Edoardo told Franca:

"When we get home, we will have to find out who's behind Paolo. Why did he settle for half? Franca, I must learn to use a pistol."

5

Once again, Messina blossomed with copious flowers, palm fronds swayed and shadowed piazzas, prickly pears sprouted from bushes, and the aroma of citrus fruit infused the still air. The earth was regenerating itself. Life returned to the city; boys played soccer amid obtrusive destruction and families strolled the sickle-shaped harbor. But cafes along the bay were filled with disillusioned, unemployed men who played cards to fill the idle hours.

Edoardo and Franca were grateful to be in the safety of their domain, on the ground that Franca loved despite its problems. They knocked on Elena and Giacomo's door on the first floor apartment building and effusive tears of happiness flowed among them.

"Siete il bastone della mia vecchiaia."[20] Giacomo said, wiping away his tears.

"We are so happy you're back so soon," Elena said, embracing Giulia.

"Papa′, later we must talk."

"Of course, after dinner." Giacomo replied, noticing the urgency in Edoardo's voice.

When Giacomo heard about the crisis that had befallen them, he was livid, his face turned crimson, and he bellowed.

"How dare they? I'll find out who's behind this threat against my granddaughter. I've always been kind to everyone. Who has this vendetta against me? Or you?"

"Papa′, I never thought I could kill anyone, but I must learn to use a pistol."

"I'll teach you," volunteered Tonio.

A month later, Giacomo and Edoardo departed for Palermo, known as *Conca d'Ora,*[21] for its abundance of fruits, wheat, olive groves and vineyards. Intellectualism once flourished in Palermo from the twelfth century to the eighteenth century. Intellectuals such as Voltaire and Rousseau spent time in the courts of the aristocracy.

When they descended from the train, Don Armando Fazio had a carriage waiting for them. A driver drove them outside the city through a winding road to a spacious villa, high up in the mountains. A six-foot high, wrought iron fence surrounded the property with an abundance of cypress trees, growing against the railing, filling every gap. Flowers galore surrounded the property.

Mastiffs roamed the grounds but when the gates opened, armed guards chased the dogs away, and signaled the driver to ride on. They searched Giacomo and Edoardo, removing their pistols and assured them they would be returned to them upon their departure. Children played on a wrap-a-round balcony, waving and yelling at them. They waved back at them. A servant came out of the house, grabbed their hands and brought them inside.

Don Fazio's servant welcomed them to Palermo and led them into the library that contained an entire wall of books and manuscripts. Edoardo and Giacomo were served espresso, pastries, strega and anisette. Then Don Armando Fazio sauntered in, impeccably dressed in a beige linen suit and a brown tie with geometric designs in beige. He was an impressive, handsome man with light brown hair, flecked with gray, which he wore straight back. His green eyes glanced at them with cordiality. He smiled. They rose to their feet and Don Fazio embraced Giacomo and kissed both sides of his cheeks.

"Grazie, Don Fazio. This is my son-in-law Edoardo Privitera. I'm sure you have heard of his father Count Ruggero Privitera."

"Si, Count Ruggero Privitera … an honor. Sit down, please. Don Giacomo, I will never forget your assistance in my admission to the University of Messina."

"It was my pleasure," Giacomo stated.

Edoardo and Don Fazio studied each other, each trying to figure out the other's personality. Edoardo wondered what did Armando Fazio have to do with the threat on Giulia's life.

"Don Giacomo, I extend my condolences on the loss of your children and your land. Is there anything I can do to help?"

"Edoardo, tell Don Fazio what happened to you in America."

Armando Fazio listened and appeared sympathetic. Don Fazio expressed his regret, shook his head and declared it was a terrible thing that had happened.

"I want my granddaughter, Franca and Edoardo to live in safety. The mere thought of threats on their lives cannot be tolerated." Giacomo said.

"What do you want me to do?"

"Find out who is responsible and make sure it never happens again."

"Don Giacomo, I give you my word. I need at least two months."

"How much will it cost?"

"Don't worry about the cost."

Edoardo leaped to his feet.

"I would appreciate your honesty."

"At this time, it will cost you nothing."

"But how about later?"

Giacomo placed his hand on Edoardo's arm to cease the confrontation. Armando Fazio laughed sardonically at Edoardo's questions that unnerved him for a moment. He was not accustomed to confrontations; his word was law.

"Eh, Don Giacomo, *il mondo camina,*[22] said Fazio, shaking Giacomo's hand.

"Si, others have told us … we know the world goes on," Edoardo murmured.

On the ride back to Messina, Giacomo questioned Edoardo about Don Fazio.

"Do you trust him?"
"Papa′, after what happened between Paolo and me, I trust no one."
"We'll see," sighed Giacomo.

Giacomo was pensive and he recalled he had always dealt fairly and honestly with people. His reputation had earned him respect and power. He had been an integral part of the wealthy nobility in Messina that controlled the trading between the Occidental and Oriental worlds.

At last, Armando Fazio sent a courier with a message: he planned on coming to Messina and would like to meet at Giacomo's home. Giacomo answered he was honored and invited Don Fazio to dine with his family.

Don Fazio arrived and after dinner with the family, the men retired to the verandah. The serious conversations began.

"Now, you can speak freely." Giacomo stated.
"Don Giacomo, here is the problem. La Mana Nera wants a percentage of your business in America. Edoardo and you have made a lot of money and haven't shared your prosperity. My son is marrying a girl from the Province of Messina. I want part of your land as a wedding present for them."
"My land?"
"You'll live without fear and never have to worry about your family."
"I don't know. How much?" Giacomo queried.
"One-half, it needs much work."
"I need some time to think about it," Giacomo uttered.
"My family is coming in tomorrow for my son's engagement. I would like to know tomorrow. It will be a wedding gift for them."
"Are you aware that the land has been in my family for centuries? You'll need an army to restore the land." Giacomo told him, wiping away his tears.
"That is my concern."

Fazio stood up, extended his hand to Giacomo, and departed.

"Giacomo, let him have it. Our family's safety is more important than the land," Elena said.

Giacomo put his hands up to his head, sauntered into the bedroom, wanting to be alone, and fell asleep with his thoughts. When he awoke, he concluded it would it would be a desperate act, handing half of his property to Don Fazio. His ancestors' struggle for the land haunted him. Yet, on the other hand, his only son was dead, the land lay fallow, and he lacked the strength for a new beginning.

Don Fazio came in the morning and waited for Giacomo's handshake that sealed their agreement.

"You have my word that your family will be free from terror. I will tell all parties involved that you are indeed a man of honor."

6

With rumors of war, Italian forces invaded Libya in 1911, at the behest of Prime Minister Giovanni Giolitti, who hoped to distract Italians from internal problems. Some opposed the colonization of Libya, but the prime minister assumed it was a land for Italian emigrants. But, a young, ardent imperialist Benito Mussolini condemned the war as a crime against humanity. In a sense, Italians were returning to their ancient Roman roots.

"Papa', look at the newspaper. We have invaded Libya and chased the Ottoman Turks out. There has been a great deal of slaughter. Although the Turks fled, we have been ruthless … killing men, raping women, and putting Libyans in camps."

"Such outrageous behavior" Giacomo gestured, raising his hands in futility.

"Papa', teach me Arabic. When things quiet down, people will need linens and fabrics; then I'll go.

"Don't rush it. It could be very dangerous. At the dock, I heard Omar Mukhtar, a teacher of the Koran, is leading the guerillas. But, he has been fair in his treatment of the Italians."

Some Sicilian men signed up for duty in Libya, but Edoardo had other plans. He remained in Messina, despite the fact that he and Giacomo's factories had closed for lack of business. He studied Arabic with Giacomo, preparing for the day when he could sail to Libya. As Giacomo read newspapers from Milan, he expressed concern about Benito Mussolini, a Socialist, who said: *We Socialists are not Italians, we are Europeans.*

"What nonsense!" Giacomo exclaimed.
"He wants to be a Caesar," Edoardo concluded.

Two years later, Edoardo boarded a ship for Libya, three hundred and fifty miles from Sicily. With the invasion, Italians had built roads, installed irrigation systems, developed Libya's port, and Italian men married Libyan women. The ship stopped overnight at Pantelleria, an island between Sicily and North Africa, picking up passengers who were anxious to leave the penal colony harbored on the island.

Three days later, Edoardo reached Tripolitania, where a Roman stronghold had existed in ancient times. He descended the ship and asked the driver where he could find a good hotel.

"Italiano?"
"Si. Piacere, mi chiamo Edoardo Privitera."

And they shook hands.

"I'll take you to the Italian community."

When they reached the Italianate hotel, the clerk welcomed Edoardo, spoke Italian not Arabic to him with a warning:

"Do not look or speak to the women. It is dangerous."
"I'm not interested in their women. I am a merchant. I sell linens and fabrics."
"Buona fortuna."[23]

Edoardo thanked him, getting the key to his room, unpacked his suitcase and left the hotel later in the afternoon when the sun went down. He walked along concrete walks, past piazzas and stores, where Italians had planted trees and graced their stores with an abundance of flowers.

He entered a fabric shop, when an entourage of Libyan women followed him, holding their toddlers. Sneaking a glance, he found the young women alluring and mysterious with their almond-shaped, black eyes peering above their veils.

One of the elderly women yelled so quickly that Edoardo could not grasp what she was saying.

"What's wrong?" Edoardo asked the shopkeeper.
"You have to go outside while they shop."

Edoardo bowed in deference to the older woman in charge and she nodded in appreciation.

Meanwhile, he strolled around the city and entered a cafe′, where he heard Italian voices. He sat down, ordered lunch with a glass of red wine.

"Signore, don't eat alone, sit with us. Where are you from?"
"Grazie, from Sicily … Messina."
"There are a lot of Sicilians here."
"May I ask how Italian men are allowed to marry Libyan women?
"Sure, they convert to Islam."
"Really?"

They nodded.

On the tenth day of his trip, Edoardo was elated with the orders of merchandise. He decided to tour the area and asked a fellow Sicilian whom he would recommend.

"Hassan, he speaks some Italian."
"And I speak Arabic." Edoardo replied.
"Hassan, please come here. Permit me to introduce Signore Privitera."
"Signore, a pleasure, do you want a tour of our area?" Hassan smiled.

His front teeth had a wide gap; his trimmed, black beard was interspersed with gray, his black eyebrows hung over his eyes and his robes flowed as he walked.

"Si, grazie." Edoardo replied, bowing his head.

After touring the city, Hassan asked him if he would like to see the Bedouins encampment.

"Is it safe?"
"Signore, you are with me."
"Hassan, it would be a great honor."

Hassan grinned and bowed to him.

At sunset, they arrived in the desert out side the city as Bedouins tended their sheep and horses while their camels bellowed. Hassan led Edoardo close to the camels and Edoardo realized they were seven feet tall, larger than he anticipated. He backed away from their fetidness as Hassan roared with laughter, bending in half, and Edoardo joined him in the laughter.

"Would you like to ride one?" Hassan asked.
"No, thank you."

Suddenly the camel spat at them and Edoardo yelled out.

"Is he angry at me?"
"No. May I ask, what is wrong with your eye?" Hassan asked.

Edoardo explained.

Hassan embraced him, invited him to dine with his family on roast lamb in the family's tent. Large torches provided lighting and Hassan invited Edoardo to sit on a rug. When the women served dinner, he respectfully lowered his eyes. The men nodded to each other, appreciative of his respect and knowledge of their ways.

"Edoardo, my uncle said you speak Arabic with a Sicilian accent."

Edoardo grinned. All eyes and ears were focused on him as he explained that Sicily flourished under Arab rule from the eighth century to the eleventh century. Palermo was their capital where a beautiful mosque still exists.

"The Sicilian language has inflections of Arabic."

They were astounded, and patted him on the back. Suddenly, a man placed a kaffiyeh on Edoardo's head amid resounding laughter. Abruptly, their laughter came to an end. The Bedouins leaped to their feel, goading Edoardo to follow suit. Their leader, Sheik Al-ibrahm Nufusa rode his black stallion through the camp, stopping at Hassan's family tent. The men bowed to him as he jumped off his horse, walked toward Edoardo, and removed his sword from his sheath, placing the sword into the sand. The sheik was a tall, gaunt man, a handsome figure in a black robe and kaffiyeh, edged in gold. His piercing black eyes gazed at Edoardo with suspicion. Edoardo pulled the kaffiyeh off.

"You may wear it. You look well in it."

Then Hassan rattled on about Edoardo, where he came from and how he became a friend, respectful of their ways.

"I have been to the port of Messina … beautiful island," the sheik stated.

"Thank you."

"You have earned a seat at our table for your respect of our culture and language."

Edoardo bowed his head.

The next moment, the sheik's black eyes bored into Edoardo, who suddenly felt fear crawling up his spine at the change of mood.

"We are tired of invaders. We will rule ourselves and rid our country of the Italians under the leadership of Omar Mukhtar."

"I agree with you. I do not approve of my country's invasion. Why, Sicily had been invaded for twenty-five hundred years."

"I know Sicily's history, but you should warn your fellow Italians."

"I will," replied Edoardo."

Edoardo's lips quavered and he shuddered under the cold starry sky. He glanced at the sheik with awe and thought: he is a zealot!

"Salaam, Signore Privitera. May Allah be with you."

"Salaam, Sheik Al-ibrahm Nafusa, and may Allah be with you."

Edoardo bent over, touching his heart, lips and forehead in deference to his ways.

"Have a good journey," said the sheik.

He jumped on his black stallion, disappearing into the darkness and reached his huge tent with giant torches, where guards stood with swords unsheathed, surrounding the tent.

The Bedouins gathered around Edoardo, embraced him and applauded his behavior that had impressed the sheik. Then Edoardo departed the camp with Hassan, who drove him back to the hotel and refused the money Edoardo had offered him.

"You are a friend."
"Thank you. Good night"

The next day, Edoardo joined Italians in a cafe´, reveled in his adventurous day, and cautioned them about the sheik's warning. At first, they doubted his existence, but Hassan had told him the sheik was rarely seen. He was a mysterious figure.

"He is a very impressive man … almost mystical," Edoardo told them.

They scoffed at him.

"They are desert people. We have machines and we built their roads and irrigation systems. In fact, they should be grateful we invaded them. We brought them into the twentieth century."
"Don't ignore the warnings. It's frightening."
"Edoardo, don't you understand, we have the weapons."

Two weeks later, the discordant sound of gunshots awakened Edoardo. He jumped out of bed, dressed, packed his suitcases, and ran down into the lobby, where bedlam ruled. Bedouins had unsheathed their swords, bellowing ancient curses upon the Italians, whose use of guns was not as effective as the Bedouins' skill with swords. Those Italians, who had assimilated with the Libyans and wore robes and kaffiyehs, had been spared.

A hand gripped Edoardo's shoulder: Hassan! During the time Edoardo had spent with him, he appeared as a man of jocularity, but now he saw his true nature, a man of augury, with a divine mission to rid Libya of Italians.

"Signore Privitera, our leader has ordered your safe departure."
"Hassan, does it have to be this way … all this bloodshed?"

"The Italians started this; we are defending ourselves," his faced etched in anger.

"Please express my gratitude to Sheik Al-ibrahm Nafusa."

"Yes. Now we must hurry."

Hassan led him through crowds of Libyans surrounding the ship, where Italians lined up, anxious to board. Hassan explained the sheik's orders and he was permitted to pass, escorting Edoardo to his cabin.

"For your protection, do not leave the ship or your cabin until you are out at sea."

"Hassan, Salaam, thank you. I hope all turns out well."

"Inshallah."[24]

The roar of gunshots, screams and butchery unnerved Edoardo; he wondered if he would leave Libya alive. Finally, at sunrise, a deadly stillness ensued and the ship sailed for the long voyage home. He left his cabin, went to the upper deck, where men lay with bleeding wounds, bandaged heads, and missing limbs. They yearned to return to Italy, where they would receive proper medical care.

Eight days later, authorities heard about the slaughter and medics met the incoming ship. Edoardo sighed with relief as the full moon reflected upon the sea and the top of Mount Etna, capped with a blanket of snow that glistened. The stars glittered in the midnight blue sky and he was happy to be home.

7

Edoardo reached home, haggard, bearded, and sighed with relief. Giacomo had heard about the turmoil in Libya, but had refrained from relating the news to Franca and Elena, who worried about his long journey. Now they welcomed him home. Giulia ran into Edoardo's arms; he picked her up and held her close. Franca embraced him.

"Did you have any luck?" Giacomo asked.

Edoardo opened his brief case, piled with orders and threw them into the fireplace.

"Why are you burning them?"

"Papa', I was happy to get out alive. Thanks to you, I knew how to respect them and that guaranteed my safety. No doubt, they are interesting people, but the slaughter was incredible on both sides."

Then, he opened his suitcase, displayed the kaffiyeh and the sword of Islam, a gift from Hassan.

"Madonna! You can get your body ripped open with that," Giacomo exclaimed.

"That's the point," Edoardo said, shaking his head.

Edoardo expressed his concern over the business Giacomo and he had lost since the factories had shut down. Giacomo assured him not to worry and stated he had been selling parcels of land to peasants.

"But Papa′, I don't want your money."

"Edoardo, Elena, Franca, Giulia and you are the only family I have left."

Life was peaceful once again. But, in 1914, Archduke Ferdinand of Sarajevo was murdered, which eventually led to World War I. By December of 1914, Mussolini turned from Socialism to Fascism. He blessed Ferdinand's murderers as benefactors of mankind, wanting to show the world that Italians were capable of a Great War and the image of Italians as pleasure-seekers and unwarlike would be obliterated.

"Edoardo, I have bad news. They are going to draft not only Italians, but Italian-Americans who are visiting here."

"I'm no good to them with one eye. Besides, remember the old adage, *better pigs than soldiers*," Edoardo stated.

Giacomo shook his head, grinning.

"We have always volunteered; we do not want to be recruited."

With World War I, travel on the high seas was prohibited. Edoardo devoted himself to Giulia, spoke English constantly to her, and watched her blossom into a lovely girl. She attended a convent high school, prepared for her graduation for outstanding achievements at the age of seventeen, and grappled with her first corset.

"Mamma, I can't move."

"Never mind, you will have lovely posture."

The servant placed her white organdy dress over head, used a buttonhook for the twenty tiny loops from the back of her neck to her waist, and combed her waist-length, dark brown hair loose, tucking a white organdy bow in her hair. She swung around for her mother's approval, flashing her amber eyes.

"Giulia, you're beautiful."

"We're proud of you," Edoardo stated, and kissed her.

Then she went downstairs to her grandparents' apartment, paraded in front of them, kissed them and waited for their blessing. They touched her head.

"Dio ti benedica," they said in unison.[25]
"Grazie, Ava e Avu,"[26] she replied.

After the ceremonies, they dined and Edoardo informed Giacomo and Elena they were going to Rome to enroll Giulia at the University of Rome and search for an apartment.

"Please come with us," Edoardo implored.
"Not his time. I have peasants who want to buy land."

And so they journeyed to Rome, found an apartment on Via Veneto, and toured the city with its ocher and café au lait buildings. When they stood in from of the Victor Emmanuele II Monument, Giulia giggled.

"It resembles a cake with too much icing."
"I never thought of it that way," mused Franca.

In September, Giulia began her first year at the University of Rome. Franca remained with her, volunteering at the Trastevere clinic, while Edoardo departed for America. Shortly before Christmas, he returned. They awaited the arrival of Elena and Giacomo for the performance of Bizet's *Carmen* at the Rome Opera House, where distinguished guests and patrons gathered.

Edoardo strolled in with Giulia on one side and Franca on the other side, attracting attention. Edoardo always wore his black patch on his eye when he was out in public, which added a certain distinction to his appearance, in his top hat and tails. Franca had her hair, now sprinkled with gray, cut short in the latest style. She wore a silk, black evening gown with a short, black mink jacket.

Opera lovers stared at Giulia in her low-cut, black panne velvet gown, revealing her full breasts. Her dark brown hair was coiled around her face; her profile appeared sculpted with her straight nose and jutting chin, which balanced her face. She wore three-inch, black high heels, elevating her five-foot, five-inch frame.

Her patrician grandparents were behind her. Elena wore a royal velvet gown with diamond earrings and necklace with a full length, mink coat. Despite Giacomo's slight limp, he walked straight as a ramrod. They were led to their box on the first tier, speaking only Italian, mindful of their Sicilian heritage, which was discriminated against in the societies of Rome and Central and Northern Italy.

Rome had secular societies and intruding upon them was an imprecation of their unwritten code. Across from their box, sat the Black Romans; haughty, preeminent residents, proud of their lineage as descendants of the nobility who had built nearly six hundred churches and palazzos in Rome, ingratiating themselves with the Papacy, gaining power and wealth.

During intermission, the family joined the crowd as white-gloved waiters served champagne, while men and women gazed blatantly at Giulia. Elena whispered to Giacomo,

"With her beauty, intelligence and education, she will marry a man of position and wealth."

"Of course," replied Giacomo, crossing his middle finger over his index finger.

After the opera, they dined at a quaint restaurant near the opera house and Giacomo proposed a toast to Giulia, singing to her sotto voce:

Sicilian Brunette, there's none like you,
With your passionate eyes, like the Conca d'Ora,
You can conquer any man …

"Avu, that was lovely."

She leaned over and kissed her grandfather.

The following day, flowers and letters arrived in abundance as suitors also sent marriage proposals.

"Rome has discovered you," said Elena, thrilled with the outpouring of proposals.

"I'm only marrying for love."

"Well, you need security, too. Love goes out the window when you struggle," added Franca.

"Mamma, I would never marry an uneducated man."

Once again Edoardo returned to America, scheduled two visits per year. He remained in his hotel room, ordered room service, and met salespeople in the hotel; he avoided any old acquaintances. When he went back home, he spent time with France and Giulia. During the summer months, they were with Elena and Giacomo at the new villa Giacomo had built.

Three years later, Giulia graduated as a linquist, proficient in English as well as French. She was offered a position at the university teaching English with an opportunity to earn a doctorate.

On a blustery day in October, Edoardo rose early as teeming rain pelted the windows, but frost blocked his view and he wiped the windows.

"What a dreary day."

"Papa´, why are you up so early? Giulia asked.

"I'm worried about the day's events. Stay inside today."

"No classes today. My friends and I have plans to walk in the parade as part of the *March on Rome*."

"I'd rather you didn't go."

"Edoardo, it's part of history. I've been reading a lot about Mussolini and I'm joining the Fascist party," Franca interrupted.

"Please don't. You're only asking for trouble."

"Well, I'll see."

Meanwhile, throngs gathered throughout the city while men in black shirts assembled in a state of expectancy, camped beyond the city. Forty thousand men arrived from Tuscany, waited at Monterando, fifteen miles from Rome, strong, organized and prepared to seize the main railway through Italy's spine.

Westward of Civtavecchia, the old port of Rome, Blackshirts were puffed up with Fascism, in a state of euphoria, arriving from Pisa, Lucca and Carrara. Their objective: also, the railway. In the South in Capua, Neapolitan Blackshirts huddled together in frigid weather, and lacked food, weapons and orders. By late dawn, Blackshirts occupied the railways, post offices and military barracks.

Civilians converged upon the crowd, embraced soldiers, singing the Fascist song dedicated to the youth of Italy.

Giovinezza! Giovinezza! Primavera di bellezza …
Youth! Youth! The beauty of spring …

Men, women and children leaned over balconies and verandahs, singing along. Despite the bitter cold, young boys ran out into the streets without their jackets and flanked soldiers, joining them in song. After all, they were the youth of Italy and were entitled to celebrate Il Duce's March on Rome in 1922.

"Edoardo, let's go."
"No, you are looking for trouble."

They remained secluded in their apartment, in awe and fear of the scene unfolding before them. Romans gravitated toward the center of the spectacle in wagons, carts, bicycles, trucks, horses and donkeys. Finally, curiosity took hold of Edoardo; he pushed the white sheer curtains to the side, opened the window and shook his head. Women threw flowers at the soldiers, kissing and hugging them while men poured red wine on the street, perhaps a harbinger of bloodshed.

"Papa´, can't we rent a carriage? It is so exciting."
"Edoardo, let's go. History is being made right in front of us."
"All right, but we must be careful. It's rather frightening."
"You worry too much," Franca said, kissing him.

They managed to find a carriage, but remained on the periphery. Romans shouted Mussolini's name with admiration, awe and reverence as if he were some kind of deity. Edoardo fumed. How could Italians revere such a man? Crowds prohibited the driver from getting through, and they returned to their apartment.

As they walked down the hallway of their apartment building, something was wrong. Their door was opened; drawers had been ransacked; their closets emptied and Franca's jewelry and fur jacket had been stolen.

"That is why we need Mussolini. People have said they can leave their doors open without fear of robbery," she said holding back her tears.

"I'd call the police but how can you find one in this crowd?" Edoardo said.

"We'll have to buy some clothes. They even stole our blankets."

"I hope I can find a store open," Edoardo said.

The next morning, the weather was still dismal and Edoardo heard men hawking newspapers. He went out on the balcony, yelled down for a newspaper, threw a few liras, and backed away when the man hurled a rolled newspaper up onto the balcony. He unfolded the newspaper and read the headlines:

IL DUCE PLANS MEETING WITH KING OF ITALY AT THE QUIRINALE PALAZZO

"Povera Italia,"[27] Edoardo murmured.

In the meantime, Mussolini prepared for his meeting with King Emmanuele III. He wore a black shirt, black trousers, black morning coat; covered his head with a black bowler hat; glanced down at his worn-out spats, and dusted them with talcum powder.

Romans walked side by side with Mussolini and his soldiers, a five-hour walk, passed the Piazza di Popolo along Corso Umberto to Piazza Venezia. They climbed the steep canyon on Via 14 Novembre, paused in front of the Quirinale Palazzo, and then Mussolini joined the king on the balcony. Underneath, soldiers and a frenzied populace waved palm branches to their hero as a symbol of victory. The rotund dictator beamed, jutted out his chin, and spoke; the crowd roared:

IL DUCE! IL DUCE!

The spellbound crown threw kisses at Mussolini. Exhilarated by his speech, they hailed him as the New Caesar with his promise that Italy would be restored to her former grandeur and ancient glory.

Suddenly, a knock on the door startled them, a telegram from Elena. Giacomo had had the last rites of the church and she urged them to return home immediately. Edoardo sighed, anxious to leave the chaos in Rome, but saddened over the news.

"Papa′, I love Avu so much. I hope he—," Giulia wept.
"We all love him," Edoardo replied and embraced Giulia who leaned against his shoulder.

When they reached Messina, Giacomo Raimondi lay in his massive bed with a painting of Christ in His mother's arms hanging over the bed. Elena sat by his side while Tonio stood at the foot of the bed. The priest lit candles and led Elena and Tonio in prayer.

Franca, Edoardo and Giulia entered the apartment, interrupted the rosary and when Elena saw them, she sobbed. For a moment, Giacomo opened his eyes, smiled wistfully at his family, at peace that they arrived before his demise. He grabbed Elena's hand and kissed it.

"I love you," she murmured.
"Mi'amora, soon I will be with Roberto and Maddalena," he moaned.

He let go of Elena's hand, death spasms engulfed him; he grabbed his chest and expired.

Tears coursed down his family's cheeks while Tonio got on his knees and wept without restraint, disconsolate over his friend's death. For three days and nights, dignitaries and contadini paid their respects, and to Franca's astonishment, Don Armando Fazio sauntered in. She recalled his onerous actions and wanted to scream at him:

"We don't want you here," but she held back her tongue.

He bent down and kissed Elena, offered his condolences, and spoke about Giacomo as a man on honor, whom he had respected. Franca squirmed in her chair. He left as quietly as he came in.

On the fourth day of morning, a High Mass was solemnized in the Madonna of the Letters Cathedral. A band followed the cortege, playing solemn music until they reached the ancestry cemetery of the Raimondi family, where Giacomo rested next to his great-grandparents, grandparents, parents, his son, Roberto and daughter, Maddalena. Large marble angels surrounded and protected their burial ground.

8

With the void in Elena's life, she begged Giulia not to return to Rome. For a moment, Giulia hesitated but then agreed. Her grandparents had given up so much for her and her parents' safety. Edoardo was delighted about her decision, stating the chaos in Rome was disastrous and he worried about her safety.

Giulia found employment at the University of Messina teaching English to graduate students who planned on emigrating to America and Australia. Her grandmother waited for her daily return. She listened to Giulia's stories about students who flirted with her, offering her an exciting life abroad. Elena roared laughing.

"Mamma, it's good to hear you laugh again."

Elena's lined face bore the enervation of her losses. At times, she spoke about the past as if it were the present. She still possessed her frail beauty; her silver hair crowned her bony, delicate features but her prior high-energy level had dwindled. Something gnawed at her constantly and she needed reassurance from Franca.

"I know Edoardo would like to move to America, but please don't go until I die."

"Mamma, I have no intention of moving there. I like it here."

One morning before class, Giulia was summoned to the head of the language department. Professore Riccardo Leone leaped to his feet. His hands trembled at the sight of her and he grabbed his quill pen to steady his hands.

"She's so beautiful," he thought.

"I was concerned about your students. How are you managing?"

"Sometimes they get bored, so I double their work. Professore, is that all"

"Signorina, may I call upon your family?"

She glanced at him perplexed; she never thought of him as a prospective husband.

"No, I'm sorry. Excuse me; I have to get back to my students."

Professore Leone's eyes revealed his disappointment. Giulia gave him a second glance; he was of medium height, slim, a narrow face, aquiline nose, a receding hairline, and a pleasant sort of a man. But no way could she be near him. When she fell in love, it had to be passionate and exciting.

When she returned home, she told her parents and grandmother about the professor.

"Let's invite him for dinner," her grandmother spurted out.

"Now, Ava, don't get any ideas. In Sicily, one doesn't invite a man for dinner unless there are thoughts of marriage. You told me that."

Elena laughed.

"He could be useful to you," Franca said.

"Oh, Mamma, I can't. I don't want to give him hope."

"Franca, leave her alone. When she meets the right one, we'll know."

"Thank you, Papa′."

The next day, Giulia received a message: Professore Leone wished to see her.

"Not again," she thought.

She went to his office, knocked on the door, and he welcomed her in.

"I apologize for my behavior. But you are so beautiful, I couldn't help myself."
"No apology is necessary. Professore Leone, I must get back to my students."
"If I can be of any help to you, let me know."

She departed.

A few weeks later, Professore Leone knocked on Giulia's classroom door, apologized for the interruption, and walked in with a young man who resembled him. But that young man was dashing, extremely handsome, with almond-shaped charcoal eyes that locked into her amber eyes. Her knees wobbled, her heart fluttered and she held onto her desk to steady herself. What was happening to her?

"Signorina, this is my brother, Alissandru. He will join your class."
"Welcome to the class, Signore Leone."
"You are as beautiful as my brother has told me."
"Signore Leone, please sit down."

She turned away from his penetrable gaze that scanned her body, undressing her mentally. A sense of mortification overcame her; she felt naked before him. Yet, feelings of warmth churned inside of her, wanting to touch him, kiss him and hold him close to her. There was an undeniable attraction for a man she had just met. A man she felt she had known, yet, she had never met before! It was strange, foreboding, forbidding, and exciting. He shook her hand, held onto it, and she pulled it away, embarrassed at the pleasure she derived from his presence.

His brother, Riccardo, noticed the current vitality flowing between them. They appeared ethereal, transcending reality, totally absorbed in each other. Alissandru had unleashed a passion within Giulia that Riccardo had never seen, as if they belonged to another dimension.

For the rest of the afternoon, Giulia was incapable of teaching. Alissandru stood up and walked towards her. She noticed his knife-edged trousers, his tweed jacket, his lanky body, his perfect teeth, straight nose, black hair, and charcoal eyes. He had an air about him, inured in self-confidence. He was perfect! What would it be like to kiss him, make love to him with all the fervor that lay dormant within her, and then lay spent in his arms with amorous words flowing from his lips? She sighed.

"May I wait for you?
"Yes."

When she left the building, Alissandru paced back and forth, but Tonio was there as well; her eyes drifted between them. Tonio suspected there was something going on and held the door open for her. Usually, Giulia ran to the carriage, but she hesitated.

"Tonio, I want you to meet one of my students, Alissandru Leone."

They shook hands and Giulia concluded it was best to go home with Tonio.

"I'll see you tomorrow, Signore Leone."
"Si, Signorina, domani."

As they rode home, Giulia discussed Alissandru with Tonio.

"Just be careful. You must marry someone worthy of you."

That night sleep eluded Giulia. She saw Alissandru's face before her, his lips upon hers, his hands caressed her body, and she clutched her pillow, twisting and turning it all night. She panicked for a moment: suppose he was just flirting with her. Finally, rays of sun poured into her bedroom. She jumped out of bed, opened her armoire, tried on four dresses, and settled for a blue silk dress with an ivory silk collar and cuffs. The servant styled her hair into a single braid.

"You look beautiful. Anything special going on?" Her grandmother asked.
"No, Ava. Where's Papa′ and Mamma?"
"Your father is opening a factory and your mother went with him."
"Ava, I met Professore Leone's brother … he's the one."
"My goodness! That's wonderful. But, be cautious."
"Don't say anything to Mamma and Papa′, yet."

Elena nodded.

Tonio drove her to the university, where students lolled inside the black iron fence that was twelve feet high. The university, a Gothic ocher building, was impressive in its simplicity, facing the law courts across the street. The piazza had gracious cypress trees, an abundance of flowers, and children played around the fountains with spittle hitting their faces amid their laughter.

Alissandru stood there, one hand in his pocket. When he saw Giulia, he ran to her, his eyes penetrated into her eyes, his scent intoxicated her, and she was flustered with his nearness.

"Buon giorno, Signorina. You look lovely."
"Thank you," she replied, walking ahead of him, but he caught up with her.
"I have to see you."
"I know."
"Something's happened between us, totally beyond our control."

She smiled.

"I'll meet you after class for an espresso."

When she entered the classroom, there was a message from Riccardo Leone. She grimaced.

"What does he want with me?"

She entered his office and his face revealed his adoration for her. Turning away, she directed her gaze on the garden outside his window.

"Signorina, I fell in love with you the first time I met you."
"Please, I don't want to hear that."
"I saw what happened between Alissandru and you. But, I am warning you, he is a ladies' man."
"Aren't all men until they marry or meet the right woman?"
"Damn it! He is not for you. I'm sorry."

She turned around, unwilling to hear his imprecations about Alissandru for his own motives.

"Professore, I don't think this is any of your business."

She left his office and concluded if she received a message from him again, she would ignore it.

Returning to her classroom, Alissandru stood up and carried her briefcase to her desk. She thanked him and fumbled with the students' papers. His nearness unleashed such sexual arousal within her. No one had ever reached the deepest recess of her soul until that day. She had never-ending thoughts that they had met before … somewhere, sometime … but where? Could it have been in a previous life? What nonsense! Her imagination was running wild.

"I haven't slept since I met you."
"Neither have I."
"May I meet your family?"
"No, we hardly know each other."

Someone banged on the classroom door and Giulia saw Tonio's face leaning against the glass top of the door.

"Tonio, what is wrong?"
"Your grandmother" … he couldn't finish.
"Ava?"
Tears trickled down his face.

When Giulia arrived home, she stiffened with fear at the sight of her grandmother, who appeared comatose, barely breathing. Dottore Rossi warned them that the time was near for the cessation of her life. Franca, Edoardo, Giulia and Tonio flanked her bed, tears poured out of them. Edoardo grabbed Franca's hand as Elena's breathing became belabored; her chest heaved and her head dropped to the side.

"She's gone," murmured Franca.

Dottore Rossi nodded.

"Ava, sweet Ava," Giulia cried.
"Giulia, she's gone. She's with Avu," Edoardo consoled her.

With the death of Elena Raimondi, an era had ended. The light, the bulwark and the glory of the family had passed into history. At her funeral, the residents of Messina paid their respects to a lady whom they had admired for her graciousness and generosity. Now she joined her husband, son, and daughter in their ancestral cemetery.

9

Two weeks later, Giulia returned to the classroom, a portrait in black, her hair tied back with a black ribbon. Alissandru stood up and expressed the class' condolences. She thanked him and began teaching. But Alissandru's eyes swept over her body, devouring her beauty and for a moment, she disliked the power he wielded over her with his sensuality. When class ended, he was the last one in the room and swaggered over to her.

"I've missed you."

She stood up, backing away, fearful if he came closer, she would succumb to his charms.

"I'm not going to hurt you. We knew from the moment we met, didn't we?"

"Yes."

"May I call on your parents?"

"No, it's too soon."

"I understand," he replied.

He kissed her hand and leaned over and brushed her lips.

A month later, Giulia asked her parents if she could invite Alissandru for dinner. Edoardo was pleased; Franca was cautious.

"What do you know about him?"

"He is Professore Leone's brother. He graduated from the University of Messina and he is an architect."

"Why is he studying English with you? Franca asked.

"Someday, he'd like to go to America. His family is listed in the Nobilario di Sicilia," she added enthusiastically.

"Sounds like a nice young man. Invite him for Sunday dinner."

"Thank you, Papa´."

Alissandru was elated at the invitation, meeting Giulia with a floodgate of love for her. She put her arms around his shoulders; he pulled her closer to him, wanting her to be united with him, in body and in soul. Their lips met, gently, and then furiously, kissing with unyielding passion. Tonio knocked on the door, saw them and walked away.

"Tonio won't say anything. I trust him."

"Are you sure?"

"Yes, he told me my parents used to sneak kisses all the time before they were married."

Alissandru laughed.

Returning home, Giulia changed into her riding outfit, pulled her horse out of the stable, and climbed on top of it.

"Don't be long," Franca called out, instructing Tonio to follow her, always fearing the sword of Damocles hung over her.

Giulia met her girlfriend, Maria, in the piazza. As they trotted along, Giulia spoke about her love for Alissandru. Suddenly, she turned around at the sound of a racing horse: Alissandru!

He slowed down his horse, grabbed the reins of Giulia's horse and they trotted ahead, waving to Maria. He jumped off his horse, tethered his and Giulia's horse to the railing and moved close to her, lifting her face to his lips.

"Tonio is watching somewhere," she giggled.

"Let's sit down and talk."

"Alissandru, Riccardo told me you have traveled a great deal."

"Only throughout Italy, Sardinia and Corsica. I'd really like to go to America. One can become stagnate in our society."

"I think you are right, but my parents had a bad experience there when I was little."

"What happened?"

"La Mana Nera threatened to kill me."

"What is the difference between them and the Mafia?"

"They're Italians who terrorize other Italians, especially newly arrived immigrants. Well, I'd better get home. See you on Sunday."

"I can't wait."

They climbed on their horses and each headed in opposite directions.

Giulia caught up to Tonio, riding alongside the carriage. When they reached home, she jumped off her horse and ran inside.

"Mamma, I saw Alissandru while I was riding. Oh, I'm so in love with him."

"Now, don't rush anything. We have to check his background to see if there's any idiocy or insanity or serous illness that runs in his family."

Giulia slumped onto the sofa, removed her boots and sat stupefied and numb. Naturally, she was aware of the nobility's search into a person's background before marriage. But she could not ask Alissandru, who was a proud man and would be offended.

"I'll ask Riccardo."

Riccardo beamed when Giulia knocked on his door and welcomed her in. She avoided his lovesick gaze and explained the purpose of her visit.

"I understand. Before my sisters got married, my parents checked into my brothers-in-law's families. Our family is not as high up on the scale of nobility as yours, but we are listed. We all went to college and my sisters are teachers.

He explained the family originated from Parma many generations ago, settled in Novara, in the province of Messina. There were all landowners, but the land had been destroyed in the 1908 earthquake.

"We haven't had any awful diseases, insanity or idiocy in our history."

"Thank you, Riccardo."

"If you ever need me, I'm here."

On Sunday afternoon, Alissandru arrived at one o'clock, dressed in brown britches, a beige shirt, a tan cashmere jacket, and a dark brown suede hat cocked to the side of his head. Edoardo, Franca and Tonio welcomed him, impressed with his appearance. He, indeed, dressed like a gentleman, resembling the Prince of Messina, who had perished in the earthquake. Edoardo told him to have a seat, but he was fidgety and nervous, preferring to stand. He glanced at Franca, who stood aloof, her blue eyes penetrated through him. He felt ill at ease, wanting to leave.

"She doesn't like me. Why? Maybe it is my imagination."

Giulia strolled into the living room and apologized that she kept him waiting. His throat knotted at the sight of her; his heart thumped to the beat of love, a love he must possess. Walking close to him, she wore a burgundy wool-riding outfit with a blouse with variegated shades of pink and burgundy, and a burgundy slouch hat.

"Shall we ride before dinner?"

"You're so beautiful," he whispered.

"Oh yes, that would be wonderful."

While they rode their horses through the city, cool breezes caressed their faces and their eyes focused on each other. He grabbed the reins and halted the horses, jumped off and lifted her down. He held her close but his eyes mirrored some kind of distress. He maintained a mask of spurious politeness. What was wrong? Had she offended him in some way that she did not realize?

"Your mother doesn't like me," he blurted out.

"That's not true. She is very reserved until she gets to know people. Please don't spoil this day."

"I guess you're right."

He jumped on his horse, galloping away from Giulia, who was well known for her horsemanship. She sped ahead of him, glancing back at him, smiling. He caught up with her and they trotted alongside each other. They spoke about their aspirations; the cloud that hung over them for a moment had dissipated.

"We better go; dinner is probably ready."

They returned to Giulia's home, sat down for dinner, and during dinner Franca asked a pivotal question.

"Where do you work? I understand you are an architect."

Alissandru dropped his fork, clenched his jaw, and disquietude pervaded the room. Giulia stared at Franca with incredulity while Alissandru took a deep breath and responded.

"The government wants to rebuild buildings that were destroyed in the earthquake and I'll be involved with the projects. We are waiting for funds."

"You can't depend on government, we can attest to that."

"Signora, I answered your question," he tersely replied.

He stood up, excused himself, and Giulia linked her arm through his and walked outside with him.

"Franca, what's got into you? You are never rude. He is a fine young man, intelligent, handsome—

"I only asked where he worked."

"You made him feel uncomfortable."

"I have a premonition about him. I was born with a 'veil', and the peasants believe one who is, can see the future."

"What? Nonsense! You just met him. What is a veil?"

"A thin tissue over a person's face when they are born."

"Edoardo, that's true. I believe it as well."

"Tonio! Really? You believe in that superstition?" Edoardo asked.

"Yes," he said, never blinking.

"I think that's ridiculous," said Edoardo, shaking his head.

The following day, Giulia dressed as meticulous as usual, glancing outside at the morning sky, where tufted clouds hung overhead. The sun peeked through, reflecting upon the azure sea. Since her parents had opened the factory, they left early at dawn, and Giulia was relieved she did not have to face her mother and answer a myriad of questions. Tonio opened the carriage door, noticed her lack of enthusiasm, and wondered what happened. Usually, she was effusive, exuberant and smiled constantly, but not on that morning.

Suddenly, the still of the morning was interrupted with the sound of a horse galloping toward the carriage. It was Alissandru. He jumped off, tethered his horse to the carriage and climbed inside. Giulia glowed at the sight of him. Tonio realized the depth of her love and wondered if they could be happy. Maybe things would work out well for her. A love like that was rare and beautiful, but frightening to him. Did Franca's fears deserve credibility? Looking at them and the love shining on their faces, he began doubting Franca's concern.

Tonio drove along the sea, passed the Madonna of the Port, where residents boarded the ferry for their return to work in Northern Italy, Switzerland and Germany. Reggio di Calabria, with its sun-baked, colossal mountains of porous rocks loomed in the distance. When the ferry reached the boot of Italy, verdant mountains and plants with an abundance of flowers coloring the earth appeared.

"I love watching the ships and ferries," Giulia said.

"How about you marry me and we move to America?"

"Alissandru, that is presumptuous of you. You must ask for her hand," Tonio exclaimed.

"I apologize," he murmured.

"I accept", she whispered.

Alissandru went through the customary procedure and presented Giulia with a round-cut diamond ring. He concluded he would tolerate Franca for Giulia's sake, but he could never have affection for her. She had humiliated him.

Three months later, Giulia prepared for her wedding. She wore an ankle-length, ivory satin gown with narrow, tapered sleeves, and an ivory satin headpiece with an attached veil. Franca peeked in while the servant fixed her hair and put on her headpiece. Franca presented her with a bouquet of cascading white lilies.

"Mamma, thank you for your understanding. If I didn't marry Alissandru, there would have been no other."

Franca touched her bosom, she found Giulia's intense love for Alissandru frightening and alarming. She realized she had offended him, but it was the eternal quest of a parent concerned with a suitable husband for a daughter.

At the wedding, Giulia's eyes were glued to Alissandru's eyes. Riccardo, his best man, stood at his brother's side, while her friend Maria was her maid of honor. Riccardo concluded:

"I've never seen such passion. They do belong together."

After the reception, sunset settled upon the city and Giulia and Alissandru departed for Taormina, a town high up in the Peloritani Mountains. A myriad of flowers graced the town such as dwarf apple flowers called fiore di mele, barba di giove (Jupiter's beard), and a glorious white flower with plumes of pink and brown penciled leaves spread like Prince of Wales feathers, each branch a yard long. Taormina, with its remnants of Greek culture, provided a haven for honeymooners with its warm days and balmy nights, where the gods resided.

Alissandru brought the horses to a halt in front of a terra cotta hotel with large arches and graceful palm in huge, terra cotta pots. The owner of the hotel welcomed them, ordered an attendant to bring their carriage to the stables in the rear of the hotel. Then he led them to their suite overlooking the cascading mountains.

After dining, the full moon lit the darkened skies and they returned to their suite. Alissandru locked the door, shutting out the world, only wanting Giulia in his arms. He poured two glasses of champagne and proposed a toast.

"To us and our love …"
"Yes, forever. We have been given a special gift," she sighed.

He freed the combs from her hair, removed her white satin negligee, and covered her breast with her dark lustrous hair, breathless at the sight of her voluptuous body.

"You are exquisite," he moaned.
"Alissandru, teach me how to love you."

Moonbeams flickered through the partially opened shutters and Alissandru extinguished the candles. He moved closer to Giulia who trembled as his body molded against hers, his maleness rubbed against her thigh. His lips came down upon her expectant lips; tongues swirled around each other's mouths, savoring the champagne. He led her to the bed, his kisses covered her body and her nipples hardened under his lips. She ran her fingers up and down his lean body, urging him to enter her, wanting to feel him inside of her. Their bodies moving to exquisite rhythms of passion, soaring them into another realm, and he exploded in her with a whirlwind of ecstasy. Spent, they lay in each other's arms, their love fulfilled; his hands glided along her body.

"I love you," his voice murmured, kissing her neck.

"I'll love you forever, until I die."

In the morning, Alissandru opened the shutters. He called out to Giulia as falcons and hawks swooped through the mountains, their powerful wings controlling their ballistic flights, soaring upward and downward onto perches of red cliffs, overlooking the Ionian Sea. Mount Etna, a formidable, powerful force in the distance, spewed out fumes and reminded the residents the volcano still ruled the island.

"Beautiful," Alissandru remarked, holding Giulia close to him.

For two glorious weeks, Giulia and Alissandru basked in the splendor, the majesty and ethereal beauty of Taormina, where stars touched the mountaintops, illuminated the dark blue skies, and where legend had it that the gods resided in Elysian fields. Giulia packed but appeared sadden, murmuring,

"I wish we could stay here forever … I'm afraid."

"Giulia, it's a beautiful place, but we have to get back to the real world. Why are you afraid?"

"I don't know. I feel we will lose the love we have. There's magic here."

"Giulia, what we have can never be taken away. The gods have blessed us."

"I hope so."

10

Messina, in its decline since the great earthquake, had become a poverty-stricken city with destruction from the earthquake still abounding. Unemployed young men had become impatient with her static society without opportunity, departing from the island in droves, sailing to Argentina, Brazil, Australia, and America. While Alissandru worked in the cathedrals restoring facades and repairing stained glass windows and statuary, he yearned to design new buildings and homes; but that was impossible.

Edoardo had been biding his time since Elena's death and his patience dwindled as well. He scorned the poor ancestry who still lived in the nineteenth century, unwilling or unable to accept modernity, clinging to old ways, hoping for revitalization of their society that was part of the past.

At the dinner table, Edoardo brought up the subject that he knew would distress Franca, but he had decided it was time for the family to move.

"Move to America permanently?" She queried.

"No, we will have our home here. Alissandru, America is a young country and with your talent, you will do well."

"Why don't we move to Northern Italy?" Franca asked.

"Franca, things aren't great there either. Besides, I have to go to America and check my investments."

"Giulia, what do you think?" Her father asked.

"I don't know. I'm not sure."

"It will take at least fifty years until the area is restored. Think about it."

"I'd like to go." Alissandru stated.

"Papa', so would I." Giulia replied, smiling at Alissandru.

"Everything and anything to please him," thought Franca.

Sleep eluded Franca that night. The thought of leaving her beloved city, with its memories of her distinguished family, distressed her. At dawn she awakened, made coffee, poured some into a cup, added hot milk, and stirred it until it resembled a whirlpool. Tonio put his hand upon hers.

"I think it's mixed."

"Sit with me. If we go to America, would you come with us?"

"Franca, I am an old man. Besides, my family is buried here."

"All right, then stay in the apartment and we'll rent the other two."

"You'll be back, won't you?"

"Of course."

"Franca, I will miss you. I love you and your family."

Franca stood up, embraced him, and they clung to each other.

Three months later, Giulia and Alissandru spent a week with his family in Novara. Tears coursed down Riccardo's face as he wished them well. Alissandru embraced him and said,

"I hope you find the right woman."

"I have but she fell in love with you," he thought.

The family prepared for their departure and their trunks were loaded onto the ferry. They stood at the railing of the ferry, waving at Tonio, staring at the water rippling beneath them, leaving Sicily as they crossed the Strait of Messina. Were they introspective about their departure? Only Franca, whose thoughts of Ancient Sicily were pervasive. She spoke out loud, with an orator's tongue.

"Beloved Sicilia, Nature has given you great beauty and great sorrow. Your earth has been ravaged so often by Nature and the greed of men. Your land has been seared with the torrid heat, scorching your earth. Yet, when you blossomed, you were a *Garden of Eden*, with your abundance of wheat, fruits, vegetables, vineyards and glorious plants and flowers."

All faces glanced at her, tears rolling down their cheeks, anticipating more from her. She continued:

"We have become embittered at times, unable to handle the harshness of your Nature. But when your acrimony subsided, your beauty consoled us. Help our people to deal with modernity in this resplendent, historical land that has nurtured us. This land that Cicero, the great Roman orator, declared in ancient times: 'Sicily is the breadbasket of the Roman Empire, the granary of Italy, and the first jewel in Rome's imperial crown.'"

Passengers moved closer to Franca, wanting to grab her hand, but Edoardo stood in front of her, shaking his head. Then he knew somehow that he would never see Sicily again, and cried out:

"*Sicilia Bedda,* your land and people suffer under Nature's cruelty; earthquakes destroy you and Sicilians create strife with their fellow man. Yet, your beauty comes through with the good people who toil the land and love the beauty of your sea, mountains and skies. This is the land where Aristotle vacationed, where Plato spent time at the court of Dionysius the Elder of Siracusa, and where Archimedes, the Greek mathematician, physicist and inventor, was born and lived."

Everyone sobbed. Now they turned their back on Sicily and glanced forward to Reggio di Calabria, with their eyes toward the future.

Aboard ship, Franca and Edoardo retired early while Giulia and Alissandru had a second honeymoon; danced until the early morning and discussed their plans for the future. Giulia had doubts about their departure, but now with Alissandru's exuberance and verve, doubts floated out to sea. During the night, the ship rolled back and forth, awakened Franca who was terrified of rough seas, but Edoardo slept soundly.

The sun had risen and Franca glanced through the porthole. She aroused Edoardo at the sight of mountainous waves overlapping and battering the ship. Bullhorns resounded throughout the ship; stewards pounded passengers' doors, warning them to put on their life jackets as the fierce winds intensified. Edoardo and Franca grabbed their money belts, dressed warmly, and knocked on Giulia and Alissandru's door.

"Hurry! Follow us, holding hands," Edoardo warned.

They wound through the sea of humanity into the dining room, wavered through debris of broken dishes and glasses amid wails of terrified children in their parents' arms, snaked through turned over tables and chairs, holding onto a railing and finally reached the upper deck.

Stewards tied passengers to the railings on the deck. Voluminous waves whipped them; their faces ached from the incessant thrashing and passengers vomited, excreting fountains of emesis. At that moment, Franca and Edoardo relived the earthquake, when the earth moved beneath them, wondering what would happen to them.

Now stewards webbed Giulia and Alissandru to the railing with rope. They cowered at the site of a gigantic, roaring wave, resembling a boom ready to strike them dead. Giulia turned her face away from Alissandru, regurgitating, and collapsed, pulling Alissandru down with her. Relentless waves pounded them as breathing became difficult. They huddled together for three hours.

Eventually, the ocean ceased its convulsions. The winds eased up and despite copious clouds, the sun spread it glory like a giant eagle. Stewards untied passengers, called out for a stretcher for Giulia, who refused it, stating she wanted to go back to their cabin, where the doctor followed her.

"Doctor, there is nothing wrong with me. I'm tired and pregnant."
"Congratulations. Rest. I'll take care of the others."
"Thank you."

Alissandru came in, bent down near her, and grabbed her hand.

"The doctor told me, it's wonderful. What a beating we took; I hope the baby will be okay. I asked the steward and he said your parents are back in their cabin. They are upset, but all right."
"We'll tell them later. Let them rest as well."

Five days later, the ship crawled into the New York City harbor. Alissandru stared at the towering skyscrapers, an architect's dream. He grabbed Giulia's hand, kissed it, and brushed her lips.

"I'm going to like it here. It makes me feel alive."

"Alissandru, Giulia, I thought you'd like to spend a week here by yourselves. I have business to take care of and then we are going to Camden, where there is an Italian community, and find a home. I'll get your room number before we leave and call you."

Alissandru smiled at Giulia, excited by the idea, and thanked Edoardo.

"One thing I ask of you, don't go to Little Italy."

Alissandru had a quizzical look on his face, but nonetheless, would comply with Edoardo's request. When Giulia was alone with him, she told him the reason.

"I can't believe that! How could anyone harm a hair on your beautiful head?"

"That was a long time ago," she shrugged.

11

Camden, New Jersey, a city near the Cooper River, had a lovely residential area. Edoardo decided staying away from New York City would be a safeguard for his family, and facilitate Alissandru's search for employment. He could take the bus to Philadelphia. They rented a home, furnished it, and waited for Giulia and Alissandru's arrival.

Giulia called various architectural firms in Philadelphia, made appointments for Alissandru, and accompanied him on his first trip. She waited outside while he presented his credentials. Secretaries fawned over him, but the employers were not impressed with his diploma from the University of Messina. The interview ended with:

"We cannot use you at this time."

As he walked outside toward Giulia, she saw his discomfiture, but refrained from questioning him.

"They have never heard of Messina. Don't they know anything about world geography?"

"There are other firms who can use your talent."

On the daily treks, Alissandru brooded, became disheartened, silent, tense and withdrawn. Giulia, bursting with life, yearned for his nearness, his arms around her, his lips upon hers, wanting him to be happy for the life that came from their love. His aloofness sent dread through her, and for a moment, she regretted leaving Sicily. When she spoke English, he became impatient with her.

"Alissandru, if you speak English fluently, you will have a better chance to find work."

"I don't have the patience right now."

Franca and Edoardo noticed the rift between them. Edoardo warned Franca not to interfere. Moving to America required a period of adjustment for a new culture, a different way of life.

"As soon as he finds work, they should get their own place," stated Franca.

"I agree," Edoardo replied.

In the midst of their adjustment in America, Franca yearned for her home and missed the university, where she had spent so many hours. She organized a club, propagating Fascism and Benito Mussolini, who would restore Italy to its former ancient glory. She stated a half-million men emigrated from Italy every year, leaving families and seeking employment. On Sundays, she spoke at a park, where families strolled with their children.

"We women are equal to men in intelligence, and as mothers we must supervise the development of our children. We should love and respect our husbands, but we should be free from their domination. One of the reasons I agree with Mussolini's policies is enforced education up to the age of sixteen years of age. Poor women are burdened with large families; they have six, seven or even more children. Whereas, city women are selective, choosing to have three or four children."

Applause resounded through the crowd, only by women, while men yelled out:

"Troublemaker! Troublemaker!"

Edoardo ran up to her, protecting her, then the men backed off.

"Franca, it's dangerous for you to talk like that. Please stop it."

"I hate to see women with such large families and not enough money to feed or clothe them."

"Franca, it's their problem, not ours."

They returned home and Edoardo opened the mail. Franca's life had been threatened with hate spewing out of the letters about her speeches, promoting women's causes. She was warned to cease her speeches. He panicked.

"Franca, you have to stop it. Don't go out without me. It's terrifying. I want peace. We've got to get out of this town."

"I'm sorry. I guess people want the status quo, at least the men do."

"Mamma, I agree with you. Alissandru, dinner is ready."

"I'm not hungry. I'll go out later for a bite."

"Alissandru, please. I'll go with you."

"I want to go out alone."

Sadness masked Giulia's face as he left the house. Edoardo rose to his feet and embraced her.

"He's probably homesick. Give him time."

"Stop catering to him. He should cater to you." Franca told her.

Giulia's wistful glance broke their hearts, but they refrained from further comments.

That night, Giulia and Alissandru slept miles apart, not a word passed between them. She understood his anxiety about employment, but not his moodiness. In the morning, she insisted that they discuss the problem.

"You have to be patient. Look what my father went through."

"Giulia, I'm not a patient man."

From then on, Alissandru went on his excursions alone and Giulia found some respite and peace away from him. She walked the park, passed rows of tulips and daffodils that lay bent in the warm breeze, sat on a bench and wept. Alissandru was not the man she had married; he frightened her with his remoteness and moods. That evening, he came home after another rejection.

"Americans don't like Italians. I keep telling them it's Italian, not eye-talian."

"Overlook it. Sometimes you make mistakes in English. After the baby is born, maybe we should move to Philadelphia. You could take courses so you can get a license here."

"Courses! I'm an architect! I feel inferior here; an educated man and they won't hire me! There was another man there and he was upset as well. The prejudice seems to be against the Italians and Jews."

"I guess we have to become Americanized," Giulia said.

And she left him stewing in his sorrow and self-pity.

Franca and Edoardo heard Alissandru's voice, laced with anger, and it jarred their nerves. Perhaps Alissandru should return home alone. They knew Giulia loved him too much and she would go with him. Confused and bewildered, they wondered what they could do. Nothing.

As Giulia's time grew near, her parents hired a woman to cook and clean.

"Mamma, thank you. Things will be just fine when Alissandru finds work. There is prejudice against Italians."

"Also against other nationalities … that's life," retorted Franca.

Later that afternoon, clouds blocked out the heat of the day. Giulia went into the backyard, folded clothes, and placed them into a rattan basket and suddenly stopped; strong back pains brought her to her knees.

"Mamma! I'm in labor."

If Franca had restrained her emotions during post-mortems and her years at the clinic, now her well of courage dried up, watching Giulia cringe, holding onto the kitchen sink during the throes of labor. In between her pains, Giulia went upstairs to her bedroom, glancing out the window, watching people getting off the bus. She longed for Alissandru to be with her in that moment to watch the fruit of their love being born.

Alissandru came home, pushed opened the screen door, calling Giulia's name as he climbed every other step, went into the bedroom, expressed his love for her, and tears welled in his eyes.

"Forgive me; I've been unfit to live with."

She looked up into his eyes, contented that he had manifested his love for her and that's all that mattered.

"I'm sorry I didn't get here sooner."
"Alissandru, look at how lovely she is. She looks like you."
"She's lovely. We should name her after my mother."
"There are enough Marias in Italy. How about we change the M to D?
"Daria, I like that."

The doctor departed and left the nurse to assist Giulia.

A few days later, Alissandru continued his treks in his search for work. Without telling Giulia or his in-laws, he took a train to New York City, venturing from one office to another but without success. He knew he had exceptional talent and there was no place for him to use it. Perhaps they should have gone to California or Argentina or Australia? Wherever they went, they needed money.

Upon his return to Camden, Giulia noticed the desperation in his eyes. He was sullen, chain-smoked, refused dinner and sulked in their bedroom. Giulia handed the baby to Franca, went upstairs, and opened the door.

"We must talk; don't shut me out. I'm willing to do whatever makes you happy. Do you want to go home?"
"No."
"Sometimes, I think that would be the best thing."
"And live in poverty?"
"Well, not exactly poverty. Let's devise some kind of plan."
"I don't want to go home. Leave me alone."

She slammed the door shut, went downstairs and sobbed. Franca and Edoardo frowned at each other, but did not say a word. Standing on each side of her, they kissed her.

Hot, humid days brought residents outside on their porches, seeking relief but there was none. Edoardo decided they should spend two weeks in Atlantic City; he wanted to get out of Camden. Perhaps a change of scenery, on the beach with ocean air, would be beneficial to all. On the daily excursion train to Atlantic City, Alissandru held the baby, conversed with Giulia, and thanked Edoardo for his kindness.

"We're staying at the hotel where we stayed on our honeymoon." Franca said, smiling and sighing.

Perhaps some peace could flow between them.

Giulia and Alissandru spent their days languishing on the beach, rollicking in the water, laughing as Alissandru rode the waves to shore, imitating other young men.

"It's beautiful here. Now, I'd like to live here." Alissandru said with content.

"I would, too." Giulia replied.

Meanwhile, Franca and Edoardo took the baby for a carriage ride into the Italian neighborhood. They looked over the different stores; spoke to residents, wanting to know if the neighborhood needed a linen shop. They shook their heads and pointed to a store on the next block. They walked back to the hotel and Edoardo decided they should venture up to the Boardwalk and rent a store. As they went in one store and out the other, the rents were prohibitive.

"Franca, perhaps we should live here for a while and then make a decision after we learn about the area. We've got to get out of Camden. When Alissandru finds work, he can take the train. We'll tell them at dinner."

Alissandru and Giulia were excited with the news, living at the shore with its beautiful hotels, shops, and restaurants, was different than life in Camden. Besides they heard it was a wonderful place to raise children.

They found a house in Ventnor, a suburb of Atlantic City, facing the beach and ocean. Franca was exhausted from the move and Edoardo thought she needed a change.

"Go home and see how things are … and see Tonio." Edoardo said.

"Come with me."

"No, I won't leave Giulia and the baby. He hasn't changed. He is very difficult to talk to. I wanted to reassure him, but it was futile."

Franca wept in his arms and buried her head on his shoulder. Giulia entered the room and hugged them. She realized it had been difficult for them, and her mother needed to get away from all the dissension.

"Mamma, give my love to Tonio. If you see Riccardo, tell him we are fine."

"Lie to him?" Franca asked.

Giulia turned away.

On the day of her departure, Edoardo rode the train with Franca to New York City. Each one pensive about conditions at home.

"Edoardo, she should divorce him. This is America."

"Divorce? Maybe. I don't think she will ever leave him." He retorted.

12

Aboard ship, Franca welcomed the solitude and respite from the stress in the household. She yearned to see Messina, touch the soil, pick an orange from a tree in the backyard, and watch the ships crossing the strait. Most importantly, visit her family's graves. When she descended from the ferry, Tonio called out to her. She ran to embrace him and neither one uttered a word.

"Oh, Tonio, how are you? I've missed you."

She had never realized how aged Tonio looked until that moment. With a mass of white hair and furrowed bronze face, his mouth appeared cavernous without teeth, and he faltered when he walked.

"Franca, why are you alone?"

"Lots of problems, I'll tell you later."

"Is everyone well?"

"Yes, I told you in the letter Giulia had a girl … Daria, beautiful baby."

"And how is Alissandru?"

"He can't find employment. He's a very moody man. I do admit there's prejudice against foreigners."

"It's probably temporary. Edoardo told me stories about the difficult time he had."

"That's true. It's a different culture, but when things improve, Alissandru can be very successful."

"Tonio, I hope so, with all my heart. She loves him too much."

"Too much?"

"Yes."

As they rode to the apartment, Franca noticed the morose conditions throughout the city. Streets were deserted, stores emptied, old men loitered in piazzas or sat in front of taverns. Where were the young people? Could it be possible that they all left? And where were the flotilla of ships that she watched growing up, going through the strait?

"It's depressing. Young people leaving in droves." Tonio said.

"Despite all the problems, it's wonderful being home." Franca told him.

Tonio prepared dinner for them, set the table with linens and silver, and opened a bottle of wine.

"Have you seen Dottore Rossi or Alissandru's brother?"

"I don't go out much."

"Are the people in the other apartments paying you rent?"

"Sometimes, the men are out of work."

"We'll talk about it later."

At dawn, the bullhorns awakened Franca. She walked out to the verandah and watched the ships sailing by. Tonio joined her.

"There they are. I was so sad when I didn't see the flotilla. This is what I miss most of all."

"Are you going to sell your properties?"

"I won't sell this building, only the villette and the remaining acres. Suppose we want to come back. I should get a lawyer to make sure the tenants pay the rent. You need it to live on."

In the afternoon, Franca visited Dottore Rossi's home and his daughter welcomed her in and led her to his bedroom, where he lay quietly. Franca touched his hand, stifling her tears and he opened his eyes.

"Dottore, Dottore, it's Franca."

"Oh, Franca, how wonderful to see you. I've been so sick. How's the family?"

"Cosi, cosi. Giulia had a baby girl."

"I'm happy for your family. Messina is not the lovely city we were raised in. Life was beautiful then. The earthquake has ruined us."

"It will take time and the city will be restored to its former beauty."

She bent down, kissed his forehead and hugged him. His frail body trembled and she knew he didn't have long to live.

"You were like a daughter to me. You should have been a doctor."

"Dottore, that was a millennium ago."

He wept.

"I've had a full life. Avogghia[28] … Addio, Franca."

He turned his face away from her and she walked out, shaking with grief.

"Addio, Dottore. I love you."

As Franca went to the carriage, tears spurted out, blinding her, and she hung her head. The rank of death hung over her doctor, her friend, her mentor, and she would miss him tremendously.

The following day, Tonio and Franca headed for the interior. She emblazoned the view on her mind, every foot of the highway, mountainsides with familiar houses and sites, and land with distinctive markings. Then she smiled, recalled the annual treks in June to their villa, the joy she shared with her family, and the bounty of her father's land. Crossing her arms around her shoulders, she needed a protective shield for those special memories, now fading into the recesses of her mind.

Tonio drove on and they notices six young girls skipping and singing, their bronze skin and white teeth glistening. Franca smiled. She asked Tonio to stop while she waved to them, and they waved back to her.

"Tonio, there's the face of Sicily, strong, pretty and independent."

They reached the gates of her family's cemetery, where the Raimondi name stood out and two huge marble angels guarded the graves. Franca knelt down, placed flowers at her parents' graves, picked up a stone, and scratched *addio* on the tombstones of her brother and sister as well.

"Our past is now severed."

Tonio helped her up and they held onto each other. She wondered how her family had been so secure, loving and happy, but then splintered into a billion pieces with devastation and death.

"Tonio, I'd like to see Maria and Costanza's graves, please."

He could not speak and led her down the road, where she placed flowers on their graves.

On the way back, she wanted to go to the university to see Riccardo Leone. The activity around the school pleased her. Students lolled around, exuberant in their discussions, and hope resounded within her. That was life: young people with enthusiasm. When she entered, she walked through the halls and reached Riccardo's office. He saw her through the glass top of the door.

"Signora Privitera, welcome home. Are you alone?"

"Yes, how are you."

"Fine, thank you. Alissandru wrote to me and told me about the baby. He's having problems finding work. He sounds very depressed."

"Well, it isn't easy for Giulia."

"I'm sorry. What can I do?"

"Nothing and don't tell him we talked; he'll take it out on her."

"I'm sorry. They're so in love."

"Giulia is the one really in love."

"Signora Privitera, what do you mean?"

"Never mind. Addio, Riccardo."

Tonio and Franca returned to the apartment. Their upstairs neighbors invited them for dinner and apologized for their late payments. How could she ask for the money when their husbands are out of work?

"When you get the money, give it to Tonio. Please take care of him. If anything happens, bury him near his family and take the expense out of the rent." She whispered.

The next morning, Tonio packed a lunch of prosciutto, provolone, olives, bread, and a bottle of wine. They departed for the villa where Franca surveyed the land; she had about ten acres left surrounding the house. The rest of her father's land was dotted with small houses with gardens, but the sheer beauty of verdant, unpopulated land with fruits, vegetables and wheat, was gone. Tonio opened the villa, smelled the musty, dank smell of an empty house, and tried opening the boarded windows.

"Don't bother, let's eat outside, like the old days."

Now, it was time for Franca's journey back to America and she told Tonio she would visit once a year. His throat knotted and he knew he would never see her again. He held onto her as tears streamed down their faces. She ascended the ferry, waved to him and turned away. She hid her tears, gazed at the blue sea and fixed the view in her mind and heart. Faltering, she held onto the railing, glanced up at Mount Etna, supreme and majestic, and wondered if she would ever see that view again.

13

Meanwhile, in Atlantic City, Edoardo read the morning newspaper and became concerned with the news. A perfidiousness was spreading throughout America; warehouses bulged with merchandise that did not move, causing cessation of production and loss of jobs. Display windows rarely changed and slowly, businesses began closing. He ridiculed any possible disaster, confident in the American way of life. He must transfer his funds to an Atlantic City bank before he picked Franca up at the docks.

Sleep escaped him that night. He rose at 5:00 a.m. and boarded the 6:00 a.m. train to Manhattan. He consoled himself that any purported disaster he had read in the newspaper was just a method of selling newspapers. During the years he had spent in Messina, he never doubted for a moment that his money was secure in America.

When he arrived at Grand Central Station, he hailed a taxicab to the bank, where men were queued up, shoving each other, trying to get ahead of one another.

"What's going on?" he asked.

No answer. Suddenly the bank's door slammed shut. The dissonant sounds of screams, curses and fulmination against the bank and its officials shocked Edoardo. Throngs converged in front of the bank, pushing Edoardo out of line. Fights ensued among the desperate people who attempted to break down the steel doors. Men pounded the doors, their knuckles split opened, blood splattered over their clothes; their violent outbursts went unheeded and terror spread like a creeping monster.

Edoardo stood glued to the ground, inert and terrified; men pushed him to the right and to the left as if he were a puppet. He could not think or feel. What should he do? He glanced at his pocket watch; he had an hour before Franca's arrival. He circumvented the faces of desperation, yelling to a taxicab driver.

"Take me to Wall Street."
"Sir, haven't you heard."
"Anything worse than this?"
"The stock market has crashed; people have lost millions."

Edoardo slumped into the seat, a lump in his throat at the nightmare unfolding.

"Take me there," he ordered.
"Yes, Sir."

Men hawked newspapers about the day's events and when the driver stopped at a light, Edoardo jumped out and bought a paper.

EXTRA! EXTRA! READ ALL ABOUT IT!
STOCK MARKET CRASHES! BANKS CLOSED!

Edoardo got out near Wall Street, where pandemonium ruled. People ran around in circles, looking for some way to gain entrance to the building, but the doors were sealed as guards set up barricades. He was horrified at the sight of people jumping out of the skyscrapers and backed away quickly, fearful of being crushed. He knew he had to hurry to meet Franca.

Throughout the city and country, the news had traveled like an anaconda, slowly but powerful, eating the souls of men. Franca paced the docks, searching for Edoardo who yelled out to her.

"Here I am! Here I am!" he sobbed.
"Thank God you are all right. Tesoro, we will manage."

"Everything's lost. I should have withdrawn the money. I loved the American way, but now everything is gone."

"We'll be all right. We've survived worse than this. Please, Edoardo, let's get out of here."

Aboard the train to Atlantic City, Edoardo rattled on about his losses, what he should have done and cited the peasants in Sicily with their innate distrust of government and authority per se.

"Edoardo, stop it! You are going to drive yourself crazy. I didn't marry you for your money," she said grabbing his hand.

"I love you, Franca."

Upon their return to Ventnor, Giulia saw the despair on her parents' faces, but words of consolation were futile. At that moment, Alissandru came in, concerned over the day's events.

"My parents lost everything."

"I'm sorry. What can I do?"

"Sorry? Can't you assure them that all will be well?"

"Giulia, what do you want from me?"

"A kind word … you're incapable of that."

"You complain about everything I say or do."

Alissandru slammed the door as he left. Giulia sat with her parents, poured a cordial glass of strega and they discussed the situation.

"Mamma, how was Messina?"

"No good. Tonio's close to death and Dottore Rossi is dying. Messina looked dead, except for activity at the university."

"Did you see Riccardo?"

"Yes, he knows how things are, but I told him not to write to Alissandru about what I told him."

"Should we go back?"

"Giulia, with what and to what?" Edoardo interrupted.

She hung her head, ashamed; her thoughts were always on Alissandru, what he needed and what he wanted. Now that had to stop. Daria awakened, crying for her, and she ran upstairs. The door opened and Alissandru returned, went up to the bedroom, where Giulia sat in her daughter's room, rocking Daria who had fallen asleep. He picked Daria up and put her in the crib.

"Giulia, what do you want from me?"
"Warmth and some kind words. They've been good to you."

He clenched his jaw and slammed the bureau with his fist. Daria cried out.

"You woke her. Grow up and start acting like a man."
"Do you want me to sit down and cry with them?"
"All I want from you is concern for their well-being. You never hug or kiss them."
"I'm not that type."

He turned, ran downstairs and out the door, walking to the Boardwalk.

He came back an hour later and Giulia pretended she was sleeping. He put his arm around her and she burst out crying.

"Oh, how I wish we were in Taormina. It was special there."
"Taormina was a dream, not the real world. Stop talking about it."

Alissandru discontinued his daily trips to Philadelphia. Most architectural offices had closed their doors, and those that were still opened, maintained one or two architects on their payroll. He walked the streets of Atlantic City, dazed, bewildered and suddenly stopped. He saw islanders lined up at soup kitchens; despair and elusive employment had degenerated the souls of men. Fear overcame him and he ran up to the Boardwalk. Majestic hotels graced the Boardwalk, elegantly dressed tourists strolled along, and he was in his milieu. He leaned against the railing, gazed at the ocean, inhaled the fresh air, and watched the passing parade. A sense of well-being came over him. He stopped at a drugstore for a sandwich and coffee, and then returned home at midnight.

"Where have you been? I was worried."
"Giulia, I needed time alone."
"You need time alone!" she yelled.

Edoardo and Franca heard her; he fumed and she hated him more each day.

"Franca, we have to live alone. I'm looking for a small store in the Italian neighborhood. We'll sell freshly roasted coffee, cookies and candies. Hopefully, there's an apartment behind the store."

"How about Giulia and Alissandru?"

"We'll give them money for a couple months rent. It's a good thing I had cash saved."

"Perhaps being alone is the answer; he'll take responsibility for his family."

Franca was pleased that Edoardo had regained his verve and strength.

At breakfast the following morning, Edoardo discussed his plan. Alissandru concluded it was right for them to be on their own. Edoardo handed Giulia an envelope, but she was worried about her parents being alone, away from her and her family. Totally befuddled and concerned, she knew she had to take the money.

Franca and Edoardo strolled through the Italian neighborhood and found a store with an apartment in the rear, directly across the street from St. Martin's Church. Whereas, Giulia and Alissandru found a five-room, two story house on South Texas Avenue, an extended part of the Italian neighborhood.

Alissandru swallowed his pride, gave up his suits for work clothes, and found work as a house painter, carpenter and tile setter. Each time he pounded nails or filled tiles with grout, he bemoaned his wasted education and talent. When he came home, he didn't speak to Giulia; he bathed, put on a suit with a white shirt and tie, contented, and sat down for dinner.

After she put Daria to bed, Giulia bathed and dressed up for him, knowing how much he loved beautiful clothes on her as well. She hated herself for catering to his whims, but she needed his love as one needs food for sustenance; he was her lifeline. At first, she believed him, but then rumors about his illicit affairs reached her parents. And they belched their rancor against him!

"He has a beautiful woman of superior intelligence, who works like a peasant for him, and he replaces her with whores!" Franca exclaimed.

"I hope she leaves him now. She won't tolerate such nonsense."

"I hope so, Edoardo, I hope so. Don't let on that we know just yet."

Giulia visited her parents daily, but on Friday, Edoardo was out delivering coffee orders to restaurants. Franca wanted to talk to her alone.

"Giulia, your father and I are very upset about the whores."

"Mamma, they are not whores, they're neighbors."

"Leave him. Divorce him! Where's your dignity and self-respect. How can you tolerate such nonsense?"

"Maybe something is wrong with me. I love him and always will. We are destined to be together … forever."

"I don't believe that."

"I do, no doubt at all."

On her way home, Giulia stopped at the 5 & 10-cent store and bought rouge and lipstick. Since Alissandru liked American women, she would dress and wear makeup like they do. After she prepared dinner, she went upstairs, bathed Daria and herself, and dressed in a tight-fitting silk dress that skimmed her figure. She pulled her hair back and wore a headband and then, applied rouge and lipstick.

"Well, I look like an American."

While she waited for Alissandru, she poured herself a glass of wine, smoked her miniature pipe, and he sauntered in an hour late for dinner. She stood up, moved in a sensual manner, and he stared at her.

"Where are you going looking like that?"

"I'm waiting for you."

"Why are you wearing lipstick?"

"It's American. Besides, I like it and I feel pretty. The women you go out with wear it and you like it."

"I wish you wouldn't wear it. You are beautiful without it."

"Apparently, not beautiful enough for you."

"I'll see you later. I have an appointment."

"Why, Alissandru, are you doing this to us? I cook and clean like a peasant, yet I try to keep myself nice, wanting to look glamorous for you. What do you want, a divorce?"

"No, I don't want a divorce."

"What do you get from these women?"

"They shower praise upon me, like the way I dress, tell me that I am handsome …"

"But you are a married man with a child, not some kind of gigolo. Grow up, because I won't be around here forever."

"Look, I'll be right back. I have to give an estimate."

Ten minutes later, he returned, poured himself a glass of wine, picked on his cold dinner while Giulia put on the radio and sat in the living room. He came towards her, sat down, and tried to kiss her, but she shook her head.

"I must admit that you are very desirable. You look beautiful."

"Alissandru, I want to recapture the love we had, a love I felt was blessed by the gods. We must talk."

"You and that Greek mythology."

"You know myths come from real life. If one receives a gift, one cherishes it or else you anger the gods."

He grabbed her hand, led her upstairs, and it appeared as though they had rekindled the passion they once had. She moaned with absolute love for him.

They lay spent and she questioned him about other men.

"Suppose I dated like you do, what would you do?

"Don't you dare! I don't know what I would do if I found you with another man."

"How do you think I feel? Just remember that."

She had sown seeds of doubt, not that she ever wanted to be with another man, but if he thought about it, perhaps, he would stop cheating on her.

In the meantime, Franca and Edoardo had a sense of belonging in the Italian neighborhood, with its familiar sounds and pungent aromas. Most storekeepers had apartments behind or above their shops. Houses had porches and balconies, graced with pots of basil and parsley. Those who could not afford pots used discarded spaghetti boxes. No doubt it was an insular neighborhood, where residents' needs were met in a radius of five blocks with school, church, clothing stores, grocery and butcher shops, a doctor, a lawyer, shoemakers, dressmakers, restaurants and bars.

But on Giulia's daily visits, her parents noticed a difference in her appearance. She was haggard, somber, her hair disheveled and she looked bedraggled.

"Giulia, what can we do to help you?" Edoardo asked.

"I want to go home. I don't like it here. Alissandru is different … I've tried so hard."

"Leave him! We'll find a larger place. Business is improving."

"I can't. I'm pregnant."

Franca's heart stopped: another child! How could they afford it? She held onto the counter and bit her tongue. A customer came in for cookies and Giulia left.

Giulia pushed the carriage, smiling at neighbors, anxious to get home, retreat from the world, and hide her broken heart that had splintered into a million pieces. She had not told Alissandru she was pregnant for fear of upsetting him. The last time they made love was three months ago and her efforts to save her marriage had failed. The marriage had degenerated almost to hatred for each other; she had become cold and distant and he went out every night.

Often times, when Alissandru did come home, Daria tugged at his pants; he picked her up, kissed her, and put him on his lap.

"Daddy has to bathe, I won't be long."

Later he came down in his suit, put Daria on his lap again and combed her hair. Giulia melted for a moment; his tenderness with Daria moved her to tears.

"Alissandru, I spoke to my parents. They'll go home when we are ready."

"I don't want to go home. When this depression is over, I'll be able to make a lot of money."

"I want you to know, I'm pregnant."

"Damn it, we don't need another child right now."

"I didn't get pregnant alone. Get out of my sight and out of my life!"

14

The following morning, Giulia came downstairs with Daria, made breakfast, and looked around for Alissandru. He was gone! Perhaps her life would change without him. His liaisons were an apparent attempt at healing his bruised ego, since he was unable to work as an architect. But, at lunchtime, he walked in, much to her chagrin, hugged her, kissed her, expressed his love for her, and spoke words of endearment that she had longed to hear for months.

"Giulia, I'm sorry, I love you."
"Alissandru, sometimes I think you love yourself more."

His lips found hers, and for a moment, the illusory vision of Taormina filled their hearts. He touched her face; tears glistened in his charcoal eyes, knowing full well, her love was unconditional. He murmured how beautiful she was when Daria squeezed herself between them.

"Mommy, Daddy, love you."

They glanced at each other and Alissandru picked her up and put her to bed.

On her daily walks to her parents' store, they noticed the difference in Giulia. She bloomed with child and was ebullient in her conversations. She never mentioned Alissandru and they never asked about him.

Six months later, when Giulia gave birth to a son at the Atlantic City Hospital, Alissandru could not hide his elation, showering Giulia with affection and love.

"I love you so much. A son, how wonderful."
"I named Daria, you name our son."
"Carlo, after my father."

Franca and Edoardo arrived at the hospital, beamed at the news, and placed their hatred for Alissandru in reverse, attempting to form some kind of rapport with him. After they left Giulia, they soon discovered peace was an aberration to him. When they offered to care for Daria, Alissandru replied,

"They will stay with our neighbor."
"Why? Franca asked, bewildered.
"Because I prefer it that way."
"Alissandru, what have we done to you? We've been kind to you" Edoardo asked.

No reply. They turned, leaving despondent, wary, and wondered why he hated them. But they concluded the hatred was reciprocal.

Ten days later, Giulia came home with her son. Franca and Edoardo hired a woman for a week to clean and cook for her. They visited Giulia and the children when Alissandru went to work. They refrained from asking any questions.

Eventually, Giulia resumed her daily treks to her store. They came outside to glance at the baby in a wooden carriage.

"What happened to the English pram we bought for Daria?"
"We needed money and I sold it."

Franca was livid, her blue eyes tearing, and she unleashed her fury.

"How can you, a daughter of nobility, place your baby in a second-hand carriage?"

If Franca had slapped Giulia, the pain could not have been worse than her admonition. Tears streamed down Giulia'a face, and Daria pulled on her mother's coat.

"Go inside with Nonno.[29]"

Giulia wiped her tears, embraced Franca, took a deep breath and explained.

"Mamma, I obtained this carriage honestly and my children will remember their mother as an honorable woman."

Shame overpowered Franca for her haughtiness, stunned with Giulia's statement that sounded prophetic.

"Forgive me, forgive me, you have nobility of character and dignity despite adversity."

"Mamma, I understand. I had the best of everything and now I have nothing for my children." I cannot give them half of what I had."

In the meantime, Edoardo played with Daria and saw that Giulia prepared to leave. He put on Daria's coat and hat and she twirled around in her navy blue coat that Giulia had made from Alissandru's old coat.

"Mommy made it for me."

"You look beautiful," said Franca, amazed at Giulia's ability to adapt in the midst of need.

Giulia returned home with groceries, carried the baby inside and told Daria to let her know if the baby cried while she took the wash off the lines. Frigid air had frozen the clothes on the line. Giulia unpinned the clothes and dropped them into the basket, where they stood like toy soldiers. She fed and bathed the children, tidied up the house, prepared diner, set the table with a linen cloth, and put on a black silk dress that she made. Alissandru ran into the house, nodded to her, went upstairs, bathed and changed into a suit.

"I hate those damn work clothes."

"I don't blame you. You look like a movie star when you're dressed."

He grinned but never reciprocated the compliment. He sat down and poured wine for both of them, cut the veal, chewed it and spit it out.

"Can't you buy a better grade of veal?"
"Is it that bad?"
"It's terrible."

She glared at him with contempt. Since the baby's birth, nine months ago, his dark moods bore the cloak of lamentations, critical of her in every way.

"You're a rotten bastard," she cried out.
"I'm sorry. I just said …"
"Sometimes, you are so nasty."
"Mannagia![30]"
"Alissandru, get out of my life. I've walked on eggshells since I married you."

Alissandru grabbed his topcoat, slammed the door shut, and went out into the darkness. He walked up to the Boardwalk and stood there, contemplating his past and his future. He concluded he should not have married. Although he loved Giulia and the children, he disliked the responsibility of a family, preferring freedom to do what he wanted, when he wanted.

Meanwhile Daria heard the ruckus, climbed down the stairs on her buttocks and ran into Giulia's arms.

"Mommy, is Daddy mad again?"

Giulia held her close, grieved that her precocious daughter had overheard the argument. She put her to bed, remaining with her until she fell asleep. She took off her dress, put on a housedress and began cleaning the kitchen. The front door opened, the wind blew from the living room into the kitchen and that ill wind brought Alissandru, who stood there, throwing his topcoat on the couch.

"Alissandru, I'm leaving you. I think it's best for you and for me. I'll get a housekeeper for the children while I work and live with my parents until I can afford my own place."
"Huh! You think you'll find a job just like that," he said, snapping his fingers.

"I'll try and I'd appreciate it if you leave now."

"I have to find a room to rent."

And he went out. She locked the door and went to bed.

The next morning, she brought the children to her parents, explained her decision, and they were pleased with her assertiveness. She boarded a trolley to Atlantic City High School on Albany Avenue, filled out applications for a Latin, French, Italian or English teacher, and showed the administrator her diploma from the University of Rome.

"Very impressive. Right now, I may have a day now and then as a substitute, but that's all I can do."

"I really need a full-time position. Please keep me in mind."

"Yes, I will."

She returned to the store; her parents saw her downtrodden look and refrained from any questions.

"I think if we lived near a university, I'd have more opportunity. When the baby is a little older, I'll move to Philadelphia."

"We'll go with you as long as he isn't with you."

March winds blew through the island; dreary days and nights lingered on. Alissandru had not moved out, coming and going as he pleased, leaving money on the kitchen table, and periodically, pleading with her to forgive him. She had become insensitive to his repetitive imploring that they rekindle their marriage.

"I can live without you," she told him with assurance.

He stared at her with incredulity; the one thing he had always been certain about was her love. She went about her chores, humming a tune, but inwardly, her stomach churned.

"Have you met someone else?"

When she did not reply, he stormed out of the house.

On Sunday morning, Franca and Edoardo entered St. Martin's Church, blessed themselves with holy water from the marble font, genuflected and slipped into a pew. Still a distinguished couple, parishioners turned and nodded to them. During Mass, a woman tapped Franca on the shoulder.

"I must speak to you after Mass."

"Yes, of course," replied Franca.

"Something's wrong with Giulia," Franca whispered to Edoardo.

Father Damiano, pastor of St. Martin's Parish, droned on and on during the homily. Franca became irritated, unnerved, and turned and spoke to the woman.

"We're leaving. We'll wait for you in our shop."

The next twenty minutes seemed like infinity to them until the woman came in, ordered a pound of coffee, and placed a quarter on the counter, which Edoardo returned to her.

"Signora, Signore, thank you. I'm sorry to tell you this, but you should know. Your son-in-law beats your daughter."

"What! He beats her!" Franca exclaimed.

Edoardo turned pale and rushed the woman out of the store and called a taxicab.

"Lazzarone![31] I'll kill him! I'll kill him!" Edoardo shouted.

When they arrived at the house, Edoardo pushed the door open and Franca shrieked at the sight of Giulia. Her lovely face had hues of dark blue and purple; she sat in a chair, weeping, holding Carlo in her arms, while Daria leaned against her.

"You're leaving now. I thought you decided to divorce him," Edoardo said, furious and exasperated with her tolerance for his nonsense and now, physical abuse.

"Papa', I need the money he earns until I see my way clear to move to Philadelphia. But, I am afraid of him."

"And you work like a peasant for his 'majesty'," groaned Franca and then she sobbed.

"Where is he?"

"Papa', I don't know."

"He's destroying you and you are allowing it. Think about your children; he sure doesn't."

"I guess I still love him. I've always felt we were destined to be together."

"*Merda*! Love! Love is what your father shows me." Franca screamed.

At that moment, Alissandru pushed the door open and Edoardo shoved him outside, whirling his walking cane as a weapon. Alissandru backed away.

"You rotten bastard! Get out of Giulia's life. You don't give a damn about her or your children!"

"Leave our home," Alissandru said, his voice cold, remote, and his steely eyes sent shivers through Edoardo.

Edoardo called out to Giulia.

"Are you coming with us?"

"No, Papa´. I've been a burden to you long enough."

"Giulia! A burden? You are a burden away from us; we're constantly worrying about you."

Alissandru smirked at Edoardo and Franca, arrogant, flaunting his influence over Giulia. Edoardo rushed toward him, balled his fist, and Giulia leaped between them.

"Papa´, your eye, I don't want anything to happen to it. Please go home. I'll call you later."

He straightened his patch, grabbed his walking cane and Franca's arm, tears streaming down their faces and a general malaise overcame them. How could this nightmare happen to Giulia and her children, and to them?

From that day forward, Giulia's daily treks to her parents' store revealed a servile, besieged, slovenly woman; her hair in disarray, her silk stockings had holes in them and her shoes leaned outward when she walked.

"Look at you! Giulia, do you see what's happening to you? He's destroying you."

"I know. There's nothing I can do. The happiest day of my life will be the day I die." She murmured.

Franca could not look at her as she departed. Turning around, she went into the store and screamed:

"She didn't think I heard her. Edoardo, she said the day she dies will be the happiest day of her life."

Edoardo and Franca held onto each other, their tears intermingled. They remained huddled together until the telephone rang; a customer ordered coffee. They went through the rituals: roast the coffee, grind it, and carefully package it amidst their broken hearts.

15

On Thursdays and Fridays, Edoardo and Franca roasted coffee beans, ground and bagged them and Edoardo delivered them to restaurants. One Friday, upon his return from delivering, he inquired if Franca had heard from Giulia. She said she had not.

"I'm going over there."

He knocked on the door, pushed it open, and saw Giulia on her knees, scrubbing the floor. His stomach dropped, appalled at the sight of her soiled housedress. She wiped her hands and jumped to her feet.

"Where's the *grand signore*?"

"Papa', he lives around the corner on South California Avenue. I don't know the address but it is a duplex."

"I'll kill the bastard!"

"Don't bother, I don't want him anymore. I've been such a fool."

"Finalmente! Come live with us. I'll look around for a larger store and living quarters."

She shook her head.

"I don't believe you! You must live with us."

Edoardo left the house, walked at a rapid pace, reached South California Avenue, and looked for a duplex. He saw Alissandru sitting on a wicker rocking chair, lighting a cigarette, and unfolding a newspaper. A woman came out of the house, handed him a glass of lemonade and stood behind him. She rubbed her pendulous breasts against him, giggling over some humorous remark he had said to her.

"Goddamit! He's witty and charming in front of others. Fucking bastard! I wish I were a killer, but I'm not."

Alissandru caught a glimpse of Edoardo and lit another cigarette from the one he was smoking. Edoardo flipped the cigarette out of his mouth.

"You sonofabitch, I'm tired of you, your moods, and the way you treat my daughter. You don't deserve her."

"Alexander, don't listen to him."

"Oh, he's Alexander now."

Then Edoardo pointed his finger an inch away from the woman's nose.

"And you, Madam, use your dalliance on someone else, that is, if your husband can't get it up."

"Alexander, what's dalliance mean?"

"Oh, shut up. Sometimes you are so stupid."

She spun around, her buttocks rose up and down, to the rhythm of the Victrola playing the Black Bottom.

"Stay out of my life. I'm tired of your interference." Alissandru barked.

"You're scum. She should not have married you."

"I knew you didn't want her to marry me."

"Once you were married, what was the use?"

Alissandru ran up the porch, into the house, packed his belongings, and returned home. Giulia was cold, distant and indifferent to his pleadings of reconciliation. He left money on the kitchen table and changed into his work clothes. He worked sporadically, as some men did during the Depression.

Now Giulia's beautiful smile had long since withered. Her well of courage had shriveled up and she wept at the slightest provocation. She avoided her neighbors, who informed her periodically about Alissandru's affairs. He had become well know for his vigor and women yearned for a night or a moment with him. And they pursued him.

Giulia told herself she did not care what he did or with whom he made love, but deep inside, it tore her apart. Now her concerns lay with her children, who suffered under the brunt of animosity. Determined to move to Philadelphia, she made the decision to move when Carlo was two years old. But at night, alone in bed, she still yearned for his arms around her, his lips searching for hers. Why couldn't she get over him? She hated him, yet she loved him.

The next evening, Alissandru dressed in his impeccable manner with a high shirt collar, beautiful silk tie, navy blue suit, and went out. She never asked where he was going or what he was doing. Each led separate lives, yet, together because of their children and lack of money. She fed and bathed the children, put on the radio, and got out the ironing board. She heated the cast iron on the gas range and unrolled one of Daria's dresses.

The door flung open; it was Alissandru. Her heart thumped, her lips quivered, and her hands trembled with fear. Why was he home so early?

"Giulia, we have to talk."

"It's over. Don't you realize it's over? I want a divorce."

"You don't mean that," he said, moving toward her, using his artfulness that he used on women.

"I'm working like a common laborer. Do you think it's easy for me?"

"Oh, stop it. Poor you."

Tears coursed down her cheeks, hating herself for revealing her vulnerability toward him. Then disquietude pervaded the room as Alissandru strode back and forth like a man ready to explode, and then flipped his cigarette into the sink. He came near her, put his arms around her, but she pushed him away. The passion that once encompassed her body and soul and intensified her desire for him was gone. She had conquered her obsession for him.

"I'm free of you and your wiles!"

She wept with tears of joy, visibly glowing with renewed strength.

"I don't believe you."
"Alissandru, I pity you."
"I don't need your pity," he replied.

Turning livid, clenching his jaw, he knocked her on the floor, kicking her over and over again. She crawled to the corner of the room, grabbed the broom, stood up, and fended off his attack.

"What a joke life has played upon me. I really believed we were destined to be together."
"Giulia, we are meant to be together. Give me a chance."
"I told you, it's over."

He picked up the cast iron, aimed for the wall, but missed and hit Giulia on the head. She fell backward, held onto a chair, dazed, blood oozed down her face, and she screamed.

"Get out! I hate you."

He left cursing and slamming the door. She sat on the couch, holding her head and sobbing.

Meanwhile, Daria heard the commotion but hesitated; she went to the bathroom, flushed the toilet, hoping the gurgling would cover up the noise. Standing at the head of the stairway, she listened. It was quiet, but now and again she heard her mother sobbing. She held the railing and climbed down the stairs, and saw her mother holding an ice bag over her head.

"Mamma, Mamma, are you hurt?
"Lovely Daria, I'm all right. Guess what? We're going to live with Nonna and Nonno."
"I love them the whole world."
"So do I."

Putting Daria to bed, she kissed her and left the room as tears rolled down her face. Carlo cried; she went to him, cradled him in her arm until he fell back asleep. Giulia bathed, put on her nightgown, and slumped on the bed. Her head throbbed with excruciating pain, and she didn't know which way to turn or what to do. She slipped under the covers; perhaps she needed a good night's rest. But then she sobbed over Alissandru. Once in Taormina, he had loved her with equal fervor, but she, herself, had become a prisoner of love consumed with him. Now she was liberated from the entanglement of the web of love. She fell asleep.

During the night, the pain in her head had intensified. She got out of bed, dressed, straightened out the kitchen, put some ice on her head and looked outside. The fog was dissipating and dawn shed its light upon the city. She waited for her neighbor's shades to rise and ran across the street.

"Please, I'm very sick, terrible pain. Watch my children. I called my parents and an ambulance. Thank you."

"I hope you are all right."

The driver assisted Giulia onto a stretcher, reaching the emergency room of the Atlantic City Hospital, where patients lined up around the nurse's desk. Giulia was rolled into a room, examined, and the doctor ordered the nurse to put her in a room with patients who had typhoid fever. At that moment, Franca and Edoardo pushed their way inside the room before she was taken away. Giulia vomited and then lost consciousness. Franca cleaned her up and she came to.

"Doctor, my daughter does not have typhoid fever."

"Ma'am, how do you know?"

"In Italy, I worked with people who had the disease. Have you given her a thorough examination?"

"Look, Lady, we're busy. We have an epidemic of typhoid and she'll have to be quarantined."

The burly doctor turned his back on her, exhausted from working sixteen hours a day, seven days a week, and tired of listening to emotional immigrants. Franca shoved him aside, examined Giulia's abdomen and questioned Giulia. Then she saw Giulia's head and she yelled to the doctor.

"Listen to me. She doesn't have a rash on her stomach. She has a subdural hematoma from a blow to her head."

"Whoever did this should be arrested. Nurse, move her into another room." The doctor ordered.

"No arrest, Mamma, Papa´. Please think of the children."

Giulia implored them.

"Oh Giulia, he has to pay for what he's done."

"I beg you …"

Tears poured out of her, beautiful, sweet Giulia close to death. Their only child was dying in front of her. They remained at Giulia's side, watched her lovely face contorting with pain, and hatred for Alissandru distended within them.

"Mamma, Papa′, I'm getting a divorce. I don't care what anyone thinks. That's what made him so angry. He never thought I would leave him."

"Get well, first, and then we'll make plans." Franca said, kissing her hand.

"If something happens, take care of my children."

She sobbed uncontrollably and they sobbed with her. Edoardo bowed his head in prayer.

"She can't die! It would be dreadful and horrific beyond comprehension."

They remained at Giulia's side, dozed off, but awakened when she moaned with pain; furious about falling asleep, knowing each moment with Giulia was precious. Edoardo pulled aside the drapes and the streetlights were shrouded with morning mist. Then the sun burst out, radiating the city and they saw the ocean, calm, serene and beautiful.

Edoardo waited for the elevator and when the door slid open, Alissandru walked out. Edoardo sneered at him, bursting with hatred, wanting to berate him in front of the nurses and doctors. His eyes portrayed the venom coming out of him. Alissandru ignored him, rushed to Giulia's room, and was shocked at her pallor, revealing the mask of death. Franca stiffened.

"I'd like to speak to my wife alone."

"Mamma, just for a moment."

"What's wrong?"

"When you threw that iron, it caused a subdural hematoma."

"I'm sorry. I meant to hit the wall."

"Alissandru, it's too late. At one time, I thought you were a loving, affectionate, and kind man. What happened?"

"I guess because I wanted to work as an architect and become successful."

"Things have been difficult for everyone, but your behavior has been horrendous. I've been embarrassed so many times by neighbors talking about your affairs."

"I am so sorry. I love you," he bowed his head and wept.

"I would have given my life for you. You're a foolish man. I believe we should have remained in Messina and visited Taormina. We would not have been rich, but we would have been happy. Please don't ever forget Taormina; it was so lovely."

His body was racked with guilt, remorse, and sorrow for the woman he had truly loved and abused. Tears moistened his face as he waited for the elevator. Franca did not glance at him and returned to Giulia's room, where she shook with cries of despair.

"Oh Giulia, what can I do for you?"

"Mamma, it's too late for me but my children …"

Meanwhile, Alissandru went to Anna Triento, Franca and Edoardo's neighbor, who cared for the children. Anna was twenty years old with blonde hair, protuberant brown eyes, and a smile on her face at all times. Alissandru thanked her and kissed his children. Suddenly, Edoardo was there, his face a mask of fury and condemnation.

"Anna, I told you the children aren't allowed to see them."

"What's wrong with you? Their mother is close to death and you will not allow them to be with their grandparents?"

"Yes, and I don't care to discuss it any longer."

On the fourth day of Giulia's hospitalization, she cried out for her children, wanting to love them and kiss them for the last time. The doctor denied her request because of the typhoid fever epidemic, and ordered the nurse to wheel her down to the lobby, where Anna waited with the children. Daria ran to her mother, kissing and hugging her, and asking her when she was coming home. How could she answer that she was not coming home? Edoardo placed Carlo in Giulia's lap; she kissed him with fervor, alternating with Daria.

"Mamma, quando vieni a casa?"[32]

Whenever Daria was upset, she spoke Italian and her grandparents recognized her need to be consoled.

"My darlings, I love you. I love you."

She motioned to the nurse to take her back to her room.

Franca helped the nurse put Giulia back in bed, unable to hold back the copious tears. Giulia glanced at her mother and shook her head. Then her head fell to the side and she expired. Franca held her and kissed her.

"E′morte [33] … morte," murmured Franca, leaning over her body.
"Oh no, our beautiful Giulia," Edoardo cried out.

They flanked the bed, each one held her hand, kissed her checks, her hair, and spoke about her childhood and the joy she had brought them. The doctor came in, pronounced her dead and asked if they wanted an autopsy performed.

"No one will desecrate our daughter's body." Franca lamented.
"But Franca, we should know the truth."
"Her husband did this, didn't he?"
"No, Doctor, she fell and hit her head."

Edoardo lied, remembering their promise to Giulia.

"I'm sorry, but we must do a postmortem to be certain of the cause of death."

Orderlies brought Giulia's body to the morgue and her parents ambled home in a daze, unable to fathom that Giulia was truly dead.

In the meantime, Alissandru rushed into Giulia's room and her body was gone.

"Nurse! Nurse! Where is my wife?"
"She died. She is in pathology; the doctor requested an autopsy."

He flinched. How dare he? He was her husband. He shuddered and left the hospital. Later that evening, the doctor called Franca, confirmed her diagnosis of a subdural hematoma and offered his condolences.

"Thank you, Doctor."

When Franca and Edoardo went home, they called Anna. They told her they wanted to have the funeral for Giulia and would she intercede on their behalf and call Alissandru. He agreed.

Two days later, Alissandru entered the funeral parlor, wanting to be alone with Giulia's body. With his body and mind tormented with guilt, he sobbed. He touched her beautiful hair, her lips, her face and tranquility cloaked her face. She looked young and lovely, lovelier than she had been in months. But she was young, only twenty-eight years old.

"What am I going to do without you? My nerves have been frazzled."

He turned around and thought he heard a voice say:

"Poor you, you're always making excuses."

He ran out of the funeral parlor, spooked with his guilt.

Soft breezes caressed the island and dusk cloaked the city with a golden mantle of hues of orange. A dark gray hearse crawled along the cobblestone street. The undertaker taped his horn, warning children, who grabbed their baseballs and bats and scurried onto the sidewalk. In front of the Privitera's store, the black and white striped awning had been drawn back, lights reflected on large, square jars of green coffee beans, curlicue candles, and pastel-covered almonds and cookies.

The florist placed a spray of white gladioli, sprinkled with pink roses on the screen door, while the funeral director and his associates carried the casket through the store into the living room. Edoardo and Franca sat slumped in their leather chairs, while the director raised the lid and arranged the flowers inside and outside of the casket.

"I'll be back later," said the director.

Edoardo locked the front door, trudged toward the casket and watched Franca comb Giulia's hair and smooth out the wrinkles in her pink satin negligee and robe. Then she took her mother's pearl rosary beads, the ones her mother had given her when she married Edoardo, and wove them in Giulia's fingers.

"Edoardo, the strain is gone from her face but she was much too young to die."

Someone knocked on the door, interrupting their private mournful moments.

"Who is it?"
"It's Alissandru. Please let me see her."

Edoardo relented. Alissandru slumbered to the casket, wearing a black suit with a black armband on his left arm.

"Why did you let him in here?" Franca asked.
"Please let me explain. It was an accident."
"Accident! You kicked her down! You abused her and destroyed her. For God's sake, you didn't want her. Why didn't you let her go?"

He leaned over the casket; bit his bottom lip, his tears falling upon Giulia's face and murmured,

"I'm sorry. I loved you."

Neighbors started drifting in and out, through the store, into the living room, and exited through the kitchen door. Anna Triento pushed through the crown, holding Daria's hand and carrying Carlo.

"Anna, what are you doing?"
"He wants the children to see her."
"How cruel."

But it was too late. Alissandru grabbed Carlo who cried for his mother while Daria stared at her mother's supine body. She struggled with her tears and trepidations, pushing her disheveled hair off her face. She reached into the casket, touched her mother's frigid hand, pulled back, and called her.

"Mamma, svegliate, e´ Daria."[34]

Neighbors' hearts were ripped apart with the pathos unfolding before them and the doleful cries of the children. Franca grabbed Carlo out of Alissandru's arms, shielded his eyes while Edoardo picked up Daria, and asked

Anna to take them home. They were relieved when everyone left, leaving them to spend the night at their daughter's side.

At sunrise, Franca started to unwind her mother's pearl rosary beads, but then decided to leave them. Neighbors knocked on the door, brought in fruit, fresh Italian bread, and coffee.

Meanwhile, Father Damiano stood at the altar waiting for the parishioners to be seated as they awaited Giulia's body. An old world priest, he was robust, authoritative, personified a paternal figure to his parishioners, and commanded respect from his flock. He strolled through the neighborhood in his faded, black cassock, black coat, and doffed his biretta to the women. His black shoes were highly polished, although they had been soled and resoled. During the winter months, he left the rectory with a white, woolen scarf covering his mouth because of his susceptibility to sore throats and colds. Boys attending St. Martin's School dreaded the sight of him. If he caught them misbehaving, he pinched their cheeks and hung on to them until they yelled out in pain.

The funeral director led Edoardo and Franca to the first pew on the right side, while Alissandru sat on the left side with bowed head. Father Damiano gazed sternly at the altar boys and warned them to follow his instructions. He sung the High Mass in Latin, articulated the homily in Italian, and extolled Giulia's virtues as a wife, mother, and daughter, moving the congregation to tears.

The choir sang the dirge and the Mass ended amid quiet sounds of mourning. The funeral director led neighbors with cars to the Pleasantville cemetery, seven miles away. Edoardo and Franca placed a pink rose on Giulia's casket and Alissandru placed a red rose.

"Rest in peace, our beloved Giulia", they said as they held onto each other sobbing.

16

A week later, Alissandru called upon Father Damiano at the rectory and his housekeeper expressed her sorrow for his loss. He sat down while she summoned the pastor. He gazed at the mahogany cabinets lining the walls to the ceiling, containing baptismal, communion, confirmation, marriage and death certificates, of which many were suicides during the Great Depression.

"Alissandru, what can I do for you."

"Father, my neighbors are helping me with my children, but I can't impose upon them any longer. I've found steady work. Do you know of a good orphanage?"

"A good orphanage!" Father Damiano's voice raised an octave.

"Yes."

"Your in-laws are such good people, surely they will help you."

"Leave them out of this."

"Don't you have any family here?"

"No, they are all in Italy."

"Well, I will see what I can do. Alissandru, where have you found work? Not many parishioners are working; it's been awful."

He had found work in an auction house, repairing antiques, jewelry, sculptures and paintings in an exclusive shop on the Boardwalk.

After he departed, Father Damiano walked two doors away to Franca and Edoardo's store, where they sat in a stupor, weary, distraught, and unable to fathom the reality of Giulia's death. But when the pastor told them of Alissandru's plans, implacable rage overcame them.

"That despicable man killed her and now he's going to make the children suffer."

"Signora, that's a terrible thing to say," the priest's eyes opened up like two full moons.

"It's the truth," explained Edoardo.

Edoardo called a taxicab; they went to Alissandru's house and pounded on the door. Daria peered out of the window, waved to them, jumping up and down with excitement.

"Nonna! Nonno! Where's Mommy?"

"Daria, stop that," Alissandru said.

Edoardo opened the door, unable to speak through his vale of tears.

"I beg of you, put the children's welfare above our bitterness," pleaded Franca.

"You don't know what you are doing. I grew up in an orphanage and you cannot imagine how terrible it is," implored Edoardo.

Alissandru's handsome face stiffened, his charcoal eyes narrowed, and he pointed to the door.

"Leave my home and stop interfering."

"Why, you cold-blooded bastard."

Edoardo's strident voice bellowed throughout the house. Daria cried out and ran toward them. But Alissandru's voice penetrated through her, warning her, and she backed away. Edoardo grabbed Franca's hand and they departed, fraught with despair, tottering home in silence.

Soon after his encounter with his in-laws, Alissandru placed Daria and Carlo in a boarding house on Iowa Avenue. Word about the deplorable conditions reached their grandparents. They closed the store, called a taxicab, and arrived at a rickety house on Iowa and the bay, with broken-down furniture strewn about the porch. A rotund man stood on the porch, yawning, his bushy eyebrows overlapped his bloodshot eyes, and he guzzled down a bottle of beer with his one hand. Moments later, a woman emerged in a flowery housedress with a dingy, white slip hanging under the dress, brushing her legs, mapped with varicose veins. She rearranged the furniture and swept the porch in a mock attempt at cleanliness. Her husband grinned at her, winked, and pulled up his pants that kept slipping off his corpulent belly. He grabbed her flaccid buttocks and pushed her into the house, laughing and slamming the door shut.

Edoardo and Franca reached the height of vexation at the sight of their grandchildren. He unwound the rusty chain on the gate, evaded piles of trash and old tires, and cleared a path. Toddlers sat in playpens, playing in their own excrement while swatting at flies and mosquitoes that invaded the island from the land breezes across the bay. Edoardo covered the garbage pail, squeamish over the maggots crawling inside and outside of the pail. Carlo gripped the playpen, irked with the tenacity of the greenhead, and flailed his arms. He fell down as his feces squeezed out of his diaper. Daria sat on a wooden bench, her torn yellow dress stained with grape soda. She bit her petulant mouth, on the verge of tears, and then she saw her grandparents.

"Nonna, are you taking me and Carlo home?"

Franca sat down, placed Daria on her lap, hugged and kissed her and combed her dark brown hair, so much like Giulia's; her throat knotted, unable to speak.

"Where's Mommy? Tell her we want to go home."

"Daria, Mommy's on a long trip. Nonno and I want you to come home, but your father won't let you."

In the meantime, Edoardo hosed Carlo's playpen, pulled a diaper off the clothesline and changed him. The other children cried from the heat as well as the bites from the greenheads and mosquitoes. Edoardo held Carlo close to him, his throat sucked dry, hindering his speech. The boarding house owner stepped inside and fulminated against them for their intrusion on his property.

"What the hell you doin' here?"

"Mister, we're the grandparents. How dare you mistreat these children?"

"Get the hell out of here and don't come back. Aliss—can't pronounce those damn foreign names—he said you ain't allowed to see the kids."

"This place is a pigsty … for animals. At least, you could keep it clean. I'm taking them out of here."

"Don't you dare! I'll call the police."

"Edoardo, please don't argue with him; he might take it out on the children."

They kissed the children and departed.

They trudged to Pacific Avenue, the pitiful cries and anguish of their grandchildren reverberated through them. How much worse could things get? Climbing onto a jitney, they got off at Ohio and Pacific Avenues. They went to the Marlborough-Blenheim Hotel, a turn-of-the century hotel that resembled a Moorish Castle, where exclusive shops faced the Boardwalk. Alissandru leaned against the doorway of the auction house, watching the parade of tourists, and then saw his in-laws. He panicked, pulled out a cigarette, cupped his hands and lit it.

"Alissandru, we saw the children. We beg you to put aside your hatred for us and take them out of that place. It's a pigpen." Edoardo pleaded.

"It looked all right when I was there. I go once a week."

His face appeared etched in ice, his eyes frightened them; he was capable of anything, lacking compassion and emotion. Would their grandchildren bear the brunt of his callousness?

"Leave me alone. Stay out of my life."

A rolling chair driver asked them if they wanted a ride, Edoardo nodded, and they rode to Mississippi Avenue, disconsolate, bewildered, and sought out a neighborhood attorney. Pity surged within him for their plight.

"He's the father and there is nothing you can do."

"Unless we prove he's responsible for her death?"

"Signora, there are rumors in the neighborhood, but can you prove it?"

Edoardo shook his head, recalled their promise to Giulia, and asked the attorney to drop the matter. Edoardo asked if he could call the authorities and have the boarding house closed. The attorney said yes and waived his fee.

Three days later, Alissandru received a telephone call; the Board of Health had shut down the boarding house and he must pick up his children. He did and went to see Father Damiano.

"It's urgent. I have to find a place for them."

"Alissandru, there's a place about seventy-five miles away. It's called St. Martin's Orphanage."

"Good, the farther away, the better. When can I take them?

"Mid-August."

Alissandru left a donation on his desk and departed with his children. He avoided going near their grandparents' store; instead he returned home. He sought out his neighbor and offered her ten dollars a week for each child. She agreed.

Franca and Edoardo roasted coffee; the aroma filtered through the neighborhood. But, the sight of Father Damiano unnerved them. What bad news did he have this time?

"The children will be going to an orphanage in August. The place is in Hopewell, New Jersey, about seventy-five miles away from home."

"We'll never see our grandchildren ... Giulia's children," Edoardo sobbed.

"Seventy-five miles!" Franca cried out, wiping her face with her apron.

"I'm sorry,"

"Father, thank you for telling us."

17

In August, the island sweltered with humid, hot weather. Tourists and islanders converged on the soft beige sands, swam in the dark green ocean, and sought relief from the muggy weather.

Alissandru packed his children's clothes, borrowed a car, and drove to Franca and Edoardo's store. He carried Carlo, held Daria's hand, but she pulled away from him and ran into her grandmother's arms. Alissandru placed Carlo in Edoardo's arms, stating:

"They're leaving. I thought you'd like to see them. I'll be back in fifteen minutes."

"Alissandru, please let us take care of them. We beg you," implored Edoardo.

"Too much for you."

"That's ridiculous."

Alissandru did not respond and left.

Daria wiped her grandmother's tear-strained face, forced her mouth into a smile, and Franca trembled, fearing their incarceration would have a deleterious effect on the children without love or family.

"Nonna, next time you go on vacation with us?"
"Thank you, Daria, Nonna and Nonno would love to go with you."

She had dreadful thoughts about what they should have done to Alissandru; then she rationalized that they could have landed in prison. And what about the children? The thought of their grandparents as common criminals would be a horrendous legacy.

Alissandru returned and put his children into the car. They journeyed to the Sourland Mountains in Hopewell, New Jersey, reaching St. Martin's Orphanage, where acres of land rolled into a carpet of green landscaped hills with manicured hedges and graceful elms fluttering, prodded by gentle breezes. The guards opened the gate and Alissandru drove through a winding, tarred road with austere buildings in the background. Puffs of white clouds hung over the starkness, tipping the mountains, and sunset colored the skies.

"Isn't it pretty here? Alissandru asked Daria.
"I wanna go home."
"This is your home," he tersely replied.
"I wanna live with Nonna and Nonno."
"You can't."

She pouted and slithered back down in her seat, crying softly.

Alissandru parked in front of the main building, where a nun came out, greeted the children and him. He picked up Carlo who slept, and handed him to the nun. But Daria sulked and refused to leave the car.

"Come on, Daria."
"Papa′, andiamo a casa."[35]
"She's bi-lingual."
"Yes, Sister, she's very precocious."
"Daria!"

His penetrable gaze bore into her, a warning to behave, and she got out of the car.

"Mr. Leone, the older ones are rebellious when they first come here. Come inside, Mother Regina is expecting you."

Mother Regina stood behind a large, mahogany desk with folded arms underneath her starched collar; her face swathed in white and a white rope girdled her brown habit. Daria kept her eyes downcast, glancing at her reflection in the polished black and white checkered floor. She tugged at Alissandru's pants.

"I don't like it here."
"Mr. Leone, she'll get used to it."
"Daria is three and a half years old and Carlo's a year and a half."
"That will be fifteen dollars a month per child."
"That's fine."
"Sister Agnes will give you a tour of the grounds."

A pudgy, red-faced, freckled nun led Alissandru and his children through the building, showed him the nursery, where he handed Carlo over to the nun, who fussed over him.

"Daria, kiss your brother good-bye."
"No, non mi lasciare!"[36]

Sister Agnes gripped Daria's hand; she tried squirming out of her grip but alas, there was no escape.

"Once she meets the other children, she'll be fine."

Alissandru bent down, kissed her cheek, walked away, and she wiped her face with the back of her hand. He never glanced back, entered the car, and drove through the great iron gates. Daria squirmed out of Sister Agnes' grip and ran and climbed the fence, screaming for her father. The guard lifted her off and handed her to the nun. She yielded to Sister Agnes' hold and spun around at the clangor of the gates that sealed her and Carlo's future.

Sister Agnes led her to the dormitory, a massive room with thirty beds neatly made, and she pointed to Daria's bed.

"Now we'll go to the dining room."

Daria was terrified of the surroundings, stifled her tears and waited for instructions. Sister pointed to her seat. Girls lined up with their plates, laughing and screeching with delight. Daria covered her ears from the incessant dissonance, the discordant sounds of pots and broken dishes and glasses. Daria's stomach churned at the sight of string beans covered with a lumpy cream sauce and a boiled potato. She glanced around, hoping no one was watching, and dumped the food on the floor.

"Daria, the bread and butter is good and here's an apple." A girl in charge of young children told her.

Now Sister Agnes clapped her hands, signaled that dinner was over, and the girls stood up. They carried their plates, scraped off morsels of food into two huge garbage cans for the farm animals and piled the dishes near the sink. Then she motioned to Daria to follow the girls into the dormitory. She was handed a towel, a washrag, and a toothbrush. After she brushed her teeth, two heavy hands swooped her up, undressed her, and threw her into the bathtub.

"I can bathe myself," she whined.
"Girls, leave her alone," ordered Sister Agnes.

She peed, stirred the bath water and bathed. After she dried herself, she ran into the dormitory, slid under the sheets, and felt something furry writhing against her leg. She leaped out of bed and a sinuous cat followed her. The roar of laughing was deafening and Daria cried out for her mother.

"Mamma, dove siete?"[37]
"She's a foreigner," remarked the girl in the next bed.
"Leave her alone," yelled Sister Agnes.
"Yes, Sister," a resounding chorus replied.

Sister Agnes put Daria into bed, left the dormitory, and balled fists faced Daria from all directions. She sat up for a moment, trembled at the sight of menacing fists around her, and slid under the covers. In the morning, after breakfast, Daria followed girls her age into the schoolyard amid giggles and jeers at her, an initiation for newcomers. She found a corner, sat down, crossed her legs, bit her nails until they bled, and suddenly a shadow hovered over her.

"Stop biting your nails."
"I wanna go home."
"Aw, shut up. For a little girl, you sure have a big mouth. This is it, get used to it. Some of us are here because our parents are dead and some of us

are here because our mothers are dead and our fathers don't want us. Which one are you?"

"Not gonna tell you."
"So, who cares?"

Daria curled up near the hedges and dozed off for a moment. When the lunch bell rang, she ignored it while girls scurried into the building through the warren of corridors. A figure in brown blocked out the sunlight, her long brown habit blew from late summer breezes. Sister Agnes stood rigid, arms akimbo, resembling an eagle about to scoop her up with its claws.

"Get up."

Daria bounced up and lagged behind the nun who rebuked her.

"Pick up your feet when you walk."
"Yes, Sister."
"Well, that's more like it."

Six weeks later, brisk autumn winds whipped through the grounds, denuded trees with leaves falling on yellowed lawns. As yet, Daria had not adjusted, stifling her tears at night, yearning for her mother, crying sotto voce:

"Mamma, Mamma."

Once a month, on Sunday afternoons, children who had living relatives gathered in the auditorium, in a state of expectancy. At the sound of her name, Daria rushed into her grandmother's arms.

"Nonna, are you taking me home? She asked, snuggling close to Franca.
"I love you, but I can't."
"Tell Daddy, no more vacation."

The nursery nun carried in Carlo and he nestled his little body into his grandfather's arms, responding to his affection and kisses. Then he asked Daria if they saw one another. She shook her head. By now, Franca and Edoardo's hatred equaled the force of Mount Etna's eruption. The hour allotted them flew. The nun grabbed Carlo from Edoardo's arms and Sister Agnes called out to Daria.

"Mr. and Mrs. Privitera, Mother Regina wants to see you in her office," Sister Agnes said.

Mother Regina's words struck a chord of incredulity within them. Anna Triento, who had driven them there, looked puzzled.

"You're telling us that we can't see our grandchildren?"

"I am sorry. Mr. Leone has given me strict orders. Since you came quite a distance, I couldn't stop you from seeing them."

"How can you, a 'woman of God,' do this? They've lost their mother and now this. He doesn't have to know we visit."

"I can't do that."

Edoardo grabbed Franca's arm and without further utterances, he motioned to Anna to go.

"Did you hear that? We are not allowed to see them. He won't let us see them."

As Anna drove them home, she realized Alissandru was relentless in his pursuit to punish them for something. What had they done to him, but shown him kindness and generosity?

That night Daria cried herself to sleep, wet her bed, and in the morning her sheets reeked of urine. The girl in the next bed taunted her, yelling:

"Piss-face, piss-face! Hey, girls, she needs a diaper!"

"Shut up, meanie," returned Daria, realizing that she was learning the lingua franca of the orphanage very quickly.

Cold, blustery winds roared through the acreage of land. To Daria's surprise, her father visited them and fussed over them but only Carlo responded to Alissandru's affection. He noticed Daria had been subdued; she only spoke when spoken to and appeared to be different from the child whom he had left with her precocity. He summoned Sister Agnes, dismayed at Daria's emaciated body. Sister explained she would not eat or make friends and spoke about her mother and grandparents.

"Mr. Leone, she is a very bright child. Why can't she live with her grandparents?"

"She cannot. That's all there is to it."

"Daddy, we saw Nonna and Nonno."

"You allowed them to see the children … after I had given you strict orders?"

"Mr. Leone, it was an act of charity."

"Don't let it happen again."

He placed Daria on his lap to kiss her good-bye. She slithered off his lap, curled her lips, and tears poured down her cheeks.

"Now be a good girl, eat, and make friends. This is your home."

And so Alissandru Leone left his children in the care of strangers. Carlo had adjusted because he did not remember what home was like, while Daria put her memories in the recesses of her mind and fended for herself.

18

Back in Atlantic City, Franca closed the store for the afternoon, called a taxicab, and went to the Atlantic City Hospital. Two weeks prior, doctors had removed Edoardo's prostate gland. He was placed in a ward, surrounded with seven men who groaned, cursed, prayed, and sought respite from their pain. Franca drew the curtain around his bed, trying to shut out the smells and voices of death. She embraced him, still a dignified, handsome man with his white hair and black and gray moustache; he left his eye patch home, refusing to wear it. His face had the gray mask of impending death, and she trembled. She puffed his pillow up and caressed his cheek with the back of her hand.

"Edoardo, I love you."

"I adore you. Let's be honest. We both know that I am dying."

Tears dripped out of Franca's blue eyes that he loved so much. He held her hand, diverted his face from hers, glanced at the ceiling, and wept. She rested her head on his chest and he stroked her salt and pepper hair that she wore in a braid, encircling her face.

"Franca, my love."

"Don't give up; I need you."

"Oh Tesoro, we had a wonderful life, despite the tragedies. When Giulia died, our hearts died with her. Why didn't he die instead of her?"

They held onto each other, knowing the end was near, and he gently pushed her away.

"I've always prayed that I would go before you. You are a strong woman and our grandchildren need you."

He winced. His face contorted with pain and Franca drew open the curtain and called out for the nurse. The nurse administered a shot of morphine.

"Go home. I don't want you here when it happens."
"Please, my darling, I love you. I don't want to leave."
"I beg you, leave now."

She agreed, wiped her tears, and departed forlorn, wondering how she could live without him, his love, his gentleness, and kindness. Walking home, her breathing became belabored as tears hindered her walk. A terrible loneliness engulfed her; she needed to shut herself off from the world and think about him and Giulia.

When she entered the store, she locked the door and went to the used baby grand piano Edoardo had purchased, despite her objections that they couldn't afford it. But their lives had become depressed, bewildered and without hope. At least when Franca played the piano, it invigorated him, giving him a glimpse of life and hope for the future.

That night, Edoardo died. Two days later, the same dark gray hearse crawled through the narrow, cobblestone streets, the second time within nine months, and stopped in front of the coffee store, while the bells of St. Martin's Church pealed noon.

"Signora, I came early as you requested."

The funeral director and his assistants wheeled the casket in, raised the lid and left. Franca locked the door, stared at Edoardo, wanting to touch him, but that would confirm his death. She sat at her piano, played his favorite Scarlatti sonatas, closed the piano and leaned over.

"My darling Edoardo, what will I do without you?"

Yet, she hadn't touched him. She slumped into her leather chair and spoke to him about her love for him. Finally, she stood near him, touched his petrified hand and his full head of white hair, the only part of him that felt alive. She glanced at Giulia's photograph in her riding outfit.

"You are together now. How I wish I were with you."

A knock on the door ended her moments with Edoardo. The darkened skies were full of clouds and nary a star shown. She shivered and then realized it was time for the viewing. Anna came in and refrained from any utterance of sorrow or condolences. Knowing full well the pain in Franca's heart, she sat with her as neighbors paid their respects.

Suddenly Alissandru came in, stood before Franca, extended his condolences but she ignored him, acting as if he did not exist. He bowed his head, went to Edoardo's casket, knelt down and made the Sign of the Cross, exiting quickly. Edoardo was buried next to his beloved daughter. Franca returned home, spent and sapped of her vim and vitality. Death would have been welcomed, but Edoardo's words haunted her and inexorable rage and hatred for Alissandru fueled her renewed strength.

Meanwhile, at the orphanage, Sister Agnes took Daria aside and explained that her grandfather was in heaven with her mother. Frightened, she cried out:

"Nonna's all alone."
"Your grandmother?"
"Yes."

At dinner, Daria left her food untouched and Sister Agnes excused her as she ran to the bathroom, where she found solace, sitting on the toilet. Then the sounds of laughter startled her. She garnered herself for the usual round of battles with the girls who were relentless in their torment, pinching her until her body turned black and blue. Then they held her down in the tub; the water covered her head. She had learned to control her breathing so she did not gasp for air. This displeased them and they released her. She retaliated, scratched their faces, grappled with them and stomped on their feet, running naked through the dormitory into Sister Agnes' arms.

"Sister, they hurt me all the time."
She snuggled into Sister Agnes' arms.

"Girls, whoever is responsible, come here!"

No one came forward and she asked Daria to pick out the girls. She shook her head. But with her assertiveness, Daria became reclusive, keeping her distance from those girls who ruled cliques. Slowly, they stopped tormenting her; she had been initiated and now she was one of them.

On Sunday, Alissandru visited his children. He was pleased with Carlo's development but concerned with Daria's fragility and total withdrawal from him. A glimmer of guilt surfaced and he touched her face.

"Aren't you glad to see me?"

She shrugged, sat on the floor and played with Carlo. Then her almond-shaped, charcoal eyes, so much like his, glanced up at him.

"Why doesn't Nonna come here?"
"She's sick."

Her eyes misted, recalling amorphous figures of her mother and grandfather, but her grandmother's face was imprinted on her mind, remembering her braid, encircling her head.

"I'm leaving. I won't be back for a long time."
"Bye."

And she ran away from him. Alissandru was pleased with her behavior. She did not ask constant questions and to his surprise, had adjusted to the orphanage, a world unwanted but thrusted upon her brother and her by his selfishness.

19

Alissandru purchased a 1927 Buick Sedan and was on his way to Pittsburgh, Pennsylvania, where he had contracts renovating cathedrals with vaulted ceilings, stain glass windows, and statuary. A new world of independence opened up for him and at thirty years of age, he felt young and alive again. He anglicized his name to Alexander.

As he dined one evening, the hostess, a beautiful young brunette, flirted with him and asked if he was married.

"Not married," he replied, failing to mention he was widowed and had two children.

"Handsome man like you not married? I'll be finished in an hour. Will you wait for me?"

"My pleasure," he smiled.

She invited him up to her apartment. They had torrid sex but when she reached an orgasm she yelled out:

"Mi′ amore"

He leaped out of bed, put on his shorts and glanced at her with surprise.

"You didn't say you were Italian."
"I'm not. I'm French and English."
"But you said 'my love' in Italian."
"Alexander, that is your imagination. I don't understand one word of Italian.
"Are you telling me the truth?"
"Yes. Say, you are strange. You'd better leave right now."

He dressed and ran out of her apartment, returned to his place and sleep eluded him. Was it guilt? Ridiculous! Giulia was dead; he was entitled to his freedom and to be with any woman he chose without remorse. Or was Giulia right when she said they were destined to be together forever? That's absurd, he reiterated over and over again.

The following night, he went into an Irish Pub. The owner, a stunning blonde with blue eyes, sat with him, bought him a drink and between courses, slid in beside him. She asked him where he was from and conversation flowed between them. Later, she told the bartender she was leaving, to close up the place, and if he needed her to call her apartment.

She had noticed that Alissandru drank red wine at her restaurant, so when they entered her apartment, she poured him a glass.

"Alexander, you should be in the movies. With your accent, you sound so sensual."
"Thank you, but I'm an architect and haven't been able to find work."
"Things are difficult right now."

She put on the radio and slid into his arms and they danced around her living room. She was enamored with him but he was cautious; he did not want to spoil the evening. She raised her lips and led him to the bedroom, where she undressed, ready to give herself to him. They had passionate sex and when she climaxed, she screamed:

"Mi′ amore"

He pulled out of her, held his head, wondering if he was losing his mind.

"Leslie, where did you learn Italian?"

"Eye-talian? I don't know a single word of Eye-talian."
"Why did you say mi´ amore?"
"Who me? You are out of your mind. You'd better see a doctor."
"Maybe I should. I apologize."

He walked the streets of Pittsburgh all night, sloshing through the snow, despondent. He stood under a streetlight, lit a cigarette and wondered what was happening to him. Was Giulia haunting him, tormenting him, or seeking vengeance?

For weeks, he avoided any trysts, working ten hours a day until he fell into bed exhausted. Then a tall, beautiful redhead came into the cathedral as he worked. He could not keep his eyes off her; she was gorgeous with green eyes and a slim figure. She flirted with him despite his dirty work clothes.

"If I go out with someone totally different, it probably won't happen again." He thought.
"How do you do? He asked.
"Fine, thank you. You do beautiful work. I've been here a couple of times."
"Sorry, I did not notice. My name is Alexander. Please excuse my appearance."

They chatted for a short time and Alexander invited her for dinner.

"I'd love to. Here's my telephone number and address."
"Wait. Your name?"
"Carol Anderson."
"Carol, you are lovely."

She blushed and thanked him.

He drove up to her home, dressed in a navy blue suit, navy topcoat, and navy Stetson hat. She met him at the door, introduced him to her mother who was impressed with him.

"Mother, I won't be late."
"Mrs. Anderson, nice to have met you."
"Thank you. Have a wonderful dinner. Where are you going?"
"Carol, would you like to go to Dante's Restaurant?"
"Sounds wonderful."

While driving to the restaurant, he told Carol that he was widowed but did not mention children. They dined at Dante's Restaurant and after dinner he invited her up to his apartment.

"I won't touch you, you are safe. I don't force myself on anyone."

"With your looks and class, you don't have to. I'm sure the women pursue you."

After they entered his apartment, he put on the Victrola and played the famous Italian singer, Carlo Butti's recording of *Guitarra Romana.*

"What romantic music."

"I'm glad you like it. Would you like a cocktail?"

"Yes, thank you."

Later, they sat on the couch, she succumbed to the amorous music, moved near him, kissed and touched him, and his member bulged in his pants. Then she stood up, stripped, danced around, and he exclaimed.

"You're a natural redhead."

"Let's go in the bedroom."

Alissandru could not hide his excitement. Finally, he could have a perfect night of lovemaking with a beautiful woman. He smothered her body with kisses, entered her, and she curled up with passion, crying out:

"Mi′ amore, someday in Taormina."

He rolled over her, put on his robe, apologized and said he was ill, and helped her dress.

"What's wrong with you? She asked.

"I'd better see a doctor. My wife's tormenting me, won't allow me to be with another women. What the hell am I saying? I'm an intelligent, educated man."

"But you told me she was dead."

"She is, but she believed we were destined to be together forever and ever … and beyond."

"Wow! That's scary. Why don't you go see a gypsy?"

"A gypsy? That's nonsense."

"What do you have to lose?

"No, that's not for me. I don't believe in that stuff."

The next evening, he walked around a pavilion, pushed his collar up as snow began to fall. A gypsy stood behind a dimly lit store window and beckoned him. At first he ignored her; then changed his mind and went in. She asked him to sit down and lit candles. He felt as if he were at his own viewing. She studied him for a few minutes, examined his hands, and asked for three dollars up front.

"Ah, she's still around you. She can't rest in peace."

"This is crazy. Why did I bother coming in here?"

"The problem is you are a troubled man. What have you done to her?"

He leaped to his feet, ran outside into the street; a man possessed with his own guilt and called out:

"Giulia, I'm sorry. Forgive me, let me live."

20

Four years had passed since Alissandru's last visit to the orphanage, when he told Daria he was going away for a long time. Still emaciated from her lack of eating, she filled up on bread loaded with butter, fruit, lumpy wheatena, and occasionally, a hot dog. She excelled in school, became mentally strong and realized her ability, which earned affection and respect from the nuns.

One day during class, Daria was summoned to Mother Regina's office. A mask of spurious curiosity covered up the fear as her hands trembled, her confidence dwindled, and she wondered what was wrong. Only children with problems were called into her office. She gingerly knocked on the door and Mother Superior gave her permission to enter and sit down.

"I have wonderful news for you. Meet Mr. and Mrs. Pifle; you are going to live with them."

Daria leaped to her feet, gripped Mother Regina's desk, and avoided the smile of the couple.

"No, I'm not."
"Watch your manners. They will be your foster parents."
"And I'll be their servant."
"Where did you hear that nonsense? Naturally, you'll have chores."

"The kids talk about it. And I have a brother, will he go with me?"

"No, only you. I've told Mr. and Mrs. Pifle what a wonderful student you are."

"No, Mother, I don't want to leave here. I'm only half-an-orphan and someday my father will take me and my brother home."

"Daria, your father gave me permission to board you with Mr. and Mrs. Pifle."

"He did? Why?" Her lips quivered with disbelief.

"So you can live in a home."

"I ain't going anywhere! I want to live here until my father takes me home."

"Your English is awful. Remember, *ain't fell into a bucket of paint.*"

"I say *ain't* when I'm mad. I know, angry, only dogs get mad."

Mother Regina sighed with relief; at least their teaching was not in vain.

"You are excused."

"Mother Regina, thank you."

She glanced back at the couple, hoping her behavior had been a detriment, and they would find someone else.

Once outside, she ran like a deer in flight, stopped suddenly and noticed tulips, daffodils, and hyacinths popping out of the earth. She looked around and no one was in sight. She bent down and picked up a cluster of hyacinths, inhaled the fragrance and placed it in her uniform pocket. Standing up, she reflected upon the expansive grounds, the austere buildings, and the manifold of trees, and grinned. She walked around, smug and confident with a mantle of security; she was home. That night when she climbed into bed, she shrouded herself with her sheet and blanket and hummed the song she had learned when she first arrived at the orphanage.

Be it ever so humble,
There's no place like home.
My mother is dead,
My father's gone away.

She had a benign sleep, trying to remember her grandmother, who was only an amorphous figure.

Spring departed and hot summer days emblazoned the acreage of land. Girls sat inside a giant gazebo, laughing and gobbling down roasted chickens, hot dogs and potato salad. Skunks found shelter underneath and girls stomped on the platform to lure them out into the open. The skunks, discernible with their black and white stripes, retaliated by releasing their powerful, foul odor, which forced the girls to back off. Pinching their noses, they fell to the ground laughing.

With summer's end and the arrival of frigid winds, the children were confined to their dormitories. When they saw a profusion of tufted clouds covering the mountains, they were elated. The skies were expectant with snow that would fall during the night and blanket the grounds, allowing them hours of play and frolic in the fresh snow the following morning.

Shortly before Christmas, a contingent of women from St. Martin's Parish visited the five children from Atlantic County. Anna Triento sought out Daria and Carlo. Daria glanced at her with reticence and indifference until she explained she was a friend of their grandmother who had sent them presents.

"Whatever you do, don't tell your father I was here or tell him about the presents. Do you see him?"

"No," Daria replied.

Daria unwound her gift, removed the paper and folded it, screeching with delight.

"It's the first present that I have ever got. This is the most beautiful dress in the whole world."

She placed the wool, scotch-plaid dress against her, touched the black velvet trim on the collar and puff sleeve. Carlo unwound his gift; a navy blue suit with short pants, navy blue knee socks, a white shirt and a red bow tie. He put the suit against him.

"How did my grandmother know our sizes?"

"She called Sister Agnes."

Their faced glowed with happiness. Anna's throat felt like it had been pricked with thorns, kissing and hugging them and enjoying their rapt expressions.

"How's our grandmother? I used to call her something else."
"Nonna"
"Nonna, Nonna," repeated Daria, liking the sound.

When Anna departed, she left two forlorn children who had experienced a touch of love and affection, of which they had long been deprived.

21

During the next few years, Carlo and Daria never saw their father or each other. A high cyclone fence separated boys and girls, intensifying the chasm that separated them. The blustery winds and snows vanished once again. With the emergence of spring, girls played hopscotch and jumped rope while the younger boys played baseball and the older ones cut the lawns.

Daria discarded her oversized brown coat and ventured outside. She glanced down at her small breasts, defined waist, and her charcoal eyes flashed with excitement; she was growing up. Her luxuriant, dark brown hair reached her waist and it was a source of pride to her.

Carlo, now eleven years old, had a slight build, sandy brown hair, brown eyes and a mischievous smile. But there were rumors about his aberrant behavior, which included disobedience and belligerency towards the nuns. He was summoned to the disciplinarian's office and he shuddered and paced back and forth until the "giant" gave him permission to enter his domain.

"Leone, get in here!"
"Mr. J-Johnson, I'm s-sorry." A penitent gaze was upon his face.
"Too late, you were warned." Johnson said.

Johnson stood six-feet, four inches tall with a ruddy complexion, reddish-brown hair with wisps of gray at the temples. He overshadowed Carlo who stared up at his protruding eyes and saw mucous hanging from his nostrils. Johnson wiped his nose with his hand, grabbed the horsewhip from the wall and swung at Carlo's legs. Carlo dashed through his legs, ran like a cheetah, and landed in the woods surrounding the orphanage. Mr. Johnson flailed his whip, leaped quantum steps and his gruff voice ranted and raved about the little ruffian who had dared to defy him.

"Boys, help me weed out Leone."

Meanwhile, Carlo peered through the bushes, cringed at Johnson's raucous voice, crawled farther away, and cracked a twig.

"He's around here!" One of the boys hollered.

"Soon the bears and mountain lions will come out and they will be mighty hungry," said Johnson, winking at the boys.

Carlo's ears perked up; he glanced around, spotted raccoons, squirrels and rabbits scampering about but he did not move. Suddenly a big, fat hand grabbed him by the neck as if he were a rag doll; his legs dangled, his arms lashed out, fighting only the air. Johnson held onto him, thrashing his legs and buttocks until Carlo cried out in pain.

"Now, you'll behave."

With all the commotion, girls ran toward the fence that separated the girls from the boys. Daria saw Carlo crying and holding onto his legs. She funneled her fingers through the fence, climbed up and tried to jump over, when someone grabbed her and put her down; she looked up into Mother Regina's stern face.

"You big oaf! Stop hurting my brother!" Daria screamed through her tears.

"Mr. Johnson, enough! Sometimes, you get carried away with your duties."

Mother Regina realized Johnson relished his empowerment role as a disciplinarian. His bovine, insouciant manner ignored the boys who begged for forgiveness.

"Yes, Mother Regina, but no dinner for him."

Daria pressed her face against the fence, etched with the twisted, galvanized wire, and called out to Carlo who waved to her and fled to the bathroom. He patted his welts with cold water, headed to the dormitory and flung himself on his bed.

"Hate him, hate this place," he mumbled as his legs ached in pain.

Falling asleep, the aroma of roasting meat tempted his palate; his stomach gurgled. He glanced around the empty dorm and followed the trail that led to the nun's dining room on the lower level of the children's dining room. He stooped down and saw a succulent roast beef surrounded with potatoes and carrots. He licked his lips and rotated his tongue, and the aroma wafted through the window. He crept away, holding his stomach and returned to the dormitory. In the morning, he gulped down two servings of lumpy, cooked cereal and ate four slices of bread with creamy butter.

Now snow flurries glistened, webbed in white showers over the trees, coating rolling hills with mantles of snow. Daria wiped the steam from the windows, glanced outside, and a full moon lit the grounds with a blanket of serenity. She giggled as nocturnal animals scurried around, leaving tiny tracks, which revealed the presence of crows' feet, while raccoons forged trails. Deer stood still, frozen in time, then the movements of others animals forced them to retreat.

"Someday, I'll be free like you," she murmured.

Spring burst out with an array of flowers, the fragrance of honeysuckle infused the air and children remained outside until orange hues of sunset glowed across the skies. Sleep escaped Daria so she tiptoed to the entrance and sneaked outside; the air was heavy with clouds of moisture. She strolled the grounds, avoided the lanterns that were sentinels, and watched spotted owls perched on trees, awaiting their dinner: leaping rabbits and small birds. Despite her fear of animals, the night air was invigorating, and then she returned to the dormitory.

The next day, during recess, girls rejoiced, squealing, exhilarated as they oscillated on the swings with warm breezes caressing their faces. Daria threw back her head; her long, dark brown hair cascaded and touched the ground. Her orphan-mate Sally called out to her.

"Come on, Daria, stand behind me and you'll fly."
"Oh no, we could get into trouble."
"Sister threatens us all the time, but she's not around."

Daria perused the grounds, her eyes went up and down and across the buildings; no one was around. She stood on the swing; flying higher and higher, freed from restrictions, and Sally's and her laughter reverberated throughout the playground.

"Daria Leone! Didn't you hear my warnings?"
"Yes, Sister. I'm sorry. I'll go to confession."
"Too late for that, sometimes drastic measures are needed. Sally, you were seated; you're excused."

Daria backed off, trembling, her teeth chattered, even though she was perspiring, and she wondered what kind of punishment Sister would deem appropriate. Slowly, girls formed a semi-circle around her, as Sister Marian's crimson face erupted with veins. Her neck and face were swathed in starched white cotton and topped with a brown veil. She removed a pair of scissors from her pocket, then Daria sought deliverance, but where could she run? The sun glistened upon the scissors and Daria wondered if they were a harbinger of her punishment. Would she cut her uniform? Sister grabbed Daria's beautiful, dark brown hair and Daria shrieked.

"Please, not my hair."
"Stand still or I'll cut it all off."

Daria hung her head and acquiesced. She stood meek, reticent and compliant outwardly, but inwardly, she churned with odium for Sister Marian, who slashed her hair in different directions.

"I hate you! I hate you!

Sister ignored her outburst. Clip, clip, clip echoed through Daria's mind. Then Sister wiped the scissors with her fingers and placed them back into her pocket.

"Girls, you've just learned a lesson."

Daria glanced down at the tarred playground; the sun reflected on the red highlights in her hair. She scooped up her hair, placed it in the apron of her uniform and ran. Then dropping her apron, she touched her head, still running and left a trail of dark hair. She entered the building, zigzagged through the corridors until she reached the bathroom, where she peeked in the mirror, removed hair from her mouth, and sobbed.

"I'm so ugly."

Trudging out of the bathroom, she climbed into bed, wrapped the sheet around her head, and hummed the usual song, omitting the first two lines.

My mother is dead.
And my father's gone away.

Sleep provided respite from her defilement.

In the morning, the din of the girls awakened her, but Daria did not stir from underneath the sheets. Her orphan-mate, Sally, touched her arm and Daria peered out, still covering her head.

"Thank you for not tattle-tailing on me. Oh gosh, Sister is coming."
"Daria, get up!"

Her imperious voice paralyzed Daria with terror. Sister pulled the sheets off her while Daria grappled with her. Her charcoal eyes glowered at Sister Marian who shoved her out of bed.

"It's time to get up."
"Please, I don't want to."
"Get up!"

Daria plodded through the congestion of girls who snickered at her. Their laughter reverberated from all directions while Daria stood in front of the mirror, combing the hair she had left, over and over again.

"Hey, Leone, you look like a boy; you're in the wrong bathroom."

Daria lunged at the instigator and a brawl ensued among those who were sympathetic to Daria and the vicious girls. Then the voice of the authority bellowed throughout the hallway: Sister Marian. Instant quietude prevailed.

She ordered the girls to put on their veils and line up for Mass. Daria obeyed. She thought of running away. Where could she go? Her Nonna lived far, far away. Other kids had done it and some ended up in reform school as delinquents.

After years of living and working in Pennsylvania and Ohio, Alissandru arrived in Philadelphia to live with a cousin, Vincenzo Conforto, who moved to America from Novara, Sicily, Alissandru's hometown. He had not been feeling well, nor had he married, and he stated he did not want a stepmother for his children. He led a monastic life since his last incident with the stunning redhead he had found so beguiling and, yet, left her like a madman, roaming the streets, afraid to touch a woman. He believed that Giulia would torment him for the rest of his life. Yet, he yearned for the qualities in a woman that Giulia possessed: beauty, intelligence, education, class, but especially love. Once he had the best a woman could give a man, but he had destroyed her and neglected his children.

While Vincenzo and he dined, Alissandru bent over in excruciating pain and went to the bathroom; blood spurted out from his mouth and rectum.

"Call an ambulance, please hurry," he yelled.

After four days at St Agnes Hospital, the doctor diagnosed his illness: cancer of the stomach. Alissandru was roiled and astonished at his diagnosis; his mind swirled with the news and plans for his children.

"It can't be. I haven't been feeling well, but cancer?"
"Get a second opinion," his doctor advised.

He consulted with another doctor, who arrived at the same conclusion.

"How long do I have?"
"Possibly a year."

Alissandru asked to be discharged, amid his doctor's protestation; he had a lot of things to do concerning his children. That night he dreamed about Giulia, who looked lovely in a white negligee like the one she wore on their honeymoon. She smiled, glided through the sky and he reached out for her, weeping, but she never spoke to him. He woke up, concluding, it was a phantasmagoria.

Vincenzo picked him up and drove them to his home.

"Alissandru, what are you going to do about your children?"

"They'll keep them there until they are eighteen."

"What's wrong with you? Do they know about their Sicilian heritage and Italian culture? I'm sure they don't. You can't leave them there to rot."

Alissandru excused himself and prepared for a trip to Atlantic City.

22

Cold, capricious weather with over-laden clouds concealed blue skies during the last days of March. Alissandru climbed down from the excursion train, stood in front of St. Martin's Church and walked to Franca's store. She sat in her overstuffed, leather chair; waiting for customers and intermittently, stoked the coals in the potbelly stoves. The bells of St. Martin's Church tolled: twelve noon. She blessed herself, removed her rosary beads from her apron pocket and recited the rosary. Then she could not believe her eyes: it's him! He tapped the frosted window; she stood up, her body stiffened at the sight of him, her face hooded in fury. Alissandru! What did he want: Was there something wrong with the children?

He opened the door, extended his hand to her, which she ignored. He was still a handsome man, despite dark circles underneath his eyes, and dressed elegantly in a brown cashmere coat with a dark brown Stetson hat. Franca's hands trembled; stabilizing herself, she placed both hands on the counter and glared at him with such hatred. He had been the cause of such misery and now he stood before her. Alissandru squirmed at the venom oozing out of her and turned his gaze away from her.

"How are you?" He asked, removing his hat.

"Do you really care? Apparently, you are doing fine. You dress like a prince while your children rot in that place."

"I have stomach cancer," his voice trailing at her gelid expression.

Franca smirked at the news, picked up her shawl and placed it over her shoulders.

"What do you want from me? Compassion? Didn't you ever wonder why we didn't have you arrested for Giulia's death?"

"It was an accident. I don't want to talk about it."

"She made us promise not to press charges. She loved you so much; a love beyond reality. And what you did to the children, disposing of them without any concern for their well-being."

"Believe me; I have spent many sleepless nights."

"Who gives a damn about you? What flows through your veins?

"I had to work and it would have been too much for you."

"That's nonsense and you know it. You hated us but what did we do to you?"

"I don't want to talk about the past. I'm here concerning the children?"

He told her the children were coming home in June, after the school year. He rented a house in the cul de sac near Milano's Restaurant. Then he put on his hat and left without further utterance.

At the orphanage, Dario and Carlo were summoned into Mother Regina's office. They fidgeted as they waited for permission to enter and each wondered what the other had done.

"Children, come in. I have wonderful news for you. You are going home."

Daria leaped to her feet, gripped Mother Regina's desk, and for a moment, her happiness turned to skepticism.

"Honest to God?"

"We don't use God's name lightly. Yes, you are going home. Your father will be here in four days. You're excused."

"Thank you, Mother," they replied in unison.

They walked out hand in hand, ruminating about home. Carlo appeared perplexed.

"I wonder if it's like we see in the movies."

"I guess."

Then they separated, glowed outwardly, and Daria skipped along the concrete path, singing:

"We're going home ..."

Girls clustered around her, envy and pathos clouded their faces. Daria discontinued her singing as her orphan-mate Sally came toward her, hugged her, and wished her well.

"Your hair will grow and you'll look pretty again."
"Thanks. Do you have any family?
"No, I'll have to stay here until I'm eighteen," said Sally, her eyes misting and walked away.

Daria gulped and realized she was so lucky; even her shorn head did not disparage her joy. She ran to the dormitory, found a calendar, and marked the first day of the last three days of her confinement. She returned to her classroom, finished her chores, counted books, alphabetized them, and raced around as if she were caught in a whirlwind.

"Daria, calm down. Whew! You're excused."
"Sister, I'm going home."
"I know. God bless you."

Daria grinned.

On the day of the children's departure, Daria placed her toothbrush and a pair of panties into a small, brown paper bag. She ran to Mother Regina's office, waited outside for Carlo who took quantum leaps toward her, and together they sat on the concrete steps. A black car drove up, Alissandru parked the car, and walked to Mother Regina's office, where two emaciated children sat, huddled together, giggling. He shielded his eyes from the midday sun and faltered for a moment.

"They can't be my children. They resemble children of war, emaciated and pathetic, and the little girl's hair is sheared."

Daria wore a faded, blue cotton dress with pink rosebuds on the white collar, reaching her laced, brown shoes, while Carlo wore a clean, tattered white shirt and short blue pants that drooped on him. She stood up, twisted the bottom of her dress into a roll, dropping it when her father came toward them.

"Is that our father?" Carlo asked.
"Yes."

Alissandru ambled toward them, smiling, and Daria noticed his charcoal eyes sunk into his thin face; his forehead seemed higher than she had remembered.

"Daria, Carlo, are you happy that you're going home? Say, what happened to your hair?"
"It's okay. I was disobedient and had to be punished."

Mother Regina watched the encounter, ventured outside, nodded to Alissandru, and explained the rules.

"Couldn't you have done something less barbaric?"
"And you, Mr. Leone, couldn't you have done more for your children? Until my dying day, I will never forget the pain on their grandparents' faces when I told them you had forbidden them from seeing their grandchildren."
"I don't want to hear any more. Carlo, Daria, get in the car."

Unexpectedly, a crowd assembled around them and waved goodbye as Alissandru drove through the great iron gates. The children whirled around at the sound of the gates, the usual clamorous noise that had shut them off from the world.

While they were driving, the children remained silent, waiting for their father to speak. But Alissandru's discomfiture and pain thwarted any conversation. Now Daria was ready to burst, curious about her grandmother.

"How is she?"
"Do you remember her?"
"Huh! Huh! She had a candy store."
"I can't believe you remember the store."

Daria smiled.

When they reached Hammonton, New Jersey, thirty miles from Atlantic City, Alissandru veered off the road and stopped at a restaurant, where there were huge pictures of various sandwiches in the windows. He leaned over the steering wheel, moaned as fierce spasms gripped him. He reached into his pocket, popped a pill in his mouth and motioned the children to go inside. Daria and Carlo looked at each other, worried their father would collapse. He motioned for them to go on. The aroma of food lured them inside and Alissandru followed them inside the restaurant.

"Daddy, can we have one of those?" Daria asked, pointing to a ham sandwich with Swiss cheese, lettuce, tomato and mayonnaise on rye bread.

"Yes. Miss, I'll have soft boiled eggs."

Alissandru watched as his children feasted on their sandwiches, enjoying every morsel with exuberance and zest as if it was manna from the gods. He fought back the tears and memories of Giulia surfaced.

"Where have all the years gone? We had such promise, hope, and love. With the time I have left, I'll do my best for them."

"Daddy, what did you say?"

"Daria, just mumbling."

Alissandru reached the Albany Avenue Bridge in Atlantic City and his children squealed with delight at the sight of the dark green waters of the bay, shimmering with the sun's last countenance of the day. Houses on the bay had boat slips, where men removed canvasses from their land-locked boats, scraped moss from the bottom and sides of their boats, getting ready to paint them. Sailboats skimmed underneath the bridge that opened for those who sailed through with yachts and sailing ships. Young boys sat on wooden bulkheads, dangling their feet, battling with minnows that squiggled while they attached them to hooks, using cord. Men used bamboo rods, pulling their lines taut and slackened them when boats sailed by.

"Daddy, it looks like fun here," exclaimed Carlo.

"It sure does. Carlo, we'll learn to swim. Daddy, guess what? I can hold my breath under water."

"Where did you learn that?"

"When I was little, the kids tried to drown me. So, I held my breath, didn't cry, and they didn't have fun."

Daria grinned, proud that she had won the battle.

"Yeah, Daddy, the giant was the meanest."
"Giant?"

Carlo explained.

Pangs of guilt eroded Alissandru's conscience and pierced his heart like an arrow, realizing he had left his children to fend for themselves. He had disposed of them as if they were someone else's children. They had suffered the consequences of his selfishness.

"Giulia, Giulia, I'm sorry," he thought.

Now Alissandru drove through the entrance, around a monument, where a Greek Temple with Corinthian columns housed a statue depicting Liberty and Distress, dedicated to World War I veterans. Then he passed the Atlantic City High School, drove to the Boardwalk, where the children caught a glimpse of the dark green ocean with frothy waves.
"Daria, a real ocean," Carlo said.
"Oh, it's so exciting. Daddy, may we get out?"

He shook his head, ashamed of their tattered clothes and frail bodies.

"Your grandmother is waiting for you."

Alissandru reached the Italian neighborhood on Mississippi Avenue, where storefronts displayed fruits and vegetables, round balls of provolone and dried red peppers hung from the ceilings. The aroma of fresh-baked bread permeated the neighborhood. Women checked their purses before they shopped for the day's dinner.

Children ran in and out of the corner drug store that contained a long marble counter, and held onto their double-dipped ice cream cones that melted faster than they could lick them. Boys and girls flirted with one another until their parents glanced in their direction; the girls acted demure while the boys acted disinterested. They passed a family clothier, a shoemaker, a butcher shop, St. Martin's Church and Garibaldi Hall. Women sat on the steps of Garibaldi Hall, watching their children, knitting sweaters, earning a few dollars from a merchant who sold them on the Boardwalk to wealthy clientele.

Alissandru beeped his horn, looking for a parking place. He passed Rienzi's Fish Market, where the owner's son, a dwarf, sat on a red wooden bench, awaiting the smiles of good fortune. Neighbors chatted with him as his fish-shaped, black eyes twinkled. His rotund body vibrated with laughter, as he joked with teenage boys. Alissandru made a u-turn, passed several stores built side by side, that lined the narrow cobblestone street. People queued up in front of Petrillo's Bakery, waiting for hot bread that cost seven cents a loaf. The redolence of fried meatballs and sausage stimulated Daria and Carlo's appetite. Closing their eyes, they inhaled the delectable aroma over and over again. Children ran in and out of their homes, invaded their mother's gravy pots, grabbed a meatball or sausage on fresh bread and headed for the beach.

Alissandru swerved the car for the excursion train from Philadelphia and Camden as the conductor tooted the horn.

"That's her store!" Daria exclaimed.
"I can't believe you have recognized it. Do you remember your mother?"
"No."

Women leaned over balconies and verandahs amid flower pots filled with geraniums, daisies, cockscombs, scarlet poppies, and an abundance of pungent basil and broadleaf parsley. All eyes focused on Franca's store as Alissandru emerged from the car with his children. They wondered how Franca would react to her grandchildren's homecoming and the encounter with Alissandru, whom she hated. He told the children to go ahead and they ran into Franca's opened arms. She wept and blurted out in the Sicilian language.

"Figghi bedde da Mamma,[38] I'm so happy to see you, to have you home. I've longed for this day."

Alissandru, despite his hidden emotions, gulped and wiped away his tears with his handkerchief.

"Che successo con le sue capelli?"[39] She asked, in formal Italian.

He explained.

"You have made your children suffer unnecessarily."

Ignoring her admonition, he told her to send the children to his house after dinner.

The children followed Franca into the living room, where a portrait of their mother, in her riding outfit, set on the piano.

"Who's that beautiful lady? I see her in my dreams all the time."
"You do. That is your mother."

Franca sat down, weeping, and Daria went over to her, kissed her cheek.

"Don't cry, I don't remember her."
"How could you, you were a baby?" Franca said.

She led them into the kitchen, pointed to chairs set around a large, round table, set with a linen tablecloth and linen napkins. The children inhaled the aroma of food. Franca placed a bowl of romaine salad, a large dish of pasta, meatballs, sausage, a bracioli, and twisted loaves of Italian bread with sesame seeds. Daria and Carlo stared at the food and their stomachs churned with hunger.

"Eat all that you want, but eat slowly. I don't want you to get sick."

They ate with such zest as if they had been deprived of food for many years. Franca couldn't eat as she watched them relishing every morsel.

"No-na, this is the bestest food in the whole world." Carlo said, holding his stomach.
"It's Non-na," replied Franca, laughing.
"Sure is, Nonna." Daria chimed in.

Daria stood up, piled the dishes and placed them in the sink.

"Daria, it's been a long day. Go to your father's house and I'll see you tomorrow for leftovers."

When Franca was alone, she slumped into her armchair reflecting upon the children and Giulia. She sobbed at the turn of events that had created such an upheaval, splintering their lives.

Carlo and Daria held hands as they crossed the street, walked through the cul de sac, knocked on the door with caution, and Alissandru called out to them. He stood up, held the door open and they waited for permission to enter. His face dribbled with tears.

"May we come in?"

"Daria, Carlo, of course."

"Daddy, are you sad because we came home?"

"Oh Daria, no. I'm happy. I'm not feeling well. Come, I'll show you your rooms."

Gripping the banister, he trembled, and Daria stood behind him, prepared to break the fall. He reached the top of the steps and showed Daria her room. She was astonished at what she saw. She touched the white frame bed, white chest of drawers, and flung herself on the white chenille spread, splashed with pink rosebuds.

"Is this really mine?"

"Yes," said Alissandru, smiling.

"Wow! I can't wait to go to sleep."

"Take your bath while I show Carlo his room."

Carlo followed his father, tiptoeing into his room, fearful of treading on someone else's property, touched the maple dresser and bed, and took his shoes off. Then, he crawled underneath the blue chenille spread, cuddling himself.

"Get out of bed and take your bath."

"Thanks, Daddy."

After they bathed, they put on their pajamas and hugged and kissed their father. He held them close, knowing how happy they were to be out of the orphanage.

Alissandru went downstairs, lay on the couch, regained an elusive peace, and hoped that the "angel of death" would delay his demise for the sake of the children. He dozed off but footsteps aroused his semi-conscious sleep. Daria walked with her arms extended, her nightly ritual, and passed him without saying a word. He followed her, waved his hand before her eyes, but she turned around and went back upstairs to bed.

"She's a sleepwalker. I'd better lock the doors at night."

In the morning, he prepared breakfast, which consisted of orange juice, bacon and eggs, and toasted Italian bread.

"No more lumpy cereal," said Daria, grinning at Carlo, and then she glanced at her father.

"Nonna wants us to eat dinner with her every night? May we?"

"Yes, of course."

Despite Daria's sense of freedom and happiness, she noticed an impenetrable wall between her father and grandmother. She asked her grandmother why her father didn't dine with them, but Franca gave her an elusive response. And her father's reply:

"I'm not well enough to go out."

Mary Gatta, a neighbor, acted as mediator between Franca and Alissandru, regarding the children. She washed and ironed the children's clothes, cooked dinner for Alissandru, and eased his burden, despite the fact that she had eight children of her own. Mary felt deeply about the family's troubles, recalling Giulia's suffering under Alissandru's fury and her early demise at his hands. She shuddered, remembering when he had kicked her in the vagina repeatedly during the early days of a pregnancy, and she lost the baby. Since Mary lived right next door to the Leones, it was difficult to avoid the fracas.

Mary reported to Franca on Alissandru's progressive illness that racked his body with tortuous pain; but if she tried softening Franca's heart, it was a futile attempt. She lacked the least bit of sympathy for him and hatred distended within her. Only love for her grandchildren kept her alive.

"Let him suffer the way Giulia and my grandchildren have."

During the night, Alissandru's outcries of pain distressed Daria and Carlo, awakening them. They wanted to help him, but what could they do? Soon they became accustomed to his nocturnal sobs of distress. One night his outburst terrified Daria; she climbed down the steps and saw her father holding her mother's photograph, murmuring to her.

"Giulia, my beautiful Giulia, who can tempt Fate? Whose unyielding force directs our lives? Please forgive me. How I wish we were in Taormina. I wonder how your mother will manage after I'm gone."

Daria wept for her father, herself, and for Carlo, but she knew in the recesses of her mind that her grandmother would be there for them. She had to be!

The next evening, Franca noticed creeping despair on the children's faces. They had lost their alacrity and a cloud of solemnity hung over them.

"Nonna, is our father dying?"

"Daria, he's very sick."

"I heard him cry out last night. He said, 'how will she manage?'"

"He meant me. Don't worry; you will never go back there."

"Another thing, where's Taormina?"

"In Sicily. Your mother and father spent their honeymoon there. Where did you hear about it?

"Daddy said he wishes he was there."

She did not respond.

The children breathed deeply; they were freed from the shackles of the institution, the clangor of the gates, and lumpy cereal. They ate their dinner with animation, hugging and kissing Franca, secure in her love.

23

Tourists departed from the shores of Atlantic City, leaving the flotsam to the pigeons and sea gulls. Islanders were delighted; now they had the Boardwalk, beach, and ocean to themselves. The children of St. Martin's Parish returned to school. Daria and Carlo's excitement was tempered with concern and nervousness, hoping for acceptance among the students. After they dressed, Alissandru looked them over and nodded with approval. Carlo wore long, navy cotton pants with a white shirt and blue tie, while Daria wore a navy blue, cotton dress with a white collar and white cuffs on shorts sleeves. Her father touched her cheeks.

"Your mother wore something like this when we first met."

Daria gazed up into her father's sunken, dark eyes, bursting with a question that haunted her.

"How did my mother die?"

His pallid face turned crimson, the muscles in his thin neck bulged, and a few minutes later, he answered her.

"Typhoid fever, there was an epidemic."
"Oh, Carlo, let's go."

Holding hands, they crossed the street and entered school and agreed to meet outside after the half-day session. Franca stood in front of her window, waiting for them; they turned around and she waved at them.

In class, Daria sat frozen to her seat, not wanting to attract attention, wishing she could hide. The other girls had long, finger curls and beautiful wavy hair. Daria touched her head.

"What an ugly haircut!"

She leaped to her feet, ready to battle the girl behind her. The nun interceded and Daria sat in her seat.

"Daddy, a kid made fun of me. I'm really ugly, aren't I?"

"No, you're lovely. Someday, mark my words; you'll be the prettiest girl in the neighborhood. You have your mother's hair."

He choked up.

"Really?"

"Yes. And I won't be there to see you," he thought.

Suddenly, Alissandru keeled over, the pain had intensified, exacerbated to the point that was unbearable, and no longer subsided.

"Call the doctor, hurry."

Twenty minutes later, the doctor arrived and Alissandru told the children to walk over to their grandmother's while he spoke to the doctor.

"Alissandru, you have to go to the hospital."

"No, I want to spend my last days with my children."

"It's going to get worse."

"Double the medication … anything to keep me going."

When Franca saw the children, they had the mask of desolation on their faces. Daria explained to her grandmother that her father was very ill and the doctor came to the house. When they returned to their father, Franca called Father Damiano. He visited Alissandru and cited that he needed hospital care, but he refused to leave his home or his children.

Thanksgiving Day came and went. On a crisp, cold night, the full moon appeared translucent, peeped through the clouds, and snow blanketed the island, glistening under the streetlights. Stillness enveloped the island, except for an occasional trolley car on Atlantic Avenue, interrupting the peacefulness. Carlo and Daria were in bed, but she was unable to sleep, as her father lay on the couch, seeking relief from his unyielding, tortuous pain. She heard him yell and pity surged within her. How could she help him? Should she call Franca? No, her father might get angry. Finally, he fell asleep and that was her chance. She ran and banged on Franca's door.

"Please help him. He's in terrible pain."

Franca dressed, put on her black cape, and held onto Daria as they trudged to the rectory. Father Damiano answered the door, preparing for the 6:00 a.m. Mass.

"Father, he should be in the hospital. He needs heavy doses of morphine. He's near the end."

"I'll hear his confession, bring him Holy Communion and administer last rights."

Franca agreed. Daria walked to her father's home, ran up the cul de sac and peered into the house. The couch was empty; her father had gone to bed.

An hour later, Father Damiano knocked on the door. Daria let him in and pointed upstairs to her father's bedroom. As he climbed the stairs, the priest froze for a moment, cowering at the sound of horrid cries of agony. Alissandru sat up in bed, extended his bony hand to the priest, and apologized for his stubble of a beard.

"Alissandru, I brought the Holy Eucharist."

He stammered his thanks, his voice hoarse and barely audible.

Father Damiano placed a white stole around his neck, opened a white linen cloth, and placed a candle into a holder before a crucifix. Alissandru's raspy voice evoked tears from the priest, who heard his sin of omission against the children and his cruelty to Giulia. But, he did not acknowledge her subsequent death. The priest administered Extreme Unction, the last right of the Roman Catholic Church, and Alissandru slumped back into his pillow.

"There is a hospital on the outskirts of Philadelphia for cancer patients. Maybe they can help you."

"What is the name of the hospital?"

"Sacred Heart Hospital"

"I never heard of it. Can you help me?"

"Yes."

The time dragged on for Alissandru, now weighing one hundred and twenty pounds, with insufferable, endless pain. He waited each day to hear if there was a bed for him at Sacred Heart Hospital. Father Damiano had told him there was a chance for a cure. He called his cousin, Vincenzo Conforto, asking him to call the hospital. Vincenzo visited the hospital but could not tell Alissandru the truth. Why destroy the little hope he had left? The sign at the hospital read:

SACRED HEART HOSPTIAL FOR THE INCURABLES

With Alissandru's torment, his patience with his children dwindled to a trickle. One day, he received a note from Carlo's teacher about his behavior, tardiness, and absenteeism. As weak as he was, he swung at Carlo with his belt, yelling at him.

"You caused your mother's death and you won't kill me."

Carlo gawked at him with incredulity, thrashing his head from side to side. He recalled the stories his grandmother had related about his mother; he revered her memory.

"No, I didn't do anything to her."

He ran upstairs, flung himself on the bed and wept without restraint.

Daria glared at her father, a pathetic man, whose temper had reached the summit of irrevocable cruelty, and she ran to her grandmother's.

"That's an outrage! When Carlo started to walk, your father was cleaning his pants and left Carlo alone for a moment. Carlo drank the cleaning fluid and nearly died. It was your father's fault. He twists events to cover his own guilt."

"Nonna, Daddy said Mommy died from typhoid fever."

"Nonsense, I can't talk about it now. Someday, I will tell you."

On Palm Sunday, throngs besieged the island for its annual fashion show on the Boardwalk. The sun emblazoned the cloudless sky and merchants were enthralled; money would jungle in their cash registers. Alissandru prepared for his trip to the hospital and explained to Daria and Carlo he would get well and would be back soon. Also, he told them they must go to college as he and their mother had.

He hadn't worn a suit in months and when he put on his jacket, it hung on him. Disgusted, he threw it aside and slipped into his pajamas and robe again. Daria and Carlo flanked him on his tortuous trek to the street. They held their heads down while neighborhood men rushed to his aid, shocked at the sight of the former, handsome, dashing man, whom they envied, reduced to one hundred pounds of bones. His deep-set eyes resembled two black marbles, his beard sharpened his spectral appearance, and his skeletal frame faltered.

His cousin Vincenzo arrived from Philadelphia, disguised his shock at the sight of Alissandru, smiled at the children, and introduced himself as their cousin. Vincenzo picked Alissandru up, put him in the back of the car, placed a pillow in back of his head, and he waved a languid hand to his children. Lateral glances went from Alissandru to his children, and finally, to Franca's store. Would she come outside to see him off? She saw his cousin lift Alissandru into the car and she, herself, was amazed at the transformation.

Alissandru asked Vincenzo to drive in front of the store, craning his neck for a view of her. Their eyes locked for a moment, she spun around, nearly falling, went over to the piano, ran her thumb along the keyboard, banged on middle C with a vengeance, and played a glissando, murmuring.

"It's over."

The crowd dispersed and Carlo and Daria ran to Franca's store, secure in her presence and love; she held them close and sensed their wretchedness. After all, they were losing their father, but what kind of father had he been?

During the ride to Philadelphia, Alissandru's pain was agonizing. Each time Vincenzo shifted gears, he cried out and moved from side to find a comfortable position. But he had no flesh to cushion his movements and could not find a modicum of comfort. They finally reached the hospital on the outskirts of Philadelphia. Alissandru struggled to sit up, then read the inscription above the entrance that foretold his future and fell back onto the pillow.

"Vincenzo, why didn't you tell me? Did my mother-in-law have something to do with this?"

"Not that I know of. But you need care and comfort. How much pain can you take?"

Tears spurted out of Alissandru's eyes. Vincenzo, a slender man with a receding hairline, olive skin and black eyes, wept with him. Vincenzo picked him up and carried him inside where a nun waited with a gurney, and rolled him into a ward with bed after bed of dying men. An abysmal solitude inundated Alissandru; he shuddered and envisioned the end of his life.

"Vincenzo, wheel me out to the hallway. I want to call my mother-in-law. Please dial her number."

Alissandru's hand trembled, hoping she would show some consideration, but a cold, heartless woman reacted to his call.

"*Vossia,* I'm in a hospital for the incurables. Vincenzo will pick up the children on Tuesday so I can see them before I die."

"No, you can't see them."

"I'm dying and I can't see my own children?"

"Remember once we pleaded with you? You were so cruel, now they're in my care."

"I'm sorry … hello?"

She slammed the phone down.

Alissandru glanced at Vincenzo for consolation, but Vincenzo did not murmur a sound and wheeled him back to the hostel of the living dead. The smell of death infused Vincenzo's nostrils; hanging over the ward like a giant spider web, ready to catch in its filament. He wished Alissandru well and ran out of the building, inhaling the fresh air.

The nurses bathed Alissandru, put on a dingy gray hospital gown, and brought him a tray of food, which he pushed away. Men on each side of his bed uttered strange, grating sounds emanated from holes in their throats. His body rattled with fright; he focused his eyes straight ahead, wanting sleep, an eternal sleep, but cries of anguish hindered any respite. He wondered if he would scream at the end like those men beside him.

"I won't … I won't."

The next day, Vincenzo received a telephone call from Alissandru's brother, Riccardo, shocked that he was in America.

"When did you get here?'

"Several years ago. I called a friend of mine in Atlantic City and he told me that Alissandru is close to death."

"I'll wait for you and we'll go see him."

Riccardo ambled into Alissandru's room with Vincenzo, dressed as a typical college professor with his horn-rimmed glasses, brown pants and tweed jacket. Alissandru struggled to sit up and could not believe that Riccardo was in America; his mouth dropped and he sobbed. Riccardo embraced him, felt his skeletal bones and cried with him. Alissandru, whom he had envied, was now desperately ill and gaunt like an old man.

"Riccardo! Riccardo! How come I haven't seen or heard from you?"

"I called a friend of mine in Atlantic City and he told me you were ill. I tried to get in touch with you. But I understood you were in Ohio and Pennsylvania for many years. Once I went to Atlantic City and my friend told me the news about Giulia, the children, and the animosity between your mother-in-law and you."

"Did you see her?"

"I sent a message to her but she refused to see me. She's so angry at you."

"Why did you put the children in an orphanage?"

"Riccardo, please, I made a mistake."

"Giulia was so beautiful and intelligent."

Alissandru raised his languid hand, shaking his head, not wanting to discuss Giulia. His guilt had been overwhelming, dreaming about her, tormented by her. Or was his guilt tormenting him?"

For twenty-eight days, Alissandru lingered between moments of lucidity and horrendous pain, constantly begging for morphine. When he had some rest he saw Giulia, who smiled at him, looking lovely in a white satin negligee, stretching out her hand. He sat up, unable to reach her and fell back asleep.

The next day, she appeared to him again, still in her white satin negligee. She stood by his bed, touched him, and grabbed his hand, holding onto it.

"M'amore, andiamo a Taormina."[40]
"Si, Giulia, m'amore, andiamo."

Alissandru succumbed to the "angel of death" and the Mother Superior called Franca. She expressed her condolences and asked when the undertaker would pick up the body.

"Just bury him, no one will come. I suggest you use his body for an autopsy."
"But Mrs. Privitera, he should have a religious burial."
"Give it to him." And she hung up.

Riccardo was notified as well. He went to the ward, but Alissandru's body had been taken to the morgue for an autopsy.

"Nurse, who gave you the authority?"
"His mother-in-law."
"Does she want to bury him?"
"No."
"I will do it."

Riccardo hung his head and wept. He entered the chapel where he prayed for his brother and Giulia who had so much, yet tragedy struck and splintered and shattered their lives. He, himself, had never married. His love for Giulia gnawed at him but she had loved Alissandru with intensity beyond reality.

Meanwhile, in Atlantic City, Franca told Daria and Carlo about their father's death. Their eyes misted for a moment, realizing all they had now was their grandmother.

"We'll have to close his house, sell some furniture, and we'll move across the street to a larger apartment."
"Nonna, can I go over to the house now?"
"Sure, Carlo, make sure you lock the door."

Carlo dashed over, flew up the stairs, entered his father's bedroom, shuddered for a moment, and opened the armoire. The smell of moth crystals wafted out, he glanced at his father's wardrobe, and counted the suits and coats: ten suits, two cashmere coats, one black and one brown, two matching Stetson hats, and numerous shirts, ties, bathrobes, and pajamas. He tried on the brown hat, glanced in the mirror, cocked his head to the side and then flung the hat across the room, crying out.

"Daddy, how could you say I killed my mother? I loved her."

He fell asleep sobbing and twenty minutes later, awakened, ran to the bathroom and splashed cold water on his face. Then he stood in front of the armoire once again.

"In a few years, I'll be the best dressed guy in the neighborhood."

He checked the windows, grabbed the photograph of his mother in her riding outfit, kissed it, and slept with it that night.

24

For the first time in their young lives, Carlo and Daria had a sense of security with Franca, who showered them with care and love, nourishing their bodies and their minds. The new apartment behind the store was cluttered, in particular, the living room with the baby-grand piano. Franca placed a for-sale sign in her store window and advertised in the Atlantic City Evening Union. But in September of 1939, the Great Depression was still a menacing force all over the country, and the highest offer she received was fifty dollars.

She played the piano for her grandchildren, who were fascinated with the beautiful sound. Yet, she knew the piano had to be disposed of and hired neighborhood men to chop up the piano, needing wood for the winter. With each crushing blow, she cringed; tears flowed out at the sound of the discordant keys crashing to the floor.

Daria and Carlo stood mesmerized, watching their grandmother as she closed her eyes. She envisioned her patrician parents, her brother Roberto, her sister Maddalena, and Edoardo, her beloved husband. For a moment, she felt his lips upon hers and yearned for his arms to embrace her with words of consolation. Then Giulia'a memory brought a deluge of tears, but now, the grating, splintered cuts of the hatchet severed her from her past, and the last vestige of her cushioned life was merely a dream.

A month later, she received a call from a local attorney, stating he must see her. She was perplexed, what did a lawyer want with her? Alissandru had used up his money during his illness; sold his car, furnished his house, and few, at that time, could afford life insurance.

"I don't like to close the store, can you come here?"
"Yes, of course."

He informed her his client wanted to remain anonymous. However, she would receive fifty dollars a month to cover her rent, electricity, coal, and other expenses.

"Is this some kind of joke?"
"No, not at all. I assure you it is legal and honest."
"Please tell my benefactor that I appreciate his or her kindness. When he left, she slumped into her leather chair with relief. And she wondered who could be so generous toward her and the children during those difficult times?

Bitter, frosty winds skirted the island. Daria rose early, cleaned out the potbelly stoves and salvaged blue coal that had not burned. She started fires with Franca's old music sheets. She had breakfast, dressed for school, and was ready to leave when a nun came in.

"Good morning, Sister, am I late?"
"I'm not here for you but for your brother."

Franca entered the room.

"Mother Frances wants Carlo transferred to public school. We can't handle him."
"Sister, my grandchildren are orphans and shouldn't compassion be shown to them first?"

Daria cringed whenever her grandmother referred to them as orphans; it had a connotation that they were pariahs.

"Mrs. Privitera, I'm sorry."

Carlo came into the store, apologetic and kissed Franca.

"Nonna, I'm tired of the nuns; they're too strict. I'd rather go to public school."

Franca acquiesced.

"You don't have a choice, do you?"

Now St. Martin's Parish prepared for its annual procession on Mother's Day; lilies graced the three marble altars and potted plants flanked the main altar. Outside, children lined up as the sun reflected on their jovial faces. Girls wore white dresses with white veils, while boy wore navy blue suits with white shirts and powder blue ties. The majority of the children wore blue carnations and a few children with dead mothers wore white carnations, another signature of their differences. Daria threw her white carnation on the ground, stomped on it, and held her head up high. She detested those sorrowful gazes that followed the motherless children. Now she joined her classmates, singing before a statute of the Blessed Mother.

O Mary, we crown thee with blossoms today,
Queen of the May and Queen of the Angels …

Nearly all of the children's hearts were filled with the beauty of the day, the love of their own mothers, whom they embraced with fervor.

At the end of the month, Father Damiano drilled the seventh and eighth grade students in spelling and religion. First, the children stood up and he led them in the Pledge of Allegiance to the American flag on the right hand side of the room, and then turned to the Italian flag on the left side, with a salute to Benito Mussolini and the King of Italy's photographs. The class then burst out in song dedicated to the youth of Italy.

Giovinezza! Giovenezza! Primavera di bellezza—
(Youth! Youth! The beauty of spring—)

Father Damiano stood with his arms folded, nodded his approval, but his mask of severity appeared bonded on his face, with his chin jutting out.

"Geez, he looks like Mussolini." A boy shouted.

Laughter reverberated throughout the classroom. The nun turned crimson, mortified with the outburst and disrespect shown toward Father Damiano.

"Whoever said that, come up to the front."

No one stirred. The boys maintained a spurious mask of innocence and the nun ordered them to remain after school. From then on, bland faces and unutterable words became the rule, especially when the pastor entered the classroom.

When Daria was in the orphanage, the nuns considered her an intelligent, diligent student; and now at St. Martin's, she prided herself on her ability and excelled in spelling and religion contests. After school, she returned to the store and handed Franca a new pair of rosary beads that she had won in the contests.

"Thank you, Daria. I am so proud of you. You are as intelligent as your mother."

Daria was thrilled with her grandmother's response and headed to the apartment. She changed her clothes and began singing the Fascist song.

"Giovinezza! Giovinezza!

Franca was in hot pursuit.

"Where did you learn that song?"
"In school, we sing it all the time."
"You should not be singing that. Italians are behind Mussolini, in fact, I used to be a Fascist. It is dangerous. Don't sing it anymore and don't tell anyone about me."
"Why?"
"I don't know if I could be sent back to Italy. And what would happen to Carlo and you?"
"Oh, I'm sorry."

Franca embraced her, touched her chin and kissed her.

"Nonna, am I pretty like my mother?"

"You are pretty, but your mother had the kind of beauty that artists paint and poets write about."

Franca could not reveal that each time she glanced at Daria, she saw Alissandru's face, his straight nose, his almond-shaped, charcoal eyes, and his perfect white teeth. But that moment of reflection was interrupted with boys yelling and fighting. Daria ran outside and saw Carlo involved in a disturbance.

"Carlo, stop!"

But he was totally oblivious to Daria; fighting the neighborhood bully, punching him and hanging onto him like a rag doll. The bully ridiculed Carlo's combative style and dangled him before the crowd that had assembled. Daria snaked her way through the circle of boys, confronted the bully, and ordered him to put Carlo down. He did, grinning at Daria, who stretched her five-foot-two inch frame up to six feet and slammed him in the face amid snickers.

"You big citrolu[41] … leave my brother alone!"

A young man intervened, raised her arm and shouted:

"Ladies and Gentlemen, the 'terror' of Mississippi Avenue."

The applause resounded throughout the street. Daria and Carlo laughed as they pushed through the assemblage, agog over her *nom de guerre*.

"Carlo, next time pick on someone your own size."
"Me? How about you? The 'terror' of Mississippi Avenue."

St. Martin's Parish provided artistic and sporting events for children in Garibaldi Hall, which included operas, concerts, and basketball for her energetic young men. On Sundays, the boys had a make-up game which Daria attended with Carlo. Whistles resounded throughout the hall and Daria turned around, wondering who was behind her.

"They're whistling at you," said Carlo.
"Oh, no, not me," Daria turned florid, embarrassed at such attention.
"Sure they are."

Suddenly, a fourteen-year-old brunette sat next to Daria, smiling and introduced herself. She was petite like Daria, but nature had endowed her with a full bosom at an early age.

"Hi, I'm Valia Donatelli. I go to public school."
"My name is Daria."
"Maybe after the school year, we can meet at the beach."
"Sure, I'd like that."

Boys encircled them and Daria blushed while Valia basked in the attention. Daria pushed her way through, climbed down the bleachers and went home.

Now, in her last year at St. Martin's, Daria anticipated her graduation with one problem, no money for her dress and hat. She could not ask her grandmother and thought about approaching her teacher, Sister Clarissa. She was the embodiment of Sister Marian at the orphanage: strict, unyielding, grim, and a formidable force behind her desk. Daria concluded:

"I'll wait until she's in a good mood, which in never."

Since it was Friday, Sister Clarissa instructed the children in fire drills; her voice droned on and on. Daria became bored, squirming in her seat, twisting and turning, and Sister's ire surfaced. For a moment, Daria thought she was back in the orphanage; she saw Sister Marian's crimson face, her neck swathed in white, and veins popping out of her temples, but instead of a brown veil, she pushed back her black veil off her face.

"Daria, do you have worms inside of you?"

Daria burst out laughing, her classmates joined in, and chaos ensued, but that was an abomination to the teacher, who wanted constant control. Daria's eyes met hers in a battle of will, which unnerved Sister Clarissa. She went over to Daria, ordered to put her hands on the desk, which she did without flinching or moving a muscle. With her heavy ruler, Sister beat Daria's knuckles. Daria did not cry out but grabbed the ruler, stood up, flung it across the room and went home. Students commented about her audacity sotto voce, and Sister scolded them.

"No whispering."
"Yes, Sister," they responded in unison.

Franca gazed at Daria with concern.

"You're home early."
"Yes, Nonna, fire drills."

That night sleep eluded Daria, old fears surfaced, but she had the weekend for reflection. On Monday, she feigned illness and Franca examined her.

"You're not sick, what's wrong?"

Daria explained.

"I'll go with you."

Daria paced the hallway while her grandmother explained her formative years and hardships to the nun. Sister relented and Daria was allowed back in class. She tiptoed to her desk, kept her eyes down, and avoided Sister Clarissa's dour face. But if Daria had speculated that Sister had forgiven her, she deluded herself; whenever she raised her hand to answer questions, Sister ignored her.

The future graduates of St. Martin reveled in their forthcoming plans for graduation and Sister Clarissa explained the girls' dresses and hats were twenty-five dollars. Daria cringed and after class approached the nun.

"Sister, I can't afford to graduate, please just give me my diploma." She whispered.
"I'll speak to Mother Frances."
"Thank you, Sister."

In the morning, Daria was summoned to Mother Frances' office. She was a gentle woman with a sweet, kind face; she still retained her Italian accent, and put Daria at ease.

"Daria, you must be part of graduation."
"Mother, it doesn't matter to me."
"I'll give you the dress and hat. Do you think your grandmother can buy your shoes and stockings?"
"Mother, I don't want charity."
"It's my pleasure, not charity."

"Honestly?"
"Yes, my child."
"Thank you."

Mother Frances wept after Daria left her office. She admired Daria's self-respect and regretted Carlo's dismissal from St. Martin's.

Daria went back to her classroom, beaming, intoxicated with thoughts of graduating in a beautiful dress and hat. Even the enmity between Sister Clarissa and her did not disparage her happiness. When she told her grandmother, Franca hugged and kissed her, impressed with her innate dignity and maturity.

"I'll buy you silk underwear as well."
"Gee, Nonna, that's swell. I'm so lucky."
"You and Carlo deserve happiness, but I am concerned about him."

At that moment, Carlo strolled in, despondent, sullen, eyes downcast, and went to his bedroom with Daria pursuing him.

"Carlo, what's wrong?"
"I'm going to be left back."
"Well, what do you expect? You hooky school and you don't study. Ask your teacher if you can make it up this summer. I'll help you. How many courses?"
"Two, but I want to be free this summer."
"Free! And left back!"

Daria gesticulated and exasperated at his moodiness and aberrant behavior, slammed his door shut.

Gentle winds prodded billowing waves toward the sandy beige beaches, in its perpetual ebb and flow. Daria spent time on the beach, bronzing herself with the sun's countenance, glowing inwardly and outwardly. She bathed, washed and set her hair, placed her clothes methodically on her bed. Then she put on her white silk brassiere, white silk panties, white slip, and stockings. Picking up her sandals, she smelled the newness and put them on. The grand moment arrived; she slipped on her powder blue, silk taffeta dress with short, puffed sleeves, turned around in front of the mirror and smiled at her reflection. She placed her powder blue picture hat on, tilted her face from side to side, and was pleased with her appearance.

"Daria, hurry."

"Nonna, take a look. Now am I as pretty as my mother?"

"Yes, and she would have been proud of you."

"Nonna, I see her in my dreams all the time. Daddy and she are together."

Franca gulped, staggered for a moment, and stifled her tears.

Family, friends and neighbors gathered outside and inside of the church, expecting the graduates, who were lead by Mother Frances to the inside for the High Mass. After Mass, Father Damiano called each graduate to the altar, tapped their faces, and handed them their diplomas. When Mother Frances clapped, the graduates headed for the schoolyard for their formal photograph. As the girls walked out of the church, Mother Frances handed each girl a dozen American beauty roses. Daria shook her head, but Mother Frances put the roses in her arms, touched her face and Daria smiled at her with gratitude. She touched the velvety petals, compared the darkness and richness of the color against her powder blue taffeta dress, and sighed.

"This is the happiest day of my life," she murmured.

Later the crowds assembled in Garibaldi Hall for refreshments and congratulations from relatives. In her search for Carlo and Franca, Daria bumped into Sister Clarissa, whose face revealed her funereal, wrathful gaze. Her animosity toward Daria still simmered; she grabbed the roses out of Daria's arms.

"Since you didn't pay for them, I'll put them on the Blessed Mother's altar."

Daria stared at her, shocked, confounded, and glared at the malcontent nun with incredulity. Gnashing her teeth, she pulled off her hat, dropped it on the floor and stomped on it, zigzagging through the oceans of happiness. Her breathing became belabored, her throat narrowed, unable to spew out words, and Franca caught her and held her close to her bosom.

"Calm down, don't try to talk."

She took a deep breath and spilled out her vilification.

"Go home; I'll be there in a few minutes."

Daria ran through the crowd, crossed the street, entered her bedroom, and pulled off her dress, shredding it until it resembled spun silk; she gingerly removed her sandals and placed them in a box. Meanwhile, Franca seethed as she searched for Sister Clarissa, but collided into Mother Frances, fulminating, related what Sister Clarissa had done.

"Signora Privitera, I am so sorry. Wait, I'll get them."
"No, give them to the devil."
"I am truly sorry."
"You've been kind to Daria and I appreciate it."

She returned home, where she found Daria weeping in her bedroom; she sat on the bed and pushed her sodden hair off her face.

"Daria, when I taught Latin and Greek literature, one of my favorite poets was Pindar, the Poet Laureate, who lived in the fifth century before Christ. During difficult times, his words penetrate my heart and soul. He said, 'with God's help, may I still love what is beautiful and strive for what is attainable.'"
"That sounds pretty, but I don't understand what it means."
"Memorize it, keep those words in your heart and mind as a guideline throughout your life. Someday, you'll understand what it means."

Daria sat up, closed her eyes, and memorized those words of wisdom that came from her beloved grandmother.

Mother Frances searched for Sister Clarissa and admonished her for her outrageous behavior.

"Get those roses and throw them in the trashcan. You harbor vengeance in your heart; that was an evil act."

Sister Clarissa bowed her head, wept, and followed her instructions.

25

With languid, summer days upon the island, Daria and Carlo relished the freedom from constant regimentation. They put on their bathing suits, strolled passed the poolroom, where men sat outside smoking Di Nobili cigars and spat their brown saliva into brass spittoons. The "lungers" smacked their lips, scanned Daria's figure with lecherous gazes, and whistled. Daria wore a two-piece, yellow bathing suit with a multicolored hula skirt. Despite her revealing bathing suit, she walked with dignity.

"Hey, you guys, cut it out. She's my sister."
"Yeah, Carlo, we know. She's growing up."
"Let's hurry, they make me sick."

Daria walked at a harried pace.

They reached Convention Hall at Mississippi Avenue and the Boardwalk. Carlo ran ahead of her, leaped over the pavilion, landed on the sand, rolling in it, and ran to the ocean. Temperate winds stroked the island and the ocean swelled with gentle waves. Daria sunk her feet into the sand, discarded her hula skirt, and put on her yellow bathing cap and bathing slippers.

"Daria," Valia Donatelli called out to her.
"Hi Valia, let's go in the water."

Before Valia responded, Daria dove into a wave and swam out and met Carlo. During the short time that they were in Atlantic City, they had a sense of freedom in the ocean. Daria soon earned the reputation as the "Italian mermaid" for her innate swimming ability; equaling the boys' skills, riding ways side by side with them. A long time ago, she had learned survival underwater, losing her fear, and now she was drawn to the ocean's elixir with an unsurpassed tranquility. She rode a wave back to the shore, bumped into Valia, laughing and exhilarated by the ride.

"Valia, why didn't you come in?"
"I only go to my knees. Boy, you're a fish."

Daria rolled in the sand, covered every bit of her body, warding off the chill.

"How can you stand all that sand on you?"
"I love it. It gives me an excuse to swim again."

Suddenly, boys surrounded them; Valia flirted with them while Daria moved toward the water, mute and reticent.

"Daria, wait up, don't be shy. The guys will think you're a snob."
"What do I say to them? I only know how to talk about swimming."
"C'mon, after you wash off, we'll take a walk."

While they walked, Valia explained about petting and how babies are born. Daria's mouth remained agape, mesmerized with the knowledge unfolding before her.

"Do you mean priest, nuns and the Pope were born the same way?"
"Sure. Say, where have you been? Sorry, I forgot."
"Boys and girls were separated; I never spoke to a boy."

They returned to Mississippi Avenue beach. The lifeguards dragged their boats into the water, a daily routine at 3:00 p.m., allowing swimmers to venture farther out into the ocean. Carlo and Daria dashed into the water, swam out to the boats, heaved themselves on board, dove off, and swam back to shore, waving their appreciation to the lifeguards.

During dinner, Franca explained to the children that they were having a guest, a music professor, who only taught talented children. His father had been the family's photographer in Messina. While Franca waited for the professor, Carlo and Daria walked to the corner store for lemon water ice. Upon their return, Franca conversed with a bald-headed man, with dark hair down to the nape of his neck. His nose slightly swooped down, his big, brown eyes focused on Daria, and she disliked him immediately. He had the same lecherous glance that the neighborhood men had, when they looked at her.

"Che bella."[42]

Franca raised her eyebrows as a warning to him and a rapid discussion ensued between them.

Professor Ruggero Nicotra excused himself, went into Carlo's bedroom and changed into his pajamas; he came out, holding his pajama top closed because buttons were missing.

"I'll sew buttons on for you," said Franca.
"No, I like to hold it."
"Ruggero, you're a strange man."

He grinned.

Professor Ruggero Nicotra was a nocturnal visitor during the summer; fear of the police promulgated his late visits. Nonetheless, Franca enjoyed his intellectualism, reflected upon their days in Messina but he constantly complained to her about the absence of the piano.

"How could you have chopped it up? Don't you miss playing?"
"Stop it! Yes, I miss it. But life has been difficult for us. Someone is sending me fifty dollars a month. Say, is it you?
"No, Franca, I couldn't afford that. Some of my students can't afford to pay me."

Professore Nicotra strolled the Boardwalk at night, dressed in black, blending in with the darkness, avoiding streetlights. He passed the Central Pier, where once he had his music studio, until he got into trouble. Later that night, upon his return, Daria awakened at the sound of strident voices. Why are they arguing?

"Ruggero, you should not walk on the Boardwalk. The police are looking for you; they have a warrant out for your arrest. I don't want to get into trouble. I have my grandchildren to think about."

"I'll go crazy hanging around here. I think of her all the time."

"What you did to her was terrible."

"Terrible? We were in love."

Professor Nicotra had fallen in love with one of his students, a girl of seventeen and he was fifty-five years old. Her parents accused him of debauching the morals of a child, but he denied the accusation.

"Her parents caused her to have a nervous breakdown. We were happy together."

"Ruggero, for God's sake, you could be her grandfather."

"Her parents did not have to put her into an insane asylum to get away from me. She loved me and I adored her."

"Ruggero, find someone your own age."

Daria sneaked back into bed; she had a feeling the professore was strange and now she realized her assessment of him was correct. In the morning, the sound of her neighbor's radio roused Daria from her sleep. Rising, she went to the bathroom and upon her return, left her door unlocked, falling asleep again. Then she felt a hand crawling up her nightgown, and another hand muffled her cry. The professore!

"You're lovely. I adore young girls. When I go back to New York, is there anything I can buy for you?"

"Nonna!"

His hand slipped off for a second, but then he clamped down again as she squirmed and kicked, and her fiery eyes smoldered with hatred. He touched her breasts, and during his prurient act, his hand moved, and Daria bashed his face with all her strength.

"You're a pig! Besides, you're nuts!"

Franca ran in, whacked him on the head with Edoardo's walking stick, jabbed his chest, and he apologized for him behavior.

"Degenerate! The filth of the earth! *Maladetto*! I'm calling the police. How could you touch my granddaughter? Because of our friendship, I invited you into my home. Now get out. I don't ever want to see you again!"

"Franca, don't call the police. You can get into trouble because I stayed with you. I can't help myself; I like young girls.

The professore dressed, packed his bag, and departed. Daria bathed and scrubbed off his dirty hands.

Now summer came to an abrupt end. Daria prepared for her first day at Atlantic City High School, whereas Carlo repeated sixth grade. Daria cautioned him to study and behave himself.

"Don't preach to me; you know I hate it."

"Carlo, you have to get an education."

And she walked away from him.

Daria met Valia in the cafeteria. Daria only drank a glass of water and saved her allowance of a nickel for a cherry coke after school. Kids congregated in a neighborhood hangout and jitterbugged to music from a jukebox. Somehow, word got to her counselor that she never ate lunch. She was summoned to her office and was handed a book of tickets. Daria stood up, stiffened, pursed her lips, and placed them on the desk.

"I don't want charity."

"Lots of poor kids use them," the counselor told her, adding, "I see your grandmother is raising you. No parents?"

"No."

Daria raised her eyes to the ceiling, tired of answering the same question.

"Thank you, but I don't want everyone to know that I'm poor."

"No shame in that."

"Isn't there?"

And she walked out of the office, her dignity and self-respect in tact, proud of her stance. Since the incident with the roses at her graduation, charity toward her was not an attribute but a detriment.

26

Wintry winds blew across the island and in that December of 1941, the Japanese bombed Pearl Harbor and America was plunged into World War II. Atlantic City's young men were sent off to various destinations around the world. Streetlights and Boardwalk lights remained off at night for fear of enemy ships and U-boats that promulgated the use of Civil Defense, with the Coast Guard patrolling the beach and the Boardwalk. Commodities such as sugar, coffee, and meat were rationed as well as gasoline; the government allotted stamps and coupons for those items. A "black market" surfaced and flourished.

Franca's business declined; residents now purchased their coffee in tin cans. She decided to close the store, sold her roaster and coffee grinder to a wholesale coffee dealer who would display them as relics. A housing project opened two blocks away from the store and Franca qualified for residency. Daria and Carlo jumped with delight at the news that their house had central heating and no longer would they have to save blue coal that did not burn, and start fires in the potbelly stoves.

Since Daria discarded uniforms, she became aware of beautiful clothes the girls wore at school. She applied for a job as a bus girl at the fashionable Shelburne Hotel, a hotel that catered to wealthy clientele, working after school and on weekends. A new world opened up for Daria. She was exposed to a life of opulence, dazzled with the women who strolled into the mirrored dining room in their mink, sable, and chinchilla coats, with jewels glistening on the ears, fingers, and wrists, that blinded her with their beauty. When Daria told her grandmother about the opulence, explaining the clothes, furs, jewelry, and beautiful women, Franca put her hand on her shoulder.

"Don't ever feel inadequate, you are a blueblood. You come from nobility."

"We are so poor, I feel silly saying that, here in America. Nonna, were you rich like those ladies?"

"Rich? I guess so, but it's not just money. It's breeding, education, and lineage."

"Before Daddy went away, he told us we must go to college."

"With what? I can teach you many things. You have a good mind, always asking questions."

"Daddy used to get angry when I asked questions."

"He was angry at the world."

Daria lowered her head; her grandmother hated her father and seldom mentioned his name. But when Daria mentioned him, a cloud of fury masked her face, and then Daria would stop asking questions about him.

At the end of the school year, Daria worked full time at the hotel with Valia. They shared a room with other bus girls, where they changed into their uniforms and relaxed before going into the dining room. In between lunch and dinner, Daria went for a swim while Valia wet her feet. After they served dinner, Valia and Daria dressed up in the sophisticated styles of the Forties with draped dresses, opera-length gloves, and feathers or flowers nestled in their hair. They dined in the fashionable restaurants and emulated the women they served and admired at the hotel. Once a week, they went to the Knife and Fork Inn, a restaurant and bar on Albany Avenue near the Boardwalk. They walked in with assurance, placed a cigarette in their holders, and lit up.

"A dry Manhattan, please."

After they were served, they kicked each other, holding back their laughter. If men glanced their way, they ignored the admiration, acted snobbish, holding their noses up, and when they left, they roared at their antics all the way home.

Summer ended, tourists departed from the island's shores, and Daria still worked after school and on the weekends. Valia joined her, riding the tired aged horses along the shore with sea gulls screeching above them. But when smarting particles of sand stung their faces and blustery winds hindered their riding, they ceased riding until the spring.

On a bitter, wintry morning, snow blanketed the island with a mantle of white. Daria trudged to school, through the park across the street, near the high school, that resembled a fairyland with denuded trees bent with graceful elegance, creating a surrealistic setting. She removed her galoshes, went to her locker, and settled in her homeroom, when she received a message to report to her counselor's office.

"Daria, your grandmother had a heart attack."

Fear slithered up her spine, a sense of foreboding overcame her; she ran outside, jumped on a trolley car, and got off at Ohio and Atlantic Avenues. She reached the emergency room, where Franca was under an oxygen mask, cloaked in gentility and sweetness that Daria loved about her. The nurse removed her mask.

"Nonna," she choked up.
"I'm feeling better. I'm diabetic and I had a heart attack."
"Nonna, we need you."
"I'm not dying until you're settled. Go home and keep an eye on Carlo."

During Franca's ten days at the hospital, Daria went to school, worked, and tried keeping an eye on Carlo. On Saturday night, he came home at 1:00 a.m. with disheveled hair, torn clothes, and his face bruised. She unleashed her rage and castigated him for fighting.

"Carlo, can't you walk away from trouble? I'm on edge all the time, worrying something is going to happen to you."
"Nobody is gonna mess with me."
"Yeah, I know you're tough," she said sarcastically, adding, "but Nonna's in the hospital and she worries about you."

He ignored her, ran upstairs, grabbed his long razor that he usually sharpened on a strap to shave, and came after her. She stood her ground, not wanting to show the fear that overcame her, and calmly stated:

"Carlo, if you hurt me, who will look after you."

He backed away, his eyes misted, and he apologized.

Franca came home and spent her days in her overstuffed, leather chair near the window, where sunbeams streamed through the Venetian blinds. She read and re-read her books on Greek and Roman literature, with bits of brown paper falling onto her lap. When Daria was home, she instructed her and quoted concise statements relevant to a good life. At times, Daria became impatient, not fully understanding her teaching, longing to be out in the world of her classmates who had fun playing and dancing. But soon she realized girls her age were silly; somehow she had bypassed normal teenage years and matured beyond her years.

During the winter months, Franca found solace when she listened to the opera broadcast on the radio from the Metropolitan Opera House. She sang the arias in the various languages and related stories to Daria who tried to hide her impatience. Soon Daria loved classical music and opera, which delighted her grandmother.

On Memorial Day, parishioners of St. Martin's Parish visited the graves of their loved ones in the Pleasantville cemetery. Daria asked her grandmother if she could go with a neighbor and place flowers on her mother and grandfather's graves.

"I know Daddy is buried in Philadelphia."
"I don't believe in such practices."
"Please, just once. It'll make me feel close to them."
"I said 'no' and that's final."

Daria pondered her grandmother's decision, which was totally adverse to what the neighbors did. Was she hiding something?

During the summer months, Franca's dreary existence was stimulated; educated Italians sought her company for the sheer pleasure of her intellectualism, articulation and discussion of world events. Her face sparkled when she reminisced about her life in Messina, her family, Edoardo, her love, but she hesitated on Giulia's name, fearing a deluge of tears. They dubbed her *La Messinessa*, the lady from Messina. And upon their departure, they left a forlorn, distraught woman who survived on her lovely memories and for her grandchildren.

Daria relished her exposure to the world beyond the neighborhood and savored the freedom, which allowed her verve and vitality to bloom. She spoke to educated people, which pleased her grandmother. But soon the ugly head of gossip spread throughout the neighborhood about her sensual mode of dress. One night, she sneaked into the house and her grandmother stood there, waiting for an explanation. She reprimanded her for coming in late and criticized her style of dressing that belied her sixteen years of age.

"Nonna, I've never felt like a child. You know that I'm mature for my age."

"I know you are but you dress too sexy. I worry about men who might take advantage of you. You don't have a father or brother to protect you and men know that."

"Nonna, I'm a good girl and no one is going to take advantage of me."

Tourists and islanders streamed into the Million Dollar Pier, between Arkansas and Missouri Avenues on the Boardwalk, to hear the sounds of the Big Bands. Daria wore a sleeveless, princess-style, navy dress that skimmed her figure. In her hair, she used two "donuts" to form two chignons at the nape of her neck, and a "rat" for her pompadour. She nestled feathers on the left side of her head and wore matching opera-length gloves. Valia wore a low-cut, pink dress with spaghetti straps, revealing her full bosom.

They scanned the ballroom and young men gravitated toward them, flirting with them. Daria maintained her reserve but Valia delighted in the attention, flirting back. The young sophisticates sauntered around the ballroom like movies stars, sleek dancers slid across the burnished floor, while the sound of music overcame the roar of the ocean. Handsome young men from South Philadelphia arrived en masse, wearing "zoot-zuits with double-breasted jackets, pegged pants, dangling watch chains, and box-toed, suede shoes, with their hair slicked back with pomade. When they chose a girl to dance with, they jutted their chins and the girls knew it was a sign, slid into their arms, and danced the rumba or jitterbug.

Valia nudged Daria, whispering to her that a young man had been staring at her; he had blonde hair, blue eyes and wore white slacks with a navy blazer and white shoes.

"May I have this dance?"

"No, thank you."

"Daria, you should have said yes. You have to flirt with the guys."

"Valia, I can't," replied Daria, trying to overcome her timidity that was a detriment to popularity, according to Valia.

"That guy's coming back."

"Miss, may I have the honor this time?"

"Yes," and glanced at Valia who winked.

His arms encircled Daria and led her around the dance floor, holding her close, much to Daria's discomfort.

"Daria, you are beautiful."

"How do you know my name?"

"Mother and I are staying at the hotel and I asked the maitre d' for your name."

"And your name?"

"Roger Anderson. I'm from Boston and I'll be attending Harvard in the fall."

"Thē Harvard?" Daria gulped.

"Yes, tell me about yourself."

"Not much to tell."

The band scattered for intermission; dancers ventured outside on the Boardwalk alongside the pier, leaning against the railing for fresh air and to cool down. Daria and Roger leaned over the railing, glanced at the waves breaking around the pilings, and saw lovers sneaking kisses underneath the Boardwalk. He bent down, kissed her lips, put his arms around her, and his hand grabbed her breast.

"Take your hand off me. I'm not someone to play with."

She spun around, reentered the ballroom, and laughed at Valia dancing the tango with a "zoot-zuitor," attracting attention with her exotic and artistic movements. Then someone tapped her on the shoulder.

"Say, Babe, how about a dance?"

"If you call me Babe once more, I'll stomp on your suede shoes."

"Geez, I'm sorry. I'm Phil. May I have this dance?"

"I'm Daria. Yes, wait a minute."

She removed the "rat" and the "donut" from her hair, combed her hair and pulled off her gloves. He led her to the center of the ballroom, where they jitterbugged; he spun her around, picked her up, slid her between his legs, and hurled her over his shoulders. When she stood up, she was dizzy but elated. He escorted her back to her seat, thanked her, and kissed her hand.

"You're a classy dame. Sorry, I mean girl."
"Thank you. You're a terrific dancer."
"So are you."

Then Valia and she walked home, exhausted and barefooted, carrying their three-inch, Dorsay pumps, and laughing about the guys they met that night.

When she returned home, Franca paced the floor, tears trickling down her face.

"Carlo's been arrested. Go to the police station and ask for Detective McDermott."
"What did he do?"
"He stole five dollars."
"Five dollars! I'd better change."

The streets were empty as she ran to Atlantic Avenue, jumped on an empty trolley, got off at Tennessee Avenue, entered the building, and a policeman led her to the detective's office.

"He's busy. I'll take you to your brother. Miss, where are your parents?
"No parents, just my grandmother."

He led her through a narrow, dingy hallway. Her eyes misted, her heart pounded and she caught glimpses of men lying on cots, groaning, mumbling and cursing. Then, someone shouted at Daria.

"What's a pretty kid like you doing here?"
"Shut up, Smitty," yelled the policeman.

Daria kept her eyes straight ahead, avoiding the faces of the prisoners.

"There he is, the wild one. You have fifteen minutes."

When Daria saw Carlo, she held onto the bars of the cell, appalled at the sight of him. His eyes were black and blue, one half-shut, his nose pushed aside, and he held his broken ribs.

"Who did this to you?"

"The police. Detective McDermott was preaching to me, asked me if I believed in God and I said, 'there was no God', then they beat me up."

He removed his shirt, his back had gashes covered with coagulated blood, and she extended her hand through the bars; he held on and they wept together.

"He better behave himself or face the consequences," stated Detective McDermott.

"They didn't have to beat him up!"

"Miss, come with me."

He led her to his office that reeked of stale cigar smoke mixed with a mixture of mildew. His desk was cluttered with papers and photographs of missing children lined the walls. He sat down, lit a cigar, and Daria gagged from the smoke. He apologized and opened the window.

"Miss, how old are you?"

"Sixteen."

"He's tough and gets nasty. Aren't you aware of the problems he gives his grandmother?"

Daria's mouth drooped; she lowered her eyes and could not answer. She excused herself and went home crying, feeling lonely and helpless. Her grandmother waited for her, her handkerchief sodden with tears.

"Nonna, he's hurt. They beat him up. Please don't go there. It's scary."

"What will happen to him?

Daria and Franca had a sleepless night. In the morning, the police brought Carlo home with a warning:

"Next time he goes to a detention center."

Franca closed her eyes for a moment, upset at his handsome face that was battered and bruised; she opened her arms to him.

"Carlo, you know what's right or wrong. Please behave yourself. I love you and I would have given you five dollars. What was the purpose of stealing?"

He sobbed and went up to his room.

The next morning, Daria poured juice for customers and placed rolls and butter on a dish for Roger Anderson's mother.

"Good morning, Mrs. Anderson, how are you today?"
"Fine."

For a moment, Daria resented her rude, pithy response, but her job required good mornings, good afternoons and good evenings. Mrs. Anderson belonged to a different era; she wore long dresses and skirts, hats piled on her head with flowers and ribbons, high-laced shoes and a dour face that matched her antiquated wardrobe.

Daria walked to the linen closet, joked with the waiter about Mrs. Anderson, whose sour disposition was well established with the waiters.

"Daria, one morning, she was so miserable and demanding, I spit in her grapefruit juice."
"Oh, no."
"Yeah, the motto is … always be nice to your waiter and waitress."

Daria laughed and then a familiar face stood in the doorway: Roger Anderson.

"Good morning, Daria. Please accept my apology for my behavior."
"I accept it. I just served your mother; does she ever smile?"
"Once in a while. How about meeting me down the beach after lunch?"

She hesitated for a moment and then agreed.

Daria met him on the beach in a two-piece, black velvet suit with a black, straw picture hat and his eyes mirrored his admiration.

"You're gorgeous. How old are you?"
"Sixteen."
"You'll be a junior in September?"

"Yes."

They held hands and strolled along the water's edge, picking up seaweed and popping the tiny bubbles. She threw her hat onto the sand and they dove into the ocean, swimming side by side. He grabbed her arms and she paddled her legs while he pulled her.

"Can you go out to dinner with me tonight? Do you have to ask your parents?"

"I don't have parents; I live with my grandmother. Yes, I can go. It'll have to be after work, about nine o'clock."

"Fine. I'm looking forward to it."

She smiled. He was behaving like a gentleman and she was pleased.

Roger parked his red convertible near the back entrance of the hotel and watched Daria weave through the garbage cans and trashcans, holding her nose. She wore a black silk dress with a black lace bib, revealing slight cleavage, and a white straw hat with velvet trim, complimenting her dress. He leaped out of his car and opened the door for her.

"You came out the wrong door; you look beautiful."

"Thank you."

They dined at the Knife and Fork Inn and Daria ordered her dry Manhattan while he ordered rye and ginger ale.

"I guess we look old enough to get served," he said, proposing a toast.

"To our future."

She glanced at him, flabbergasted, eyed him with suspicion, and wondered what he was up to?

"Roger, may I ask you how old you mother is?"

"Fifty-eight. I was a change-of-life baby."

After dinner, Roger drove to the Inlet, where he parked in Lover's Lane, and kissed her lips. She kept calm, but then his hands crept up her dress. She turned livid, bashed him in the face, opened the door, and stepped outside, looking for a taxicab.

"Just because I don't have parents, you can't take advantage of me. I told you before, I'm not a plaything. All that baloney about our future!"

"What are you saving it for?"

"Damn it! Not for a creep like you. Why don't you go to the Chalfonte Alley and get yourself a prostitute!"

"Maybe I will."

Daria got into the taxicab, went home, and removed her high heels before she entered the house. Franca sat there, dazed, and placed her wet handkerchief into her pocket.

"He's been arrested and they brought him to a detention center in Egg Harbor City."

"What did he do?"

"Same thing, fighting and stealing."

"Nonna, what can we do?"

Franca opened her arms in despair and weariness masked her face.

"Nonna, he's always angry. I don't understand."

"Daria, I don't know what the answer is."

Franca sat on her leather chair the entire night and called out:

"Oh Edoardo, I wish you were here. What will happen to him?"

In the early morning, Daria came downstairs and saw Franca sitting in her chair; her head slumped to one side.

"Nonna, Nonna," and she gently straightened her head.

"I'm all right, I fell asleep."

"Are you sure?"

"Yes, I'm fine. Daria, I need to go grocery shopping today and I just don't feel up to it. I'll place orders with Marco and Tillie and would you please pick it up."

"Sure, Nonna."

Daria stayed home from school and Franca called in her orders. Daria stopped at the butcher's, where the owner, Marco, stood behind the counter, extending his fat hand to her, which she ignored. Marco was a rotund man with reddish-brown hair and brown eyes; his face resembled a red ball from imbibing excess wine. He was known for his lechery throughout the neighborhood. He dealt in black market meat and sugar and residents tolerated his nonsense because of their needs.

"Where've you been? You've grown up."

She disregarded his questions, glanced at him with disgust; his thick neck bulged out of his starched white shirt and his lascivious smile curdled her blood. Again, he tried to grab her hand, but she squirmed out of his grip. She avoided his salacious smile and kept her eyes down, circling the sawdust on the floor and wiping her sullied hand on her dress.

"Marco, I'm in a hurry."
"Aw, be patient."

As he scanned her figure, he leaned over and whispered:

"I wanna know something … can you show my son the ropes?"

His corpulent body vibrated and his thunderous laughter resounded through the store; his spineless employees laughed with him, fearful of losing their jobs.

Daria glared at him, met his bloodshot eyes in a battle of will, and inexorable rage enveloped her.

"Damnit! You're a first-class jerk. Why don't you do the world a favor and drop dead!"
"Guys, look at her, a spitfire!"
"Give me my grandmother's order."

She threw the money on the counter, slammed the door, and wept. Marco's mordant mouth had cheapened her, but her sharp tongue had cut through his salacity. There was no sense telling her grandmother, she had enough to handle with Carlo.

She passed Rienzi's Fish Market, sat down with Joey, the little man, whose mother came outside and embraced Daria. When her father died, Mrs. Rienzi outfitted Daria with a wardrobe, even though she had eight children of her own. Her husband had fishnets on the Million Dollar Pier, where he hauled in tons of fish daily; they were the wealthiest family in the neighborhood.

Next, Daria went to Tillie the Chicken Lady, who owned a grocery store. Her main source of income came from her roosters and chickens, which crowed and cackled all day long in their coops. Tillie was a lanky lady with gray hair and brown eyes. She wore a housedress with a bloodied apron and covered her head with a turban. She spoke to her roosters and chickens in Italian and they cackled and crowed back to her. Tillie was married without children but she doted upon her husband who had a *sickness*. He periodically ran off with a *spring chicken* from outside of the neighborhood and returned home to Tillie when he ran out of money.

"Hi Tillie, do you have Nonna's springer?"
"I'll get it. I'm running a little late."

She raised the lip of her coop, grabbed a chicken and mumbled as she pulled its neck, envisioning her husband in her grip. Daria laughed at her expression, turned away and sat on the stoop while Tillie plucked the feathers from the dead chicken.

Suddenly, Tillie saw her husband, Tom, strolling down the street, nattily dressed and suntanned; he nodded to Daria and entered the store. Tillie's heart raced at the sight of him; her head throbbed, she threw off her turban and bloodied apron, leaving Daria's chicken half-plucked. She leaned against her husband's broad shoulders, her toothless, cavernous mouth opened wide. He excused himself, went to the bathroom, and changed his clothes while Tillie finished plucking Daria's chicken.

"Thanks, Tillie, see you later."

Tillie closed the store, went into the bathroom, showered and splashed herself with dime-store perfume, and put on a fresh housedress. She grabbed Tom and forced him into the bedroom. He vowed he would never leave her *coup* again; nor would she give him money for his *young chickens*. She was his chicken and they belonged together.

Daria returned home and Franca was upset at the cost.

"Nonna, I'm quitting school and working full time."
"Don't, you'll regret it. Don't spend so much money on clothes."
"I spoke to a girl who said she earned a hundred dollars a week."
"Really? It's a big step."

"Nonna, we need the money."

"Promise me that you will keep on learning and in difficult times, remember you come from class, intelligence and nobility."

Franca reiterated they came from nobility, a past completely foreign to Daria.

Now Daria's life was untethered; the money she earned eased Franca's burden. She was able to purchase the beautiful clothes she yearned for; she recalled her father's impressive wardrobe.

"I must take after him," she thought.

During the Christmas holidays, Roger Anderson and his mother came to the hotel. When Daria saw them, her lips curled in revulsion. But she thought about her job and maintained the specious manner of courtesy. She poured water in their glasses, smiling, and Mrs. Anderson's sourpuss face did not change an iota. She nodded at Roger and walked away, with him in pursuit.

"May I see you later?"

"No."

"Just for coffee on your break."

She relented and met him at a little coffee house on the Boardwalk.

"Daria, I want to spend every moment with you while I'm here."

"What for?"

"I'm in love with you."

"Well, I'm not in love with you. I have to go now."

When Daria returned home, she told Franca about Roger.

"You'll meet the right one someday. I know it's too soon to talk about certain things, but you should know that after hunger and thirst, one pubic hair is the next strongest force in the world."

"Geez, Nonna, that's awful."

"Just preparing you for the future," Franca replied nonchalantly.

"I understand."

Then she told Daria that Carlo was coming home and Daria crossed her fingers.

27

The chasm of anger, frustration, and anxiety between Carlo and Daria now appeared filled with hope and love. He had grown taller with a lean body and a Greco-Roman face, a combination of his parents. Franca was pleased at the change within him; it appeared he had lost his bitterness. Through Detective McDermott's intervention, Carlo enrolled in vocational school, where he would learn to be a carpenter.

Daria had to get another job, since she was fired from the Shelburne Hotel, and the union sent her to the Claridge Hotel between Ohio and Indiana Avenues. Tranquility reigned in the household and for the first time, Daria noticed her grandmother's contentment.

One afternoon, Carlo came home from school, cleaned his pants near the gas range, while Franca was upstairs changing the beds. The cleaning fluid had splattered onto the range, blew up in Carlo's face, and set him on fire. The howling curdled her blood and Franca came down the steps, fearing the worst. She pulled off the tablecloth, wrapped it around Carlo, trying to stanch the fire. He threw it off, screaming at her to keep her distance, fearing she would get burned. He ran outside, rolled himself on the lawn, then fled like a cheetah to the Atlantic City Hospital's emergency room, four blocks away, and collapsed on the floor. Franca's words stuck in her throat; by the time they came out, it was too late.

"Wait, I'll call the ambulance!"

Franca called Daria at work and faltered on her words. She told her to come home immediately. Daria got excused, hailed a taxicab, and told the driver to wait.

"He doesn't listen. I warned him not to get near the range."

When they reached the emergency room, terror clutched their hearts. France tottered at the sounds of hideous outcries that sent shivers through her. Daria went ahead of her grandmother and found Carlo thrashing on the bed while nurses gently stripped off his clothing, cautious not to pull his flesh. The malodorous odor of burnt flesh permeated the room. His eyelashes, eyebrows and hair were singed and the doctor gave him a shot of morphine. While he dozed off, they scraped the hanging flesh and his body appeared as if a hunter had skinned him alive.

Daria and her grandmother comforted each other; then, Franca recalled the burn victims after the earthquake. She shuddered for Carlo and the pain he would endure, beyond his comprehension and her own sorrow.

"Miss, take your grandmother home. We'll take care of him." The doctor said, glancing at the crew of nurses surrounding him.

As they walked home, each wondered why Carlo was intent upon self-destruction.

The following day, between the lunch and dinner shifts, Daria went to the hospital. She was allowed ten minutes and geared herself for the worse scenario. She sobbed. His flesh resembled freshly cut beef and he writhed in pain, shouting for heaven to hear him. The nurse ran in, gave him a shot of morphine, and before he became drowsy, he asked about Franca. She did not answer him, but touched his arm with her right hand and wiped her tears with her left hand.

Daria visited Carlo during the months of his recuperation, but she also resumed her life beyond the neighborhood. She was seventeen years old but felt ancient with the responsibilities thrusted upon her. One summer evening after work, Valia and she strolled the Boardwalk, with a full moon lighting their way, reflecting a line of shimmering lights that rippled on the water.

America was still in the throes of war. The Coast Guard patrolled the beach and Civil Defense men walked the Boardwalk. Islanders drove their cars with headlights painted half-black and parked behind the Sea and Sand Club on Stenton Avenue. Daria and Valia stopped in front of a club and Valia nudged Daria.

"Let's see if we can get served."
"No, I think they have gambling inside."

The manager lit the way for customers with a flashlight, directed away from the ocean.

"Girls, coming in?"
"No, we're not allowed in gambling joints," replied Daria.

Valia poked her in the ribs and she walked up to the manager.

"We can come in for a drink."
"Fine, I'll seat you."

The front lounge had a musical bar with an ebony piano, glistening on a revolving platform. The walls were covered with musical notes on beige fabric. The name *Raf* was scrolled in purple and magenta on a beige carpeting.

"Who's Raf?" Daria asked.
"My brother, he owns the joint. Sit here so I can keep an eye on you. I'm Victor Caselli."
"I'm Daria Leone and this is my friend, Valia Donatelli."
"I know you; you're the kid whose grandmother had the coffee store. I think you girls are too young to drink."
"Victor, we're old enough. Kids grow up." Valia replied, kicking Daria.

Although the lights were dim, Daria stared at Victor for a moment.

"I have one brown eye and one blue eye," Victor said, grinning.
"Sorry, I didn't mean to stare."

Valia gazed around, smiling, while Daria kept her eyes straight ahead. They finished their rum and coca-cola and asked the bartender for the check. He shook his head and pointed to Victor. They thanked him and he escorted them to the door. Daria smiled at him; he had a kindness and gentleness about him that she had not seen in other guys. Strolling down Stenton Avenue, they spoke about their first visit to a nightclub. Daria thought about Victor who was a well-built man of medium height with a pugilistic nose, a cleft chin, a sheepish grin, and blonde hair.

"Valia, he's cute."
"He is. He liked you."

The following morning, while Daria waited for a jitney at Mississippi and Pacific Avenue, someone kept blowing the horn. It was Victor Caselli!

"Want a ride?"
"Yes, thanks."

She got into the car, smiled broadly at him, and studied him for a moment. If he was good-looking at night, he was handsome and younger looking in the daylight.

"Are you really Italian?" Daria asked.
"Full-blooded. Where do you work?"
"The Claridge."
"How about dinner some night?"
"Are you married?" She had to ask; often times married men asked her out.
"No, I've been waiting for you."

She blushed and thanked him for the ride.

That night when she got off work, he was waiting for her.

"Let's go to Kent's Restaurant for a sandwich."
"Thank you, I'm starving."

While they waited for their order, Victor spoke about the house he grew up in and the people he knew. She felt safe in his company and relished the calmness and serenity. He did not utter obscenities or speak in a scabrous manner.

"Victor, you're nice. Another guy would have tried to grab me, touch my breasts—", she put her hand on her mouth, laughing, but embarrassed at her own statement.

He roared; his laughter bellowed way down from his diaphragm and customers surrounding them laughed with him.

"You're a breath of fresh air and beautiful, too."

"I am?"

"Yeah, and you're not a schemer. I meet so many phony broads."

"Victor, one time I went out with this guy for dinner. He kept pawing me and used the f-word."

"What did you do?"

"I picked up a tray of glasses nearby and threw the whole tray at him. Boy, did I run."

He laughed hysterically.

From that day on, Daria and Victor met every week. Rumors floated through the neighborhood about them, which reach Franca who pounced on her.

"What are you doing with those dregs of society … gamblers. And he is much older than you."

"Nonna, he's only ten years older. Wasn't Nonno ten years older than you? He's a kind, gentle man and I feel safe with him."

"Just be careful … until you marry."

"I will."

On their next day off, Victor picked her up at the corner near her house about 5:00 p.m. and drove to Philip's Inn, an exclusive Italian restaurant on the White Horse Pike, leading out of the city. While they dined, he spoke about the closeness between his brother and him, and he asked her about Carlo; he was fully aware of his problems. Daria changed the subject, speaking about Carlo pained her, causing her melancholy, which she tried to avoid. After dinner, they walked to the parking lot, when suddenly thunder sounded the night, filaments of lightning created daylight over the surrounding verdant shrubs and trees, and torrential rains pelted the car.

"Daria, we'll wait until it eases us. How old are you? The truth."

"Seventeen."

"Are you kidding? I could be arrested, you're jail-bait."

"Victor, I've never felt young."

The rains subsided, Victor drove Daria home, reached her corner, and they saw a woman pacing back and forth. She wore a black cape and hat and wisps of silver hair peeked out from her hat. She hesitated under the streetlights.

"Oh my God, it's my grandmother."
"I'll explain why you were late."
"No, don't. I'll get out here."

Daria bypassed her grandmother, scampered into the house, and ran upstairs into her bedroom. Guilt eroded her and she came downstairs and explained her tardiness.

"Prostitutes stay out late. I'm sending for that man."
"Please, don't. I don't want to be forced into a marriage."
"I want to meet him. He will respect you more if he meets me."

Daria called Victor to forewarn him, but to her amazement, he was pleased. He was an old-fashion guy at heart and her grandmother was justified in protecting her. On Sunday afternoon, while Daria worked, Franca awaited Victor's arrival. She set the table with fresh fruit, pastries, a bottle of strega and a bottle of anisette, and prepared coffee.

Victor knocked on the door, carrying flowers for Franca, and Franca welcomed him in. She studied him for a moment; the portrayal of a gangster and gambler had been deceptive. He wore a beige suit, white shirt and brown tie, and Franca was pleased with her first impression.

"Victor, welcome to my home. I am Signora Privitera."
"Signora, thank you. It's an honor to meet you."

The living room had a burgundy mohair couch, an overstuffed, leather chair, a spindle-legged desk, a floor lamp and a radio. Franca let him to the kitchen and Victor resembled a toy soldier, obeying his sergeant's orders. Franca chortled.

"Make yourself comfortable. Do you understand Italian?"
"Sort of."
"Do you know that Daria's parents are dead?"

"Yes, in fact, my father died when I was ten years old and my mother died when I was sixteen."

"I'm sorry. Daria and you have a lot in common. Do you have honorable intentions?"

"Yes, Signora."

"Well, I'm glad to hear that. Daria is a 'rose' and you have my permission to date."

"Thanks."

He stood up and embraced Franca; a spate of tears flowed down her face.

"Signora, what's wrong?"

"Just thinking about Daria's mother."

After enjoying Franca's hospitality, Victor departed, thanking her. Daria called her grandmother, anxious to hear about the meeting.

"I like him. He is kind and affectionate."

"I'm glad. See you later."

That night, Victor met Daria after work. The fountains in front of the Claridge Hotel spouted green water and resembled graceful Chinese elms. Clouds hung overhead, suspended like cotton balls and a slivered moon peeked through the movement of clouds. Soldiers sent to Atlantic City for rest and relaxation, walked the Boardwalk. Daria asked Victor why he had not been drafted.

"I'm 4F. When I was a kid, some guy shot a bee-bee gun, hit my eye, and I lost the vision in my brown eye. It was a freak accident."

"I'm sorry."

Daria shuddered, snuggled up close to him and they held hands as they strolled the Boardwalk.

In August of 1945, World War II had ended and islanders reveled in the news. Lights went on once again and people rejoiced, dancing through the streets and on the Boardwalk, with renewed hope for the future. Some servicemen received a hero's welcome, while others returned with the wounds and scars of war. Memorials of those who were missing and dead joined the dead of World War I in the park across from the high school. Neon signs glittered again and fear of invading German submarines drifted from the island's shores.

Daria met Victor at the Sea and Sand Club and joined the festivities in celebration of the war's end. Then he led her to Raf's office for an introduction. Raf was a lanky man, with dark hair and eyes, and a cigarette dangled from the side of his mouth. Although he was a handsome man, he appeared to be a formidable man and bore little resemblance to Victor. It was obvious that Victor admired his brother. Neither one had gone beyond eighth grade, yet, Raf owned one of the largest nightclub and gambling casinos on the island. No doubt, he was a powerful, well-respected man because he never refused any one or any organization a favor.

"Nice meeting you, kid." Raf said, and that was the extent of their meeting.

"C'mon, Daria, I'll show you the casino."

"Are you a gambler."

"No, not really, the house always wins. But, I play cards occasionally and I'm a craps dealer"

"Do you ever get raided?"

"Once in a while. It's a way of life here. Besides, my brother pays off politicians and cops. He even has the State Police in his pocket."

Victor explained the island's two-month economy provided less than a decent living and gambling supplemented islanders' income. Then he led her to a house on the street. Entering, he pushed a button, a door opened, and they crossed a bridge into another house. Diehard gamblers were hunched over tables played poker, chemin de fer, craps, and women played roulette wheels. Gambling was the great equalizer, men and women were addicted to the fast money made and lost.

"I've never seen anything like this before."

"Gambling is all over the city. I'll take you home now. I don't want your grandmother to worry. I had an extra key made for you to my apartment, in case, Valia and you would like to hangout there."

She eyed him with suspicion.

"Don't worry, I've sown my oats."

She put her hand out.

After work, Valia and she went to Victor's apartment, where Daria experienced a sense of maturity. She glanced around the living room, which had a hunter green couch, a lipstick red couch, and a small oriental rug with the same colors. The bedroom contained twin beds, a chest of drawers, a bureau, and a chair. The apartment also had a bathroom and a kitchen that had a window box that Victor used during the winter months.

"Valia, it's cozy."
"Sure is. Someone's knocking."

Daria opened the door.

"Hello, I brought sandwiches and coffee. Do you like the place?"
"I love it and you have great taste."

After they ate, Valia left. Daria hugged Victor, secure in his arms. He stroked her hair, his lips kissed hers, and Daria's tongue sought his and he backed away.

"Where did you learn to French-kiss?"
"I read True Romances to learn how to kiss. Was it all right?"
"I loved it. I'm nuts about you, will you marry me?"
"Yes, but I have to ask Nonna."
"Tomorrow we'll tell her."
"I think we should wait."
"We can't have secrets. What's wrong?"
"Carlo has been arrested and he's being sent to reform school."
"You're not alone. I'm with you."
"Let's tell Nonna then."

Franca sat in her nightgown and robe, her gray braids reached her shoulders, and when they walked in, she stood up. Victor embraced and kissed her and asked for Daria's hand in marriage.

"Yes, you may marry Daria. God bless you both."

For a moment, Daria noticed relief on Franca's face. She recalled her grandmother's words: she would not leave the earth until Daria was settled.

28

On a brisk, wintry day in February, cold ocean breezes blew across the island. Franca welcomed Carlo home and gave him the news. Although Franca was delighted, she glanced at Carlo and saw the perennial mask of glumness covering his face. If only she could erase his pain.

"Carlo, you have to give Daria away. I'll get you a nice suit."
"Thanks, Nonna."

Daria and Victor prepared for their marriage at St. Martin's Church. Father Damiano had died and the new pastor, Father Giorgio, delighted parishioners with his charming smile, easygoing manner, and black eyes that twinkled when he smiled and when he was disturbed. He had clumps of black hair, growing in different directions, which he constantly pushed down.

Daria wore an ivory wool dress, trimmed in ivory satin, with an ivory wool coat and matching cloche. When Franca saw her, pride swelled within her and she handed Daria a small box. Daria gasped at the diamond earrings.

"I saved them for you," Franca said, choking back the tears.
"Thank you, Nonna."
"Your mother would have been proud of you."
"And my father?"

"Let's leave now."

Daria wondered why her father's name brought up such pain and animosity. She only knew half-truths and bits and pieces of what occurred. Someday, she had to find out what happened, no matter how painful the truth would be.

Carlo came downstairs, dressed in a black suit and his sandy-brown hair neatly combed. Still handsome albeit with scars on his face, yet his eyes never lost their melancholy. Daria dismissed his underlying pain; that day belonged to Victor and her.

Usually neighbors gathered in church for weddings, funerals, confirmations and graduations, but the frigid weather kept parishioners in their homes. The church was empty, except for Raf, who was Victor's best man, and Valia, the maid of honor. After the ceremony, they had dinner at Milano's Restaurant, across from the church. Later Daria changed into a black chesterfield coat, black velvet beret, and Victor looked at his wife with admiration.

"I married a movie star."

"Did you notice how pleased my grandmother looked?"

"Yes, and Carlo's a good kid; he's just got to grow up."

For a moment, the old despair clouded Daria's mind for her brother and herself. She must place him in the recesses of her mind and look forward to a new life.

On the train to New York City, Victor teased her about reading True Romances.

"With all those glamorous women that come in the club, you must have learned a lot from them."

"Can't compare to you. Don't you realize who and what you are? You are bi-lingual, beautiful, and intelligent. I love it when you speak to your grandmother in Italian."

"How about tri-lingual? I speak Sicilian, too," she laughed.

"Then you know three languages."

She smiled at him and he touched her cheek. He had a sheepish smile, which she found appealing and the cast in his injured eye fascinated her as well.

They reached Grand Central Station in Manhattan and Victor hailed a taxicab to a hotel off Times Square. They unpacked and dressed for dinner at Lou Walters' Latin Quarter. Ann Corio, the Burlesque Queen, was the main attraction, stripping to sensual music. Later they danced until two o'clock in the morning, their bodies molded together as one.

"Let's go, Honey, I can't hold out much longer."

Back in their hotel, Victor ordered cocktails for them, ran the water in the bathtub, and asked her to bathe with him. She glanced askance at him, gulped, smiled impishly and undressed. Her body still had a smattering of a tan from her two-piece bathing suit, but her buttocks and breasts appeared sculpted in marble.

"I'm crazy about you, you're gorgeous."
"I love you, too."

During bathing, they lathered each other's bodies, discovered their sensitive areas that aroused their passion. His lips met hers, his hand cupped her breasts for his lips, but then she pushed him away.

"I just want to model my nightgown for you."

And she twirled around in an ivory satin gown that skimmed her figure.

"You look beautiful, now come over here."

He put on the radio, they danced around the room and his lips came down upon her receptive mouth.

"You're worth waiting for."

When he dimmed the lights, rays of neon lights beamed through the Venetian blinds and he slid her nightgown off, fondled her breasts, and her nipples hardened under his gentle touch. She was so close to him, felt his erection, and he pulled her toward the bed. He entered her and they were one, moaning and spiraling into ecstasy with tremors of passion and love exploding for each other.

"Daria, I love you. Did I hurt you?"

"A little, but it was as beautiful as I imagined."

During the next few days, they toured Manhattan, visited museums, rode a carriage through Central Park, and then Daria had a special request: she wanted to see an opera. The scheduled opera for the evening was Bizet's Carmen. Victor paid the cashier extra money for good seats without reservations. Daria was captivated by the elegantly dressed men and women, remembering her grandmother's description of evenings at the opera.

"Victor, my grandparents had a reserved box here."

"You're kidding?"

"No, I'm not."

The orchestra revved up and Daria was enthralled, especially when Carmen danced on the table at the gypsies' canteen. She squirmed in her seat, wishing she could join the singers and dancers.

"This is so exciting?"

"It's more fun watching you. The guys at the club won't believe me when I tell them I saw an opera."

"I can't wait to tell Nonna."

Their honeymoon ended and upon their return to Atlantic City, their happiness splintered. Franca sat in her chair weeping, despondent and wondering what could she do for Carlo. He violated his parole and officers returned him to reform school.

"Did you have a nice time?" Franca asked as a formality.

"Terrific, we saw an—" her voice trailing.

Victor nudged her not to continue; he felt such pathos for Franca.

"Signora, I mean Nonna, we'll go visit him as soon as we're allowed."

"Thank you, Victor, you are very kind."

Six weeks later, Daria and Victor drove to the reform school, fifty miles away. Daria lacked the will to see Carlo whose *record* kept spinning and scratching her grandmother's and her life with no respite. As they reached the reform school, it resembled a farm, a pastoral sea of tranquility with landscaped slopes, grazing cows, and young men in uniforms mowing the lawn. Inside the reception room, prison guards stood remote, yet, vigilant as young men lined up for expectant visitors.

Once again at the sight of him, sorrow surfaced with Daria for her brother, the string of affection still hung between them. Carlo thanked Victor for coming.

"How's Nonna?"

"Every time you get into trouble, you ask me about Nonna. Why don't you consider her feelings before and not after you do something wrong?"

His penitent gaze masked his face and he sobbed. But Daria had reached the summit, tired of his problems that he brought unto himself. Victor glanced around and shuddered at the young men who resembled hardened criminals, while others looked like altar boys, including Carlo, who would become fodder for the strong, dominant leaders.

"Carlo, aren't you scared?"

"Victor, I can take care of myself."

"Carlo, I know I'm preaching, but get on with your life, forget the past; there's a wonderful world out there." Daria pleaded.

"I still hate preaching."

"Carlo, she's trying to help you. This place gives me the creeps."

"No worse than the orphanage," he retorted.

The guards signaled the time was up. Daria and Victor watched Carlo exit through the steel door and he waved a languid hand to them. They saw a desperate, terrified look on his face.

"He's scared shitless," said Victor.

Grabbing Daria's hand, he led her to the car. They drove home in silence.

During the next six months, Daria visited her grandmother as usual and noticed her pallor and deterioration.

"I'm calling the doctor."

"My foot hurts, maybe my sugar is high. Carlo called and he is coming home. He sounds as if he's changed."

"I hope so. Nonna, I have great news. I'm going to have a baby."

"Oh, how wonderful. Go upstairs and in my bureau, third drawer from the bottom, there's a wallet; bring it down."

"First, I'll call the doctor."

Daria handed her grandmother the wallet. Franca removed a hundred dollar bill and handed it to Daria.

"I can't take it."

"You must. Buy an English pram for your baby. I hurt your mother's feelings when she bought a second-hand carriage for Carlo. So trivial, I've regretted my outburst since the day I said it.

"Wait until the baby is born."

"No, take it now."

Daria bent down, kissed Franca and moved a chair near her. Thinking sometimes silence was the best consolation, they sat quietly together; each one reflective on their future. Daria thought about her baby, while Franca thought about Carlo and death.

A month later, Franca prepared dinner for herself and Carlo. The pot fell out of her grip, she slumped to the floor, held her chest while Carlo called the ambulance and Daria, who met him in the emergency room. Their grandmother was under an oxygen tent, but at the sound of her grandchildren, she pointed to her eyeglasses. The nurse put them on and raised the tent.

"Daria, Carlo, my diabetes if very high. My heart is not good and the doctors are concerned about my foot. It's gangrenous and they may have to remove it."

"Oh no," moaned Daria.

"Nonna, don't let them do that to you," cried Carlo.

"Nurse, please do me one favor. I want my grandchildren to walk me to the sun porch."

"You can't do that."

"Please, it's my last wish," she whispered.

Daria and Carlo flanked their grandmother, who walked with the last remnant of her dignity in tact, and the nurse followed them with a wheelchair and an oxygen tank. Franca put out her arms, Daria was on one side and Carlo on the other. They kissed her soft cheek, tasted the salt from her tears, and told her they needed her. As they departed, they waved to her and she forced back the tears.

Now Franca touched the wilted poinsettia, weeping, but then regained her strength. She waved down to her grandchildren, closed the window, and knocked the poinsettia plant down.

"We're both dying. At last, peace."

"Mrs. Privitera, you must go back now. It's dangerous. I could get into trouble. Besides, Father Giorgio is here from St. Martin's Church."

"I'm ready."

Father Giorgio stood in the doorway between life and death, unnerved about the scene unfolding in the room with its laments. He came over to Franca, wrapped the curtain around her bed and heard her confession, gave her Holy Communion and granted her Extreme Unction. He could not wait to get out of there amid the tragic sounds of suffering. Franca bowed to him in deference for his kindness and his explanation of a better life from the trials and tribulations of the earth.

Sleep eluded Daria, worried about her grandmother; the thought of losing a foot was an abhorrence. Finally, at 5:00 a. m., Victor came home and she was dressing.

"It's dark out there. What are you doing?"

"I've got to see her before surgery."

"Take the car. I'll get changed and grab a jitney."

The streets were deserted with an eerie silence, and Daria had a feeling of desolation and foreboding. She parked the car on Michigan Avenue, ran to the entrance and reached Franca's room. When she saw Daria, her face lit up like an angel, peaceful and ethereal.

"Daria, Daria …"

Daria raised the oxygen tent at Franca's request, kissed her forehead, repeated that she loved her and thanked her for caring about Carlo and her.

"You've turned out to be lovely. I wish you had know your mother; she was wonderful."

"Like you."

"No, I've been haughty at times, but she had a humility about her. She was beautiful and brilliant but did not flaunt it."

"And Daddy?"

"I didn't like him, but he was equally intelligent. He had class, I hate to admit, but he was mean."

"I'm sorry."

"Listen, Daria, you come from class and intelligence. It's has to come through you and your children. You have a wonderful mind, use it well."

"Nonna, I love you."

Daria joined Victor as Carlo spoke to Franca.

"Nonna, don't go. I need you."

"Carlo, for your own sake, behave yourself. You come from class and intelligence. Think about it. I beg you."

"I know. I know."

Victor and Daria paced the floor, drank coffee, smoked cigarettes, and after three hours, the doctor emerged, wiping off the perspiration from his forehead.

"She lived through the surgery, but then her heart gave way. I'm sorry. She knew the risk. I've never seen anyone at peace before surgery, almost as if she welcomed death."

Daria was not surprised; she had been in a state of expectancy. Carlo and Daria wept for their grandmother, a noble lady, who loved them unconditionally. She had saved them from the orphanage after Alissandru's death and she had taught them so much. Victor held Daria close and extended his hand to Carlo.

"She was some lady," he murmured.

"Victor, I have to get the doctor."

"What's wrong?"

"I want her buried with her foot."

"Is that necessary?"

"Yes."

The doctor stated Franca's foot was in the lab and he would call down.

"Doctor, we'd like to see her."
"Of course, Mrs. Caselli."

Franca's body was covered with a sheet, the indentation of her missing foot churned Daria's stomach. As she wept, she removed the sheet from Franca's face that looked serene and peaceful. She and Carlo kissed her, whispered good-bye, and told her they loved her.

Now Victor discussed the funeral and Daria and Carlo stared at each other. They had never attended a funeral or knew what happened to their mother and grandfather. They knew that Alissandru was buried somewhere in the Philadelphia area.

"First, we have to find out if she had a plot. Where are your parents and grandfather buried?" Victor queried.

"Daddy died in Philadelphia. That's all I know."
"They must be buried in the Pleasantville cemetery. Haven't you ever visited their graves?"
"No, Nonna wouldn't allow us."

So now began the search through Franca's papers. Daria found the document signed by King Umberto I, which had given her grandfather legitimacy. She found her mother and father's wedding certificate, and a document that entitles her father a share in his parents' land in Novara, Sicily. Where was her grandmother's title to her land that so often spoke about?

Then she probed Franca's drawers and found a box with undergarments and a dress. Then her eyes opened wide at a journal that contained a folded letter which Daria unfolded.

Dear Daria and Carlo,

I know that you are saddened by my death, but I'm at peace. Bury me in these clothes, next to your mother and grandfather. Remember that I loved you.

Nonna

Daria reclined on Franca's bed and tears poured out as she read Franca's journal. She wrote about her earlier life with love and security, the earthquake that had destroyed her father's land, and the loss of her sister and brother. She stated that their father was buried in Holy Cross Cemetery in Philadelphia, and he was responsible for their mother's death.

"Carlo, come up here. I want you to read Nonna's journal."

"Not now."

"But Carlo, she tells us that Daddy was responsible for out mother's death."

"Leave me alone. I don't feel like reading."

Daria placed the journal near her coat, dialed the undertaker's number, and explained her grandmother's last request. An hour later, he called back.

"Your mother and grandfather are buried in Potter's field."

"What's that?"

"A pauper's grave."

"You mean for poor people?"

"Yes, Mrs. Caselli."

Daria dropped the telephone; she sat in her grandmother's leather chair and read. Now she understood why she had forbidden them from visiting the graves. Yet, she wanted to be buried near her mother and grandfather. Although the news was devastating, she had to adhere to her grandmother's last wish.

On the evening of the viewing, Daria stood by Franca's casket, intertwined her rosary beads around her stiff fingers, noticed her shoes, and both of her feet looked normal. She sighed. Neighbors streamed in and out and suddenly Daria saw a man who resembled her father walking toward her. He appeared about fifty-seven years of age, but he had a shorter stature and wore eyeglasses.

"Daria, Carlo, I'm your Uncle Riccardo, your father's brother."

"Yes," Daria replied, wanting to ask why he had come.

"I want to speak to you alone after the viewing."

The funeral parlor emptied out and Riccardo Leone explained he had visited their father and buried him when he died. Tears misted Carlo and Daria's eyes; at least, he did not die alone.

"We should hate him for what he did to our mother and to us, but somehow we can't."

"Daria, he regretted his behavior, believe me."

"It's over. I'm tired of talking about it." Carlo said.

"Carlo, you must read Nonna's journal."

He walked away, annoyed with her insistence.

Riccardo spoke of his love for Giulia and how she fell madly in love with Alissandru. Daria interrupted him.

"Why didn't you visit us and try to help Nonna? We were so alone."

"I tried to see her but she wouldn't see me. Daria, didn't she receive a monthly check?"

"You're the one!"

"Yes, your father implored me to help. He loved your mother."

"Oh sure, Nonna said he had other women."

"Didn't mean a thing, times were difficult and that was some kind of outlet for him."

"Explain why he put us away."

"Daria, I can't."

In the morning, fierce winds buffeted the island and billowing clouds hung in the sky. Franca's Mass was held at St. Martin's and a few neighbors joined the funeral procession to the cemetery. Daria stared at the markers in Potter's Field, only numbers, and no names of the diseased. Glancing at the pussy willows, a sense of renewal overcame her, as the willows swayed to the rhythm of the winds, with wild flowers ready to burst with life. She cried softly, her teeth chattered, and she murmured.

"A nonentity's grave for such wonderful, educated people."

Daria's adrenaline soared, angry, hurt, and she wondered why Fate had given her family and her such heartache.

"Is my illustrious family to end among the weeds? No! Nonna, I promise to educate myself and the children I hope to have in the memory of our family."

"Daria, that's a big promise." Victor said.

"I know."

Daria held her Chesterfield coat closed, but her protruding abdomen interfered with its closure. Blustery winds blew her black mantilla to the ground, resembling a huge, black butterfly. The sun peeked through the clouds and glistened on Daria's dark brown hair with red highlights. Victor retrieved her mantilla and he held it until she pinned it back on.

Carlo, an island unto himself, feared treading on his mother and grandfather's grave and stood back. Riccardo placed his hand on his shoulder, as bored, gravediggers leaned on their shovels, chatted, and swigged on miniature bottles of liquor. Their disrespect, apathy and odious behavior enraged Daria.

"You don't realize my grandmother was a noble lady with an unconquerable spirit. If you only knew her, you would have doffed your hats to her."

"I agree," Victor said, and doffed his hat.

Carlo and Daria placed a red rose on Franca's pine box. Then, Daria picked up a pussy willow bursting with life, and gently blew the catkins away. She turned and vowed never to return, abiding by her grandmother's wishes.

"Don't visit the graves, we're not there."

Riccardo returned with Daria and Victor to their apartment. Riccardo asked Carlo if he'd like to live in Philadelphia; Carlo glanced at his uncle, a stranger, and declined his offer.

"I'm seventeen; I'd rather be on my own."

"Here is my card, if you ever need me. And Daria, I'd appreciate it if you call me once in a while. With the war over, I'll start going back to Messina during the summer months. Things are bad there and we have a large family that needs help. The destruction was terrible."

"Uncle Riccardo, someday, I'd love to go to Messina."

"That would be wonderful," he replied, departing and wishing them well.

Daria glanced around at the apartment and guilt eroded with her. There was no room for Carlo and he would have to live alone. But she had an underlying fear that his anomalous behavior could hinder her marriage, recalling what her grandmother advised: married people should live alone.

Carlo went home and Daria told him she would see him the following day, when the two of them would go through the house. But at ten o'clock that evening, Carlo telephoned; he had been arrested for theft, stealing tools from a builder. Daria's hand shook, unbelieving. She unleashed her fury, her rancor, and accused him of dishonoring their grandmother's name on the day of the funeral.

"What's wrong with you? I can't take any more!"

"I'm sorry. Can you visit me tomorrow?"

"No!" And she slammed the telephone down.

"Daria, why are you so angry?" Victor asked.

"Victor, I'm tired of his problems. My God, he didn't let her grave get cold."

She sobbed.

In the morning, Daria went to her grandmother's house and started emptying drawers. She looked at Carlo's room with the unmade bed, locked the house, stifling her tears, and drove to city hall. Carlo was mute, remote, and in a foul mood, and she abstained from any castigation. What could she say to him that she had not already said? And why was she compelled to visit him, despite the berating she gave him and her impatience with him? Her baby kicked, the new life within her needed her attention, and she left Carlo to his fate.

Two weeks later, Carlo called her to come for the hearing, which she did. The police cited his battles with policemen, his parole violation, and his reprehensible act on the day of his grandmother's funeral. Carlo's court-appointed attorney advised him to plead guilty and depend upon the mercy of the court. The judge reviewed his record and deemed strong, punitive measures were needed. Apparently, he had not learned his lesson and no mercy was shown him.

"One year in Trenton State Prison."

"He's only seventeen!" Her outburst fell on an emptied courtroom.

"M'am, didn't his attorney know his age?" The guard asked, and told her she had to leave.

She scurried to the judge's chambers and the clerk was unavailable. If Carlo had any grievances, his attorney should file a motion with the court.

Frantic, she ran through the hallways, looking for Carlo's lawyer, and spewed out her anxiety.

"He told me he was eighteen."
"He'll be eighteen next October. Can't you tell the judge now?"
"No, there are certain procedures we must follow. Excuse me."

Daria ran outside and leaned against the building for support; her mind swirling with ideas how to help Carlo, but none were suitable or feasible. She closed her eyes, inhaled the fresh air, but when she opened them, she saw Carlo, flanked by police, shackled, handcuffed, and shoved in a paddy wagon. A trolley car went by, blocked her screams, and she went home downtrodden.

As she unlocked the door, wretchedness besieged her, slumping down into a chair, she cried quietly. Then Victor got out of his bed, rubbing his eyes and yawned.

"What happened?"
"A year in Trenton State Prison."
"What? He's not old enough for that place. It's for killers and really tough guys. They'll slaughter him."
"Oh my God, I've got to see the judge."

In the morning, Daria dressed with care, hoping to impress the judge with her refinement. She arrived at the courthouse before it opened and knocked on his chamber door.

"Please, five minutes, hear me out."
"Mrs. Caselli, come in. Your brother is a troublemaker; this has been going on for a long time. Do you know he fought seven policemen, not one, but seven!"
"And they beat him up unmercifully."
"He'll learn his lesson in the *big house*. I can't do anything until the proper papers are filed. It will take about six weeks."
"Your Honor, by that time, he'll be dead."
"Excuse me; I have to be in court. Take my advice, you have a nice husband, you're a lovely girl, and you're going to have a baby. Forget about him, he's on a path of destruction. Were you in the orphanage with him?"
"Yes, Your Honor."
"Heed my advice."

Six weeks later, Carlo had not been released and Daria and Victor drove to Trenton State Prison. He parked the car while Daria stood there gazing at the towering, gray stone buildings that sent shivers up her spine.

"The devil's residence," she murmured.

Daria was enveloped in the morbidity of the massive edifice and perceived impending doom for Carlo; guards were perched above and they ruled that monstrous tomb with their guns.

"Scary, isn't it, Honey?"
"Yes, Victor."

He clutched her arm and Daria waddled on the side of him. Guards stood behind the huge steel doors, examined her bag, and frisked Victor. Another guard led them into a cobweb filled room with a twenty-foot ceiling. A single bulb hung overhead and the dingy walls seemed to close in on them. Victor urged her to sit down but she declined, recoiling at the glass partition, separating prisoners from visitors.

Then Carlo shuffled into the room, clothed in a black and white striped dingy garb that drooped on him. He splayed his hands on the heavy glass panel, his face etched in terror and Daria trembled. His head had been sheared like a sheep and the one single bulb reflected upon his shaved head.

"What have they done to you?" Daria bellowed.

With terror in his voice, he whispered:

"This is what they do to new prisoners. I've been fumigated, men beat me up, and they raped me."
"Raped you? I don't understand."
"Daria, I'll explain it later," stated Victor, nervously.

She stood up; her back ached from bending over and speaking through a six-inch by twelve inch opening. Why did she want to protect Carlo, when he sought self-destruction? If only she could forget him and go on with her life. Carlo wiped his tears with his shirtsleeve, sobbing until his heart was ready to burst, and Daria knew his spirit had been broken.

"I spoke to the judge and he said it would take six weeks to transfer you. Have you heard anything, yet? Why did you tell your lawyer you were eighteen? You could have saved yourself from this hell?"

He shook his head to the first question and shrugged to the last.

The guard placed a heavy hand on Carlo's shoulder, whose eyes darted between Victor and Daria. He turned around, foot-dragged back into the tomb of perversion, with the guard at his side. Daria and Victor scurried out of there at a harried pace, anxious to get out of the musty, dank air. On the way home, Victor explained about a man raping a man and his eyes mirrored his distress.

"If he fights them, it could get worse."
"I don't understand him."
"Neither do I," replied Victor.

Carlo's imprisonment pervaded their thoughts and they considered his incarceration in Trenton State Prison a travesty of justice. Daria touched her abdomen.

"You're going to be a lawyer."

Victor also touched her.

"Your mommy is very ambitious."

And they had a moment of alacrity.

The next morning, Daria rose at dawn, had breakfast, bathed, dressed and arrived at the judge's chambers. She gulped on her words.

"Your Honor, they raped him."
"Mrs. Caselli, that place is not a country club and that's what happens in those places. There is more bad news; you had better sit down."

She did and glanced at him with anxiety.

"Your brother is in the hospital. He rejected the older men's advances and they beat him into unconsciousness. He's a tough one. I'm sorry."
"So am I, Your Honor."

That night Daria's sleep was thwarted with dreams about her parents. Her mother wore an ivory negligee and her father had a navy blue robe on; they wept unrestrained. Daria thought her dreams of her parents had ended many years ago. What did they mean? She sat up and queried.

"What can I do?"

But they had disappeared once again. She sat up, bewildered, and felt her baby moving; she got out of bed and ate breakfast, nourishing herself and her baby who needed her.

Two weeks later, she received a call from Carlo. He had been sent back to the farm and was feeling better.

"Please, Carlo, behave yourself."

29

Daria and Victor concentrated on preparations for their baby's birth. In mid-July, Atlantic City prospered with tourists en masse and Victor was concerned about leaving Daria alone. She joined him for dinner at the club, wearing a black, chiffon maternity dress and pulled her dark brown hair back with a black ribbon. He fawned over her, told her she looked beautiful, maternal, and appeared ready to pop out the baby. After dinner, he brought her into the casino and told her to sit at the craps table while he put on his horn-rimmed glasses and dealt craps.

"You look like a scholar in those glasses," she whispered.

He shook his head, not to interrupt him, as his fingers moved deftly as he counted money. She was impressed with his dexterity.

Suddenly, a contingent of State Troopers surrounded the club and casino. Victor stuffed the money into his jacket that was lined with pockets. He leaped across the craps table, grabbed Daria's arm and pressed a hidden button in the wall, which enabled them to slide through an opening that led to the basement.

"Don't make a sound. My brother and I are the only ones who know about this hideout."

Two hours passed, they were holed-up in the basement, and then Daria bent over, moaning, sharp pains contorted her face, and then the pain subsided.

"Victor, I'm starting labor. I don't want our baby born in a gambling joint."

"Shh, it won't be long now."

The sound of activity came to a halt and the sirens were gone. Victor pushed a button, the wall moved, and the passage led them outside. He left his car for fear of police still lingering and they walked to the corner and hopped a jitney to the Atlantic City Hospital.

Twelve hours later, Daria gave birth to a son, who was placed in her arms. She touched his bruised face from the forceps, intertwined her fingers through his tiny fingers, and kissed him on the forehead. The experience of giving birth created instant maternal love, which surpassed anything she could have imagined.

When she returned to her room, Victor was there with a dozen American Beauty roses. He smiled, then hugged and kissed her.

"Was it rough?"

"Yes, but he's worth it. He looks like you."

"My brother's so excited. He wants the baby named after him. He has no intentions of marrying."

Silence … dead silence.

"Well, what do you think?

"I've seen him three times, never had a conversation with him, and he wants our baby named after him. Raffaello Caselli, that's a mouthful. There could only be one Raf."

"I guess you're right. I don't like juniors. What do you want?"

"Richard, after Richard the Lion-Hearted, it sounds strong. He launched the Third Crusade from Messina."

"You're reading too many books. I like it."

She smiled wistfully at him and he melted with love for her.

Daria soon realized she had uprooted Raf's power over Victor. At Richard's christening, he treated Daria like a nonentity, speaking about the baby as my "brother's kid." Yet, Raf's power puzzled Daria; waters parted when he entered a restaurant, bar or some elegant party. His appearance was noted in the Atlantic City Daily Press, where notables hovered around him and coveted his friendship for his influence in the political and entertainment arena. He was photographed with famous movie stars, politicians, nightclub entertainers who performed at his club, and granted favors to all who asked. He relished it, fueled his hubris, which also gave him power and indebted people to him. And Victor swelled with pride when he spoke about his brother's achievements.

Now the moment came that Daria promised her grandmother; she purchased a gray-beige English pram for her baby. She strolled the Boardwalk beaming with pride, having fulfilled her grandmother's request. Upon her return to the apartment, she checked her mail and there was a letter from Carlo stating he was coming home. A week later, he arrived at the apartment and she wished him well and embraced him. His appearance distressed Daria, he resembled a boxer with his straight nose pushed aside, one eye half-shut and a bitterness still lingered within him.

"Have dinner with us every night." Daria said.

"I'll help you find a room in the old neighborhood. Since everyone knows you, I think it will be good for you. I'll help you get work as a carpenter."

"Victor, I'll find my own place and my own work. I'll go to the Carpenter's Union."

"Fine, good luck."

When Victor and Daria celebrated Richard's first birthday, Victor told her that his brother was engaged to Joyce Barrett, a willowy girl with limpid green eyes, straight flaxen hair, who exuded confidence with an air of self-importance. She had been a starlet in Hollywood and returned to Atlantic City a personage.

Joyce and Raf's wedding was the social event of the year. They were married in a judge's chamber and a reception was held at the Sea and Sand Club. Guests arrived in chauffeured limousines, tawdry cars, and Rolls Royces and the parade of automobiles extended from Pacific Avenue to the Boardwalk. The seven-foot, seven-inch doorman greeted guests in a navy blue uniform with epaulets, white satin cording across his broad chest, and a navy blue turban with gold tassels. He smiled broadly and endeared himself to the guests.

Four hundred guests gathered at the club, in anticipation of the bride and groom's entrance. Raf swaggered in with Joyce, wearing a navy blue tuxedo, while Joyce wore a mauve taffeta gown with tulip sleeves, a mauve silk flower tucked in her hair and her one-carat diamond earrings caught the reflection of the lights.

Daria met Victor at the club and he escorted her to the showroom. Small tables had been replaced by large, round tables, seating ten guests. Magenta satin covered the tables with an overlay of sheer white linen; large centerpieces contained mauve roses, interspersed with bluebells of Scotland and baby's breath.

The backdrop on the stage glittered with tiny, silver-sequined musical notes and ten strolling violinists weaved through the tables, performing special requests.

"Ladies and gentlemen, Mr. and Mrs. Raf Caselli!"

Guests rose to their feet, applauding the union; Raf and Joyce mingled with their guests, beaming and shaking hands. When they stopped in front of Victor and Daria's table, they continued on to the next table.

"We didn't get a chance to say our congratulations." Daria exclaimed.

Victor shrugged, appeared offended but did not say a word. After a sumptuous dinner, the guests danced until 4:00 a.m., with Joyce and Raf leading the crowd. The following day, they flew to California for their honeymoon.

Raf's reputation and power soared; he became internationally well known for his club and casino and his connections ranged far and wide. Joyce and he invited judges, senators, congressmen, prominent lawyers, wealthy businessmen, and a plethora of entertainers to the club and private parties. Only influential or wealthy people were considered suitable as part of their entourage and social milieu.

Although Victor worked at the club, Daria and he were never invited to any of their affairs. Daria's self-respect was very important to her; besides she preferred the quiet life, reading and studying all the time. She built an invisible wall around her as a protective shield. Whereas, Victor felt the brunt of his brother's exclusions, but hid his deep distress.

Daria became pregnant again, much to their delight. Victor scanned their apartment.

"We've got to get a house."
"But how? We need a down payment."
"I'll ask Raf, he owes me."

She appeared skeptical about Raf's generosity, but she did not utter a disparaging word to deter Victor's enthusiasm. He went to the club, sought out Raf, who was in his office, where the usual men groveled around him and emulated him. One man stood against the wall, smoking a Havana cigar; he touched his tripe-like complexion from a bad case of acne and pushed his hand through his dyed black hair, while showgirls pranced in and out for Raf's approval. The man whistled at the girls and moved toward them like an animal in heat, preparing for an attack.

"Damn it! Don't you have any class?" Raf barked.
"That's hot stuff."
"Beat it, I'm busy."

Victor roared with laughter. The man was a *horses' ass* and threw his weight around the club, ordering waiters, waitresses and bartenders to do his bidding because Raf was his friend.

"That guy's a real jerk. I'm glad you told him off. I have to talk to you alone."
"Sure, let's go outside."

They walked out on the Boardwalk and faced the ocean, leaning on the railing and watching the waves pounding the shore.

"Daria's pregnant and we need a house. Can you lend me two grand?"
"No, I gotta 'big nut' with the revue."
"Only two thousand dollars … with all the money you make."

Victor stared at him with contempt, fuming, and incredulous.

"I'm the only one you can trust. Why, that's piss money to you. I could have stolen plenty from you, but my loyalty and honesty means nothing to you. Those idiots, those goofballs can get anything out of you, as long as they tell you how great you are and kiss your ass."

"I can't do it."

Raf turned and went to his office, while Victor went home and gave Daria the news; she was relieved. With Raf's refusal, Victor maintained independence and she assured Victor something would happen. People liked Victor and spoke highly of him.

"He throws me a bone once in a while and he tells people how much he loves me."

"He loves his dog, too. Don't you see he wants you to be totally dependent upon him?"

"But I'm married now and have a family."

"It doesn't matter to him. He needs his lackeys."

At work that evening, Victor worked without his usual enthusiasm and concern for Raf's business. The hostess, Courtney Fields, a stunning redhead and friend of Victor's, inquired if Raf had given him the money. Victor told her what transpired.

"I have an idea."

"Don't go to him."

"I wouldn't do that."

When Courtney's boyfriend came into the club, she explained Victor's circumstances, and he wrote out a check for $5,000.00, which he handed to Victor.

"Thanks, but I can't take your money."

"Listen, not everyone reveres your brother. You're a good guy; pay me a hundred dollars a month without interest. Is that a fair deal?"

"It's great, thanks. I've got to call my wife."

Daria was ecstatic at the news and when Victor went home, he grabbed Richard, held him close, and told him.

"Richard, we're moving to Margate."

Three months later, they found their *palazzo* and happiness overwhelmed them as they danced through the house with Richard in Victor's arms.

"This will always be our palazzo." Daria said as they had a three-way hug.

"I'd better get back to work."

In the meantime, Carlo visited Daria periodically. He appeared to have lost his obduracy, regained his good looks, albeit more rugged, but, his eyes were still glossed over with that familiar pathetic gaze. He told her he was getting married and Daria was elated. Perhaps, a wife and family would erase the perennial sadness and give him a *raison d'etre*.

When Daria gave birth to another son, Michael, Victor's elation reached the summit. The baby resembled Daria with his dark hair and eyes. He brought three-year old Richard to the hospital to meet his brother and to present roses to Daria.

"Richard, they are so beautiful. Thank you."

"I love you, Mommy."

Two months later, the news spread around town that Joyce was pregnant. Raf purchased a house in the Parkway section of Margate, an exclusive area. The Dutch colonial house had wide steps leading to a verandah, the living and dining rooms had fireplaces, and there were five bedrooms and four bathrooms upstairs.

Victor asked Daria to build some kind of rapport with Joyce and Raf and send them a card, wishing them good luck in their home. She agreed but it was an act of futility. There was no response or invitation to their house-warming party.

After the Christmas holiday, revelers gathered at the Sea and Sand Club, the place to be on New Year's Eve. Tables were at a premium, but fifty seats were reserved for Raf and his entourage. Affluent friends and acquaintances, according to their position and wealth, had the privilege of sitting near Joyce and Raf. He needed *angels*, lenders, since he was a heavy gambler and they could supply him from ten thousand to one hundred thousand dollars in one clip.

At twelve o'clock, the orchestra played Auld Lang Syne and Victor called Daria, wishing she could be there with him.

"It's okay, Happy New Year to us."

"I have to hang up; there are lots of people waiting to use the phone."

Shortly thereafter, tongues wagged about the relationship between brothers and their wives. Some rumors stated that Daria and Joyce did not get along while others gossiped that Raf disliked Daria.

"Victor, why is your brother mean to you and me?"

"I dated Joyce."

"No. Are you kidding?"

"No. Her parents did not like the idea since I worked in a gambling joint and a nightclub. They went to Raf and asked him to stop it. Well, he started dating her, but she wanted to be a movie star. He made a call and made arrangements for her in Hollywood but nothing happened. She got some bit parts."

"Were you in love with her?"

"No, she's pretty but she wanted the best and I could not afford her."

Now winter relinquished its frost to the freshness of spring. Tulips, daffodils and hyacinths popped out of the earth and tourists arrived for the annual Easter parade. Joyce Caselli gave birth to a son and Raf reached his pinnacle: he produced a son! When Victor told Daria, he was genuinely happy for Raf.

"Now, he'll have his Raffaello," Daria said.

"No, it's too Italian. She wants him to be called Brett."

Three days later, Joyce developed a staph infection that dashed Raf's and her happiness. Her body burst out with boils, blisters and pustules. She ordered the nurse to remove the mirror from her room and put a sign on the door: no visitors allowed. During her pregnancy, she became vexed with her body that blew out of proportion. Now her face and figure, albeit for a short time, bore little resemblance to the beauty queen she had been. She directed her frustration to her baby boy. Things did not augur well for her little son, now in the care of a nurse and housekeeper, while she remained in the hospital for three months.

Joyce had not wanted children, but Raf insisted he wanted a boy; ostensibly, his ego needed a son. After all, his brother, Victor, had two sons. Besides, she was madly in love with him. But, during her hospital stay, Raf only visited a couple of times a week, socializing all night at the club with his friends and sleeping during the day.

"I had a son for you and look what I'm going through."

"You're driving me nuts. What do you want from me? I have a business to run."

"Affection and some attention."

"I'm not that type. You should know that by now."

Upon her return home, she seldom glanced at her son. She concentrated on her body, hired a masseuse, purchased a new wardrobe, and to her amazement, Raf gave her a full-length mink coat. Gradually, her beauty was restored and they resumed their social whirl. She accepted Raf on his terms; there could be no other way.

30

Daria saw Carlo, occasionally, as she was involved with her family and home in Margate. Victor learned through the nightclub grapevine that Carlo's labor brought him meager earnings; he worked at bars and drank his earnings. Often times, he sought Victor and asked him for money. One evening, Carlo sat at a bar in the Inlet, where unsavory characters hung out, competed with one another, drinking shots of whiskey with beer chaser. Someone started an argument with Carlo and punched him in the face. By the time Carlo finished with his opponent, the man regretted his behavior; he was battered, bloodied and begged for mercy.

Customers applauded Carlo's fighting skills and cheered him on; they shook his hand and wanted to be his friend. A bulky man with a pitted complexion approached Carlo and his cold, obdurate eyes even unnerved Carlo, who noticed his finger was missing.

"I could use you, you got guts. You can make a lot of money."

"Yeah, what do I have to do?"

"Meet me here tomorrow night, before you start drinking. I'll test you."

Carlo returned the next evening, rationalizing he had nothing to lose. The man waited for him in a 1955 Cadillac and introduced himself.

"I'm Frank the Monk and you're Carlo Leone."
"Where the hell did you get a name like that?"
"When I was younger, I wanted to be a missionary."

Carlo could not envision such a mean-spirited man as a priest. The man drove to the Northside of Atlantic City, reached a huge garage, with four late model cars parked in front. Men gathered inside the garage and Frank the Monk introduced Carlo. They shook hands with Carlo and welcomed him.

Then a tall, buxom blonde strolled into the garage, her large breasts barely covered, and she wore a dress that skimmed over her figure. She leaned over and one of her breasts popped out; she laughed as she placed it back. Frank the Monk kissed her and patted her buttocks.

"Hi Honey, who's the new guy?"
"Mabel, meet Carlo. One tough dude."

Carlo extended his hand to her.

"Is he allowed to be in on the fun?"
"Sure, if he wants to."

Four men unzipped their flies and Mabel performed oral sex on each of them as they vied for the largest erection, which Mabel measured with quarters. Fourteen quarters won the bet. Then the men peed, shot their urine for the longest distance and Carlo gasped in amazement. He had old-fashion principles of propriety and the scene repulsed him.

"What the hell's going on here? It's not my idea of fun."
"Hey, Carlo, lighten up," Frank the Monk said.
"I don't like that shit, let's get on with business."
"You can make a thousand dollars."
"Yeah, doing what?"
"Fellows, bring him out."

Two men led a man out with his arms tied, his legs shackled, his mouth taped, and they shoved him in a chair; his pants were soaked with his urine. Carlo stared at the man; he knew him! Frank the Monk handed Carlo a gun.

"Shoot him."

"First of all, I don't know how to use a gun. Besides, I know him and like him."

"I thought you had guts."

"I'm a fighter, not a killer."

"Well, Leone, I can't use you. Here's a C-note, keep your mouth shut."

"No thanks. I'd appreciate it if this doesn't leak out. Let's shake on it."

And he shook hands with the rest of the men, thinking:

"It's better to be on their good side."

Carlo hitchhiked back to the bar, ordered a whiskey, grateful that he did not have a killer's instinct.

Daria invited Carlo and his wife, Eve, occasionally for dinner. But, she could not tolerate the dissension between them; they argued, overdosed on liquor, and Eve exclaimed she wanted a house like Victor and Daria's, which Carlo was incapable of giving her. One evening, Eve called Daria, screaming that Carlo had been stabbed and he would not permit doctors to work on him until Daria's arrival. She called her baby-sitter and garnered herself for the worst scenario.

When she arrived at the hospital Carlo huddled in a corner, his arms and chest covered in blood. His bloodshot eyes looked at her with that familiar pitiful gaze. She shuddered; nothing had changed with him. Would he ever lead a normal life? Will it ever end?

"Carlo, the doctor wants to help you, you could bleed to death."

"Daria, will you stay here with me?"

"Yes."

Nurses washed Carlo, removed as much as they could of congealed blood while the doctor injected him with morphine. Daria held his hand while the doctor cleaned his wound, a three-inch gash. In an attempt to kill him, the assailant had inserted the knife downward, missing his heart. As the doctor sutured him, he fell asleep and Daria left.

While she drove home, spent from the ordeal, she realized that Carlo considered her an ersatz mother, despite the two years difference in their ages. She reflected upon his endless problems, his apparent self-destruction, and wondered if she could break through the glacier of despair that imprisoned him.

She arrived home, touched the walls as if to bless them. In her *palazzo*, she found solace from the outside world. Richard and Michael ran into her arms and kissed her. When they went to bed, she sat down at her piano, a luxury Victor had agreed upon, when she related the story about her grandmother's piano. As she played, her grandmother's words reverberated through her mind.

"Educate yourself … educate yourself."

And she did, unlocking her mind, a new world unfolded before her, unleashing her intelligence and potential. She gained confidence in her abilities, absorbing knowledge, and she was never satiated with what she was learning. She wanted more and more until she became obsessed with collecting books, especially, esoteric ones. At times, she recalled her father's legacy.

"You must go to college as your mother and I did."

But that dream would be directed to her children. She would instill within them the love of learning and the love of books.

Now the summer came to an abrupt end with tourists exiting the island in droves. With the departure, Victor had some nights off, which gave them nights of lovemaking. She became pregnant and they were thrilled. In July, Daria gave birth to a daughter. Victor sent her a dozen pink roses and followed the florist in. He grinned from ear to ear, kissed and hugged her, and happiness oozed out of him.

"She's so fragile, only five-pounds, six ounces." Victor said, glowing.

"Isn't she adorable? Let's name her Marisa." Daria exclaimed.

"That's pretty. My brother was disappointed it wasn't another boy."

"He was disappointed!" Daria sat up in her bed.

"He just commented."

But Raf's comment infuriated her. Victor had not broken loose from Raf's domination, an invisible cord bound them together and Victor still rendered fealty to Raf.

"Victor, sometimes I feel like we live with a third person, he wants, he says … I don't care about him."

"He's still my brother. Look how you run for Carlo."

Daria refrained from further discussion.

The next day, Victor brought Richard, now eight years old, and Michael, now five, to the nursery. The nurse picked up Marisa and they waved to her. Later Victor led them to Daria's room, where she had fallen asleep, and her sons touched her arm.

"Mommy, Mommy," they whispered.

"Hi, did you see your sister?"

"Uh, uh, look at your fingers." Richard grinned with that sheepish smile like Victor's.

Victor had placed a fishtail diamond ring on her left hand and a clustered, diamond dinner ring on her right hand.

"Oh Victor, they are so beautiful, beyond my wildest dreams, but, we can't afford them."

"I want you to have them. The salesman comes into the club and I'll pay them off every week."

Their eyes locked in love and they embraced their sons with a four-way hug.

Now Daria's devotion to her family was extraordinary, totally dedicated to their education and well-being. Their home was filled with laughter and love as she tried to give her children a sense of security, which Carlo and she missed out on. During the summer months, she leisurely walked the Margate Beach with them, passing the fishing pier that jutted out into the ocean and appeared to be held up with matchsticks. Men and women fished for croakers, weakfish, flounders and striped bass. Then she and the children rode their rafts together, laughing as they reached shore.

On Sunday afternoon, they returned home and Victor was euphoric, beaming with enthusiasm, and hugged her and the children.

"Some guy just called me. There's an intimate bar for sale that I've been interested in. One catch, my brother has to co-sign."

"Oh no," moaned Daria.

"Maybe he'll be in a good mood and co-sign it."

Daria had a pit in her stomach, the euphoria they had for a few minutes had trickled down to utter disappointment. Perhaps, Raf might want Victor to have his own place. Victor went to Raf's office, jubilant, bursting with excitement, and he explained the opportunity. Raf played solitaire, kept his head down, and then shoved the cards off his desk.

"No way!" He banged his desk, pounded his chest, and his face turned shades of red.

"I need you here. Besides, you can't make it on your own."

"You are always lousing me up. You tell everybody I make more money than you, which only idiots believe, and you've got plenty of those around you. And don't tell the fucking world that you support my family and me. I work my balls off and never get a vacation or a bonus."

"I won't sign. Here's some money to help you out."

Victor looked at four fifty-dollar bills and pushed them off the desk.

"What am I suppose to do with that? I told you before; you can't buy my loyalty or my honesty. Daria thinks we can make it."

"That's your problem, you listen to her. No woman will ever tell me what to do."

"What bullshit. How come you named your son Brett instead of Raffaello?"

"Victor, you have to stay. I won't sign. I'll try to give you a salary."

"You've treated me like shit for a long time. Get yourself a fucking mule. I've had it."

Victor turned around, ran to his car, relieved he had stood up to Raf, whose persuasive powers were well known. When Victor told Daria every detail of the encounter, she hugged him.

"I'm proud of you. Something will happen. I can do waitress work; we don't want to lose our home."

"No, I don't want you to do waitress work, be patient."

Victor sat in front of the television and Daria sat on his lap, touched his face, and asked him what was wrong.

"He took care of me since we were young."

"But you made it up to him. Victor, my grandmother often said that nobody works for nothing."

In the meantime, Daria received a luncheon invitation from Joyce that puzzled her. Why send her an invitation now? What was her motive? Perhaps she invited Daria at Raf's bidding since he constantly called Victor, asking him to return, but Victor hung up on him, fearing that he might relent to Raf's pleading.

"Victor, something is fishy."

"No, I don't think so. I heard he misses me and probably wants to make up."

"I'd rather not go to the luncheon."

"Please go for my sake."

"Okay, but I'm not going to be comfortable."

"Look, you're beautiful, classy, have a great figure, dress well, and when you open your mouth, people are aware of your intelligence."

The following week, Daria drove to Joyce and Raf's house, climbed the steps to the verandah and her hand trembled as she rang the doorbell. To her surprise, Joyce answered the doorbell; her eyes perused her clothes, and then rested upon her face.

"Hello, Daria, welcome."

"Thank you, Joyce."

Then she led Daria into the living room and introduced her.

"This is Daria, Raf's brother's wife."

"Well, that makes us sisters-in-law." Daria replied, holding her head high, almost in defiance.

"Oh, that's true," Joyce replied, her lips quavering, slightly uncomfortable that Daria had said what she could not say.

The maid served cocktails, such as orange blossoms and manhattans, and Daria chose an orange blossom, sipping it, as all eyes were upon her. Then she recalled her grandmother's advice: when you are among people who are intimidating, look at them between their eyes; it unnerves them. Joyce squirmed, holding her manhattan, and directed her gaze toward the other women.

There were those who admired Daria and smiled kindly toward her; but, there were those who found her intimidating when she discussed a topic of importance. Joyce led the women into the dining room with mirrored walls and crystal chandeliers, where they were served a lobster salad with capers dotting the top. Daria picked up her seafood fork and dropped it at the howling that came from the second floor. She cringed! It sounded like a child in pain. All eyes were on Joyce who giggled, while her guests looked at her with astonishment, wanting some kind of explanation. Was her son hurt and why didn't she run upstairs and care for him?

"Joyce, what was that awful sound?" A guest queried, while the other women stared at Joyce.

"It's my kid, he drives me crazy. I strapped him to his bed. He'll stop yelling."

"Shouldn't you go up and see if he's all right?" Another woman asked.

"No, I'll do it later."

Daria leaped to her feet, her eyes met Joyce's with virulence and tears spurted out of her eyes.

"How can you do that to your son? That's so cruel."

"It's none of your goddamn business."

Daria slithered back onto her chair, embarrassed at her outburst. She could not tolerate injustice to children, creating fury and pathos within her.

"You're right, it isn't, but keeping your son tied up like an animal is horrific, beyond anything I can imagine. It's inhumane."

Daria excused herself and left the house. As she drove home, she wondered if Brett Caselli would grow up unhinged like Carlo or would he be strong like Daria and overcome an abusive parent. His opulent home should have been a haven for him, but it was a nether world between heaven and hell. She wept for the eight-year-old boy whose mother lacked the capacity to love him. She wiped her tears before entering her home.

"You're early. How did it go?"

"A disaster, I shouldn't have gone."

She proceeded to tell Victor what had occurred, he was in disbelief, but then he sobbed without restraint.

"When my brother was eight years old, he stole some things from a neighbor. My father whipped him and chained him to a post outside, leaving him out all night in the cold."

"My God, what brutality. Why does Raf allow her to strap him to the bed if he suffered at your father's hands?"

"I don't know. It was terrible."

"How did you father treat you?"

"I was the apple of his eye. I behaved myself."

"That's why Raf treats you so badly. He resented your father's love for you."

"Daria, I don't want to hear that psychological crap."

"It seems true. And you feel guilty about your father's cruelty and that's why you stood by Raf."

The next day, Daria unfolded the morning newspaper and Carlo's name was conspicuous; he was involved in another brawl. After treatment at the hospital, he was sent to a detoxification center. Daria cringed. She could not insulate herself and her family against the notoriety; it appeared to be an impossible feat. Was she being selfish? But that time, she did not receive a call for help and she breathed a sigh of relief.

Later that day, Daria went shopping in the Italian neighborhood for delicacies and she ran into Mary Gatta; they embraced.

"He still gets into trouble. I saw his name in the paper."

"I know."

"He'll never be right. Your father cursed him."

"Oh Mary, that's awful, only superstition. When did he curse him?"

"When he drank the cleaning fluid."

"Mary, for God's sake, Carlo was only a year old. It was my father's fault. I can't talk about it."

She walked to her car, drove to Margate, and stopped at the beach. She watched sea gulls screeching above her, while some were perched above the rocks; pigeons forage through the flotsam, and huge waves billowed with foam as thick as whipped cream. Closing her eyes, she breathed deeply, inhaling the fresh air, and rid herself of her bellicosity.

Two days later, Victor received a telephone call. There was a bar and restaurant on Margate's Barbary coast near the bay; he could have fifty percent as good will because of his reputation as a family man and his experience and good name during the years at the Sea and Sand Club. But, he needed the initial down payment of twenty-two thousand dollars. Victor telephoned a few people and got the money.

The restaurant and bar became known as Victor's Restaurant and Yacht Club. After extensive renovations, the opening was held on Memorial Day weekend. To Victor's amazement, two hundred islanders attended the first night, and yachts pulled up on the bay, where an outdoor dining room and bar was decorated in blue and white with accents of red. At night, lights surrounded the building, reflecting on the rippling water of the bay. Victor's Restaurant and Yacht Club became the popular hangout for the citizens of Ventnor, Margate, and Longport. Daria and Victor were thrilled with the restaurant's success.

Then Daria received a call from Father Giorgio; it concerned Carlo and it was imperative that she comes to the rectory. Her children's faces revealed their sadness and they wanted to know why she always ran for Uncle Carlo when he got into trouble. She touched their cherubic faces and explained she had a sense of duty and obligation toward him.

"I love you. I won't be long. Richard, lock the door and when Daddy calls, tell him I went to St. Martin's because of Uncle Carlo."

Father Giorgio shook Daria's hand, his twinkling black eyes and infectious smile turned ominous. He pointed to Carlo who sat in the corner near a dim light, a portrait of despair with his head bowed, and a shadowed beard added to his haggardness. Daria saw the familiar mask of wretchedness and wondered would his problems ever end.

"Daria, Carlo knows he needs psychiatric care. I called a doctor to have him admitted to an asylum."

Carlo leaped to his feet, gripped Father Giorgio's desk, and poured out his deep-rooted guilt.

"Father, I confess. I killed my mother!"

Daria sprang to her feet, astounded that the seed of guilt her father had planted a long time ago, still tormented him, festering like a sore that never healed.

"You did not! Why won't you accept the truth? Remember when I told you, you were just a baby. Think about that! How can a baby kill? You're wallowing in self-pity and I don't know why you insist on carrying the burden of matricide."

Carlo's wife sat spellbound with the revelation, while Father Giorgio blew his nose and wept, grasping for the proper words and wisdom that were elusive.

"Carlo, when you come back from the hospital, you must read Nonna's journal. I'm so tired of your problems. I have my own family to think about."

"Oh, sure, you live in a rose garden." He retorted.

She ignored his statement and wondered if he really believed that nonsense. She wanted to scream at him but kept her angst to herself.

Two days later, Daria drove Carlo to an asylum near Hammonton, New Jersey, thirty miles from Atlantic City. He was talkative, pleasant, and resolved to get well. While his wife sat in the back, mute, she listened to Carlo and Daria, who tried to include her in the conversation.

"Eve, this is a chance for Carlo and you to find happiness."

"Yeah, I suppose."

"Carlo, tell your psychiatrist about your problems, be honest with him." Daria advised.

"I will."

When they entered the asylum, Daria quivered with fear. Institutional life was still an abomination to her, but that one was worse than the orphanage. Carlo gave his name and he was led to the men's side of the asylum with Eve and Daria in pursuit. They were shown where Carlo would be housed. Daria hesitated, traumatized at the sight of men who sat around with bowed heads, muttering, wailing, and fighting the air, their hands gesticulating, while some bellowed with despair. Others danced around in a frenzy, yelling for the band to play louder and faster, while one man masturbated. Daria winced, turned around, and started walking out.

"Hey, fella, cut that out! You're in front of a lady." Carlo shouted, laughing at Daria's reaction.

"I'm leaving. Carlo, good luck."

During the ride back to Atlantic City, Eve seldom said a word, no matter how Daria tried prodding her, and she dropped her off at her apartment in Atlantic City. Twenty-eight days later, Daria received a call from Carlo and he asked for a ride back to Atlantic City, he had been discharged. She was shocked and disillusioned that his recuperation had only been a short time. When she got to the hospital, she was astonished that Carlo controlled the ward, joked with the men, and asked them to behave in front of his sister.

"Carlo, how come they let you out so soon?"

"Well, I'm not nuts like those guys."

"No, but you have deep-rooted problems. What did your psychiatrist say?"

"I have a drinking problem. But to tell you the truth, if I hadn't come here, I could have gone to jail."

She stared at him, offended, and could not believe her ears.

"It was a ruse, you used me."

"What's a ruse?"

"A gimmick."

"You didn't want me to go to jail, did you?"

She dropped him off to his apartment and handed him the journal.

"Read this, please take care of it."

She drove home to Margate, where she found peace and tranquility in her home with her children, and away from Carlo's problems and machinations. She checked her mail and found a letter from her Uncle Riccardo, asking why she had not answered his letters or notified him about her new telephone number. She sighed. Her uncle reminded her of her father; was she trying to forget her father? Then, she saw an invitation for Raf's birthday.

"Victor, look," and she handed him the invitation.

"We've got to go."

"I'm not going."

"C'mon, we have to go. I heard he misses me."

Daria acquiesced, Victor had been wonderful as far as Carlo's problems were concerned, and she realized a bond still existed between Victor and Raf.

Daria received a call from Carlo who wept and cried out.

"I didn't kill her. I didn't."

"Carlo, if you had read it before, you could have saved yourself so much grief."

"What a fool I've been. I'd love to go to Messina."

"You're an American and you're used to our way of life."

"What a lousy life," he murmured.

He finally believed the truth. Now he could have mental sustenance, peace, and perhaps, a new life with some happiness.

On the evening of Raf's party, Daria and Victor entered his home and a plethora of guests scrutinized them, wondering if the two sisters-in-law would speak to each other. After the Daria's outburst, the gossip had spread throughout the community. Raf and Joyce greeted Daria and Victor and they wished him a happy birthday. Then, they sought a corner, sheltering themselves from inquisitive faces.

"Well, Victor, what are you doing here?" A friend of Raf's asked.

Victor leaped to his feet, lunged toward him, and then retreated.

"You jerk-off, Raf happens to be my brother."

Guests gravitated toward Victor and Raf interceded, wanting to know what happened.

"He's breaking balls. Daria, let's go."

"Don't leave," Raf said.

"I can't stand your phony friends."

The car ride home was quiet; Victor dropped Daria off at the house and went to the restaurant.

"I shouldn't have wasted my time."
"Well, you tried."

The following week, Daria and Victor received an invitation to a black tie affair at the home of a prominent businessman and his wife, who frequented Victor's Restaurant. With Daria's yearning for beautiful clothes, she had learned how to sew. She made herself a tissue taffeta, black gown with glove sleeves, and chiffon rushing across her bosom and on the edge of her sleeves. She wore her hair in a French braid, tucked a black silk gardenia in her hair, and paraded before Victor.

"You look sophisticated and beautiful."
"And you look distinguished in your tux."

Although Victor's hair had turned gray, he had a youthful appearance and was still well built. Proudly, they posed before their children who ran toward them, hugging and kissing them.

"We love you. Here's the phone number, just in case. Don't stay up too late."
"Okay, Mom," Richard replied.

He was now fourteen years old and tall for his age. Michael was eleven years old and they doted upon Marisa who was six years old.

They reached the beachfront house and high tide caused the waves to overlap a few yards away, with a crescent moon hanging in the starlit sky. Victor parked the car on the lot next door to the house. They walked to the verandah, where guests lounged about and entered the house; the owners greeted them with enthusiasm.

But then the sight of Joyce and Raf unnerved Daria. The thread of animosity wound itself around them, and whispers abound. Victor nodded to Raf and lead Daria toward the living room, where she saw a concert grand piano with the lid raised. She ran her fingers along the ivory keys and said sotto voce.

"The tone must be incredible."
"Play something."
"No, I can't. I'll be embarrassed if I make a mistake."
"C'mon, Honey, you're good, show off."

"Some people don't like their guests playing their piano without permission."

"I'll get permission."

Five minutes later, he came back, and told her they were delighted that she could play. She sat down, smoothed out her gown, handed Victor her diamond rings, and played Edward Grieg's Concerto in A Minor. Her fingers glided along the piano, and she finished with a glissando; she closed her eyes.

"Nonna, that was for you."

Victor bent down, kissed her hand, and put on her rings, and whispered:

"Great! You're Atlantic City's *dark horse*. You should have seen their faces."

Daria stood up amid the applause, swallowed her saliva, breathed deeply, her hands trembled, and she felt like she was going through the Sahara Desert. Then she beamed at the realization that she had performed publicly; she had reached her zenith. No one could dispel the self-respect and confidence that swelled within her. Now, she fully understood why her grandmother had stressed education and music, despite the fact that Franca regretted she had not been able to teach Daria the piano.

Joyce, normally the center of attention, withdrew to a corner in the den with a drink, with Raf following her.

"That was some performance."

"Yes, Raf, it was. Get me another drink."

"You've had enough."

"Do me a favor … stop bragging about what great kids they have. Didn't I tell you they inherited her brains? Did you see her photo in the paper, studying Russian? Is there anybody we know that studies Russian?"

"No." He laughed adding, "But you're a smart girl."

"She's different. I know the correct fork to use, but she's what people call an intellectual, a different breed."

"Let's go home."

She stood up, zigzagging through the crowd with Raf in pursuit, and they left the party.

Daria and Victor were surrounded with guests, as well as the host and hostess, and she received accolades for her performance; one man questioned her.

"Where did you go to college?"
"I didn't. I'm self-educated."
"Impressive!"

Riding home, Victor held her hand and told her he was proud of her.

"I felt my grandmother's presence when I played. It was strange."
"It was a beautiful evening."

31

Through the ensueing years, Victor and Daria's children earned reputations as excellent students, well mannered, and likeable. Richard was tall, well built with sandy brown hair and brown eyes, and resembled Victor. After graduating from college, Richard attended Georgetown Law School in Washington, D.C. and graduated with high honors. Victor burst with pride, especially, when islanders complimented him on his fine family.

Michael, equally tall and well built, had an uncanny resemblance to his grandfather, Alissandru, with his dark hair and eyes, straight nose, and swaggered walk. He attended Marquette University in Milwaukee, Wisconsin and planned on becoming an architect.

Marisa, their daughter, was petite like Daria, and wore her straight, dark brown hair shoulder-length with bangs. Sometimes Daria studied her, a beauty like her grandmother, Giulia, with amber eyes and beautiful eyebrows. Marisa studied ballet and her teacher suggested she apply to the Julliard School of Music in New York City. But Victor, protective of her, would not allow her to be alone in Manhattan for a week, a day, or an hour.

"She plays the piano so well, let her pursue that and Italian." Victor told Daria but Marisa overheard him.

"Oh Daddy, you can trust me."

"I know that, but can I trust the young men who will pursue you. In Philadelphia, you're only an hour and a half away."

"Daddy, if I were going to do something bad, I could do it at home."

"I know that. But knowing you are in Philly makes me feel better. The Philadelphia College of Performing Arts is a great college."

"If I get in."

When Marisa played the piano, boys waited outside until she finished and would start calling her to come outside. Richard and Michael were home for semester break and ran outside.

"You guys better get away or we'll cut your dicks off."

"Mom, tell them to stop. It's embarrassing."

The boys ran away.

When Marisa graduated high school, she was accepted at the Philadelphia College of Performing Arts for the advance study of piano with a minor in the Italian language. Victor was delighted.

When Richard attended law school, he fell in love with a fellow law student, Brooke Gandolfi. Brooke was a stunning, intelligent brunette with round, brown eyes, and a slim figure. She had an instant rapport with Daria; her grandparents had raised her. When Richard brought her home to meet his family, Brooke was concerned; her mother was Jewish and her father was Italian descent. Both her parents died at an early age. Daria quickly allayed her concerns.

"We have Jewish blood, at least on my side, going back to the fifteen century."

"Mom, you never told us." Richard said.

"It never came up. It was too far back. I didn't think anyone would care. In 1492, Jews were expelled from Sicily unless they converted. Well, my grandmother's family on her father's side hated to leave the land of their ancestors, so they converted."

In September, Marisa arrived late for her first Italian class in college. The professor informed the class they were honored with the presence of Professore Emeritus Riccardo Leone from Italy, who would teach a semester. Professore Leone stood up, leaning onto a walking stick, and asked each student to introduce himself or herself. When Marisa stood up, she stated her name; he faltered for a moment, did not recognize the name, but her lovely face. She resembled Giulia, the love of his life.

"Signorina Caselli, are you related to Daria Leone Caselli?"
"Yes, she's my mother. She didn't think you still taught here."

Riccardo sat down, visibly moved, shock masked his face and he stifled his tears.

"Please stay after class. I must speak to you."
"Yes, Professore Leone."

When the class emptied, Marisa walked toward him, kissed him and he looked at her with disbelief.

"Your grandmother was a beautiful, intelligent woman. You look like her but she was taller than you. Marisa, why has your mother ignored me? This is my last year, but something keeps drawing me back here. I've been retired. I'm eighty years old, I'm tired.
"Uncle Riccardo, Mom hates to reflect upon the past."
"What has she told you?"
"Her mother died and her father placed her and Uncle Carlo into an orphanage."
"Marisa, I've got to see your mother."
"Ride home with me this weekend. I'll call my mother."

Daria and Victor welcomed her uncle and she apologized for her rudeness. She explained she hated to reiterate the past; the pain was like a sword, twisting inside of her, cutting her in half.

"Uncle Riccardo, my father was responsible for my mother's death and he was so mean to my grandparents, and to us."
"I know," he replied, crying.

She stood up, he held her close, and she saw tenderness within him that her father had lacked.

"Daria, when I go home, come with me."
"Someday, I'd like to go."
"Please, I'm an old man. Don't wait too long."

"Let me think about it. When will you leave for good?"

"I have to sell my furniture and my lease is up in March."

"I'll call you. Thank you, Uncle Riccardo."

He embraced her and wept.

Now Daria celebrated her fiftieth birthday, contented with life, and reflected upon her family and her education she received on her own with Victor's encouragement. She still continued learning, especially ancient history, philosophy, religion, and Graeco-Roman history. She wanted to study all about the Mediterranean World. She knew Sicily's history from her grandmother's teaching; she had it ingrained in her mind. She always hoped she would visit her ancestor's home.

She put on her black maillot bathing suit, glanced over her figure, dabbed make-up on her spider veins, and grabbed her black chiffon cover-up.

"Daria, come down here!" Victor yelled.

She ran downstairs, stared as the florist carried twelve dozen American beauty roses; they were perfect with a dark, rich color. Daria was overwhelmed, touched them, and recalled the velvet sensation of those roses from her graduation. She led the florist around the house as he placed them where she pointed. She held back her tears until he left; her children came in smiling and crying.

"Mom, we thought we'd replace the roses so cruelly taken away from you many years ago. Happy Birthday from all of us." Brooke, her daughter-in-law said, wiping away her own tears.

Richard, Michael, Marisa and Victor embraced her, all misty-eyed. She had told Brooke about the roses taken away from her and she had instituted the idea of abundantly replacing the roses.

"You've washed the hurt away."

"C'mon, Daria, let's go down the beach. I have your raft. Come on, kids, I'm taking the day off." Victor said, grinning.

Since her uncle's visit, she had started narrating stories about the past and reconciled her sorrow with the happiness and contentment that now existed in her life.

Several weeks later, the family's happiness disintegrated like a rotten piece of putrid fish. Now the Caselli name had been sullied with the media blasting the news. The newspaper headlines read:

DEAD MAN FOUND ON MARGATE BEACH
SON OF PROMINENT NIGHTCLUB OWNER ARRESTED
BRETT CASELLI ACCUSED OF MURDER

Daria's heart sank for Brett, whom she had only seen a few times throughout the years, and whose future had almost been predictable to her. Nonetheless, her concern lay with her own children, who had earned respect and admiration. Now the Caselli name would be put through the wringer, exploited and excoriated by the media, unleashing itself like a sullied, rapacious dragon.

Victor, Daria, and their family watched the evening news on television stations from Philadelphia, New York and locally. Brett stood with his glamorous parents at their fashionable Margate home. Victor was despondent over the news and wondered what had caused Brett to kill someone. What could have pushed him off the edge? What had precipitated such awful behavior? He knew his nephew had been raised as a privileged child, spoiled by his father's cronies, who handed him money indiscriminately and Raf ignored their behavior. Brett often drove his BMW convertible through the area, dressed well, and he inherited his father's good looks. Brett did want he wanted to do; there were never repercussions.

"Shit, what a mess. I'd better get over there." Victor said.
"Do you want me to go with you?"
"No, Daria, there's going to be a lot of media there."

Meanwhile, islanders wondered who would defend Raf's only child, F. Lee Bailey or Edward Bennett Williams, who Raf knew personally. But no one realized Raf's dire circumstances except his creditors. He had a chattel mortgage on his club and money did not flow as easily as it once had. Yet, his lifestyle still had a spurious semblance of wealth.

Cars were parked on Ventnor Avenue in Margate, surrounding Raf and Joyce's home. A police car had its flashing lights on as other police officers stood guard outside on his verandah, questioning people who entered. Victor parked his car two blocks away and when he came up the steps, the officer recognized him and let him through.

The house was crowded with acquaintances and friends who consoled the hapless parents, whose son had been arrested for murder and was incarcerated in the Mays Landing jail in Atlantic County, fourteen miles away.

Raf stood up, Victor and he embraced, and Raf whispered to him.

"Come upstairs, I need to speak with you privately."

It was like the old days, when the only one Raf could trust was his brother.

When Raf explained what he wanted, Victor was stunned, pacing back and forth.

"You're asking too much of him. He's only been a lawyer for four years. He's never handled a murder case. It would be too much pressure on him. I can help you out with some money, but I've had a big expense with my kids in college and graduate school."

"Well, it was worth it," Raf replied.

"How about that asshole that you helped through college and law school?"

"He's now into politics."

"Raf, I'll ask Richard. Strange, they don't even know each other."

"Yeah, it's a shame."

Victor call Richard, reiterated Raf's request, and Richard was shocked. In his short career, he had decided he wanted to be a personal injury attorney. Richard was not interested in defending an accused murderer, who happened to be his cousin.

"Dad, it's too much responsibility for me."

"Please, son, my brother needs his family now."

"All right, Dad, it's going to be tough. What's he like?"

"They say he can be charming, like my brother."

At seven o'clock that evening, Richard rang the bell to his uncle's home, glanced around at the once lavish home. The carpeting was threadbare, the drapes were faded with rain-soaked spots from leaving the windows opened during rainstorms, and the couches were frayed.

"Hello, Richard, sit down."

"Thanks."

"Listen, my kid's been in trouble with drinking and drugs, but murder … no way."

"Tomorrow, I'll go to the jail and talk to him. Where's Brett's mother?"

"I'm handling this, don't talk to her."

Richard drove to the county jail, showed his credentials to the guards who were posted near Brett's cell.

"Can I speak to him alone?" Richard asked.

"Mr. Caselli, he's your cousin, isn't he?"

"Yes."

Richard extended his hand to his cousin who laughed when Richard told him he was going to be his lawyer.

"No shit, you're going to defend me?"

Richard stared at him, disturbed with his alacrity or wasn't he fully cognizant of his plight: arrested for murder.

"Now tell me the truth, did you kill that guy?"

"No."

"Then, why were you arrested."

"Don't worry about it. My father will hire one of his big-time lawyer friends and I'll get off."

"Brett, you don't get it. I'm it, no big-time lawyer is coming."

"I don't believe it," Brett said smirking.

"Brett, how old are you and do you work?"

"Twenty and I do odds and ends at the club."

When Brett lit a cigarette, Richard noticed similar mannerisms like his father; he dangled it from the side of his mouth. It was obvious he wanted to be like his father, whose fame and glory belonged to a bygone era.

The meeting continued with Brett's arrogance and lack of understanding of the severity of the situation. Richard's patience dwindled and he stood up and packed up his briefcase.

"Brett, I can't make this any clearer to you. Your father is not hiring a big time lawyer to get you off. I'm it! Now tell me the fucking truth or I'm out of here."

Brett discarded his alacrity and realized Richard was telling him the truth.

"Yeah, I did it."

Reporters stood watch at Raf's house, wondering who would be the lawyer for his son, but no one of consequence entered Raf's home, only his nephew. Richard appeared before the judge with his cousin for his bail hearing. The judge set bail at two hundred and fifty thousand dollars and Raf put up his home for Brett's bail and he was released. The judge studied the young men who stood before him: one, a lawyer, the other shackled from his defiance of the law.

Richard hired an investigator to search for information about the dead young man's background. After months of inquiries, he recommended that Brett take a plea, rather than face a jury. Raf was shocked.

"Oh my God, He really killed him?"
"Yes."

Richard learned the reason for Brett's brutal behavior. He yearned for his parents' love, in particular, his father's love and affection, since his mother lacked the capacity of loving him. Therefore, Brett focused on his famous father, emulated him in every way he could. But Brett floundered, with no focus on his future, and he was a disappointment to his father.

Raf continually berated Brett in front of his friend, James Brandisi. Raf was impressed with James and often praised him. The praise Raf showered upon the friend belonged to Brett, and they were stolen, precious moments that Brett had yearned for. He could no longer contain his rage and jealousy toward James.

On the evening of the murder, Brett and James drove to the point in Longport where the ocean meets the bay. They got out of the car and walked to the end of the rocks, where they had planned to smoke a joint. In the daytime, the walk on the rock into the water is relaxing and picturesque. At night, it's isolated and dangerous. Brett and James sat on the rocks and

James lit the joint. Brett stood up and shot him in the face, chest and in his ear. Brett, robotically, pushed James into the ocean and walked back to the car. Brett ventured to Atlantic City and stopped at Treasure Island, a trendy bar and discothèque. Several hours later, he returned to his parents' home in Margate.

In the morning, fishermen on the bay reported to the marine police that an object resembling a body was floating near the marshes. James Brandisi was removed from the water; his eyes had been removed, the fish had started to feast.

The day of Brett's hearing, the media jammed the Mays Landing courtroom. Victor, Daria, Marisa, Michael, and Brooke entered the courtroom. Victor filled up with emotion when he caught eyes with Raf. Silence pervaded the courtroom and all rose when the judge entered. Richard stood at the defense attorney's table with the defendant, his cousin, Brett Caselli. Brett wore a designer jogging suit and sneaks; Richard wore a navy blue suit. Richard went through the legal formalities before the judge. The plea agreement stated that Brett would receive no more than twenty-five years in New Jersey State Prison.

"Brett Caselli, how do you plead?
"Guilty, Your Honor."

Murmurs reverberated throughout the courtroom and the judge banged his gavel. Brett turned around, gazed at his parents, and his green eyes locked into his mother's eyes. Brett would never understand why his mother did not love him. Joyce bowed her head while Raf wept for his only child. Reporters, friends, and curiosity seekers' moans and groans of shock resounded throughout the courtroom; and once again, the judge banged his gavel. Now the realization of his crime sunk into Brett like a whirlpool, pulling him down into its vortex, where he could not escape, and perhaps, drown in its swirling waters.

Sheriff's Officers handcuffed Brett and escorted him out of the courtroom.

"Dad, help me! Help me!" Brett screamed.

The courtroom became a sea of tears for the handsome, young man and his parents, who now realized the clangor of large steel gates would imprison him for years.

Daria grimaced, covered her mouth with her hands, fearing any outburst of emotion, as she recalled Carlo, when he was handcuffed and shackled. She always had an underlying fear that Carlo could have killed someone in his outburst of rage, and she was grateful he had not.

Pity surged within her for that privileged young man who had everything, but nothing in the end. She wondered how he would survive in that monstrous tomb, where evil resided. Raf and Joyce were caught up in the web of wretchedness for their only child, and left the courtroom with their friends, declining reporters' questions, and entered their car.

Victor had closed the restaurant because of the hearing and the family gathered for dinner at their home. They watched the evening news on television and saw Richard at his interview after Brett's day in court. He looked handsome, and when he spoke, he was articulate and expressed his sorrow for the victim and his cousin. Then, a reporter's question stunned Richard.

"Is it true that you did not know each other prior to the murder?"
"At this time, I think that is irrelevant. Excuse me."

The Caselli name had been besmirched, but Victor and Daria's children brought honor to the name. Victor wiped his tears and pressed Daria's hand.

"Victor, you are the 'victor.'"

He grinned that sheepish smile, which she loved, and kissed her.

Thirty days later, Brett was sentenced to twenty-five years with the possibility of parole in fifteen years.

32

With all the publicity surrounding the trial, Daria and Victor received numerous calls. Uncle Riccardo called and expressed his pride in Richard defending his cousin. He told Daria he was returning to Messina and was not coming back to America. The only reason for his endurance throughout the years was something gnawed at him, unfinished business, and he concluded it had something to do with Daria.

"Are you coming with me?"
"Yes, can Carlo go with us?"
"Oh no, I've heard too many bad things about him."

She explained the burden that Carlo had carried for years, her father's cruelty, in particular, the grievous statement of unwarranted accusation that impregnated Carlo's mind with abhorrent guilt: matricide!

"Oh, I am sorry. If you would like him to come, then he may."

Daria sat in her living room, recalled her childhood, and wondered what the impetus was for success in her life that guided her as well as her children. It always came back to the same person, her nonna. Her boundless love was like a shield of honor. The cinders in her life had burned away a long time ago, but Carlo's life had been splintered in many ways. She ran upstairs and retrieved her grandmother's journal, the pages browned and brittle. She realized what a wonderful gift her grandmother had left her, despite the tragedies.

Now it was time to write the continuation of the family's history for her children and future generations. It was time for reconciling the past with the present. She called Carlo and gave him the news. He was ecstatic.

"What about your wife?"
"We've been separated; there's nothing left between us."

At the end of April, Daria's family gathered around her and expressed their love and happiness for her. Victor had a glimmer of sadness on his face and Daria grabbed his hand.

"Carlo and I need this trip."
"I know."

Victor drove Daria and Carlo to Philadelphia, picked up their uncle, and took them to JFK airport in New York City. It was a beautiful, sunny day, with cloudless skies, and they soured away for a deeply, moving trip. In flight, Riccardo spoke about their mother, how beautiful she was, and tears trickled down his face. They realized he still loved her. Then Riccardo directed his conversation toward Carlo stating that he knew about his fights, the beatings, his incarcerations, and close encounters with death. His Atlantic City friend had sent him the newspaper clippings.

For a moment, Riccardo studied Carlo, discovered a gentleness and vulnerability that pleased him. At his grandmother's funeral, he resembled a hardened criminal, but now the bitterness had withered away. The mask of brutality had worn off from his face, and he had a noblesse about him that he had inherited but never had a chance to develop. They landed in Rome, boarded another plane to Catania, where Riccardo hired a taxicab to the city of Messina. He wanted them to stay with him at his sister's apartment, but Daria declined.

"Forgive us, but we want to stay at the Grand Hotel on Viale San Martino. That's where my grandfather stayed when he courted my grandmother."

Daria and Carlo embraced him and thanked him for the opportunity he had given them.

When Riccardo met them the next day, he was amazed at Daria's knowledge of the city and the provinces of Messina.

"Uncle Riccardo, in my dreams, I walked the streets of Messina, saw ships sail through the port, and I even imagined dancing at the parties my great-grandparents had."

"Did your grandmother describe it the way it was before the earthquake?"

"Yes."

"We'll, you're going to have a busy two weeks, and you'll have to meet your aunts, uncles, and cousins. One of my brother's is a recluse."

They strolled along the port of Messina, watched ships sailing through the straight, and ferries conveyed tourists and residents. Daria wanted to know where her great-grandparents had lived, and Riccardo pointed at the sickle-shaped harbor, where apartments now stood.

"All the palazzos were along that curve, the earthquake destroyed them all. We lived in Novara near the river, but it wasn't as bad as near the shore."

Carlo stood in awe of the infinite beauty of the sea and the majesty of the verdant mountains, while Daria inhaled the citrus aroma of orange and lemon trees. She leaned against a boulder and gazed at the palm trees with fresh fronds bursting with life.

"Nonna, you were right about the views and the beauty," she murmured.

The setting sun appeared as a giant, orange ball, topped with frothy clouds that were tinged with orange hues. Her grandmother's descriptions had been an illusory spectacle, but now reality loomed before them. Carlo put his arm around Daria.

"It's like a painting, so beautiful." He exclaimed.

"Yes, it's surreal, makes me proud of our heritage."

"Surreal? Now don't use your hi-falutin words with me."

Daria laughed. And they recited a sentence she had learned as a child, showing off her vocabulary.

"Carlo, remember this? Your vocabulary is too copious for my diminutive comprehension, so will you kindly endeavor to elucidate more explicitly."

They roared laughing with Riccardo joining in.

"Uncle Riccardo, we'd like to see our great-grandparents' graves, and the Leone cemetery."

"Things have changed. During World War II, Sicily was destroyed by the Allies' bombs. I was in America at that time, but the destruction was horrendous."

"Do you know anything about our grandmother's land?"

"Well, after the war, people manipulated documents, and boundaries were changed. It's not worth it."

"But, Uncle Riccardo, it should have gone to us."

"Daria, people have suffered so much, don't bother causing trouble."

"Daria, let it go."

"All right, Carlo, but it isn't the money. It's the idea that it belonged to Nonna and her family."

"Come on, we're going to Novara. You'll meet my brother. But first, I want you to meet someone."

Stores lined Viale San Martino, with apartments above the stores. Riccardo stopped at a small jewelry store, where an elderly man, with faded eyes, white hair, and feeble hands, was hunched over a jewelry tray. Riccardo spoke Sicilian to him and Daria and Carlo grinned; they understood every word.

"Alissandru's children," said Riccardo, holding back his tears.

"Veru?"[43] Signore Romanelli inquired.

"Si."

"Che piaciri.[44] Your father was a good friend of mine. Do they know they come from a distinguished family?"

"They know more about their mother's family. Daria, Carlo, my sister is Vice President of the Bank of Sicily, my cousin is the head of the railway throughout Sicily, another cousin is head of the Electric Company, and of course, we have several oddballs like all families."

Signore Romanelli presented Daria with a pair of gold earrings, and gave Carlo a pair of gold cufflinks. They thanked him for his kindness and generosity.

Now they were on the way to Novava, their father's birthplace, where a river flowed through the property that once included thousands of arable acres, but it was destroyed during the earthquake. Riccardo ordered the taxicab driver to stop in front of a stucco home with a Spanish tile roof and a wrap-a-round balcony, with an expansive view of the mountains with verdant trees and shrubs.

"Tomasso! It's me, Riccardo. I have a surprise for you."
"Chi e?[45]
"I figghi di Alissandru e Giulia."[46]
"Ca in Sicilia?"[46]
"Si, apri la porta!"[47]
"Apertu."[48]

They entered the foyer; the bedrooms and bathroom were on the first floor and the second floor had a large kitchen, dining and living room, overlooking the river and the land.

"Wow, would I love to live here."

Tomasso Leone was a gaunt man with deep-set, charcoal eyes; he wore riding britches, a tweed jacket, and a beige shirt with a brown ascot. He removed his hunting cap and put away his rifle. He glanced at Daria momentarily, told her she looked like her father, but then he embraced Carlo. Riccardo noticed an immediate rapport between Tomasso and Carlo.

In his youth, Tomasso married a village girl who died young and left him with two sons. Both were killed in World War II. He became a recluse, an embittered man, irascible, and did not participate in any of the family's events. No one was permitted to trespass on his property.

He told them to sit down, while he made espresso and prepared some food. Carlo went over to him and asked if he could help. Within minutes, Carlo and Tomasso roared with laughter.

"Daria, I've just seen a miracle. He hasn't laughed in years."
"Please tell him we want to see the cemetery."
"I will, but let's eat first."

Tomasso held onto Carlo's arm, walking together, deep in conversation, ignoring Daria and Riccardo until they reached the caretaker's house. They knocked on the door and he led them through the gated cemetery. Daria had a special request, she wanted a stone inscribed with her father's name, his date of birth and death. While the caretaker prepared the stone, they strolled near the river and Carlo ran his hand through the water, his eyes raised to the mountains. He sighed.

They returned to the caretaker and Daria and Carlo gazed at their father's stone with contentment. They picked up some wild flowers and arranged a bouquet in front of their father's stone.

"Rest in peace, I forgive you." Daria murmured.

Carlo sobbed, his cries echoed throughout the mountains, and his words bounced back to him.

"I forgive you for what you've done to me and my mother."

Daria and Carlo held onto each other, and Riccardo and Tomasso came over to them. Riccardo hugged Daria while Tomasso embraced Carlo, holding him close.

Riccardo explained Giulia's death, the orphanage, and the suffering Carlo had endured because of his father's accusation.

"Carlo, stay here and live with me. I need help around here."

"Uncle Tomasso, I'd like that very much. I'm at peace here, the demons are gone at last."

"Have you ever ridden a horse?"

"Sure, Uncle Tomasso, on our beaches at home."

"Wonderful, I have an outfit for you. We'll go riding."

"Uncle Riccardo, I don't want to hurt Uncle Tomasso's feelings, but we have to go to my great-grandparents' cemetery."

"Yes, he'll understand."

Tomasso insisted upon going with them, not wanting to leave Carlo. Riccardo was amazed at the transformation in his brother. At last, he prepared to leave his isolation and live again.

"Stay here tonight and in the morning, we'll go together." Tomasso said.

They reached Taormina, on the rocky red cliffs of Mount Tauro, but Mount Etna still ruled, spewing forth ink clouds of sulfuric acid, which sent chills through Daria, recalling her great aunt Maddalena's fear and her ultimate death.

"Mongibello!"

Her uncles looked at her with awe. How could she have known the ancient name the Arabs had given Mount Etna? Of course, her grandmother had told her, and she had absorbed all of Sicily's history.

Now Carlo and she were in the land of the gods in the Peloritani Mountains with its myriad flowers, graceful cypress trees, lemon and orange trees, and prickly pears. Dusk colored the mountains with hues of orange and mauve above the ancient Greek Theatre, and falcons and hawks danced their ballistic flights through the air, upward and downward, sweeping through the mountains with their gracefulness.

"Carlo, it's just like Nonna described it."

Riccardo hesitated in front of a hotel, lowered his head, and turned away.

"Uncle Riccardo, is this where they spent their honeymoon?"

"Yes, but it's been renovated."

"At least they found happiness here, if only brief moments." Her eyes moistened.

They entered the hotel, sat down in the lobby and uneasiness overcame Daria. She considered the hotel sacrosanct, where gods had poured out their blessings upon her parents, but cursed them when they left their haven.

"Uncle Riccardo, I'd like to spend the night here in the quarters my parents used."

Riccardo paused for a moment, diffident about her request, but yielded, wondering what was her motive? The owner of the hotel accommodated her since no one occupied the suite. Her uncles and Carlo slept in one large bedroom with three beds. She looked at the full moon and the starry skies with hope, then showered and went to bed, reading a book about Sicily in Sicilian. She fell asleep and then heard someone calling her name.

"Daria … Daria"

Jumping up, she opened the window and the stars glittered. She saw a radiant light in the sky and two young people smiled at her; the woman in a white satin negligee and robe, and the man in a navy blue robe.

"It's my mother, how beautiful she is, and my father is so handsome; no wonder she fell in love with him."

They waved to her and floated through the air and headed to a group of people who waited for their arrival.

"They're at peace now. Oh, Mamma e Papa', we've missed so much, rest in peace."

Departing from Taormina, Carlo's burden had been lifted, freed of the shackles of his destiny, and he found contentment and peace, at last. Daria knew the web of guilt had disintegrated from Carlo; he had unburdened the heavy load he had carried for many years. Now, he found peace in the land of his ancestors.

Riccardo instructed the driver to go to the Raimondi's cemetery, which had been partly destroyed during the war. Marble angles, with chipped noses and broken arms, still protected the cemetery, albeit lying on the ground.

Daria ordered three stones, inscribed, Franca Raimondi Privitera, beloved daughter of Elena and Giacomo Raimondi; Edoardo Privitera, beloved husband of Franca Raimondi, and Giulia Privitera Leone, their beloved daughter.

After the inscriptions were completed, Daria and Carlo knelt down, prayed for the repose of their souls, held onto each other and cried uncontrollably.

"Daria and Carlo, why, after all these years, are you subjecting yourselves to such sorrow?"

"Uncle Riccardo, we never mourned for our mother and father."

"Don't you have stones for your grandparents and mother in New Jersey?"

Daria, ashamed, could not answer in the affirmative.

"If one is buried in a pauper's grave, the State of New Jersey forbids any stone or movement of the bodies. Their spirits are here, I know it."

After spending an hour contemplating the history of their family, Daria and Carlo prepared for a plethora of dinners with cousins, aunts and uncles. Then, it was time for Daria's journey home without Carlo. He explained he had been incapable of loving any one, not even himself, with his bitterness, drinking and drugs that drowned his perennial distress.

"Carlo, be happy."
"Thanks for being there through the years."

She wept.

Daria and her uncle returned to the city of Messina and Daria gazed once more at the ships sailing by the Strait of Messina, and she ingrained the view on her mind. At the airport, Riccardo Leone's face reflected melancholy. Daria kissed him and thanked him for his generosity.

"Daria, your parents would have been proud of you. You've made me a happy man. Now I know why I kept returning to America … for Carlo, destiny. Now, I am at peace as well."

As Daria and her uncle waited for her flight, Carlo and Tomasso arrived. Carlo wore a tweed jacket, riding britches, a hunting cap, matching Tomasso's outfit. She shook her head, laughing at them, and hugged Carlo, whose flamboyance suited him.

"Good-bye," her voice trailing as she rushed toward the gate, stifling her tears.

When Daria arrived at JFK Airport, Victor and their children welcomed her home. They looked for Carlo and Daria explained what had occurred with Uncle Tomasso.

"I'm not surprised, he had an old world mentality. He loved to play bocce with the old guys in the neighborhood. He'll be happy there."

They held hands while their children retrieved Daria's bags.

At dinner the next evening, Richard, Brooke, Marisa and Michael discussed Daria's patience and tenacity with Carlo through the years.

"Well, we were rejected, locked up, terrorized in many ways, but I was able to overcome my problems; I listened to my grandmother. Whereas, Carlo dragged a boulder around for most of his life, but now that's been crushed."

"Mom, Richard and I have news. We're going to have a baby."

Daria leaped to her feet, hugged Brooke and Richard, and Michael proposed a toast.

"To the grandparents, cent'anni."
"Our first grandchild, how wonderful."

Victor and Daria walked a few blocks and she spotted the evening star below the crescent moon.

"Victor, my grandmother would say to me right now, 'the class and intelligence came through.'"
"Yes, she would. Now everyone can rest in peace."

fini

(Endnotes)

[1] It is a shame.
[1] hurry up
[2] farmers
[3] evil eye
[4] Good health and may you all live one hundred years.
[5] May you live one hundred years
[6] big mouth
[7] balls
[8] Friend
[9] Shit
[10] You're damned!
[11] Die like a dog!
[12] Burnt earth!
[13] Beautiful child of your mother
[15] fuck off
[16] Dead! Cursed earth
[17] Spit up blood
[18] Highest form of respect for grandparents and parents
[19] Black Hand
[20] You are the staff of my old age.
[21] Basin of Gold
[22] The world goes on
[23] Good luck
[24] God willing

[25] May God bless you
[26] Ancient name for grandmother and grandfather
[27] Poor Italy
[28] Enough already
[29] Grandfather
[30] Damn it
[31] Scoundrel
[32] When are you coming home
[33] She's dead
[34] Wake up
[35] Let's go home
[36] Don't leave me
[37] Where are you
[38] Beautiful children of your mother
[39] What happened to her hair
[40] My love, let's go to Taormina.
[41] cucumber
[42] What a beauty
[43] Is it true (Sicilian)
[44] What a pleasure (Sicilian)
[45] Who is it
[46] Alissandru and Giulia's children
[46] Here in Sicily
[47] Yes, open the door
[48] It's opened

www.ingramcontent.com/pod-product-compliance
Lightning Source LLC
Chambersburg PA
CBHW020612310726
48979CB00008B/1453/J

* 9 7 8 0 5 9 5 7 1 8 1 3 9 *